To Tracy,

A BOLD DECEIVER

hope yr enjoy it

By
JAMES HURD

1/9/08

Order this book online at www.trafford.com/07-1227
or email orders@trafford.com

Most Trafford titles are also available at major online book retailers.

© Copyright 2008 James Robert Hurd.

All rights reserved. No part of this publication may be reproduced, stored in a retrieval system, or transmitted, in any form or by any means, electronic, mechanical, photocopying, recording, or otherwise, without the written prior permission of the author.

Cover design by Ben Jones
Photography by Simon Smith

Note for Librarians: A cataloguing record for this book is available from Library and Archives Canada at www.collectionscanada.ca/amicus/index-e.html

Printed in Victoria, BC, Canada.

ISBN: 978-1-4251-3272-9

We at Trafford believe that it is the responsibility of us all, as both individuals and corporations, to make choices that are environmentally and socially sound. You, in turn, are supporting this responsible conduct each time you purchase a Trafford book, or make use of our publishing services. To find out how you are helping, please visit www.trafford.com/responsiblepublishing.html

Our mission is to efficiently provide the world's finest, most comprehensive book publishing service, enabling every author to experience success. To find out how to publish your book, your way, and have it available worldwide, visit us online at www.trafford.com/10510

 www.trafford.com

North America & international
toll-free: 1 888 232 4444 (USA & Canada)
phone: 250 383 6864 ♦ fax: 250 383 6804 ♦ email: info@trafford.com

The United Kingdom & Europe
phone: +44 (0)1865 722 113 ♦ local rate: 0845 230 9601
facsimile: +44 (0)1865 722 868 ♦ email: info.uk@trafford.com

10 9 8 7 6 5 4 3

For my wife Jo,
and in memory of my Grandfather,
Thomas McMinn 1915-1998

'As I was a going over
Gillgarry Mountain
I spied Colonel Farrell and
his money he was counting.
First I drew me pistol
and then I drew me rapier
Saying stand and deliver
for I am your bold deceiver.'

"Whisky in the Jar" (Traditional)

Prologue

The French poet Apollinaire wrote that memories "*are like hunting horns whose sound dies on the wind*[1]". The older the memory, the less crisp it becomes, until one day it fades altogether into the distance of time and consciousness. You see snatched glimpses, vague outlines but the detail has departed in a blur of confusion. The astute amongst you may argue that it rather depends on the nature of the memory. Some memories will stay with the individual longer than others. It is the intensity of the experience that is crucial.

As a child, I would sit on my grandfather's knee, pestering him with questions about the War. Filled with awe and wonder, he transported me back to the Royal Marines of 1943. If I closed my eyes tightly, I could picture him on Brighton pier, learning to ride a Norton motorcycle. His recollections of D-day both inspired and entertained, regardless of how many times I had heard the same account. With a sweeping gesture and a broad smile, he would recall that he had driven the length and breadth of war-torn Europe in 1945, whilst waiting to be de-mobbed; the palpable sense of relief he felt when the Americans dropped the atom bomb on Hiroshima and Nagasaki, acutely aware of his impending deployment orders to Japan.

It was not until I was older I realised there was more significance in the words he didn't speak, the memories he chose not to share – events not spoken of for half a century: the fallen comrades on that June day on the Normandy beaches; friends gunned down where only minutes earlier they had exchanged a cigarette, a joke or just an encouraging smile; the guilt that he had survived when so many others had been killed or maimed. Those memories did not fade gracefully with the distance of time. Instead, they haunted his sleeping hours, returning

---

1 Guillaume Apollinaire 1880-1918: Alcools, Cors de Chasse, st 2, 3 (1913).

in his own private nightmares. It is only now, as I have looked back, that I have questioned the effect of my childhood inquisitiveness. What must it have cost him to reawaken the ghosts of the past? He never rebuked me, but dealt with each innocent inquiry with kindness and patience. But I understand now, at least in part, the intensity of emotion those memories must have rekindled.

These thoughts have preoccupied me, as I have attempted to reawaken my own ghosts and commit them to paper. It has proved impossible for me to recall the events, which began over ten years ago now, without fully reliving them. I remember the laughter and the pain and have dredged up the forgotten disaffection, flourishing in secret in the recesses of my subconscious.

If it has cost so much, why bother? There is no simple answer; the truth is always more complicated. There are a number of reasons, not all of them noble. There is a part of me, which does not wish for the crisp Technicolor images that once endlessly replayed themselves to fade. I re-read these words and they sound detached, impersonal. Forgive me, it is Tara I do not wish to forget and yet at the same time, I need to leave her behind. I hope that by committing her story to paper, I will be relieved of the solitary burden of her memory. I am shortly to remarry. I have never hidden anything from my fiancée, but until I exorcise these ghosts, there will be three of us in this marriage.

This account is for my late brother Ben, his wife Rebecca, and their daughter and my niece Hannah, in the hope that they will understand, if not forgive.

There is also the selfish reason. Seldom do we get to witness such extraordinary events as I lived through: good and bad. Most of our lives pass us by with the depressing routine of the mundane, as the sun rises and sets; they fade from months to years without us ever really appreciating how old we have grown and how little we have achieved.

Finally, it is Tara's story, and for that reason alone it deserves to be told.

Thomas Flemming
August 2007.

31st August 1994

Following mounting speculation from Belfast and Dublin over recent days, today the news finally came that the Provisional IRA has announced a cease-fire, in their 25 year struggle to oust British rule from Northern Ireland. A spokesman released the following statement in Dublin:

"Recognising the potential of the current situation and in order to enhance the democratic peace process and underline our commitment to its success, the leadership of Óglaigh na hÉireann have decided that as of midnight, Wednesday, 31st August there will be a complete cessation of military operations. All of our units have been instructed accordingly...We believe that an opportunity to create a just and lasting peace has been created..."

The news was greeted with scenes of great jubilation in Belfast, where people flocked onto the streets in their hundreds. Flags were waved and car horns sounded in celebration at the thought that at last the killing, maiming and suffering that this part of Ireland has had to endure for so many years, might have come to an end.

Part One

Chapter One

I FIRST MET Tara in the long hot summer of 1995, as the first anniversary of the IRA cease-fire approached. A year in which it seemed to all observers, whether casual or intimate, that progress had been excruciatingly slow. The initial euphoria had faded, as the British Government prevaricated over semantics: asking whether the cease-fire was "permanent?" and then demanding actual decommissioning of terrorist weapons "as a confidence building measure," before all party talks could commence. On the streets of Northern Ireland, people had begun to experience the normality you and I take for granted. The hope remained amongst young and old that having tasted peace, no one would want ever to return to war.

At the time, I practised law. I was young and ambitious: a barrister keen to make a name for myself, which is how I came to represent Sean Keenan in his case for assault against the Cheshire Police in July 1995.

Mr Keenan's case was what is best described as a cold pizza case. You know the scenario – upon leaving the pub you have the munchies and hence purchase a pizza, loaded with pepperoni, garlic, onions and chillies. By the time you get round to eating it, your appetite has faded. You leave the half-eaten pizza, still in its box on the kitchen table, promising yourself in a drunken haze, "I'll have the rest for breakfast". But who actually eats cold pizza for breakfast? I had cases like that. You are asked to consider the merits of a case. Late at night, reading the papers, proceeding with the case seems like a good idea. Months later, when you face the prospect of a judge and in this case a jury,

A Bold Deceiver • James Hurd

you suddenly lose your appetite, wondering whatever possessed you to think you could win?

Sean Keenan was a bricklayer. He left Ireland in the early 1970's to work on the building sites of England, and later Germany. By January 1994, he was forty six and had settled with his wife and family in South Manchester. On the 15th January, he had travelled to Warrington in Cheshire to celebrate a friend's fortieth birthday – four middle-aged men on a town centre pub-crawl. Sean had drunk about four pints of beer – considerably less than his drinking partners, given his prostate condition.

After drinking up time, they wandered to the nearby takeaway. They ate salty chips with their fingers, before making their separate ways to the bus station, taxi rank or simply walking home. As Sean turned onto Scotland Road, looking for a taxi, a group of youths appeared ahead. Raised voices and shouting – four or five men in their late teens or early twenties were gathered on the opposite side of the road, some fifty feet ahead. It was not until Sean was much closer, it became clear he was witnessing a violent attack. Two assailants were kicking and punching a young man on the pavement, striking vicious blows to his head, chest and back. The victim had rolled himself up into the foetal position, struggling in vain to protect himself.

The rest of the story is taken from the court transcript of Sean Keenan's evidence. "How did you respond, once you realised an assault was taking place?" I asked him.

"I acted instinctively, the lad was getting pummelled. I ran shouting, 'leave him alone, what the hell do you think you are doing'- or words to that effect. I think my language was a little coarser on the night." Sean's cheerful admission brought a wry smile to the faces of a number of jurors sitting in Crown Square in Manchester. "As I approached, the attackers ran off. About the same time, I heard an approaching police siren. The cowards ran away even faster."

"Are you able to describe them?" I asked.

Deep in thought, Sean adjusted his tie, feeling uncomfortable in his unfamiliar new suit, purchased specially for the occasion. "One had a shaved head, and another had on a red jacket. To be honest, I was more concerned with the lad on the ground."

"What happened after the assailants disappeared?"

"The victim was bleeding from a gash on his forehead. I knelt on my hands and knees, trying to console him like – he was whimpering. I didn't want to move him, in case he had broken anything."

The courtroom was deathly hushed. Every eye was on the witness box, as his evidence built to the crucial climax I had outlined in my opening speech. Sean told me afterwards that he was nervous. He came across as a little shy – no bad thing in a witness. Too much confidence whiffs of arrogance or embellishment. "I didn't see the police van arrive, I was too busy talking to the lad. I don't know whether he could hear me or not. I heard the siren and was relieved. I thought it was the ambulance. He was drifting in and out of consciousness and I was worried about...Andy his name was."

"What happened when the police arrived?"

Sean paused for a minute, squeezing his eyes shut. "One second I was on the pavement, next to Andy, and then all hell broke loose, absolute chaos; shouting and police officers everywhere. I was physically lifted and dragged away – manhandled, as if I was the attacker. One grabbed me under the arm and yanked me backwards, punched me in the kidneys. They literally threw me into the back of the police van. I landed heavily on my right shoulder. I shouted, screamed: "what the hell's going on?"

"Did anyone answer your question?"

"It soon became clear they believed I'd done it. It was insane." Sean turned towards the jury, a smile appearing at the corners of his mouth. "I'm five foot five and weigh ten stone. I have a dodgy prostate and a bad knee. Once inside the van, I asked again: 'what the fuck is going on, I've done nothing? They ran away'. I pointed in the direction I had seen the attackers running. There were two police officers. The larger of the two – dark hair, big bloke like – grinned and sneered before punching me hard in the stomach and screaming at me to, 'shut the fuck up, you little Irish bastard.' I winced in pain and begged him to stop. He bent down and punched me repeatedly. 'Belt up you stupid Irish fucker. You're all the bloody same. You make me sick.' I was doubled up on the floor. I could hear him breathing, smell his pumping adrenaline. I tried to move, to escape, but he placed his foot on top of me. 'You won't be going anywhere now will you,' he laughed, in a mock Irish accent, before kicking me in the chest, sending me reeling."

Sean's head hung limply, straining to fight the emotion. The judge asked him if he wanted to break for a minute. Sean defiantly shook his head. "Then," he said, breathing in deeply, as if drawing on hidden energy, "he grabbed my leg. My shoe came off. The police officer started laughing. I was in agony as he started twisting my foot, back and forth, toying with me."

"What was the other officer doing?"

"He just sat there. He looked a tad uncomfortable, but he didn't raise a finger to stop his mate. I thought he was gonna push me back, bang my head on the door, but he kept twisting. 'How about a bit of your own medicine, you good for nothing little shit.' He twisted my ankle so hard I heard it snap. The pain was unbearable – absolute agony." Sean's voice trailed off, as he rubbed his eyes. "I must have passed out. The next thing I knew I was in a police cell with a doctor standing over me…"

Sean was released the following morning, after the complainant identified the men who had attacked him. Sean was not amongst them. He subsequently required an operation to repair his fractured ankle. My opponent cross-examined Sean, but failed to land any significant punches. The next witness was the police surgeon who examined Sean at the station. He confirmed his injuries, although could not comment on how they had been caused. Crucially, he did not form the impression that Mr Keenan was significantly intoxicated when examined two hours after his arrest, although he had noted the smell of alcohol on his breath. This was confirmed by Sean's three friends, who gave evidence as to his demeanour only minutes before the incident.

PC Daniel Higgs commenced his evidence the following morning. A barrel shaped man with a crew cut and bushy moustache; he had harsh, chiselled features and small dark intense eyes. He stood to attention in the witness box, arms firmly behind his back, chest pushed out, telling the jury that he had responded to an emergency call. An ambulance was required. He had no description of the assailants, only sketchy details over his radio that someone was being attacked. "At the scene, I was confronted by a man who I now know is Mr Keenan. He was drunk and abusive. He reeked of alcohol. He was leaning over the victim. My main concern was for the youth on the ground…obviously injured. Mr Keenan was hampering our efforts to assist. He was swearing and could barely stand he was that intoxicated. I was unsure whether he was the assailant or not. Given the condition of Mr Keenan, I formed the impression he could have been responsible. The logical course of action was to take him down the station. Let him sober up. Question him when he was coherent and less abusive. As I attempted to guide him towards the rear of the van, he tripped and fell over. He could barely walk straight. He must have injured his ankle. The custody sergeant arranged for a doctor. He was later taken to hospital…we were subsequently able to eliminate him from our enquiries. He was released without charge."

Higgs was one cool customer. "PC Higgs," I began. "Does it not strike you as peculiar that Mr Keenan was so drunk he could barely walk, yet the police surgeon who examined him shortly after, had no recollection of him being intoxicated?"

"He must have sobered up. I suppose Mr Keenan's leg injury helped him calm down."

"It was just under two hours later, are you saying he sobered up that much in just two hours – that his friends are all mistaken about his condition only a short time earlier?"

"When I arrested him he was heavily intoxicated," he replied calmly, not rising to my bait.

"You received a message to the effect that a group of youths had been seen running away from the scene – the prime suspects. Yet you considered Mr Keenan was also potentially one of the perpetrators?"

"I see what you are driving at, but you have to understand…" He gestured towards the jury. "I was faced with an injured man and a drunkard, hampering police officers from doing our jobs."

"How exactly did he hamper you in your duties?"

"He was hovering around the victim, shouting, just being a nuisance. The van was the safest place for him out of harm's way."

"If he was the assailant, surely he would have run away?"

"He was incoherent; too drunk to run away."

"Too drunk to hit anyone then. You've fabricated the whole story. It is a smoke screen to conceal your despicable actions."

"No sir. I have not," he replied belligerently. One of the few perks of being a barrister is grilling police officers in a way that outside a courtroom would lead to an arrest for threatening or insulting behaviour.

"He was assisting the injured man when you physically assaulted him, threw him into the back of the van and punched him in the stomach. You twisted his leg until it fractured?"

"No sir, he fell whilst intoxicated."

"You called him an Irish bastard."

A Bold Deceiver • James Hurd

"That's an absolute damned lie. I hold no feelings of animosity towards Irish people. I never said those words. And I certainly never assaulted him."

As the judge rose for lunch, I could see the puzzled faces of the jurors, asking the one question I was unable to answer. Why? Higgs didn't appear a man consumed by prejudice, sadistically attacking another for no apparent reason. I needed a motive.

In the robing room, my opponent was blunt, ever willing to point out the weaknesses in my case – even the blindingly obvious ones. "Still think he's lying Tommy boy?" I hate being called Tommy. There is nothing more calculated to annoy me. "The jury don't buy it. Your guy's just got pound signs in his eyes."

"Is that your closing speech?" I quipped.

"No, that's your complete failure to adduce any evidence to suggest a reason why an upstanding member of Her Majesty's Constabulary would embark on an unprovoked attack."

"Come on, everyone believes there are bad apples," I offered without enthusiasm.

"We'll see," he replied. "Lunch?"

"No thanks. Work to do." Cold pizza anyone?

Chapter Two

I STILL REMEMBER the first time I laid eyes on her. I had retired to the conference room to check my cross-examination for the afternoon. Fifteen minutes before we were due to recommence, there was a soft knock on the door, as I downed my second cup of canteen coffee – I needed a caffeine drip.

"Yeah?" I was too immersed to pay much attention. A young woman stood hesitantly in the doorway, reluctant to penetrate the room, anxious not to trespass on unfamiliar territory. "Can I help?" I asked, slightly perturbed.

"I was rather hoping this might help you." With a slightly embarrassed smile, she held out her slender hand. She nervously pushed her hair back behind her ear, with her free hand. She watched anxiously, as I lifted the envelope from her outstretched palm. In the split second it took to glance down, to contemplate her offering, she vanished, leaving the door slightly ajar. My recollection of our initial encounter is I am afraid, hazy on detail: dark hair and an Irish accent. Instinctively, I ripped opened the cream manila envelope, my curiosity reaching frenzy point, and extracted a newspaper cutting. I read it once, then twice – and then a third time to ensure I was not hallucinating.

I grabbed my opponent on the doorstep of the court. "I think you ought to see this," I said, thrusting him a hasty photocopy.

"You can't use this," he hissed, scanning the text. "You can't adduce new evidence halfway through a trial."

"Let's ask the judge shall we."

A Bold Deceiver • James Hurd

I addressed the judge in the absence of the jury. "Your Honour, over the course of the luncheon interval an additional piece of evidence in the form of a newspaper article has come to light."

The judge removed his glasses and began rubbing his eyes impatiently. "Mr Flemming, can you explain to me how it is that after nearly eighteen months since these proceedings were issued, this document has materialised only on the afternoon of the second day of this trial?"

"I am afraid I cannot, Your Honour. It was brought to my attention little more than twenty minutes ago." It took a further fifteen minutes to persuade the judge, despite the best endeavours of the Cheshire Constabulary, to allow me to proceed.

As the jury filed back in, I studied the public gallery, catching a brief glimpse of the woman with the envelope, sitting in the far corner of the second row. The judge scowled at me wearily. "Very well, proceed Mr Flemming."

"P.C Higgs, do you recall your whereabouts on the 20th March 1993?" The slightest hint of concern appeared on his furrowed brow. He looked a little uneasy and shuffled his weight from one foot to the other. "PC Higgs…."

Advocating attack as the best form of defence, he answered defiantly: "I remember precisely where I was on that day."

"Warrington Town Centre, the day the IRA bomb exploded?"

He nodded, his eyes avoiding mine before turning to explain to the jury. "I was in the town centre, on the Saturday before Mother's Day with my youngest daughter. We had just entered a card shop, when the blast ripped through the building." I saw his whitened knuckles gripping the edge of the witness box firmly.

"It affected you badly?" I asked, trying not to appear too harsh. Every eye in the room alighted on Higgs. He nodded again. "Do you recall giving an interview to a local newspaper in January 1994?" I handed him a copy of the cutting. He ran his eyes across the newspaper article.

"This has nothing to do with Mr Keenan. You have no right to drag any of this up." He appeared flustered, looking in vain for assistance from his barrister and the judge.

The judge looked on impatiently. "Just answer the questions please PC Higgs."

I pressed on. "You were off work for six months following that day in March 1993, suffering with Post Traumatic Stress Disorder – nightmares and flashbacks?" His shield of impregnability slipped slightly. The door was slightly ajar. When he spoke it was both moving and eloquent: a double-edged sword for me.

"I heard a deafening bang, the blast – everything happened in slow motion." His face was pained. "All hell had broken loose – shattered glass everywhere. I jumped on Gemma, my daughter, to protect her from the raining jagged fragments of glass. It was the most terrible, frightening thing I have ever experienced. You see it in the movies. But when you're there…. People were screaming and crying, blood everywhere." I watched the juror's reactions. Three of the women in the back row had tissues they were dabbing around the eyes. "Yes I was off work for months. It damn nearly destroyed my career. Yes I had nightmares. Yes it nearly cost my marriage – I came close to a nervous breakdown. Have you got a problem with that?" His voice grew stronger with indignation. "My daughter could have been killed! But that has absolutely nothing to do with why I am standing here today."

"Do you still have the nightmares PC Higgs?"

"No…well very occasionally – you never get over something like that. It changes you – beyond recognition."

"How long had you been back at work in January 1994?"

"A few months," he replied, searching for the trap in the lawyer's weasel questions.

"Were you having the nightmares then PC Higgs?"

"I don't remember, maybe…."

I cut him off. "In the interview you say, I quote, 'I felt like a raging bull in a china shop, but so powerless. I was so angry that anyone could let off a bomb in a crowded town centre. They're not human. Just animals…but the anger fades over time, you have to channel it out. Or else it eats you up inside.' Could it be PC Higgs, that on the 5th January 1994, your rage leapt out of control? An Irish accent and an injured man – teach him a lesson. Another stupid Irish fucker like the ones who planted the bomb?"

Higgs shook his head defiantly. "No."

I had one last question. "Breaking Mr Keenan's leg, punching him, twisting it till it snapped…" My voice got louder as I spoke. "Kicking him, did that ease your nightmares, PC Higgs? Did it make you feel less helpless and more powerful?"

A Bold Deceiver • James Hurd

We had less than an hour to wait, after I had sat down at the end of closing speeches to the jury. I sat nervously in my seat as the clerk of the court asked the foreman if they had reached a decision. I was busting for a pee. "We have."

"And is that the decision of you all?"

"It is. We find that the Plaintiff Sean Keenan was unlawfully assaulted." Sean was awarded a total of just under £60,000 in damages. PC Higgs had already left, perhaps sensing the writing on the wall. I looked round as soon as the jury foreman had sat down to see if I could see the woman who had handed me the cutting, but spied only an empty seat.

Chapter Three

SEAN WAS HAPPY to shower praise on anyone even remotely connected with his case, from the judge to the security guard at the entrance to the court building. "Who is she?" I demanded.

"You mean Tara? I have no idea where she dragged all that up from," he smirked. "I expect she will be in the pub. You are coming to celebrate?"

The Ox, on Liverpool Road, was pretty crowded – the usual Friday night rush for alcohol in full swing. Inside I was confronted with a mass of heaving bodies around the bar, some trying to get served, some trying to move away from the bar with their hard-earned purchases – others just mingling. The jukebox was playing some trashy one hit wonder, by whichever boy band was flavour of the day. Eventually, pint in hand I began scouring the nooks and crannies of the dimly lit interior, searching for Sean. The party was already in full swing around a table in the far corner. Sean insisted on buying Guinness for everyone in sight, whilst cracking jokes about how he had the jury eating out of his hand, a wry grin emanating from his face. He spied my approach and changed direction in mid flow. "Tom," he shouted, thrusting me into a bear hug. "Let me get you a drink." He disappeared in the general direction of the bar with a long list of drinks to buy.

"Thank you" said Kathy, Sean's wife, grasping my hand, wiping her eyes in the corners, where the faintest sign of emotion was beginning to appear.

"The credit lies elsewhere," I told her, pointing at the disappearing back of Sean. "I think that Tara is it…deserves the accolades?"

"Of course, you haven't met Tara, at least not properly?" She pulled me towards the other side of the table, where Tara was involved in an animated conversation. "Tara," she called. "Come meet Tom."

Tara made her excuses and departed from the discussion in mid-flow. I had been so absorbed earlier in the day, I had not noticed how strikingly attractive she was. Now, as she approached, her beauty captivated me; her dark shoulder length brown hair, falling loosely, with just the hint of a curl. She had large pale green eyes, which dominated her features; eyes that burned with piercing earnestness and fierce intensity. Her nose was slightly pointed, but curved at the very tip. When she laughed, her head tipped back a fraction, and her nose wrinkled, sending ripples from the corners of her mouth out in waves, which were absorbed just in front of her ear lobes. Her lips were thin but perfectly formed, proportioned exactly for her high cheekbones and pale skin. No necklace – just the freckles visible at the base of her long graceful neck, where her skin had been exposed to the sun. Her only jewellery was a silver Celtic band on her wrist. I could just discern the outline of the embroidery on her bra and the swell of her breasts. Five ten, late twenties – possibly older? She smiled politely, as she brushed her hair from her cheek, pressing it behind her ear. I noticed she did that when she was nervous.

"Mr Flemming." She spoke with a Belfast brogue, extending her hand. Our fingers entwined momentarily, our eyes meeting for an instant before she looked away, faintly embarrassed, but still venturing a smile.

"Tom." I returned her smile. "And, thank you."

"Tara O'Neil. All I did was find a newspaper cutting – you made the noble speech," she joked.

"You don't fancy helping out every time I'm in a jam do you?" I teased.

"Depends on what you are offering?" she replied, relaxing into a mischievous grin.

Sean returned carrying a tray laden with Guinness and Jameson chasers. "Looks like it could be a heavy night," I commented.

"He deserves it." Tara took a drink from Sean's outstretched hand.

"How do you know Sean?"

"Kathy and I teach at the same school."

"What do you teach?" I asked, wiping the cream from the head of the Guinness from around my mouth with the back of my hand.

"History," she replied.

"My favourite subject."

"Yeah?" Tara cast a dubious eye in my direction – weighing up whether this was the prelude to some crummy bullshit chat up routine.

"I preferred the more recent stuff – the Russian revolution to the Cold War."

"It's all relevant. Mankind's wars, revolutions, inventions, marriages, divorces, power, greed and revenge – depressing stuff."

"And womankind?"

"Only the good parts of history," she joked – enjoying the banter.

"So it's men's role in history that is depressing?"

Tara laughed. "We make the same mistakes our ancestors made when they ran around in bearskins. All our screw-ups travel down well worn paths. For all our technology, we don't get any wiser. We just figure out more efficient ways to beat the crap out of each other."

Her words were matter of fact and an awkward pause ensued. Tara appeared tense, as if she had spoken out of turn. I tried to lighten the mood, aware she suddenly felt self-conscious. "How long have you been in Manchester?"

"I moved here just before last Christmas."

"How did you find the article?" I asked, nursing my beer.

"I'm doing a Masters at Manchester University. I was doing some research a few months ago. I had to check through back issues of local papers. It was a pure coincidence – Higgs' name just seemed familiar. I copied it and then forgot all about it. I was going to tell Kathy…"

"That simple?" I asked amazed, but puzzled. I sensed the alcohol beginning to influence my brain, on an empty stomach. "How did you make the connection between the assault and Warrington?"

"Lucky guess," Tara replied, making deliberate eye contact – attempting to reinforce her sincerity.

I sipped another drink Sean had thrust upon me. "Yet you sat on it until this morning?" I think Tara could sense my slight frustration that she had chosen to reveal the story only at the last possible moment.

She paused, contemplating her words with care. "I'd forgotten all about it. Anyway, it was really none of my business," she replied with a casual swing of the shoulders, as if it was not big deal. "You guys are the professionals. For all I knew, you already had the story. Besides, maybe there was nothing in it. I would have looked an idiot."

"Why disclose it then?"

"I made the connection, when Higgs was in the witness box. Even if you had all told me to sod off and mind my own business at least I'd tried. I'm not the sort to sit and do nothing. If Sean had lost, I would have blamed myself."

I was on the point of enquiring the subject of her Masters, but the expression on Tara's face changed. Subtly, but noticeably, she retreated, as if she had revealed too much. She clearly didn't appreciate me firing questions at her. Perhaps she thought I was cross-examining her? I kicked myself. There was the signal – that look you get from a girl that you're trying your best to impress. And you know, no matter what you say or do, when she shoots that glance around the bar that asks, 'who else is out tonight?' that you've blown it. True enough, within a minute, she made her excuses and disappeared in the direction of the toilets. Upon her return, I watched her skirt gracefully around the opposite side of the bar, heading for the door, studiously avoiding looking in my direction. Whatever I had said, it had certainly caused her to make a quick exit. I stopped worrying though, as the drinks racked up.

My head was aware of the extent of my indulgence the following morning. To my surprise, as I rarely socialise with clients, I found I had agreed to go out for Sean's birthday the following Saturday. I had even written the restaurant details down on a piece of paper. I should have politely declined. If there was a subconscious part of me that had accepted, in the vain hope of a second opportunity with the intriguing woman who'd brushed me off, it was a pretty forlorn.

I arrived late at the restaurant, situated in the heart of China Town, feeling flustered – my shirt already sticking to the small of my back with the humidity of the summer evening. I despise being late to restaurants. You always end up with the seat no one else wants by the pot plant at the end of the table, which means you cannot hear a damn word being spoken by those already engrossed in conversation. You spend the entire meal pretending to understand half snatched phrases and entertaining yourself creating funny shapes with your napkin. Oh, and drinking – again.

Whether coincidence or fortuity, arriving late left only a single spare seat around a long table with perhaps eight people strewn along either side, one seat – next to Tara. Just don't blow it this time.

"Beginning to think you'd forgotten," Sean mused, "given how pissed you were the other night," his wit provoking a degree of amusement around the table.

"Don't mind me." I pulled my chair in and mouthed hellos to the mix of strange and familiar faces, which now looked up at me accusingly, as I detained them from their dim sum.

Tara held her head, leaning slightly away from me, her chin rested on her intertwined fingers, listening to a heated conversation between Manchester United fans expressing sour grapes that Blackburn Rovers had won the Premiership title. Dressed in a maroon top, the soft pale skin on her naked shoulders was both visible and inviting. Slender upper arms, with a hint of muscle tone. I dragged my eyes away reluctantly, making clear my football allegiances lay with the blue half of the city – Manchester City.

"So it's you been delaying us from our food?" she accused.

"Sorry. Hope the food is worth waiting for."

"I get so full on the starters and then can't face the rest," she replied, rotating her shoulders away from the football debate. She dropped her hands from her chin.

"I could just eat crispy duck, forget the rest."

"They've ordered the banquet." Her manner was formal – reserved. It was okay to talk banalities but personal intimacy was off the agenda. After a couple of glasses of wine though, Tara began to relax. "If I didn't know what you did for a living, I would never have put you down as a barrister."

"I'll take that as a compliment," I mumbled, tearing the remaining pork off the spare rib between my teeth.

She laughed, sipping her wine. "You're not offended?"

"Quite the opposite. Pretend you never met me before. What do you think I do?"

Tara bit her bottom lip and pushed her hair back behind her ear, her eyes glistening and her lips curling into the subtle beginnings of a smile. "Accountant?"

I rolled my eyes. "Tell me you don't give careers advice to your class."

Her smile broadened, ready with a one liner. "I tell those without moral scruples, who want to get rich: rob banks or study law."

"Okay, you win." I refilled her wineglass. "For now."

"So, seriously, I am interested. What made you become a barrister?"

The waiter cleared away the empty plates.

"I would have liked to be a musician, but I wasn't that good. Learn to live with your limitations. Discovering them, that's half the battle."

"Very profound – but…?"

"Perhaps I'm just an argumentative git," I replied cheerfully, and then thought for a moment. "As a teenager, I was and remain a huge Dylan fan. He wrote this protest song about a miscarriage of justice – a black boxer named Rubin 'Hurricane' Carter – wrongly convicted of murder. He talks about his shame that the justice system was reduced to being a game. I don't know – perhaps in my youthful exuberance I figured I could make a difference."

Tara looked bemused. "So are you making a difference?"

"Only when I get cases like Sean's. Rest of the time it's…"

Tara groaned in sympathy, twirling her wine glass stem between her fingers. "Like me marking forty essays on the causes of the French Revolution."

"Sounds gripping," I replied, rolling a duck pancake. "So why do you teach?"

"The feeling you get, when you inspire one kid. For every twenty that sit there ignoring me, staring out of the window or insulting me, there is maybe one waiting to have his or her horizons expanded, if you can reach him or her."

"So do you make a difference?"

"I spend my time filling in pieces of meaningless paper, coaching kids to pass tests, so we can achieve a league table place."

"You sound as cynical as me."

"Do you still play an instrument?" Tara asked, her body language positive, the reflection from the candle dancing in her eyes, as she moulded the dripping candle wax between her fingers.

"I play bass in a pub band – cover versions mainly. We do the odd wedding or party. What do you listen to?"

"The Doors, Joni Mitchell, I like Alanis Morisette and Van Morrison – kind of comes with the territory. You?"

"Dylan – like I said. Pink Floyd, The Who, Led Zeppelin and Neil Young."

"Do you like any female artists?"

"Chick singers?"

Tara shot me a look of bemused indignation. "Do you work with female lawyers?"

"Of course," I replied cheekily, enjoying the joke.

"Do you call them chick lawyers?"

With a straight face, I nodded confirmation, which drew a sharp response, in the form of a friendly poke in the ribs. "Seriously," I yelped. "I think Patti Smith is great."

With each passing minute, I felt drawn to her – mesmerised, the wine diminishing both our inhibitions, our faces only centimetres apart, as if we were the only two on the table.

Afterwards, I was propping up the bar with Sean, when I spied Tara saying her farewells. I took my cue and headed for the door – not all coincidences are down to chance. "Where's the best place to get a cab?" she asked.

"There's always a queue at Piccadilly Gardens. Better trying the station – I'm heading that way."

"Please yourself." Her tone was non-committal – no invitation but neither a refusal. The city was still alive with clubbers, people leaving the bars and restaurants, laughing and joking into the neon-reflected night. I walked by her side, basking in her glory, and the warm glow of alcohol.

"So given your love of Dylan, how come you're not a protest singer, rather than playing in a party band?"

"I once heard a lyric: '*I believed that rock 'n roll can really change the world, but when I bought my first guitar it was just to pick up girls.*'"

"Now that I can believe," she laughed. Her voice was soft and gentle, her tone intimate and inviting. Perhaps I mistook it for a tacit encouragement where none existed.

Tara leaned back on the metal queue dividers at the taxi rank. "You aren't really going this way are you?" She was playing the game, enjoying it – flirting with me. Her eyes were excited, alive and appeared to relish the sparring.

"I live a few miles or so that way," I confessed, pointing across the city. I'm usually pretty good at reading signals. This time heaven knows? "Listen, I've really enjoyed this evening. I wondered if we might you know, have a drink sometime?"

The question can barely have come as a surprise, but her response was as if I pulled a gun on her. Her body language altered, as she recoiled from our earlier closeness. We edged forward, as the couple in front clambered into the next available taxi. She placed her fingertips lightly on my forearm. I sensed indecision – her eyes said yes, the rest of her stubbornly refused.

"Tom," she began, the brush off glaringly imminent. "You're a sweet guy…but…" Isn't there always a but? She pressed a kiss onto my cheek, affectionate and sublime.

"But…my life's kind of complicated. I don't think it would work out – sorry."

I was about to protest, but the next cab had already drawn up to the rank. I watched in resignation as the taxi pulled away. At least she hadn't replied: 'It's not you, it's me.' Why do people say that? Do they believe that it is somehow less cruel? The truth is that it is always you – whether you've fallen out of love, met someone else, got bored or just the feeling that it is time to plough a different field. I walked down the station ramp, relishing the prospect of drowning my sorrows. So much so, I almost didn't see the taxi brake harshly and then reverse. Tara pushed down the window. Leaning out, hair blowing in the cool evening breeze, she called my name. I ran the thirty feet towards her. "What's your number," she shouted enthusiastically. I was perplexed. She was an enigma: hesitant, reluctant and eager in the space of minutes. I shouted the digits. She scribbled the number on her wrist. "I'll call," she promised, before the impatient taxi driver lurched forward again.

Chapter Four

MY LIFE WAS too busy to sit by the telephone, on the off chance that Tara might decide to place that call. Yet I could not quite expunge the intelligent, beautiful but mysterious woman who handed me newspaper articles, flirted outrageously with her eyes and then told me her life was too complicated for a drink.

It was almost the end of July, before the call I never really anticipated materialised. I was nearing the conclusion of a juicy sex discrimination Employment Tribunal, involving salacious allegations of office affairs. I had barely commenced preparing my closing submissions when the phone rang. The answer phone had already kicked in – a female voice with an accent. Quick, pick the phone up, before she hangs up. "Tom, its Tara. What are you doing tonight?"

I thought about the bundles of documents strewn across my desk. "Nothing," I lied.

"I have a spare ticket for the theatre – Richard III at the Opera House."

"Sounds great," I replied, anxious to see her under any circumstances.

"I'll meet you outside – 7.30pm." I checked my watch. I had only written the first two pages – I'd just have to get up early.

I stood outside the theatre at 7.20pm, full of trepidation, like a teenager on a first date. After a few minutes a coach pulled up and a crowd of adolescents began to disembark. I guessed they were about fourteen or fifteen, laughing and joking with one another. It's funny how when you look at any group of school kids, you recognise the same patterns, from when you were an adolescent. The group of lads who think they are hard as nails, despite their inability to grow a five o'clock shadow between them. Then there are the 'beautiful people,' a group of girls; such a turn off because they know they are attractive and flaunt it in rather a vulgar fashion – meanwhile the nerds engage in secret fantasies from afar.

I almost missed Tara descend from the coach after the uniformed hordes. You can imagine my bewilderment when she started barking orders at the herd to stay together and not to wander off. She even sounded like a teacher, which seriously scared me. Tara wore a wicked grin; guilt or amusement at the disbelief on my face. "Did I forget to mention the fifty-three chaperones?" she commented roguishly.

"It must have slipped your mind," I grimaced. What had I got myself into?

"A colleague dropped out at the last minute. So pretend we have known each other ages," she said in a hushed tone, intertwining her arm with mine. "Besides we were desperate." Tara turned her attention to the task at hand, gathering the brats round her. "Listen, everyone. This is Mr Flemming. Any problems, you can go to him."

With that, Tara strode off towards the ticket office. Suddenly my closing speech possessed a strange allure. "Excuse me sir," called a voice from my left. "Is Mrs O'Neil your girlfriend?" I almost told her instinctively to mind her own bloody business, but thought better of it, given the circumstances.

I was rescued by another member of staff. "Don't be so rude, Emma," she said reproachfully. "Sorry about that. It's very brave of you to volunteer at such short notice."

"How could I refuse such a tempting offer," I said politely. Tara reappeared with the tickets. "Nice bunch of kids," I offered half-heartedly.

"You don't have to pretend," she quipped. "I at least get paid to do this."

"What's my excuse?"

"Insanity or infatuation – I haven't decided yet."

The curtain rose: "*Now is the winter of our discontent, made glorious summer by this son of York; And all the clouds that lour'd upon our house, In the deep bosom of the ocean buried.*" I leaned towards Tara and whispered, "I guess I should have asked who else was going when you said there was a spare ticket."

"I'll make it up to you later," she promised, brushing her hand against mine for a brief moment. I queued with a mob of adolescents for ice cream during the interval, thankfully avoiding further embarrassing questions, before we resumed out seats. *"A horse! a horse! my kingdom for a horse!"*

"You have to come back on the coach – pupil teacher ratios I'm afraid," Tara enlightened me, as the curtain fell. So I hitched a ride back to where the parents were waiting to collect their little darlings, the car park darkened in the late July sky, with a pinkish hue. Had her life really become significantly less complicated over recent weeks?

"There's a good chippy, not far from here – if you're hungry?" Tara suggested. "If you're not still mad at me, that is?" Tara owned a tartan red 1967 Mk1 MGB roadster. Inside the squashed interior, a lipstick holder, makeup bag, empty polystyrene coffee cups, chocolate wrappers and various assorted papers were spread over the passenger seat. "Sorry about the mess." She swept the items off the passenger seat and onto the floor.

"Nice motor," I told her admiringly.

"I bought it from one of the other teachers last summer. I can do most things myself, but Alistair is only too willing to assist. He still really regards it as his baby." Tara studied my face. "You seem surprised that a woman knows the difference between the engine and the boot?"

I laughed. "That's not true."

"My father was a mechanic," she said, slowing for the changing traffic lights. "If I hung around too much at home, he would have me with a monkey wrench in one hand, and grease all over my face, much to my mother's annoyance. He always wanted a son, but had to make do with two daughters."

"He's retired now I guess?"

"He's dead," she replied quietly, but very matter of fact.

"Sorry," I cursed my bumbling lack of tact.

"It was a long time ago." Tara changed the subject swiftly. "Do you have brothers and sisters?"

"A brother called Ben and a sister in law, Becky. They have been married for just over three years."

We lent against the bonnet, enjoying the warm summer evening and ate fish and chips, soaked in salt, vinegar and brown sauce. "Told you I'd make it up to you."

"You really know how to show a bloke a good time."

"The way I see it," she reasoned, munching a chip, "is that I had to put up with listening to you for a day, whilst you were at work. The least I could do was to return the favour."

"Courts are public places. You could have left any time…"

"So are theatres." Touché. Tara changed the subject. "I suppose you drive a BMW or a posh little roadster…perhaps a Porsche?"

"Do I look that flash?"

Tara shrugged her shoulders, ready with the comeback. "Anything's possible."

"1961 Alvis TD21, black with red leather and chrome wire wheels."

"Never heard of them?"

"They went the same way as most of British industry in the late sixties and seventies. Great car, but the ash frame is a nightmare for rot."

"It's built of wood?"

"Classic British technology. You have to treat her with a little respect." I screwed up the white greaseproof paper. "Like an old aunt or a new lover."

Tara giggled shyly. "Is that what you're doing with me?" What could I say? "So we share a passion for old cars." It was a statement, rather than a question. "Wanna ride home?"

The evening was warm and muggy. Tara dropped the hood and started the engine. We headed back into town, a cool breeze blowing across my face. As she accelerated down the near deserted street, I pressed play on the stereo and Bruce Springsteen emerged. I hummed along with Thunder Road for a minute or so, as it crackled through the speakers, with just a hint of distortion, before finally venturing into uncharted territory. "I figured you taking my number was the thanks but no thanks routine."

"I did get the taxi to reverse."

"Most girls would you know, either just say yes or no."

"I'm not most girls," she replied bashfully, glancing in the rear view mirror. "It's been a long time since anyone asked me on a date. I didn't want to say yes…but I didn't want to say no either."

"You could have fooled me."

"Not hard – you should have seen your face," Tara said, her lips parting to form a broad cheeky grin, "when I stepped off the coach. It was an absolute picture."

Her laughter was infectious. "It wasn't quite what I anticipated in a trip to the theatre."

"You could have walked away."

"I was curious about the warped mind that figured this was a good idea."

"Security in numbers. Anyway I wanted to see how you would react."

"Did I pass?" I asked.

"You must either be mad or think I'm worth persevering with."

"Have you worked out which yet?"

"I'll let you know," she promised, turning down my street.

"You got plans for the weekend?"

"Not really – you?"

"Maybe go out on my bike if the weather holds."

"I always wanted to ride a motorbike. My mother would have thrown a fit."

"Mine did."

"You like Mexican food?" I asked, as she slowed. "Only I'm not cooking for your whole class!"

"On one condition: you take me on your bike." I opened the door, letting my hand rest delicately on hers for just a second, as it covered the gear stick, as I said goodbye.

Chapter Five

THE FOLLOWING WEEKEND granted little relief for gardeners or water companies, but was a biker's idea of heaven: warm and sunny, an almost cloudless sky. Tara eyed my 1969 Triumph T120 Bonneville and then walked over to the other side of the garage and pulled the dustsheet off my Harley Davidson Fat Boy. "I take it all back. That is flash. Look at those solid wheels."

I wheeled the Triumph out of the garage, avoiding the tray for the ubiquitous oil leaks. The bike roared into life first time. Tara donned my spare helmet and clambered onto the back. I dropped it into first and opened the throttle. Out of the city through Altrincham, along the A556 towards Mere and then down the A50 to Holmes Chapel, before eventually doubling back onto the M56 – accelerating down the slip road, sixty, seventy, eighty. Flying along in the outside lane, the wind tearing through us, buffeting us slightly, the tyres gripped the warm tarmac like glue. The engine sang in pleasure, accompanied by the harmonious roar of the twin exhaust pipes.

As we approached the airport junction, Tara tapped me on the shoulder and pointed towards the exit. I parked the bike on Ringway Road, where the road intersects with the end of the runway, the landing lights only a matter of feet away. Tara removed the helmet, her face flushed red. "That was fun," she said, shaking her hair and running her hand through it. The roar of jet engines filled the sky as a 737 flew overhead, its undercarriage visible, before gracefully reconnecting with land. "I come here occasionally – just to sit and watch the planes take off and land. Imagining the other side of the world – new cultures, people and places to see."

"They'll still drink Coca-Cola, watch CNN and support Manchester United."

"You're an old cynic." She pushed my arm in a friendly fashion. "It's a daydream: some have this fantasy about walking into their boss's office, telling him exactly what they think about his crass management skills and shoving a resignation letter under his nose. Not my style, I'd just jump on a plane and disappear. Stick two fingers up to the world, as I leave the sorry sons of bitches behind. Start afresh some place new, where the weather's just a bit warmer. Tara began humming 'Everybody's Talking', singing rhythmically, almost to herself, as another jet commenced its final approach.

"Freddie Neil," I said, joining in with her. "Although most people think Harry Nilsson wrote it because he recorded it for the film Midnight Cowboy."

Tara looked across, awoken from her daydream; snuggling close to my shoulder. "Try this one, she said, continuing the travelling theme. "We've Gotta Get Out of This Place. "

"The Animals," I replied smugly, "although of course they didn't write it. That was Cynthia Weil and Barry Mann – more famous for 'You Lost That Loving Feeling'." Defeated, she racked her brain for another. One thing I quickly learnt about Tara was how damn competitive she was, at everything. "My turn – 'Leaving On a Jet Plane'".

"Way too easy." Her face lit up with a child like glee. "John Denver. This'll stump you. 'Fly Away'". I could hear the riff in my head and knew the words to the chorus. The answer was on the tip of my tongue. The obvious puzzlement on my face was sweet music to Tara, who gloated at her victory. "You'll just have to admit I know more about music than you." There was a wicked look of mischief in her eyes. They were alight, just like the night at the taxi rank.

"Never."

"Come on – admit a chick might know more about music than you."

I shook my head vehemently. "No."

That seemed only to bolster her playfulness, before she collapsed back in a heap, laughing. "You know what?"

"What?"

"I have no idea who sang it either." My face was beside hers, only a hair's breadth between us. I reached out towards her and kissed her, tasting her sweetness – her lips responded without hesitation. And before you all feel the need to write in with the answer, I now know it's Lenny Kravitz.

The landing lights glowed brightly, stinging my eyes in the early evening sunshine. We watched in amazement, our hands covering our ears, as a 747 thundered down upon us – so close, I swear I could have touched the undercarriage. After the noise had subsided, I suddenly had a thought. "Are you Catholic or Protestant?"

"Why does that matter to you?" Tara looked surprised. "I didn't figure you as a religious type?"

"I'm not. It's just the first question that springs to mind when I think about Northern Ireland."

Tara eyed me quizzically, weighing her response. "Lapsed Catholic – I'd be there a hell of a long time if I went to confession now. But you'd think Belfast was Beirut the way it's reported over here. Most people just get on with their lives oblivious to… "

"The troubles?"

"You English are like the Americans, you prefer simple solutions: good guys and bad guys, cowboys and Indians, Catholics and Protestants. It's not about religion, although if you actually listen to what Paisley has to say you realise…"

"He's nuts?" I asked in ignorance.

"He believes that there's a Catholic conspiracy to corrupt the Protestants of Northern Ireland. It's a cloak on which to hang his bigotism. It's not theology that divides Gerry Adams and Ian Paisley, but politics. He'll fight to the bitter end to retain a monopoly on power. Let's just hope that the more moderate unionists have a little more appetite for compromise…" Her words hung in the air, floating between us like a cloud of stale cigarette smoke.

"That's the first time I have been referred to as 'you English'" I said light-heartedly, hoping to ease the tension.

Tara buried her head under my arm. "I didn't mean you personally. It just winds me up. The Government prevaricate and bluster for months on whether the cease-fire is permanent and then want the guns handed in before any talks. You have to build a peace first – not demand surrender." She stopped suddenly, in mid flow and appeared slightly embarrassed. "Just ignore me, I get carried away sometimes."

I had so many questions. Weren't there bigots on both sides? Were republicans any more peace-minded than hard line unionists? About herself: just how did studying for a Master's degree allow you to research local Manchester papers from 1994? Why was it that her life was so less complicated this month than last? I feared to probe too far in case it frightened her away.

Back home, Tara leafed through my record collection as I cleared the dishes from the table.

"I can't believe you still listen to vinyl."

"What's wrong with that?"

"A little primitive – dirty needles and you have to turn them over."

"There's something special about the size and shape of an LP. The design on the sleeve cover is large enough to be meaningful. It gets lost on a CD. Besides the sound is warmer, more attention to detail. CDs are too clinical, the sound compressed."

Tara looked amused at my passionate defence of the obsolete. "You really are retro man," she mused, as I emerged from the kitchen, clutching a bottle of Tequila. We drank to the passing of the 33rpm black plastic disc, as the last orange vestiges of sun gave way to the darkness of the night. We swayed in time to the music, my body pressing against hers, my lips searching and finding hers, intertwining, exploring – intoxicated with desire. The frantic fumbling with clasps and buttons and the trail of abandoned clothing strewn along the path to the bedroom. Sublime intensity: the softness of her skin, the scent of her perfume, as I kissed the nape of her neck; the delicateness of her touch and the eager warmth of her tongue as we made love. Afterwards as we lay contented, her head resting on my shoulder, I whispered. "Can a dumb Englishmen, ask you a question?"

"Discovered your true identity, at last?" Her words were almost emasculated by kisses.

"The cease-fire – do you think it will last?"

Tara pulled out of our embrace and brushed her hair away from her face, where it had fallen loosely over her eyes, her elbow pressed to my chest. She lifted her head, "Oh Tom, I hope so."

The following week Tara invited me over to her place. She lived on the edge of the village of Styal, just south of the airport, a few of miles from the affluence of Wilmslow and Alderley Edge, with a traditional red phone box, and a great pub – The Ship Inn. Tara's cottage, with fields to the side, was converted from a small barn situated a hundred

yards behind what was once the farmhouse. At the rear of the cottage was a second smaller outbuilding that, according to Tara, the developers could not obtain planning permission to convert. Instead, it formed a garage with stone walls, slate roof and a couple of porthole type windows, situated unevenly along the side. I calculated it could accommodate at least three cars or heaven knows how many bikes.
"Nice place."

"It's rented. Poor teacher, remember."

"Like your garden." I glanced across the neatly manicured lawns and borders.

"I'd like to convince you it was all my own handiwork. The landlord lives next door," Tara pointed in the direction of the adjacent farmhouse. "He has little else to do since his wife died. Besides, he's a bit of an old woman. Tending the front garden is just an excuse to be nosy."

Tara showed me into the living room and threw her jacket over the back of one of the chairs, before disappearing into the kitchen. I wandered around her living room, examining ornaments and trying not to pry at the open correspondence on the dresser. Tara emerged a couple of minutes later carrying two mugs of coffee and a bottle of whisky. I only made the connection in my mind, once I had reclined on her sofa. The name on the envelopes; my mind was jolted back to the night at the theatre. A comment made by one of the kids. "The other night at the theatre?" I began tentatively. "One of the kids – she called you Mrs O'Neil. And your bills…sorry I couldn't help seeing: they all say Mrs as well?"

Tara replaced her glass on the side table, every last trace of humour banished from her countenance. "That will teach me to sleep with a lawyer." There was a note of resignation in her voice. I hung my head, anxious for our eyes not to meet; the room suddenly became stifled with tension. Tara withdrew to the far end of the sofa, curling her legs, in a slightly defensive manner. "I was married once." She spoke quietly, almost a murmur – her voice choking with emotion.

"You never said."

"Do you want me to wear a sign round my neck?" she asked defensively.

"I'm sorry. I had no right to pry." Tara approached the dresser. Opening the top drawer she removed a brown envelope crammed with photographs. There was a hint of pain in her expression. Was she angry with me? Tara sorted the pictures and selected one. She handed it to me in silence. It was a man, standing in a pub, leaning against the bar, smiling – a half-empty pint of beer by his side. Tall, dark curly hair, roughly my age, wearing a shirt and a denim jacket. Strong jaw line and bright eyes. He was laughing into the camera.

"His name was Patrick. Patrick O'Neil. McCabe is my maiden name," she added, clutching the envelope tightly.

"Was?" I replied automatically, still looking at the photograph, not really picking up on the intonation.

"He's dead," she whispered, almost inaudibly. I cursed my crass insensitivity. Yet I felt elation, without the complications of an ex to compete with. Worst of all, a part of me was consumed with jealousy, over a dead man in a photograph; for the love, still obvious in his beautiful wife, upon whose sofa I was now sat.

"I'm sorry." For a moment, I thought she might cry, but that wasn't Tara's style. She didn't do vulnerability, at least not openly. Instead, she blinked her slightly reddened eyes and tried to regain her composure. She wasn't cold; I was still just too much of a stranger. After a brief interlude she unfolded the story of her own volition. "If you want to know me, you'll have to become acquainted with my baggage some time." She was reticent – her unease obvious. "We met at Queen's University. Pat was a medical student. Everyone loved Pat, whether you had known him five minutes or ten years – always the first with his wallet out at the bar and the last to leave. I think you would have got on well – except he was a Man United fan."

"I was going to say he had poor taste – but that wouldn't be true."

She began fidgeting with her hair. "It's the Irish thing: George Best and Roy Keane. After graduating, I did my teacher training, whilst Pat began the junior doctor routine. Endless hours and crazy shift work."

I felt a strange mix of emotions. A curiosity regarding what had happened, but no desire to dwell on the thought there had been anyone else. "We were married at Easter 1990. Just under a year later he was dead: February 13th 1991. Pat had just finished a night shift. He rang just after 6am to say he was running late. I never really managed to return to sleep once the phone had rang. I made breakfast and waited for the sound of his car. We would have about twenty minutes together before he went to bed and I left for work. Only this day...."

It was obvious she felt uncomfortable. "You don't need to do this."

Tara waved me away. "You'd find out sooner or later." She sipped whisky for inspiration. "Sometimes you have a feeling that everything is not quite right: a sixth sense." She gripped the arm of the sofa tightly with her hand. "I can't explain…just a sense of foreboding. I dismissed it as mad insecure paranoia. Like men always accuse women of having!"

"Never," I replied sheepishly.

"You wait till you really get to know me, then answer that question again." I reached out and placed my hand on top of hers. She made no attempt to move it. "Just as I was beginning to think I would have to catch a bus to work, the telephone rang. It wouldn't be the first time Pat had rung to say he was caught up in an emergency. I almost said, 'hello Pat.' Before I could open my mouth, there was a formal voice. It was the police. There had been a car accident. Pat was in hospital. I panicked, scrabbled around for a cab number to get me to the hospital." Tara folded her arms across her chest. "I arrived at the hospital…too late." Through dead eyes, she said quietly: "I'd have given anything to be there – to spend just a few more minutes with him. That's not much to ask, is it?" Her voice trailed off but her words hung in the air for a second. I wanted to reach out to her, but Tara staunchly maintained her distance.

Tara returned from the kitchen with a packet of cigarettes. She pushed one between her lips. She noted my surprise. "For emergencies and stressful days – I've given up, but you know how it is." Tara inhaled deeply, the end of the cigarette glowing orange. "The car appeared to have veered from the road and struck a tree. There was an inquest, which recorded a verdict of accidental death. There was a suggestion he'd fallen asleep at the wheel, after his shift. I don't buy that…"

"I'm sorry," I said. She looked up, as she crushed the cigarette end in the ash tray.

"Don't be. It was a long time ago. It just makes me so angry, still. Not being able to rationalise what happened. How could I just carry on with my life, as if nothing had happened?" Tara's words faltered. "Whilst Pat's life was taken away. He was only twenty seven. He had so much life to live. We had so much life to live," she trailed off, "when he died, I lost everything."

"Was that why you had left Ireland," I asked. The disapproving expression on her face indicated she had revealed enough about herself for one night. Tara only ever let me in so far – carefully controlled access.

"A new beginning," she replied. "Can we change the subject now?"

James Hurd • *A Bold Deceiver*

"Perhaps I should go," I offered tactfully, looking at my watch.
"Please. I really don't feel like being alone."

I remember the warmth of her tongue, the scent of her fragrance and the touch of her skin, as my fingers caressed the inside of her knee. But her passion also aroused my insecurity. Was it my face she saw when she closed her eyes, or another's?

10th August 1995

Gerry Adams, President of Sinn Féin, tonight addressed a rally outside Belfast City Hall. During his speech Mr Adams was heckled by a member of the audience, shouting, "Bring back the IRA!" In what has come to be seen as an overt threat, jumped on by the British Government and unionist politicians as evidence of bad faith in the peace process, Adams replied: "They haven't gone away, you know!"

Chapter Six

OVER THE FOLLOWING weeks, I was introduced to Tara's work colleagues, some of whom remain close friends, all these years later. Tara got to know my family, quickly striking up friendships with my brother Ben and his wife Becky. Tara came to watch the band play in a local pub and to my profound unease, got on like a house on fire with Leanne, our lead singer and my former, albeit short lived, girlfriend. That current-ex thing is both so uncomfortable you want to leave them to it, and yet dare not miss a word in case they start comparing notes. Tara and I went to Blackpool and she insisted on us experiencing every ride on the Pleasure Beach that required travelling upside down. I have no problem with speed, but I do have fundamental objections to 'entertainment' that requires being inverted. Tara, on the other hand, adored it.

Tara possessed an almost evangelical zeal for her own independence. She would struggle with a dodgy washer on a sink, or a problem with her car seemingly for hours, rather than seek assistance. She existed in a bubble of self-sufficiency that she felt unable to compromise. On an emotional level, she was reluctant to become too involved it seemed, not just with me, but with anybody on a level of intimacy beyond the superficial. That same hesitation she exhibited at the taxi rank. There were parts of her life she just didn't want to reveal, as if she had no past, prior to her arrival on this side of the Irish Sea. Having been forced to survive alone in the most arduous of circumstances, I guessed some walls were not easily dismantled.

At half term, we took a trip to Amsterdam, visiting everything from Anne Frank's house to the Sex Museum, where we giggled like helpless teenage boys, confronted with their first copy of Playboy. Our last night in Amsterdam stands out: good food and wine in a great little family run Italian place just outside the Red Light District. We then descended on a coffee-house and spent the rest of the evening becoming high as kites. Tara was hilarious when stoned, needing only the slightest prompting to degenerate into insatiable fits of laughter. The fresh air sobered us a little, our arms intertwined, reliant on each other to steer in a straight line, navigating our way back to the hotel. We crossed over a canal bridge, the neon lights of a nearby café, still half full with partying insomniacs, reflecting on the still dark water. "Thomas Flemming, I never thought I'd say this, but I do believe I am falling in love with you."

We stopped on the bridge. "You're stoned," I laughed. I took her hand in mine.

"Does that make my feelings any less valid?" a gentle hint of indignation crept into her voice.

"Can it be that Miss Independence is admitting to needing someone?" I replied, mocking her slightly.

That provoked a sharp intake of breath. "Watch it pal. I said I was falling in love with you. I did not say I *needed* you. Besides the process can easily be reversed." I kissed her cold lips. Her mouth yielded to mine for a second and then firmly rejected it. I knew what I was supposed to say. But the words just wouldn't come out right. "I…"

"Why do men find it so hard to be honest? You spend far too much of your time prevaricating as a bloody lawyer. Spit it out English boy…"

"You win," I finally capitulated. "I love you, you Irish peasant."

30th November 1995

In one of the most tangible signs of the widespread belief that peace may finally have arrived in Northern Ireland, today the first President of the United States ever to visit the province rolled into town complete with bullet proof Cadillac. Bill and Hilary Clinton arrived in Belfast to bolster the peace process. It was a triumphant visit, full of hope and good cheer for the approaching Christmas festivities, as the President addressed the crowds that had gathered to see him turn on the lights of the towering Christmas tree in Belfast City Centre.

Speaking in Londonderry earlier in the day he commented on how much the city had changed over the previous 18 months. Crossing the border is as easy as "crossing a speed bump." The "soldiers are off the streets. The city walls are open to civilians. There are no more shakedowns as you walk into a store. Daily life has become more ordinary..."

24th January 1996

The long awaited report of the International Body on Disarmament in Northern Ireland, chaired by former US Senator George Mitchell was published today. Marking a stark contrast with the British Government's demand for substantial prior decommissioning of IRA weapons, it charted a compromise between republican and unionist views, arguing that talks about a peace settlement should be held alongside talks on weapons.

In a move widely seen as an attempt to appease the Ulster Unionist party, the Prime Minister John Major, announced that there would be elections in the province. It is hoped that this will persuade the unionists to negotiate face to face with Sinn Féin, in the absence of decommissioning of terrorist weapons.

Chapter Seven

POLITICS NEVER HELD very much interest for me. However, having a girlfriend from Belfast aroused my curiosity. Bill Clinton's visit to Belfast only weeks before Christmas seemed to offer faint light at the end of the tunnel that the cease-fire might hold. This was not a blind hope. There appeared to be a coalition between the Irish Government led by Albert Reynolds, along with nationalists and republicans in the North. In addition, the Americans were prepared to assist in encouraging a dialogue. There was also a growing rapprochement between London and Dublin, which had culminated in the Downing Street Declaration in December 1993 that Britain had no self interest in remaining in Northern Ireland, and that the real issue was the consent of the majority. It had also emerged that despite John Major telling Parliament that the thought of talking to the IRA would turn his stomach, senior Government officials had indeed been conducting a secret process of negotiations with the IRA or an 'exchange of views' depending on your perspective. Republicans saw it might be possible that talking could achieve more than the armed struggle.

The doves in the IRA had long been moving the Republican Movement into a more overt political struggle since the hunger strikes of the early nineteen eighties: a slow realisation that the long war strategy had failed. After thirty years, what real progress towards a united Ireland had been made? Both sides of the paramilitary divide had stood at the edge of the precipice, peered over the abyss and had not liked what they had seen: massacres such as the IRA's fish and chip shop bomb on the Shankill Road that left ten people dead; or the UFF response in Greysteel, as gunmen shouted *"trick or treat"* firing indiscriminately into a bar, killing six and wounding thirteen.

So call a cessation and start talking? Life is never that simple. The unionists were understandably sceptical – fearing the British Government might sell them out. They wanted evidence that the war was over. The British Government, I think, was actually taken by surprise when the cease-fire was announced and had no idea how to persuade the parties to sit around the same table. Hence, we ended up with a dog's breakfast of semantics and an unrealistic demand to decommission weapons prior to any talks commencing. Republicans viewed these not as confidence building measures, but pre-conditions, obstacles to peace and a demand for complete surrender. The rankling lasted over a year with no firm date for substantive all party talks to start. In hindsight, maybe November 1995 marked the high point of optimism.

February 9th 1996

All hopes of a peaceful resolution to the conflict in Northern Ireland were shattered earlier today as a huge bomb planted in a blue lorry containing one tonne of explosives, exploded at 6.59pm under a bridge at South Quay Station, Canary Wharf in London's Docklands. The bomb, which was planted by the Provisional IRA, brought an emphatic end to their sixteen-month cease-fire.

Two people were killed when the newspaper kiosk in South Quay station collapsed during the blast. A further one hundred people were injured, dozens seriously. Police estimate that the cost of the damage to the prestigious Docklands development in the Isle of Dogs Business District is £85 million. There is tonight a scene of utter devastation at the bombsite with tonnes of smashed glass and broken masonry scattered all around, like a scene from a war zone.

On the evening of the 9th February 1996, I was slowly beginning to relax after appearing in a three day trial. It was late by the time I arrived home. I was exhausted, and despite it being Friday, I was in bed soon after 11pm. I was sound asleep when the phone rang some time shortly after 1.40am. I scrambled to pick up before the answer phone kicked in, still half asleep. "Is that Mr Thomas Flemming?" The voice was serious, but not official. There was noise in the background – music like a bar maybe.

"Yeah?" This better be good, I muttered under my breath, glancing at the time.

"I'm the manager at Parker's night-club. You know a Tara O'Neil?"

"Yes. Is there a problem?" I asked, a rising sense of panic engulfing me.

"She's collapsed and needs someone to help her home. We try and see if there is a friend or family member, before we resort to calling an ambulance. She gave us your number."

"I'll be right there."

"I'd appreciate that."

I grabbed my jeans and a T-shirt from where I had dumped them, at the end of the bed. The Alvis started first time, despite lying idle in the garage all week. I opened the window, letting in the fresh night air, figuring it would wake me up. Parker's was situated in a grotty part of town and didn't have a lot going for it, aside from a late licence. What the hell was Tara doing there? And what was wrong with her, I wondered, as I sped along the quiet roads, populated only by occasional taxis plying their trade. Under normal circumstances, she would rather have crawled home on her hands and knees, than call me for help.

The cool breeze massaged my face through the open window, as I slowed for a set of traffic lights turning to red. I flicked the radio on: 2am. I listened to the news headlines read out in a sombre voice. The IRA cease-fire was over and two people were dead. South Quay had been devastated by a terrorist bomb. I listened with sickening gall as the newscaster calmly read out the IRA statement announcing the day we desperately hoped would never come, but always feared might. It was back to war. My brain churned like an old seventy-eight gramophone record, trying to focus on the spinning label till you go dizzy. I pulled into the car park, retrieving my jacket from the back seat and walked the few hundred yards to the club. "We're closed mate," grunted the doorman, thrusting his arm across my path. I swear his biceps had a wider circumference than my thighs.

"I've come to pick someone up," I protested.

"You'll have to wait till they come out." His voice was firm but polite.

"I had a phone call from your manager. She's not well." He finally relented and gestured me inside, with a vague look of indifference. I repeated my story to the barman who disappeared for a moment and then reappeared with the manager, before returning to glass washing.

"Mr Flemming?" He looked weary and a little pissed off, his tie loose and the top button of his shirt open. "Follow me." He showed me through to a condoned off area at the far end of the bar. Tara was sat on a chair in the far corner, although sprawled, might be a more appropriate adjective. Her head was lurching forwards, her chin resting on her chest, arms splayed, hanging, as if each weighed a tonne. Her eyes were glazed and she could barely focus. The left side of her forehead was puffy and swollen, the bruise already beginning to emerge. "She fell and struck her head, but I don't think there is any lasting damage. She'll have the headache from hell tomorrow."

"I'll get her out of your way. You must have a hundred other things to do," I said apologetically.

He grunted in reply. "Too right pal."

I knelt down. "Tara, can you stand?" There was a barely perceptible nod, as she tried to focus her eyes, then gave up. Her breath reeked of alcohol and stale cigarette smoke. I lifted her up, placing her arm around my shoulder. She was like a dead weight as I tried to manoeuvre her. Just the occasional incoherent moan as I pulled her forward. The manager watched but offered no assistance. Drunken punters were par for the course, but I guess he didn't have to like them or the grief they caused. Vomit in the toilets, squabbles on the dance floor, punch ups out front, smashed glasses and verbally abusive cretins.

Finally he spoke, a little wearily. "Whatever it is you fought about – make it up. Life is too short."

"Sorry?" I replied, failing to comprehend his meaning.

"It's none of my business, except she chose my watch. You see it all in this place. Trust me, when a woman places her credit card behind the bar, before proceeding to drink the best part of a bottle and a half of vodka in under four hours and passes out on the bar, smashing half a dozen glasses in the process, it's usually about a relationship. I assumed it was you..." He shrugged his shoulders, adjusting the chair Tara had been sat in. "No offence pal."

"Thanks for the advice." I tried not to sound too sarcastic.

"Oh and when she sobers up, tell her she's barred." He delivered the punch line with a false smile and obvious relish.

"Come on Tara. Work with me. We're almost at the car." I doubt she had even the vaguest recognition of my pleas. There was no coordination, her limbs flailing in opposite directions. We struggled back to the car, with me almost carrying her. I held her steady in an upright position as I edged open the door. She flopped into the passenger seat, her head lolling forward, her eyes closing, as I fastened the seat belt around her. She remained utterly oblivious. As I drew up into her driveway, Tara wrenched the door open and threw up onto the tarmac – gut wrenching nauseating sound effects included.

Carefully avoiding the little pile of joy she had left, I carried her inside and put her to bed, before taking the hose to the driveway. I must have looked like a maniac, cleaning it up at approaching 3am. I contemplated staying, but thought better of it. I did, however, position the Aspirin helpfully by her bedside, before I departed.

On the way home, it occurred to me, in a rare moment of insight that Patrick had died in early February – was yesterday the anniversary? How was I supposed to compete with a ghost? A dead ghost who could do no wrong and who still sent his tentacles of guilt across the mortal divide.

Tara was a woman filled with contradictions. Her highs were infectious, but when depressed, she would push her food around her plate, in an empty motion staring into nothing, seemingly losing all interest in life. It all fitted neatly with my Patrick theory. After all, who could go through the experience of losing a loved one without suffering some psychological payback? She could be a bit irritable, maybe erratic but it was generally short lived, then the tightly closed flower would reopen.

I rang the doorbell the following day for what seemed like an age before there was any response. I didn't want to use the keys Tara had cut for me – I felt like I'd be intruding. I'd reached the end of the drive, by the time she opened the door, before disappearing back into the house, leaving the door ajar. The curtains were closed, shrouding the living room in a subdued half light. I opened the bedroom door. This too was in semi-darkness, with only the faint glow of the bedside lamp to illuminate the room. Tara was sitting in bed, her knees hugged tightly to her chest. "Feeling better?"

"What do you think?" Tara snapped back sullenly.

I placed my arms out in front of me. "Hey, it's okay…"

"If you've come to deliver a lecture on the evils of alcohol, don't bother."

"Actually, I was concerned about you." I tried to hide my annoyance. Tentatively, I perched on the end of the bed. In the shadow of the bedside lamp, she looked pretty rough. Her eyes were red and puffy. She looked tired and pale. Tara reached for a cigarette from the half empty pack by her side. The ashtray on the bed was already overflowing with stubbed out ends and stale ash. Tara inhaled deeply, held the smoke in her mouth for an age and exhaled through her nose in two narrow funnels of blue smoke. "Are you okay?"

"Fine." Why do women always do that, when their intonation reveals they are about as far from fine as is humanly possible? Don't they realise nothing is more calculated to wind men up? Perhaps they do…?

I edged closer, placing my hand gently on hers. Tara pulled her hand away, as if I had violated some personal sanctuary. She closed her eyes and shook her head. "Please – don't."

"Why?"

"I just… I can't do this now." Her voice was hoarse, trembling.

"Do what? I only want to help."

Tara looked up, as if seeing me for the first time. "Then please, just leave. I need to be alone." For the first time she appeared vulnerable. Like a frightened child, hiding beneath the duvet in the dark, imagining sounds from ghouls and ghosts in the unknown darkness.

I felt angry and excluded. I didn't expect her to be grateful for the night before, but some acknowledgement wouldn't go amiss. "Why won't you ever let me in?"

Tara stubbed out her cigarette a little too aggressively, spilling ash over the bed.

"Please just go Thomas," she implored me. She only ever used my full name when I was in deep shit. Her words lingered on the air like a bad smell.

My frustration grew. "You're not being very fair."

"Whoever said life was fair?" she snapped.

I should have stayed – showed that I was committed, but with Tara still sat on the bed, inspecting a blank spot on the far wall, I departed. My blood boiled, as I kicked the bike into first, and opened the throttle violently. The bike shot forwards, kicking up dust and leaving a skid mark on her driveway. I had eased into second by the time I exited the drive, the bike screaming in pain at the high revs. Fortunately, I missed the car coming the other way down the road that had to take quick evasive action. The car slammed on its brakes and tooted its horn. I accelerated away, showing the driver my gloved finger, working out my aggression on asphalt and rubber – but the relief proved only transitory. Later, I looked back on this night and wondered whether Tara was trying to provoke me into leaving? Make it easy for her, because she lacked the bottle to say straight to my face that it was over. She was welcome to her self-imposed loneliness.

Sunday February 18th 1996

Central London was tonight brought to a stand still as a bomb exploded in one of London's famous red double-decker buses in the Aldwych area. The blast which came without warning split open the bus like a tin can and hurtled shards of metal and glass through the cold and wet of Wellington Street, on the Strand. Police later said that they were thankful that it had been a Sunday as most of the nearby theatres were closed, reducing the number of people on the streets at the time of the blast.

It was later confirmed that IRA volunteer Edward O'Brian was killed in the blast whilst transporting a bomb, when it accidentally detonated. This was the third terrorist attack in the capital in 9 days following the Docklands bomb and the disarming of 5lbs of Semtex plastic explosive left in a hold-all in a phone booth on Charing Cross Road on Thursday. Scotland Yard later issued a statement asking the public to exercise increased vigilance as the IRA could strike "any time, anywhere" on the British mainland.

Chapter Eight

A WEEK OR SO after the scenes on television of the bus in Aldwych, I returned from work, in need of one of those cold beers resting in the fridge, to find Tara sat on a stool in the kitchen waiting. "It seemed crazy loitering on your doorstep, when I have a key in my pocket," she offered hesitantly.

"That's what it's there for." There was a frosty tension between us. She appeared pale and looked tired. Her disjointed burdened movement spoke only of sadness.

"Kettle's just boiled…Tea?" I nodded.

"You been waiting long?"

"A few minutes." The well thumbed newspaper by her side told a different story.

As I handed Tara the milk from the fridge, our fingers touched for a second, before we both retreated, side-stepping an otherwise awkward moment. She handed me a mug of tea and we both walked into the living room. "I didn't think I'd hear from you again."

"You can't get rid of me that easily – bad penny and all that… I'm sorry Tom."

"Me too," I replied, as a sort of reflex action. It seemed the appropriate concession to make. "For whatever I did to upset you."

"You did nothing wrong," she replied, looking rather bemused, as she sipped her tea. "I would have walked out on you. I left you with no other option."

I was determined that on whatever terms we parted, if that was to be our fate, I would press her for some kind of explanation. "I just wish you could talk to me…" I knelt in front of where she sat, cupping my hands over hers. "Why do you always shut me out?"

"I don't." Her response was swift and defensive.

"If it's over, just tell me to my face. Let's spare each other the uncomfortable silences and excruciating drawn out farewells. Just say it and be on your way…"

Tara closed her eyes tightly and shook her head gradually from side to side, her hair bouncing over her shoulders. "No." Faintly at first, almost inaudible – then louder, "you don't understand…"

"Tell me then," I almost shouted, in exasperation.

"I don't want to lose you."

"You don't have to," I implored her – her words taking the heat out of my anger.

"It's just been a difficult time…work and…"

"Bollocks." I stood and paced the floor. "You did not drink yourself to oblivion because you were stressed about work. Why can't you just tell me the truth?"

"Like you're always honest with me?" Argument rule number one: if in danger of losing, always change the subject, preferably by throwing some misdemeanour back in the face of the accusing party. It buys time to marshal your response to the substantive argument. I spun round to face her. "What the hell does that mean? Give me one instance where I have lied to you?"

Tara stood, as we exchanged verbal blows. "How about Leanne? You didn't tell me you had slept with her."

"What? It was over months before we even met…did she tell you?"

"She didn't have to. It's obvious."

"What does that mean?"

"The way she flirts with you…there's unfinished business."

"She's seeing Nick – from the band."

"I don't care." She flared her nostrils angrily, along with her accusation of infidelity. "A woman sees these things – the point is you should have told me…"

I snorted incredulously, squaring up to her. "What do you want from me? A list of every woman I have ever slept with? Perhaps we should go further, everyone I've dated, kissed, eyed in the street?"

"Of course not."

"This is not about me. You didn't get comatose the other night over

Leanne?"

Tara sank back onto the sofa, temporarily defeated. "It's just so difficult..."

I approached her, dropping to my knees in front of her, anger momentarily replaced with affection. "How bad can it be?"

"I...have got so used to lying, I do it automatically. Eventually, the lie trips off your tongue a little too easily." I watched the first tears I had seen fall from the corner of her eyes and cascade down her cheeks. "You convince yourself that is the way it actually happened. I had no idea when I first met you that I, that we...and then I never seemed to find the right time. And then, I was scared. If I told you the truth you would walk away. I should have been honest from the start, but it seemed so much easier, convenient. It saved me difficult explanations, and shielded me from the pain of well meaning but intrusive questions I had neither the strength nor inclination to deal with. I left Ireland to escape, to find a new life, a new start. Inventing a story about Pat's death seemed to make that process easier."

"Is he alive?" I asked, almost in panic.

"No – he is dead. Just not in a car crash. He was shot." Her voice was quiet but firm. I sank back into the sofa. She pulled a cigarette out from a pack in her bag and lit it. "Coming to England, it was new start for me – away from the no smoke without fire bigots, or the well meaning busy bodies, or others trying to elevate him to martyrdom. I didn't anticipate you would ask me about whether I was married. I panicked. It held such painful memories."

"How?" I asked tenderly.

"He was stopped at an army check point on his way home from the night shift. Apparently a white Sierra similar to ours had been reported stolen a couple of miles away. There were intelligence reports that it was to be used in a paramilitary attack. At the inquest, it was said that they believed the driver was reaching for a weapon. The combination of this and the alleged suspicious vehicle led them to believe he was part of a terrorist plot. Knowing Pat he was probably fiddling with the radio – reception was always bloody awful on that car. The two Paratroopers, Privates, were on their first tour of duty. One of them allegedly panicked and opened fire as he slowed at the checkpoint. Told the inquest he believed he was about to come under attack. Ten bullets fired at the car. Three bullet wounds to the chest and shoulder – he died in hospital, two days later. He never regained consciousness.

They searched the car, hey presto, no weapon. He was a doctor for fuck's sake. He patched them up, he didn't shoot them."

"I bet the shit hit the fan over that one," I remarked sombrely.

"Usual story," she snorted. "One rule for the British army and another for the rest of us. There was an 'investigation.' I'm never sure whether the aim of these things is to discover the truth or conceal it. The Para who opened fire was confined to barracks, but back on patrol within three months, whereas Pat got a life sentence and so did I. Reasonable assumption, they concluded, that the occupant of the vehicle represented a threat to the safety of the soldiers. In light of the information received there was a reasonable, albeit mistaken, belief that he was armed and intending to use the weapon. Self defence. In other words: a whitewash."

"You can't just open fire if you think something looks suspicious and may represent a potential threat?"

"They were charged initially on the basis that opening fire was an excessive use of force, but the case was quietly dropped once the outrage had died down. Swept under the carpet on the grounds of insufficient evidence."

"Why didn't they check the registration number? That would have told them if it was the stolen vehicle or not?"

"The Coroner asked the same question. The report came over the radio only a minute or so before Patrick arrived at the roadblock. Allegedly there was insufficient time to check the registration number."

"All the more reason not to fire?"

"Hey, you are preaching to the converted."

"I'm sorry," I said. Tara looked up, as she crushed her cigarette end in the ashtray.

"Don't be, it was a long time ago now. The cease-fire offered me hope that maybe no one else would have to endure the same pain. Maybe Pat's death would come to mean something, if they could establish a lasting peace – that comfortable illusion was destroyed in Docklands."

"So you went out and got hammered?"

Tara just nodded, running her hands through her hair. "You got anything to drink?"

"Scotch?" I poured two glasses and handed her one.

"So now you know why my bathroom cupboard is rammed with Prozac."

"The manager told me that we should patch up our differences.

When a woman drinks that much it is over a man."

"Sorry. It wasn't about you."

"I guessed it was Patrick."

"Oh?" She looked surprised, inquisitive yet almost afraid.

"I figured it was close to the anniversary…"

"Next week."

"And that maybe you felt guilty…." There was the slightest hesitation before Tara responded. Enough of a hesitation that later I would look back and ignore the words from her mouth and see what I regarded as the truth in the expression on her face – the perception she checked her words, before she spoke.

Tara shook her head, moving closer, the heat of the argument dissipating into affection. "He would want me to be happy…." I placed my arm around her waist, caressing her hair with my hand and kissed her. After a second, she stepped back a pace, her outstretched fingers on my lips. "Last week, I wanted to tell you, let it all out but… I just couldn't find the words. I felt so empty, as if I had nothing left – nothing left to give."

"And now?"

"Now…I need you."

Later we talked about the ending of the cease-fire. "If you ask the unionists they will tell you with a smug grin on their faces that they were right all along. It was a tactical cessation and as soon as it became clear that they were not going to win major concessions the IRA went back to war." Tara paused to sip the whisky. "The grass roots republicans agreed to this cease-fire, despite profound unease. The leadership told them that they would enter talks with the British and real concessions could be made. We had all taken the cease-fire for granted. People have got used to not worrying if their friends and family will come home of a night. This taste of normality might make people realise what they have been missing for the last thirty years. Nobody wants to go back to the bad old days…."

One other point of note regarding February 1996 is that Tara passed her bike test and bought a Kawasaki Zephyr 750 we saw advertised in the local paper.

James Hurd • *A Bold Deceiver*

29th February 1996

Just twenty days after an IRA bomb devastated the Docklands area of London, today the British Prime Minister John Major and Irish Taoiseach John Bruton announced the long awaited plans on the future of the Northern Ireland peace process, with a firm deadline of 10th June being set for the start of all party talks. It is widely believed that the setting of a firm date for all party talks is a pre-condition for any renewed IRA cease-fire.

Chapter Nine

ONE NIGHT IN late May the phone rang. We were in bed at Tara's house – I told her to ignore the call. They could leave a message. She appeared initially to concur, and then broke off. "It might be important." Tara slipped gracefully out of bed, naked. I remember watching the curves of her body, as she glided across the room and deftly grabbed the robe on the back of the door, wrapping it round her slender figure and tying the cord. I lay in bed and strained to hear her voice, trying to ascertain who the caller might be. After a couple of minutes, she had still not returned, so I followed after her into the living room.

Tara was sitting on the sofa, her knees tucked tightly towards her chest and her hands clasped together across her knees. Her knuckles were white. The same position, the same body language as that February day, months before. Her face was pale, she looked almost ghostly. It was as if a fortune-teller had told her that instead of living a long, happy and prosperous life, she would not see out the month. I felt cold all of a sudden. "What is it?" I asked. Tara was in her private cocoon. Her eyes were glazed over and she appeared not to notice. "Tara," I said, placing my hand on her knee. Her eyes flickered and appeared to focus, as she tried to regain her composure.

"It's my..." she broke off, as her voice failed her – choked with emotion. "It's my Uncle Mike – Dad's brother. A heart attack" I placed my arm around her and pulled her towards me, but she did not reciprocate.

"When?"

"When what?" She asked as if she had suddenly lost all track of the conversation.

"When did he die?"

"Oh…err – this morning."

"I am so sorry," I said, reasoning she had seen enough death already to last a lifetime.

She appeared vague about what had happened. I asked when the funeral was.

"He didn't say," she replied.

"Will you go?"

"I don't know," she whispered, her fingers nervously playing with her lower lip. I offered to accompany her, but I was left with distinct impression she wouldn't attend, which struck me as a little strange as she appeared to be so traumatised by his death. Tara appeared tense and distraught. She turned out the light without as much as a word, pulling the duvet tightly around herself. I knew that she was not sleeping. She lay awake into the early hours, and probably beyond – long after I had drifted into a fitful slumber.

30th May 1996

The people of Northern Ireland today went to the polls to elect members of a Northern Ireland Forum, which will form the basis of the all party talks due to commence on the 10th June. Despite the recent wave of renewed violence by the IRA on the British mainland, Sinn Féin polled a very respectable 15.5% of the vote, bringing them 17 seats, only four seats behind their main electoral rivals the SDLP.

There is a widely held view that the large Sinn Féin vote was the people of Northern Ireland sending a message to the IRA that they have more to gain from a totally unarmed peace strategy than a return to wanton violence.

Away from the elections it is believed that moves are underfoot in Dublin and London to try to find a formula whereby the IRA would restore their August 1994 cease-fire and allow Sinn Féin to enter all party talks before next month's deadline. It is thought that the decommissioning of terrorist weapons remains the key stumbling block.

Things came to a head about a week later. Tara appeared pre-occupied, morose, even sullen. In the nearly a year we had been together, Tara had barely mentioned her family, parents – let alone an Uncle Mike. I was puzzled that she seemed so cut up about the death of a relative she had never mentioned. "I'm worried about you," I confided.

"I'm fine," she replied, walking out of the bedroom. I followed her downstairs into the living room.

"You have not been the same since, well since you heard about your uncle."

She hesitated and then attempted to appear conciliatory. "I know you are concerned, but I'd really rather not dwell on it. Can we talk about something more cheerful?"

Regrettably, her attempt to deflect my inquisitiveness simply stoked the fire. "What is it with you?" I exploded.

"Don't do this Tom," she replied, trying to calm me down, but it was too late.

"Why not Tara? You constantly keep me in the dark. All I want is to be close to you."

My anger only inflamed her. "Where do you get off, lecturing me on relationships? I am not some blonde bimbo without a brain. This is me, this is how I am. And if you can't take that, then I was obviously mistaken about you."

"Well, I think that makes the position fairly clear. You just bottle it up inside, if that satisfies your overwhelming obsession for your fucking independence. But you will grow into a sad and lonely old woman." With that I picked up my jacket and helmet and headed for the door.

It was perhaps unfortunate timing for a full-blown row. It was Tara's birthday two days later. We were due to go out to a restaurant with a group of Tara's friends. I doubt the atmosphere between the two of us would have been particularly conducive to a good night out. Once I calmed down, however, I remembered the previous occasion this had happened and her revelations regarding Patrick's death. So I tried to ring her on a number of occasions throughout the evening, but all I heard was the same repetitive message on her answer phone. I rang again at around 11pm. To my surprise, she answered after the first ring. She must have been sat by the phone waiting. "Hello Tom."

"How did you know it was me?"

"It's been you every other time this evening," she replied sheepishly.

"I shouldn't have walked out like that the other night. I was just so frustrated… I had to…."

"Run away."

"That's not fair," I retorted, before it dawned on me that I was pouring petrol on the flames as opposed to the oils of peace.

"That's life, Tom." She still sounded very pissed off with me. Part of me wanted to retaliate and point out it was all her fault, and that I was the one with the righteous indignation. Saying sorry when you are convinced it is not your fault, is always a useful tactic. So I did my best to appear contrite.

"Listen, I don't want to fight with you."

There was silence at the end of the line. "Are you still coming tomorrow?"

"If you want me to."

"I'd like that."

I had planned to arrive early – an opportunity to expunge the tension of the previous couple of days. Regrettably, I was stuck in court out of town till late and then caught in rush hour traffic and did not arrive at the restaurant until close to 8pm. I slipped into the remaining seat at the table next to Tara, apologising for being late. "Bloody traffic." I placed my hand on her shoulder and squeezed it, as I sat down.

"You made it then? He's always long winded in court," Tara teased, to smiles around the table. Tara had a way of giving off vibes, in a subtle manner without saying anything overtly. The way she held herself, the subtle body language displayed a reservation aimed squarely at me. Although in fairness, her defensive guard dropped, with each passing glass of wine.

Afterwards, I drove Tara home. "Are you staying?" she asked, as I pulled into her drive.

"Do you want me to?" I asked, turning towards her, unfastening the seat belt.

"That depends," she replied, with a playful smirk, tongue planted firmly in her cheek, "if you are going to apologise for your outrageous behaviour the other night." She managed to keep a half straight face, before bursting into laughter, opening the car door and walking inside, not even bothering to check if I was following.

"I expect you want a drink?" she said, kicking off her shoes and producing a couple of cans of Guinness. "Look I know that I have been a bit distant over the past couple of weeks." She held out the glass, pouring the dark liquid as she spoke. "I have been pre-occupied with Mike, but there is something else." She hesitated and appeared worried. "Later this week, someone is coming to visit. Someone I have not seen since I left Ireland."

I sipped the beer, sensing her nervousness. "Who?"

"Pat's brother, Sean. He is flying to the States from Manchester and wanted to stay here beforehand. I couldn't say no."

"What's the problem?" I asked naively.

"I haven't seen him since I left Ireland. It has just kind of brought back lots of difficult memories. I left Ireland for a new start, to get away from the same old streets and faces." She paused. "Does that make sense?"

I nodded. "I still don't see the difficulty?" I asked innocently. "We'll take him out, show him the sights."

"He doesn't know…"

"About us?"

Tara nodded her head and avoided eye contact. "Pat and he were close. I just think it might be awkward. He was always so protective."

"It's been years Tara. No one expects you to still be wearing sackcloth! He will have expected you to have moved on."

"I just want to break it to him alone. He will probably be fine – I just need to see the lay of the land. It will only be for a few days."

"So I just disappear into the shadows for the week, the forbidden lover whilst you entertain another man?"

"It's not like that," she replied defensively. "Let's just cool it next week. We can go out at the weekend – take the bikes. Is it really too much to ask?" Tara saw my look of unease at the prospect.

"Please Tom, just do this for me," she asked, pleading with me, nuzzling her face close to mine and imploring me to respond in the manner she desired.

I suddenly needed some air. It was one of those lovely clear nights that you get in June. The stars were clearly visible, with only whiskers of cotton wool cloud covering the sky. We walked down the garden and then returned to sit on the patio. There was a wooden bench by the kitchen door. I opened a second beer that she had left on the table. Tara produced a cigarette pack from her shirt pocket and lit it.

"Things that bad?" I smiled.

"I'm going to give up again soon. It has just been so stressful what with work and then well, you know…" she tailed off. "Soon, I promise."

I was contemplating the stars, my arm around her, relieved that everything seemed to be returning to an even keel, although I was still not happy about the prospect of the coming week. She interrupted the silence. "Tom, promise me something?" Her voice had grown serious.

"Sure," I asked curiously.

"You don't know what it is yet," she said, her face glowing orange in the light of her burning cigarette.

"Go on."

"Next time you feel the desire to storm out of the house in frustration, please don't try and purge it from your system by riding your bike like Michael Doohan on the final lap of a Grand Prix."

"I don't," I offered half-heartedly.

"You do," she confirmed, leaning her head on my shoulder. "I saw the way you accelerated off the drive the other day, with the pebbles being sprayed in all directions. You almost hit that car."

"I'll be fine," I reassured her, exercising my male bravado, "but if it stops you worrying, I promise to take it easy."

"Thank you."

"Anyone would think that you worry about me?"

"Isn't it amazing how easily people gather the wrong impression," she quipped.

"If my numbers up, it's up," I offered lightly. "It's fate."

Tara eased away from our cosy embrace. "Don't be so bloody stupid. Fate – what is that? If someone decides to leave the pub having drunk fifteen pints and you're riding too fast, as he pulls out in front of you. As they pick up your body parts and valet your blood from his dashboard, do you think they will record your death as fate?" I could tell that she was exasperated with me by the way she was gesticulating with her hands. "There is no such thing as fate. Just stupid people," she preached, poking me in the chest.

"Hey," I said, raising my arms in self-defence. "I'm sorry. I'll be careful. I promise."

"You are so flippant, blasé about these things." She paused for a second. "I have already lost one of the only two men I have ever loved. Don't make it two."

Chapter Ten

PAT'S BROTHER FLEW to the USA on Friday morning. I booked a B&B in the Lake District for Saturday night. Tara's bike had been parked in my garage all that week, following a recent service. She telephoned me at around 7pm, saying the starter motor on her MG was, I think the technical term was, 'buggered'. She insisted I picked her up on the Zephyr, so she could give me a taste of my own medicine – making me ride pillion. I nodded hello at Tara's landlord who I now knew by sight, as I pulled into the drive, pulling up close to the out of favour MG. Tara quickly emerged from the house. "How's my baby then?"

"I'm fine."

"I meant my bike," she laughed, grabbing the handlebars and pushing the ignition button. She was cautious at first, conscious of me watching over her shoulder. As soon as we hit a straight stretch of road though, she dropped a gear and ripped the throttle open, changing back up as she hit sixty. At seventy five, a whoop of delight emitted from her helmet in front of me.

Soon after we arrived home, Ben and Becky dropped by unexpectedly, to announce in excitement that Becky was pregnant. Ben looked blissfully happy, engulfed in a grin, which stretched across his face from ear to ear, as he slipped his arm proudly around my sister in law's waist. I was going to be an uncle: my brother – a father! The champagne corks popped as we raised our glasses in celebration. I was given strict instructions not to let on to my parents. They were going to tell them over lunch on Sunday.

"He's gone now," was Tara's only reference to Sean, once Becky and Ben had left. "It re-awoke memories that I had hoped were dead and buried. I told him there was someone else on the scene. He seemed okay about us. From now on, it is just you and me, Uncle Tom," teased Tara, as I unbuttoned her blouse, caressing her shoulders, pressing my lips against her taut stomach and led her towards the bedroom.

Saturday 15th June dawned with a clear sky and bright warm sunshine. We left the city early, following the motorways north through Lancashire. It was the first long run for the Harley that summer. I had forgotten how cumbersome it could be through the bends at low speeds, but all was forgiven with the unmistakable sweet throaty grunt of the engine. Occasionally Tara would sprint off ahead, leaning low over the handlebars, before slowing for me to catch up. Eventually we settled to a steady rhythm, on the M6 cruising north toward the Lake District.

We drank coffee and stuffed our faces with eggs and bacon at the motorway services, before leaving the motorway and following the A590 and A591. We pulled over as Windermere came into sight, watching the sailing boats skim across the lake in the sunshine, listening to the reassuring peace of the water lapping the shore. As we sat together on a large rock, on the small beach, Tara appeared thoughtful, "do you ever wish you could stop time? No past and no memories. No fears – just what we can see and feel at this precise moment. Ignore the endless grind of the mundane. I do…."

Sometimes, I find myself daydreaming, back by that tranquil water's edge, in a vain attempt to recapture the contentment of that moment. Like watching a video of a football match, when you already know the score, hoping somehow your team, may still snatch victory from the jaws of defeat, before the final whistle blows.

At lunchtime, we stopped at The White Lion in Patterdale, a mile or so before Glenridding, at the lower end of Ullswater, after negotiating the truly impressive Kirkstone Pass. We sat in the beer garden thirstily drinking the cold beer in the sun. I have often since that day, tried to recall whether there was anything I could detect in Tara's behaviour that would present a clue as to the thoughts that pre-occupied her mind? Upon reflection, perhaps Tara appeared a little tense. If she was, it was no more than over previous weeks.

As we finished our lunch, the landlord's daughter tripped and fell on an uneven area of the patio, whilst carrying a fully laden tray. I distinctly recollect the noise of the shattering glass and crockery, flying through the air, dispersing and shattering on the concrete. She cut her hands and knees on the broken glass and was bleeding. Tara took her back inside the pub, emptying the first aid box in the process, as she tried to remove the slithers of glass. The pub was short staffed. I assisted the landlord to clear up the glass outside, before anyone else had an accident. The landlord refused to accept payment for our food and invited us to stay for another drink.

I visited the toilet shortly before we set off. Tara waited at the bar. As I emerged from the gents, I was vaguely aware of a television set perched high up above the bar. I have a distant faded memory of it showing the news – one of millions of items of useless information which every day my brain collates and discards. As I walked around the bar, I caught a glimpse of Tara for a solitary second. Her face was white – the colour drained away. She looked faint, almost sick. She advanced towards the door. "Are you okay?" I asked, placing my arm around her shoulder, as we strolled towards the car park. "You look pale."

"Delayed shock – I'm really quite squeamish about the sight of blood." The sun disappeared behind an ominous looking rain cloud, dark and heavy, as we continued up the A592 towards Penrith. It was still warm, even with no direct sunlight. The air was muggy almost oppressive, a storm was brewing. I could feel my 'T' shirt under my leathers, clinging to the small of my back. Despite the threat of rain we were in no hurry, as I slowed right down into the corners, easing the Harley through the bends.

Five miles further along the road, parked in a picnic lay-by, Nicholas Perry sat motionless, his head resting on the wheel of his white Austin Montego, his eyes red and bloodshot from lack of sleep, not to mention all consuming desperation. His white knuckles gripped the steering wheel then relaxed, his arms falling back loosely into his lap. With his left hand, he reached onto the unoccupied passenger seat and felt for the half empty bottle of Gordon's gin, removed from the drinks cabinet, only minutes after his world had fallen apart. His fingers came to rest on the bottle and he hungrily picked it up and twisted off the screw top. He sat and stared at it for a moment, as if concentrating intently upon the contours of the glass, then raised it to his lips. How can, in one moment, everything you regard as important in this world be shattered?

Arriving home, after working the night shift, he had opened the front door and called out to his wife as he had done every morning for the past twelve years. There had been no reply – no sound of the children playing, the television, or the radio. In the kitchen, he had missed the note propped up next to the kettle the first time. He had checked the bedroom. The bed had not been slept in. With a sense of foreboding he had scanned the empty hangers in the wardrobe. In a trance, he had opened the door to his children's room, to see that their toys were not in the usual places on the floor, or on the shelves up above the bed. He had returned to the kitchen sweeping the room with his eyes. Finally, his eyes had alighted upon the white manila envelope, upon which his name was written in her small delicate handwriting.

Perry turned his head towards the passenger seat, where the envelope now sat, next to the gin. He withdrew a single sheet of paper. "*Nick, Sorry. I can't do this anymore. I'll be in touch soon to sort out the arrangements. Let's make this as civilised as possible, for the children's sake, Janet.*" In a rare moment of activity, he wound down the window, ripped the letter up into tiny pieces and angrily threw them into the wind, where they fluttered, hanging in the air for a second before dispersing over the ground. He gulped down the gin before disposing of that too out the window. Quickly, he turned the key in the ignition. Time to act – the engine spluttered into life. He crunched the gear stick into reverse. "Civilised," he muttered to himself over and over, under his breath. "I'll give you bloody civilised." She must have gone to her mother's, he reasoned, determined to confront her, before accelerating out of the lay-by, heading south.

It started to rain – just the odd spots to begin with. I turned to look across at Tara on the Zephyr. She raised her eyebrows at the darkened skies, easing back slightly on the throttle. A couple of minutes later we approached a sharp left hand bend, with the now choppy grey water of the lake stretching out on our right. I remember braking for the corner – Tara leading the way. I changed down through the gears. In the split second after Tara had disappeared from view, it appeared: a white car. It took a second to register that he was on the wrong side of the road – my side. It dawned on me in relative calm that he was not going to stop in time. He was travelling too fast. I braked and swerved, but there was nothing I could do. He was too close. Way too close.

The following three seconds were the slowest of my entire life – freeze frame the video. I could hear no noise, apart from the thud of my heart pounding. I was utterly powerless, no longer in control. I knew the danger as a motorcycle rider, without a protective steel shell around me. The driver swerved to my right, at the last moment – too little, too late. I braced myself for the impact – the sickening thud of screeching tyres and crunching metal. My front wheel penetrated the driver's door. I was thrown over the top of the car and then…nothing, except complete and total blackness.

I remember little of the next twenty-four hours, as I drifted in and out of consciousness in the hospital ward. I have no recollection of the aftermath of the accident: ambulances, police or the passing cars that stopped to assist. I have no firm recollection of where I landed, or how I was lifted on a stretcher into the back of the ambulance, or the operation to repair my fractured left leg. Equally, I have no memory of what happened to Tara. As the anaesthetic wore off, shortly before receiving yet another shot of morphine, and disappearing into a world of soft swimming numbness, I asked whether Tara was injured?

"He is still concussed…it will make more sense tomorrow." The doctor smiled and nodded in agreement, before replacing the notes at the foot of the bed. I opened my mouth to protest, but was overcome with drug-induced heaviness.

15th June 1996

Saturday 9.20am Manchester City Centre: A traffic warden walked purposefully down Cross Street, checking vehicles for tax discs and illegal parking. On Corporation Street, she noticed a truck parked on the left hand side of the road, close to the junction with St Mary's Gate. A 7.5 tonne Ford Cargo truck, with an orange cab, white body and dark rear roller shutter with a painted name: "Jack Roberts Transport". It was parked on double yellow lines. She glanced around in vain for a delivery driver she could tell to move on. She noted the registration number, C214 ACL and wrote it in the box on her pad. She tore the ticket off her pad and placed it under the near side windscreen wiper.

9.30am: Another CCTV sweep of the city centre commenced. The operator sat high up in his cubby-hole office at the back of the Arndale Centre, lit another cigarette, and watched the bank of assembled TV

James Hurd • *A Bold Deceiver*

screens in front of him, each with a time and location in a black square in the top right hand corner. He did not notice the concealed camera high on the roof turn and sweep Corporation Street or the fact that the Ford Cargo "Jack Roberts Transport" truck was still illegally parked on double yellow lines.

9.45am: The news desk at Granada Television was quiet for a Saturday morning until a call came through from a man with an Irish accent. Using a recognised code for the IRA, the caller calmly told the news desk that a bomb had been planted and gave an approximate location. It would detonate in one hour's time. Similar calls were placed to a hospital in Manchester, a newspaper in Dublin and an office in Belfast.

10am: A lone WPC was on duty in the central shopping area when the call came over the radio that there had been a bomb warning. The location was imprecise, but she made her way towards the given area, her mind racing, as she picked up her pace to a steady jog, trying to avoid the estimated 80,000 shoppers. As she reached the bottom of Market Street, and looked around onto Corporation Street, it occurred to her that she was the first police officer at the scene. Instinctively, she scanned the area, her trained eyes looking for anything that might contain the device, the television images of South Quay, still fresh in her mind. Then she spotted it. It was the only vehicle in the vicinity – parked outside Marks & Spencer.

Her radio cackled with static and voices – it was busy. She tried again, the fear and desperation rising within her, until she realised that all across the city, officers like her were trying to either obtain or give information. Time was running out. She had to evacuate the area.

On her own initiative, she walked calmly into Marks & Spencer and informed the security guard there was a bomb and the building had to be cleared. Within seconds the evacuation had begun. She ran from aisle to aisle trying to convince people that they had to leave and this was a genuine emergency. It was an uphill struggle, as people were reluctant to leave their half-eaten pizzas and clothes they had stood in the queue to purchase. Eventually she got through on the radio to the police station and the word spread out across the city that the bomb has been located.

11.20am: The bomb exploded – just as Army Bomb Disposal Officers were in the process of using a robot device to investigate the Ford Cargo truck. The bomb was estimated to have contained somewhere between a tonne and a tonne and a half of home made explosive, primed by a small charge of Semtex. Bystanders described hearing the noise first. A loud deafening bang followed by a blast, which knocked people from their feet, shattered millions of panes of glass and dislodged masonry. People described the air as being thick with pieces of broken glass, a whirlwind of flying debris, blood and the screams of the injured.

The whole side and gable end of the Arndale Centre was "just...blown away." Windows were blown out within a half mile radius and several small fires had to be dealt with. Manchester's ambulance service said that it had dealt with 206 injured people. Ambulances and people driving private cars ferried the injured and bleeding victims to nearby hospitals. One police officer was heard to observe "this was the centre of Manchester before 11.20am. Now look: it is more like Sarajevo after an artillery bombardment."

Bad luck, coincidence or destiny – was my brother simply in the wrong place at the wrong time? What other explanation can there be as to why Ben and Becky happened to be shopping in central Manchester on Saturday 15th June 1996? Euro 96 was in full flow – football mania was sweeping Britain. That afternoon at Wembley, England would take on Scotland, needing a win after securing only a point against Switzerland. Ben and Becky had gone shopping early that Saturday morning so they could be home in time for kick-off.

I idolised the ground my brother walked upon. He was always there for me, protecting me from bullies, helping me with my homework and dragging me into adventures of tree climbing and bike riding. The wonder of my first time on the football terraces, at Maine Road, was with my big brother. I was ten years of age, a tradition, which continued for a further eighteen seasons. Ben provided my first cigarette. The first time I got drunk, he was by my side; the top shelf magazines hidden in his bedroom that I sneaked in to devour in wonder when he was out. My first motorcycle ride was on the back of Ben's 50cc Honda. I swapped my skateboard with Ben for my first guitar. I watched on in pride at his graduation and had the privilege of being the best man on his wedding day. My mother swears, as kids we were always at each other's throats – having to be pulled apart on more than one occasion with the assistance of a hosepipe. Now, I can't recall a single crossed word. And, I knew he was to be a father, before even my parents.

They had been shopping on Church Street. They knew that there was a bomb scare, but had been told it was on the other side of the city. Unbeknown to them, as they walked down Market Street they were walking not away from, but towards the device. The power of the blast surprised everyone – the distance over which it shattered glass and spewed falling masonry. The sheer force of the blast coupled with the deafening noise, knocked Becky off her feet, along with hundreds of others, minding their own business, shopping, relaxing, working, eating and drinking. In a selfless act of bravery, Ben flung himself on top of his wife and unborn child, protecting them from the splintering shards of glass that flew through the air, like hot piercing arrows.

The intensity of the blast whisked Ben high into the air, like a manmade tornado, throwing him forcefully against concrete paving slabs, like an animal spitting out a morsel of food, the taste of which it finds disagreeable. His head hit the cold slab, rendering him instantly unconscious. Seconds later, he was struck by a piece of falling masonry from a nearby building, which crushed his chest. Becky was thrown backwards like a feather in the wind, buffeted from side to side, only stopping when her back struck a bollard. She awoke to a scene from Armageddon. The familiar city of her childhood now resembled the set of a disaster movie. People crying, children screaming, sirens blasting, pedestrians staggering to their feet, sitting where they fell, dazed and confused, bleeding. Broken glass, pieces of stone, concrete, debris everywhere. Becky crawled the few yards to where Ben was lying, before passing out for a second time.

If only they had walked in the other direction. If only Ben had been flung a few feet further to the left or the right – or the falling masonry had landed in a slightly different position. If only he'd stayed in bed. If only they had decided to shop outside the city centre. If only the football had started earlier, like all those games they now play at 12.45pm for Sky TV. Fate, destiny, God's will? I have tried to philosophise, rationalise and understand – to no avail.

Part Two

Sunday 16th June 1996

Manchester is still trying to come to terms with yesterday's city centre blast, which injured almost two hundred people. Fourteen people were treated overnight in hospital and a further fifteen attended hospital on the Sunday following the blast mainly requiring treatment for shock. One unnamed man is still in intensive care. His condition is described as critical.

The police have established a security cordon around a square mile of the city centre, to prevent looting and further injury from masonry which continues to fall from the damaged buildings. The area of the blast has been left with a carpet of glass and debris, which is up to two feet deep in places. Already there was evidence of a small army of glaziers being let into the devastated area to begin the job of replacing the windows, along with repair contractors and loss assessors.

Many commented on the eerie sight of half eaten burgers and melted ice cream, still lying where they were dropped or abandoned. Initial estimates suggest that the costs of rebuilding the city centre may exceed £300 million.

17th June 1996

Whilst the clear up operation continues across Manchester, members of the public are still not being allowed back into the area. A police spokesman said that the bomb was now thought to be possibly the largest ever exploded on the British mainland.

18th June 1996

As the police carried on the massive task of trawling through numerous security and traffic management tapes gathered from across the city, they have widened their search to the route the vehicle may have taken from Cambridgeshire, where it is believed the vehicle was purchased.

Detectives have traced the origins of the white Ford Cargo truck, registration number C214 ACL, purchased via telephone from a dealer in Eye, Cambridgeshire, by an anonymous Irishmen. The buyer had rung the dealer, one Arthur Loveridge who had placed an advertisement for commercial vehicles. The transaction was effected through two phone calls. Mr Loveridge delivered the vehicle to a parking compound

A Bold Deceiver • James Hurd

in Fengate, Peterborough. He was told to deliver the vehicle at 3pm, leaving the keys hidden in the cab, which was to remain unlocked. Payment of £2000 cash was received by Mr Loveridge from a taxi driver later that Friday afternoon.

Witnesses have come forward to say that they had seen the vehicle being driven out of the compound, but no one it seems was in a position to describe the occupants of the vehicle. Police have said that the vehicle must have stopped to refuel somewhere on route to Manchester, and have appealed for garages and other businesses not to erase CCTV footage.

Chapter Eleven

AS A CHILD, I was gripped by a vivid recurring dream. I am falling, tumbling endlessly, down a bottomless chute, watching the rough dark earthen walls crammed with roots and stone shoot past me, as I hurtle downwards, impotent to forestall my impending doom. Then, in a split second, I would wake in bed. In that second before I awoke, I would be absolutely convinced I had fallen onto the bed from a great height.

Lying in my hospital bed, drifting in and out of consciousness, I was haunted by a new dream – one I could not rationalise in my groggy delirium. It is dark and cold around me. I am confused, disorientated, my senses not responding. My brain's request to move my heavy limbs meets with a negative response. I am alone yet do not feel lonely or isolated – only peace, serenity and the near certainty of death. I feel no compulsion to fight. I am resigned to my fate. Then, I feel a disturbance, a presence. I am being pulled and wrestled. Everything in me kicks back against this alien force. Finally, I lose the will to resist. I capitulate, my spirit broken. The presence holds me firmly in its grip, synchronises our actions. Then I feel sunlight and warmth as life returns, coursing through my veins. The presence comforts me, caresses me. Then it leaves me. I am quite alone.

Sunday passed in a hazy blur. I awoke at one point to see my father by my bedside. He looked troubled, the weight of the world upon his shoulders. I longed to tell him I was fine, there was no need to worry, but couldn't form the thoughts in my head into words. Where was my mother? Why did he come alone? I made a mental note to ask, shortly before I dozed off again. Around 5pm I regained consciousness. Immediately, I was aware of pain, my head pounding like a steam engine on acid. Breathing caused an intense searing pain in the left side of my chest. My right leg was sore and painful. I couldn't even feel my left leg. I could see it though, as it was engulfed by a huge white plaster of Paris cast. A nurse appeared, took my arm and measured my pulse. She smiled at me. I smiled back. She sat down when she saw that I was awake. "Good evening Thomas."

"It's Tom. Where am I?"

"Penrith Infirmary. You had a nasty accident. My name is Penny."

I felt bewildered and confused. My recall of the previous day shrouded in a cloud of mystery, half remembered words and scenes. "What happened?"

"You were involved in an accident on a motorbike. You collided with a car."

"I don't remember anything," I replied, nursing the mother of all headaches.

"Give it time." Just then my left shin twinged with pain in a sharp reminder of how lucky I was to be alive. "I'll get you something for that," offered the nurse, as she saw the pain spread across my face. "Nasty fracture to your left leg, a couple of fractured ribs, large bang on the head, a moderate concussion, and some cuts and bruises. Doctor Anderson will be along to see you soon."

"That explains why it hurts like buggery to breathe."

"Something like that, I imagine," she joked, with a wry grin on her face. "You'll be sore for a few weeks." She propped me up in bed, promising to fetch me a cup of tea.

"Nurse, my girlfriend, is she okay?"

Penny looked at me with a puzzled expression. "I'm sorry, Thomas, I mean Tom, I have no idea. As far as I know, you were the only one brought to the hospital."

"But we were together," I insisted.

"I think the chap in the other car was here, but was released into police custody last night. Now you get some rest. I'll get that cup of tea."

I was frustrated beyond belief at my inability to remember. I was certain I had been with Tara. I racked my memory to no avail.

As the anaesthetic began to wear off, I became gradually aware of my surroundings. On the other side of the ward, I could see there was an old chap in bed. He had bronchitis and his incessant coughing began to irritate me after only a couple of minutes. In the other two beds, I could make out only the shapes of bodies through the off white NHS blankets, rising and falling backwards with each new breath. Penny returned with a cup of tea and painkillers. "Your father has just been on the telephone," she said. "He is on his way."

"Was he here earlier?"

"Most of the night," she confirmed.

The nurse was only young with a gentle face, and big soft eyes. She gave me one of those reassuring comforting nurse kind of looks. "Oh, I checked to be certain. You were definitely the only person brought in by ambulance from the scene of the accident."

"Perhaps she visited whilst I was sleeping?"

Penny shook her head. "Only your father." I lay back in the bed, wallowing in helplessness as frustration took hold. Sensing my tension, the nurse added, "don't worry the police will be here soon to ask you a few questions. They will be able to sort the whole thing out." She stood up from the side of the bed, where she had been perched and walked back towards the nursing station at the far end of the ward. I glanced at her bottom through her uniform. Nothing wrong in that department then, I reasoned, with an acute sense of relief.

I lay in bed trying to ascertain which body parts I could move without pain: none. I could already feel an itch growing under my plaster. A fellow inmate turned on the television at the end of the bay. The news was on. I caught a few words, but they made no sense. "*…The clear up is under way in Manchester after yesterday's bomb that destroyed the city centre.*" That knock on the head must have been harder than I thought. I didn't hear the two uniformed police officers appear at the side of my bed.

"Mr Flemming?" The taller of the officers introduced himself. "PC Jackson and this is my colleague PC Hughes." I nodded to the other officer.

"Nasty accident you had."

"Were you there?" I asked.

"We arrived at the scene after a phone call from a member of the public."

"What happened? I can remember jack shit," I murmured, through the pain of my head, which had started to pound once again.

"We were hoping you could tell us," PC Hughes replied.

"Not at the moment," I confirmed, shaking my head slowly.

"Give it time," nodded PC Jackson sagely. "Anyway, we know it was not your fault. The other guy was three times over the limit. Stank of the alcohol when we saw him."

The question of fault in road traffic accidents was probably one of the questions I argued more than any other for a living, but my no claims bonus was the last thing on my mind. "Officer," I began, "I think, although I can't be certain, I was with my girlfriend at the time. Do you know what happened to her?"

The officers exchanged clueless glances. PC Hughes furrowed his brow. "Was she riding pillion?"

I shook my head gingerly. "She has her own bike."

"We only saw you and the driver of the Montego, and a few passers by. I have no recollection of a female on a motorcycle. I can make some enquiries if you like." I gave him her details. "Maybe she took another route?"

"Yeah I guess."

"We'll chat further in a few days. We can get your licence details then. Sort the paperwork," PC Jackson said, raising his eyebrows. I smiled back weakly. They stood to leave. "I'll say one thing for you Mr Flemming. You are one lucky man, considering..."

"Considering what?" I inquired, intrigued by his tone of voice.

"Given the force of the impact, you must have been hurled right over the car, and must have landed in the water. The bank is steep, and the water becomes very deep, very quickly. It's a wonder you didn't drown. When we got to the scene, you were on the bank. That was where the first passer by found you – laid out on your back, on the beach. It appears you managed to pull yourself out of the water, with a broken leg, broken ribs and a relatively serious head injury. Some feat – I guess somebody is watching over you. Got a guardian angel?" he offered, with a cheerful smile, as the two of them exited the ward's double doors.

I must have dozed off for a few minutes. I woke as the doctor was doing her rounds. She asked me how I felt. "Not too bad under the circumstances," I replied, as she flicked through the notes attached to the end of my bed.

The doctor examined my head and my ribs before pronouncing, "I think you will live, Mr Flemming. I have examined the X-rays. The operation was a success – you fractured the mid shaft of your tibia and fibula, which had to be manipulated under general aesthetic," she smiled, in that doctor to patient sort of way. I returned that very grateful patient to doctor smile. "Is there anything else I can get you for the night," the nurse asked, after the doctor had departed. I was about to say no, when I suddenly recalled a snippet from the earlier TV broadcast.

"Am I going mad, or did I hear that there had been a bomb in Manchester?"

"They want stringing up the lot of them."

"Who?" I asked in complete ignorance.

"The IRA – devastated the city centre. They say they will have to pull it all down – the Arndale centre and all." She disappeared and returned a minute later with a copy of one of the Sunday papers. I felt as if I was reading a science fiction or horror novel. Interesting plot, but it couldn't happen in my city, brutally violated in such a manner. I read the street names, and pictured the scene of the blast. It could so easily have been me.

I slept fitfully that night. My leg ached and every part of my body appeared to be bruised and sore. It did not help that the old man in the bed opposite snored like a fog horn. My brain simply could not switch off. Visions of the bomb swum past me, combined with an ever present worry about what had happened to Tara. What if the emergency services had missed her and she was lying wounded somewhere? What if she was dead? The thought sent a shudder down my spine. That was silly – they would have found a second bike. Where was she? And why had she abandoned me at the moment I needed her most?

I awoke to find my father at my bedside. He looked tired and haggard. "How are you feeling?"

"I know how Barry Sheen felt," I joked.

This brought a weak grin to his face. "They haven't managed to kick start your sense of humour then! What's left of your bike is being dropped back at home. Where's Tara? I thought she would have been here?"

"You and me alike," I said wearily and attempted to explain the situation.

"She'll turn up, I'm sure son." He attempted to sound reassuring, but he seemed pre-occupied. A thought suddenly popped back into my conscious mind.

"Where's Mum?" His mask of bravery slipped, revealing a very worried man.

"Manchester," he replied quietly, "with your brother and Becky…in hospital." The penny suddenly dropped.

"Oh no…tell me they weren't in the city centre on Saturday?" I asked, closing my eyes and hoping to God that I was wrong.

He nodded grimly. "I didn't know how to tell you."

I hardly dared ask the question: "They are okay though, right?"

My father held his head in his hands. "Becky was released last night. Once they were satisfied that she and the baby were okay. Some stitches for glass injuries, but they will both be fine. Ben, though…" Dad's voice faltered. "He'd not regained consciousness when I left first thing this morning. Your mother is with him."

"How bad is it?"

He grasped my hand tightly. "It's not good Tom. The doctor says he has severe internal bleeding. He's lost a lot of blood. His left lung has collapsed, where he was hit by debris and he has suffered a serious head injury. They can't rule out the possibility of brain damage. It's fifty fifty." He whispered these final words, whilst choking back the tears only a father can cry for a child in pain that he is helpless to alleviate.

I was stunned. I recalled the Friday evening we had spent together, only days earlier. It seemed so distant now. Everything had changed in the flash of an eye, from the joy we felt, as we toasted new arrivals with brimming champagne flutes. We sat in silence – neither of us had ever been particularly good at expressing our emotions. It's a bloke thing. But there was a bond between us at that moment, stronger than words. "He has to make it." I told him firmly.

"I know," he replied, his words a scarcely audible prayer.

After my father left, I couldn't concentrate. My life had been so relatively uncomplicated only a few days previously. Now, I found myself almost completely immobile, reduced to the humiliation of a bed pan, having crashed into some idiot who had been drinking. My brother was fighting for his life after a terrorist outrage and my girlfriend had disappeared. Later, the nurse wheeled over the payphone, which plugged into a socket by the side of my bed. I tried Tara's number, and listened to her voice on the answer machine, before hanging up.

Chapter Twelve

I WAS DISCHARGED the following morning in a NHS wheelchair, with a full length plaster cast, a pair of crutches, and a large box of painkillers. Taking a leak required military precision. I could just about wheel myself to the bathroom door. I then hoisted myself up on crutches, placing all my weight on my good leg and then swung round to face the toilet, hopefully avoiding the searing agony of the crutch slipping and digging into my bruised ribs. I would then have to lean on the crutches and open my fly, before repeating the process in reverse. I had only been in the sterile environment of a hospital ward for a couple of days, but the cool breeze blowing in the car park seemed the very essence of life. I sucked in the air in deep rasping gasps.

I have never been a nervous passenger, but, as I sat, my hands gripping the door handle, checking my seat belt every few seconds, I winced at every corner, just in case a car approached on the wrong side of the road. I begged my father to slow down a little. He just smiled and told me to relax; he had never had an accident in forty odd years of driving. I didn't feel like pointing out to him that neither had I until the previous Saturday.

The events of the next few hours are branded deep into the collective experience of my family. Ben was in a private room, propped up in a high dependency bed, tubes emerging from his nose, sensors attached to various parts of his torso. He wore a large bruise on the left-hand side of his forehead, shining in all the colours of the rainbow: green, yellow, blue and purple. Around the bed stood various pieces of electrical equipment, measuring his heart rate and other vital signs. A ventilator was helping him breathe. My mother was sat in a chair at the side of the bed, a magazine on her lap, which she was flicking through aimlessly, her eyes focussed on her son for the slightest sign of movement. Becky was gazing, seemingly in a trance, out of the first floor window, towards the site of Saturday's carnage. I was shocked at the lacerations on her face and arms, left by the shattered glass. Twenty stitches in her face alone. A jagged wound about four centimetres long on her left cheek dominated her appearance – the micro stitches the craft of a skilled surgeon. My mother jumped up, as my father wheeled me into the room.

"Tom," she exclaimed, rising to embrace me. I grimaced in pain, as she accidentally touched my ribs, sending a shooting pain through my upper body. "Sorry," she apologised, as she saw my reaction. "Are you okay? Sorry, I wasn't there, but…"

Becky backed away from her window vigil, kissing me on the cheek. In addition to the obvious stitches, the dark circles encompassing her eyes shouted and screamed to anyone who cared to listen that she had not slept for days.

"How is he?" I asked tentatively.

"Not good," she confirmed quietly, rubbing her hands together nervously. "He still hasn't regained consciousness. The next twenty four hours are apparently critical." She spoke in gasps, in the midst of her overwhelming fear, pushing her own trauma aside. I glanced at the slightly rounded bump of her abdomen and was consumed with emotion. I sat at my brother's bedside and gripped his hand. In a strange way he looked quite serene. I wondered if I had looked the same when I had lain unconscious?

"What happened, Tom?" my mother asked, anxious to change the subject.

"It is hard to differentiate," I began, "between what I can actually remember and what I have subsequently been told. I was hit by a drunk driver as I negotiated a bend. Apparently he was on the wrong side of the road, but I have no recollection…I was found close to the lake, on a small beach, having been thrown over the car. I only remember waking up in the hospital ward."

"What about Tara?" asked Becky, from the other side of the room, where she had resumed her watching brief on Ben.

I shook my head in frustration. "I don't know if I was alone or if

Tara was there. I've tried her home number and there is no response. The hospital said there were no visitors other than Dad, and the police say she was not at the scene when they arrived." My annoyance at my inability to remember bubbled through the surface, as my voice grew more intense.

"What did the police say?" asked Becky.

"The police and the hospital staff have diagnosed one too many bumps on the head and an imaginary biking girlfriend. The police said that they would investigate, but I was left with the distinct impression that they would simply file it."

I was interrupted by one of the machines around the bed starting to beep. A nurse rushed into the room, and ushered us all out, despite our loudly voiced concern. We waited in the corridor, whilst a number of additional nurses and doctors appeared and entered the room and closed the door. I sat in my wheelchair willing him to survive – don't give up on me now. Moments later the door flew open and the doctor emerged from the room as two porters appeared with a trolley bed on wheels. He approached Becky, as they entered the room. "Mrs Flemming?"

"Is he alright?" Becky asked, hovering anxiously outside the door.

"His heart is weak. He has suffered massive internal haemorrhaging. He is bleeding internally, losing blood into his intestines and stomach. His heart cannot cope at the moment. We have only one option: operate to try and contain the bleeding."

"Tell us honestly," my father, probed, "what are his chances?" The consultant paused for a second. He obviously hated the question and these situations, as much as the relatives feared the answers. At least when I broke bad news to clients it was only money – never life or death.

"He has only a one in two chance of surviving the operation – he is so weak. But if we do nothing…" He shook his head sternly.

I have always been sceptical about people who presented their shopping lists of requests to the God of their choice, like some great Santa Claus in the sky. Yet in that moment, I felt compelled to cry out to a God I wasn't sure existed, beseeching, no begging. It wasn't a great request, in the scale of the universe – just let my brother survive.

The operation commenced at 3pm and continued until after 6pm. Ben survived the surgery. The internal bleeding had been stemmed but his heart was still seriously compromised. The next six hours would be touch and go. Becky refused to leave the hospital and I volunteered to wait with her whilst my parents attempted to sleep. They would take the next watch in a few hours time. Becky pushed me around the hospital garden in the hazy northern sunshine. "What will we do Tom? If...how can I bring a baby up on my own?"

"Ben's a tough cookie."

She buried her head in her hands and wept. "I can't bear the thought of being without him."

"I know – neither can I."

"What have we done to deserve this Tom? We haven't lived bad lives. My unborn child, what has he or she ever done to deserve this?"

"Nothing." What rational explanation is there?

"If I ever get my hands on those bastards, I'll kill them," she spat through gritted teeth. "What do they gain from putting Ben in intensive care? I could almost understand it if Ben was a soldier. We are just ordinary people living our lives..."

"Lets hope they catch them and throw away the key," seemed a banal cliché, but then there are no comforting words, are there?

We sat by Ben's side until about 7.30pm when my parents arrived. Becky and I then went in search of a cafeteria. The cafe appeared crowded, until I realised that staff and patients alike were gathered around the television set. Tuesday the 18th June. Euro 96 had slipped entirely from my mind: England v Holland at Wembley. The jubilation that had swept Britain on the previous Saturday afternoon when England had beaten Scotland two nil had passed me, and most of Manchester, by. I had set the video, but was probably the last person in Britain to watch and marvel at Gascoigne's seventy ninth minute wonder goal, which sent the 76,864 packed in between the twin towers of the old Wembley stadium into collective joy.

All England needed was a draw against the mighty orange army of Holland. And for a few short minutes I was transported from that hospital café, away from my injured leg, Ben's operation, and my missing girlfriend, as we were swept up in national euphoria.

"*Sheringham*" boomed the commentator, "*...controls the ball well and makes a clever pass to McManaman on the right hand side. McManaman has got away, accelerating towards the Dutch penalty area. Ince is running up from midfield. McManaman to Ince, who flicks the ball into the box and runs on and...and...he has been fouled by Blind the Dutch captain,* he's been brought down. It's a penalty and the Dutch captain gets a yellow card." We watched in tense silence as Alan Shearer placed the ball on the spot. The whistle blew, Shearer ran, delivering a powerful kick. '*Goal*' sang out the commentator. Just after half time Sheringham made it two nil; six minutes later a brilliant run from Gasgcoigne who found Sheringham who passed to Shearer, who drove the ball with force past Van Der Sar. When Sheringham made it four nil the whole room erupted into cheers and chants of 'Three Lions.'

Only moments later my father appeared, his face as white as a sheet. Becky ran, sensing the worst, leaving me to loose the brake and wheel myself as fast as my throbbing ribs would allow towards the lift. As I approached the room, I could hear only the sound of Becky's voice, pleading, "no, no, no – please no." Becky was sat at Ben's bedside, squeezing his hand and pressing kisses onto his forehead. The despair on everyone faces, did not need to be articulated. My brother's tentative grip on life had slipped away. The elation felt by the rest of Britain, the nationwide happiness at our sporting triumph, contrasted so poignantly with the bitter twist of fate that befell my family, as my brother died, from coronary failure at 9.47pm. My one consolation was that he never regained consciousness. He never knew the pain of his injuries and I have never watched an international football tournament since: Beckham's kick against Argentina in 1998 or the sweet bouquet of victory in Munich in September 2001; Rooney's subsequent injuries or that red card against Portugal. The memories are still too raw, the hunting horn still too loud. Elation forever tinted with a tragic senseless death that would haunt me for years.

19th June 1996

In a statement released late last night by the Manchester Royal Infirmary, it was announced that Benjamin Flemming aged 31, from the Stockport area had died from heart failure at approximately 9.45pm. He had suffered massive internal injuries in the weekend's city centre bombing. He never regained consciousness. Police have confirmed that the bomb inquiry is now officially a murder investigation.

20th June 1996

Police have today issued descriptions of the two IRA men suspected of having planted last Saturday's bomb in central Manchester. Both wore dark hooded clothing and sunglasses. The lorry driver is described as white, aged between 20 and 30. He is of a slim build and between 5 ft 8 in and 5 ft 10in tall. He was wearing a navy blue hooded sweatshirt and a dark blue kagool type jacket. The second suspect is white and aged between 20 and 30 of medium build and is approximately 6 foot tall. He was wearing a grey hooded sweatshirt and a dark blue kagool.

Chapter Thirteen

IT IS HARD to articulate the sense of grief that enveloped my family like a dense black fog in the ensuing weeks. I moved in with Becky – she could not stand to be in the house alone. One day she and her husband had been planning to decorate the spare room as a nursery, the next day she was preparing for a wake, in a house that felt devoid of life, despite the child growing inside her. I was still pretty immobile, notwithstanding a move to crutches. I was told in the fracture clinic that I would have to wear the plaster cast for at least twelve weeks. I couldn't drive, and I certainly could not stand up in court for any length of time. I was despondent. My leg would mend – the enduring sadness of Ben's loss could not so easily be cured.

The morning after Ben died, I hobbled into the kitchen. Becky was crying, her elbows resting on the worktop, her hands supporting her head. She made a token attempt to dry her eyes, but was inconsolable. I cradled her in my arms, whilst she sobbed uncontrollably on my increasingly damp shoulder. "What am I going to do without him Tom?" she lamented through her bitter tears. "I can't do this alone. I feel as if my heart has been wrenched out. What future do we have now?" she asked, placing her hand over her growing stomach. "I have to eat for the baby, but the thought of food just makes me feel sick. How can I bring his child into this world without him?" The anguish in her eyes was almost as unbearable as the cold emptiness I felt. "How do you organise a funeral Tom?"

"Call in a firm of funeral directors and let them handle everything."

"What are your plans?" Becky asked.

I smiled. "There's not a lot I can do," I replied, pointing at my leg. "Even if I physically could go into work, I can't think straight. I need to pick up some things. I haven't been back since….Dad picked these up for me," I gestured towards my jeans and 'T' shirt.

"I'll give you a lift. It will take my mind off…" She broke off mid sentence, sitting down and wincing slightly.

"Are you okay?" I asked, with a rising note of panic.

Becky smiled briefly. "Don't be such an old woman. It's just a touch of sickness. I need to eat some breakfast – but don't really feel like it."

I handed her a glass of orange juice. "I thought it might have been a kick – you know from the baby."

"It's too soon," she said, shaking her head and reaching for the cereal packet. "A few more weeks yet according to the books."

"I'm premature in planning his football career then," I replied, attempting to keep the conversation away from funerals.

"What if it's a girl?"

"Boy or girl, they'll play for City."

"Not if I have anything to do with it – my child will play for a team that wins trophies."

"So long as he or she goes nowhere near Old Trafford!"

That brought a short lived smirk to both of our faces. I put on a brave face, but I had an uneasy feeling that we shouldn't be having this conversation. In a parallel universe, Ben and Becky were having this exact conversation about their son or daughter. It was Ben learning about his offspring's future movement in his wife's womb, not me. It was not supposed to be this way. An attentive uncle is a poor imitation for a father.

There was an unspoken sobriety when we arrived back at my house. Each of us was acutely aware of the blissful celebrations of the previous Friday. Now the two of us returned, in horrifyingly altered circumstances. There was a message on my answer phone. My immediate thought was that it must be Tara. There would be some rational explanation for the chaos of the last few days. The message had been recorded the previous evening. It was Kathy. "Tom, I am ringing about Tara. Have you seen her in the last few days? She has not been in school either yesterday or today, and she is not answering the phone. Is she okay? Give me a ring." I dialled her work number. It was just after 1pm. I was on hold for about thirty seconds before the receiver was lifted at the other end. "Kathy – it's Tom."

"Thanks for ringing. How are you?"

"Actually, things are not so good."

"It's Tara isn't it?"

"Yes and no." I explained about the accident, my amnesia and that Tara appeared to have vanished without a trace. I omitted Ben from my tale of woe. "Have you checked Tara's place?"

"She's not there. I went round last night."

As I hung up, in a curious way, I was relieved that there was some objective evidence Tara was in fact missing. At least it wasn't just in my head. Becky called from the lounge. "Oh my goodness, it's on the news." I walked into the room to see an old picture of Ben on the TV screen. "Where the hell did they get the photo?" We watched in silence as our private grief was splashed across the living rooms of the nation in a half-minute sound bite, and both felt utterly nauseous. Before we left, I hobbled into the garage. I was shocked to see the state of my mangled Harley. "Looks like you had a lucky escape," reflected Becky. The hairs on the back of my neck stood on end with the realisation that my parents could very easily have lost both their sons the previous weekend.

Later that day, I walked with the aid of my crutches into the local police station and approached the civilian receptionist, seated behind a glass partition in the small waiting area. "Can I help you?" she smiled.

"Yes, I had an accident in Penrith at the weekend and the police asked me to produce my documents at my local police station and I want to report a missing person."

She took my driving licence and insurance certificate and made photocopies and then filled out a form. "We will sort this out with Cumbria," she reassured me, before picking up the phone on her desk. "I have a Mr Flemming here. He wants to report a missing person. Someone will be with you in a minute," she replied, gesturing me towards the waiting area.

A couple of minutes later, a uniformed officer appeared through the door. He was a large man, about six feet tall with a belly that hung over his belt and a dark beard: PC Black. He led me into a nearby interview room. "They have a form for everything these days," he joked, producing his clipboard. "Name?"

"Mine or the missing person?" I could see him think smart arse, before I even finished the sentence, but he possessed a certain arrogance that irritated me.

"Yours, to start with," he replied wearily. I gave him my name and address. "And who is the missing person?" he asked nonchalantly.

"My girlfriend – Tara O'Neil." I gave him her address and details of her car and bike.

"What makes you think she is missing?"

"I have not seen her for the last five days. No one has. She's not been in work. Her colleagues are concerned."

"Maybe she went away for a few days – a holiday?"

"She is a teacher. Not in term time."

"You had an argument and she's gone to stay with friends or family?" I shook my head. "Has she any family she could have gone to? Is she from this area?"

"She's from Belfast, but I don't have any details of family members."

"When was the last time you saw her?"

I hesitated for a second. He noticed it immediately. "You're not wasting my time here are you?" he sighed casually. Yeah right, because I do this for entertainment.

"Of course not," I replied defensively, the tension rising. "It is just that well, I can't remember?"

"Oh great." He put down his pen. "I'm all ears."

I pointed at my leg. I told him the story of the accident, and he listened in silence until I finished. "I'm sure Tara was with me."

"Isn't it possible that if you are correct in your assumption that you were with Mrs O'Neil at the time of the accident, as she was on a different motorcycle, she avoided the accident altogether."

"It's a possibility."

"Look, Mr…"

"Flemming" I filled in for him, "with two ms."

"I don't mean to be rude. Think of it from our point of view. You say your girlfriend is missing. She is an adult who can do whatever she wants. You have had an accident. You think she was with you, but you're not sure. How do you know she has not gone away whilst you were in hospital for a few days?" His patience was wearing as thin as mine was. "We deal with alleged missing person cases every week. In almost all cases the alleged missing person turns up. Normally there has been a row, or a misunderstanding."

"And what if she doesn't?"

"Mr Flemming," his voice rose as he attempted to control his growing impatience. "Go home. I'm sure she will be in contact soon."

"So I am supposed to just sit and do nothing?"

"Ring her friends, family, there must be someone. If she doesn't appear in a few days, come back." I knew the police have to make decisions about priorities every day; some things always get put to the bottom of the pile. But how could he expect me to be objective about my situation – given the disappearance of Tara, the death of my brother and the plaster on my leg, which was becoming an increasing pain in the arse? I stood up, picked my crutches up and turned to leave the small interview room. "Mr Flemming, one more thing," he called. I turned back to face him. "Have you considered the possibility that she might not want to be found?"

"What do you mean?" I asked, in no mood for cryptic games.

"We see this a lot: husbands, wives, and lovers. They disappear, but they're not missing. They just can't face the person they are leaving – if you get my drift. Maybe she couldn't tell you face to face?" he reasoned none too subtly. Oh thanks for that. You just made my day.

A couple of days later, I visited Tara's cottage, searching for a clue to explain her disappearance. Possibly, I just wanted to be some place where she had been. Even though I had a key, I felt I was performing an illicit act – intruding. I inserted the key into the Yale lock, turned it, half-expecting my key not to fit, but it turned as easily as it had done on every previous occasion. The door swung open, the familiar smells and the same creaking floorboards. Ever the optimist, I called "hello," into the silence. The curtains were drawn – the room shrouded in an eerie half light, save for the orange glow which seeped in under the edges of the heavy curtains. I switched on the light and the room instantly yielded up the secrets of its darkness. The furniture in its usual positions: the sofa, the bookcase, the dresser and the CD player. I opened the dresser drawer and withdrew the envelope. The photographs of Patrick remained. I sat down on the big old armchair nearby and studied them. Tara and Patrick together in the countryside leaning against a dry stone wall and a wedding photograph. Tara looked young and carefree – so happy, vibrant. There was one photograph of her on her own. Her hair was longer, but her features instantly recognisable. I traced my finger across her face: where are you? There was no inscription on the back. I placed the photograph in my pocket, replacing the rest of the photographs in the dresser drawer. In the bedroom, I checked her wardrobe. Her clothes were hanging in their usual places along with the vague hint of a familiar fragrance.

I closed the door behind me, none the wiser. I had imagined that I would feel closer to Tara amongst her belongings. Instead, I was reminded that her possessions were a pale imitation of their owner; the sense of loss was made all the more palpable by familiarity. As I waited for a taxi, Tara's landlord and next door neighbour, Mr. Morton appeared. I saw him drop his trowel and stride purposefully across the grass, stepping over his precious borders, bursting with summer colour: fuchsia pink to primrose yellow. "I thought it was you," he snapped, without feeling the need to exchange the usual pleasantries. "Where's Mrs O'Neil?"

"Your guess is as good as mine. I haven't seen her since last weekend."

"Only she's late with the rent. She's not answering the door or the phone."

"I wish I could help, but I'm afraid I'm as much in the dark as you."

He seemed perturbed by this and considered his options for a few seconds. "Tell her, if she doesn't pay by the weekend she's out."

"I'll be sure to let her know," I answered coolly, as the taxi pulled into view. "If I ever have the opportunity," I added under my breath. I yanked a business card from my wallet, thrusting my hand in his direction. "If you see her or hear anything, would you give me a call?" He grunted and took the card without much interest, before returning to his fallen trowel.

The taxi pulled up onto the drive. Somewhere at the back of my brain, I was troubled by a feeling that I had missed an obvious clue. It was only as we turned out of the drive, the thought clicked into place. "I think I have forgotten something. Can we go back?"

"You're the boss," he replied, suppressing his obvious annoyance. Leaving the car door open, I hobbled over to the garage. I moved around to the side, where there was a window and blew away the cobwebs, peering into the darkness. I opened the doors with my key, just far enough for me to peer inside. A shaft of light illuminated the garage, revealing the Zephyr under a sheet in the far corner. I lifted the material to double check. If Tara had been on the Zephyr the previous week, she'd clearly made it home in one piece. The MG however was nowhere to be seen. When I'd picked her up, it had been parked on the drive. Either the MG was in the garage for repair or it had been fixed and Tara had reclaimed it.

On the return journey, the driver stopped outside a local bookshop and I purchased three books: one on the history of Ireland, one on the Troubles in Northern Ireland, and a third on the Provisional IRA. I desired to comprehend what it was about this tiny part of the United Kingdom, which caused so much trouble. What was this cause that was so important that my brother's life had been sacrificed for it?

Later that evening, I remembered Tara's comment about the MG on the way back from the school trip. She had purchased the car off one of her fellow teachers who assisted her with repairs. Maybe he still had it? I telephoned Kathy. "Do you know the guy who Tara bought her MG off? Tara told me that it wouldn't start, the day before the accident, I wondered if he had fixed it for her – he may have been the last to see her."

"Alistair," she replied at once. "I'll call him now." Thirty minutes later Kathy phoned back. "Tara phoned him on Friday night about 7pm and said she was having problems. He went round on Saturday morning and had a play with it. Apparently, he keeps a spare set of keys. It was only something minor, but he had to play round with the starter motor. He parked it in the garage, knowing that Tara was away for the weekend." I placed the receiver back in its handset, contemplating the first piece of the jigsaw. Tara had returned the Zephyr and had taken off – seemingly in the MG, abandoning all else in her slipstream.

Chapter Fourteen

MUCH TO MY consternation, I was compelled to sit at the front of the church, when I desired only to sit anonymously in some darkened recess, grieving in private – left to my own private thoughts, without the need to make polite conversation, or acknowledge the well meaning, "sorry to hear…." Instead, I was on public display. Crutches and a plaster cast meant it was impossible to escape those who wished, in all sincerity, to express their condolences. I listened as the organist quietly played a hymn I vaguely recognised. My heart was as cold as my brother's in the polished wooden casket only feet away. The thought of his body on the morticians slab, his organs removed to establish the cause of death – as if we had no idea what killed him? *'Amazing grace, How sweet the sound, that saved a wretch like me, I once was lost, but now am found, was blind but now I see.'* I mouthed the words – feeling sick to the pit of my stomach. I glanced along the pew. Becky wasn't making a sound, aside from the tiny sobs behind her handkerchief. My father looked stoical but sad. My mother could scarcely disguise her grief – tears distorting her carefully applied makeup. Becky's parents appeared in no better shape. Aunts and uncles, more distant relatives and rows of Ben's friends – some of whom I recognised, others just sombre pained faces, much like mine.

Usually the sermon is a cue for a doze as the same old banalities are trotted out. All things work together for the good, and how it is all part of some greater plan. I think I would have punched the vicar. Nothing good could ever come from an act of such unmitigated evil. Instead, he spoke of forgiveness. Each of us had to learn to forgive. Nothing we could do could ever bring Ben back. Long-lived bitterness would destroy us and hand another victory to the perpetrators. They were fine noble words, which fell on a stony heart. Others could forgive, understand or move on. I was consumed with anger. A curse on them all; I wanted only to hear that those bastards would be tormented in hell. I needed to cry, to fall to my knees, bang my fists on the polished floor, to scream and shout, to let the grief, anger, pain, the sense of loss and injustice, loneliness, disgust, emptiness, futility and meaninglessness flow out of me in huge gasps. I couldn't do it. Instead, I sat motionless, coldly watching the polished brass handles on the nearby wooden casket.

Afterwards, the house was stifling. Too many bodies, paper plates, empty wineglasses and half-eaten sausage rolls. The atmosphere heavy with alcohol and sorrow, subdued with claustrophobic morbid small talk. I needed some air, so retired to the quiet breeze of the garden, underneath the towering oak tree. Becky was perched on an outcrop of the trunk, all alone, her black dress flapping gently in the wind, as she pushed the hair back off her face. The stitches had dissolved and the wounds looked less livid. I doubted the scars you couldn't see would heal so quickly. "It's a bit crowded in there."

"Overwhelming, I'd say." Her eyes were red and puffy. The brave face at the church had slipped away.

"Are you alright?" I asked, which in retrospect seemed a stupid question.

"I tried to say goodbye – it's not that easy." She dabbed her eyes with a tissue. "Ben was everything to me. It's like going from a colour TV to black and white. I see the same scenes, people and places. They just look so drab… It's like someone has played a cruel trick. Any minute now, the door will open and Ben will come bouncing through, full of energy, enthusiasm and zest for life…only, it's not going to happen and I don't think I can bear that…"

I pulled a cigarette from a pack in my jacket pocket and lit it.

"I didn't know you smoked?"

"I didn't last week." I shrugged my shoulders nonchalantly. "Now… well lung cancer is the least of my worries." I exhaled strongly, feeling the initial nicotine rush go straight to my head.

"Let's have a drag."

"In your condition?"

A Bold Deceiver • James Hurd

Becky looked sternly, disapprovingly towards me, like I knew what was better for this baby than the person carrying it. Then she spoke defiantly. "This baby has no father and a mother that can't begin to face the prospect of bringing a child into this sick pointless existence that passes for life. You tell me how it can get any worse for this baby?"

I immersed myself into the books I had purchased. I was appalled at the brutality and callous wanton disregard for life, seemingly practised by a small minority of people on either side of a political and religious divide. I was shocked that life could be regarded as dispensable for political advantage. In an odd way I felt closer to Tara; we shared a common tragedy now. We had both lost a loved one to the consequences of political violence. As I read further, my thoughts turned to PC Higgs and his reaction after the bomb at Warrington and in a way I began to understand his rage.

It was hard to separate the bomb from the accident and the disappearance of Tara. I knew there was no rational connection, save that in time and space they were indistinguishable. However secure you think you are in your life, career and relationships… it's all a cruel illusion. Don't ever take it for granted. If you are lucky enough to have found happiness in this transitory world, cherish it, every waking moment. None of us have the faintest idea what tomorrow might bring. Once I had a girlfriend and a brother, who was to be a proud father…now there was just an empty void.

Chapter Fifteen

AS I BECAME more adept on my crutches, I returned to the daily grind of work. Living in Manchester made the memory of the bomb a virtual daily experience. I would walk down Deansgate and turn into St Mary's Way, observing the demolition process. The Arndale Centre – never the prettiest building in Manchester – had a gaping exposed concrete wound, adjacent to the devastated Marks & Spencer's building. Standing on Market Street, knowing it was where Becky and Ben had been at the moment of the blast, felt eerie beyond belief. My stomach screwed up in nausea, as I closed my eyes and attempted to visualise the full horror of the blast.

No matter how hard I saturated myself back into work, my thoughts always seemed to drift back to Tara. I would hear her voice across a busy pub, only for it to be someone entirely different, or spy a fleeting glimpse of the back of her head on a crowded street.

The police investigations had revealed nothing, despite my constant pestering. Hence, I decided to retrace my route on that fateful June day up towards Penrith, in an attempt to jog my still deficient memory. In addition, I wanted to meet Mr Nicholas Perry, the driver of the white Montego. In the early days after the accident, Perry became the focus of my resentment. It was he who had caused Tara to go away. If there had been no accident then maybe she would never have left. He had become a demonised two-dimensional figure – a dragon living in the cave of my subconscious. I needed to know for certain whether Tara had been there or not. In the absence of my own memory, Perry was perhaps my only shot at obtaining the truth. On a hunch, I also obtained a copy of the ambulance log.

In the subsequent weeks, I thought long and hard about Perry. I soon realised Tara would have left me regardless. I had reached a point of revelation – perhaps it had been my fault all along. Had I driven her away?

"What are you doing next weekend?" I quizzed Becky, as we sat in a beer garden, one fine late August afternoon as the sun's shadows lengthened into shades of orange. Becky stuck strictly to mineral water, her belly expanding seemingly by the day.

"Nothing special." Weekends were always the most difficult time.

"Fancy going out for the day?"

"You need a driver," she asked, her eyes fixed firmly on the graffiti which adorned my cast – now approaching its sell by date.

"It would do you good to get out," I reasoned, replacing my empty pint glass on the table.

"Okay," she capitulated, "where are we going?"

"The Lakes – maybe it will jog my memory…if Tara was there."

""Tom…" she counselled, clearly concerned about me. "Perhaps you'd be better off just accepting she's gone. There will be other women…"

I bit my lip, anxious to avoid a confrontation. "It's the not knowing. I can't rest until I know what happened, not just Tara, but the accident."

Becky's face softened to a pained frown. "Can you handle it if you discover she just walked away? Are you ready for that kind of rejection?"

"In that eventuality, I'll just have to deal with it." Becky took a slow sip of water and finished the last of the packet of crisps, and then turned perceptively to me. "There's something else to this?"

"I want to meet Perry," I replied cautiously.

"You must be mad." She was incredulous. "What are you gonna do, give him a good kicking? Don't be so stupid or you will end up on trial with him."

"He might be able to tell me what happened."

"It's in the police report?" There was a note of disapproving exasperation in her voice.

"Not everything."

"Don't they send you down for drink driving these days? I would have thought the shit would be behind bars by now." There was bile in her voice, which I am sure was not really aimed at Perry. See, I wasn't the only one with difficulties compartmentalising my troubles.

"The wheels of justice move slowly – he'll be on bail, pending a trial date." I needed her to understand. "I want to know what made him drink a bottle of gin and then decide to drive his car like a fucking dodgem. It is easy to hate a name, to pin all my frustrations on him. I'm hoping that I won't be able to do that if I see he is a real person. If I understand why…"

Becky shook her head. "If you take that logic any further, you will have me running around Northern Ireland, politely asking members of the IRA why they found it necessary to murder my husband, in the vague hope that it will help me forgive them… It simply doesn't work that way Tom." Her tone was flat and her words filled with a coldness only sorrow and loss can provoke.

I dialled Perry's number, and to my initial relief there was no reply. I let it ring for what seemed an age, but no one picked up. I tried the number quite a few times over the next few days at varying times to no avail. I decided to make it one final attempt, first thing in the morning and let the phone ring. I was just about to give up when he picked up: "Mr Perry?"

"Who is it," he asked, in a gruff voice.

"My name is Thomas Flemming. We were involved in an accident recently." There was silence at the end of the phone. "Mr Perry?" For a moment I thought he had hung up on me. "Please don't hang up."

"What do you want?"

"I…" How could words fail me at a time like this? My mouth was dry, but my palms sweaty. "Can you hear me," I enquired feebly.

"I hear you. I just don't know what to say. I've told the insurance company everything…" Unsurprisingly, he sounded defensive.

"Listen, I am sorry to ring, but I need to talk to you."

"I am sure I can tell you nothing you don't know or will hear in court," he replied icily.

"I need to talk to you. Could we meet?" There was a deathly silence at the end of the line, as he tried to figure out whether I was mad or just hell bent on violent revenge.

"Why?" There was a definite edge of caution, even suspicion in his voice.

"There are just some things about the accident I'm unsure of."

"It would make more sense if we did this through solicitors."

"Who for Mr Perry – you?" I must have sounded desperate – the emotion in my voice clear and rising.

"I am going to hang up now."

"Please listen to me. I think you owe me that much, *don't you?*" My guilt trip was paying dividends. "I can't remember anything about the accident. I don't give a shit about the police, lawyers or the bloody insurance company. I just want to ask you a few questions." I gave him my number. "I'm coming up to the Lake District at the weekend. If we could meet up then?"

An hour later he returned my call. "Where and when?"

Saturday began with the sun trying its best to break through the large patches of high cloud, which seemed to stretch out endlessly in various shades of grey and white across the morning sky. As we drove up the motorway, Becky sensed my apprehension. "Nervous?" I nodded in affirmation. "Is that in case you do remember, or the risk that you won't?"

"Both, I guess." We stopped in the same service station and ate the same ridiculously expensive breakfast complete with cholesterol levels to die for, that Tara and I had done, before heading towards Windermere.

"Now what's the last thing you remember?" probed Becky, determined to be scientific about the process. At least when she concentrated on my problems, she wasn't dwelling on her own.

"We stopped at the lake for a while and then at some pub for lunch. After that it is a blur."

We followed the A591 towards Windermere retracing our fateful route. "I think it was fairly soon after we turned off that we stopped." I watched carefully out of the window of Becky's Audi. After a couple of miles, we saw a sign for parking – one of those brown tourist signs. I turned my head, trying to jog my memory.

"Is this it?" Becky slowed the car and indicated as we turned into the parking area. I closed my eyes and in a lightening flash I was instantly back on the Harley.

"*Do you want to stop?*" *I mouthed to Tara, pointing at the sign, drawing level with her. We sat on the small shale beach and tried to see who could*

James Hurd • *A Bold Deceiver*

throw a pebble the furthest, or skim it across the surface of the lake. Her glee was barely concealed as she skimmed a stone five times.

"I beat you," she laughed, handing me another stone, eager for the challenge.

"Is this the place, Tom?" asked Becky for a second time. I nodded, unbuckling my seat belt, a warm breeze blowing on my face, as I eased myself out of the car. I hobbled down towards the water on my crutches, taking in the scenery – just as I had done before, only with a different woman. When my leg began to throb, I moved back and sat on a large boulder. Becky picked up a stone and tried in vain to make it skim across the water as it sunk straight to the depths. "Ben always used to beat me," she recalled wistfully, searching for an appropriately flat stone.

"And me, when we were kids…sorry," I said. "I didn't mean to…"

"It's okay to talk about him you know. I won't break, I promise."

"I can't square the circle. We sat here enjoying the sun. It was so peaceful. A hundred miles away at the same time, the two of you were enduring a living hell."

"I miss him Tom."

"Me too."

Once we left Windermere, heading north on the A592 up the Kirskstone Pass towards Ullswater, I sat alert and upright in the passenger seat, trying to focus on the landmarks, buildings, villages, bends in the road, the mountains, anything that would spark a memory of that journey. "Recognise anything?"

"It all looks the same to me," I replied grumpily, cursing my inability to remember. As lunchtime approached, we hatched a plan. "Look," said Becky, "we know from the police report the accident was three miles south of the A5091 turn off towards Keswick. We think you stopped for lunch, maybe at a pub. There can't be that many pubs along the route."

"Are you planning a pub crawl?" I asked her in amusement.

"I'm hoping that at least one may ring a bell as we go past," she smiled back.

We drove on, climbing into the mountains, along a narrow twisty road, searching for pubs, with Becky calling out the names. "The Queens Head?"

"Not sure…lets press on." We repeated the same process with four pubs along the route, "The Kirskstone Pass Inn: 1481 feet above sea level,"

Becky called out, but drove on, once she saw my lack of recognition. The pattern was repeated with The Brotherswater Inn, The White Lion and the Rambler's Inn in Glenridding. As we left the village, skirting the edge of the lake, it appeared we had run out of pubs. My frustration levels were rising. "This is useless, I can't remember anything."

"It will come back to you," said Becky soothingly. "Just be patient."

"Yes Doctor," I replied flippantly, as we drove parallel with the lake. Becky braked slightly to prepare for the approaching left hand bend, her hand resting on the gear stick. Bang. Technicolor flashback: I was on the Hog, easing back on the throttle, positioning myself for the bend, leaning very slightly into the corner. It was just damp, spitting with rain. I could see it so clearly, so brightly, so intense. "Stop the car," I bellowed. "This is the place."

We pulled into a lay-by, and I hobbled back along the road. For approximately fifty metres the road and the lake ran parallel. Only a small stone wall, less than two feet high, separated the asphalt from the water. A small pebbled beach jutted out into the water, marking the line where the road turned and headed up away from the lake. I almost choked. It was like an electric shock as the tightly sealed door in my brain snapped open for just an instant. I saw in my mind's eye the apex of the approaching bend. I changed down into fourth gear, squeezing both the Harley's brakes to take the corner in the wet. It was only a brief glimpse and then it was gone, as if someone had pressed the stop button on the video player an instant before Perry came into view.

I limped onto the beach, my feet and crutches crunching over the gravel. I contemplated the road above – pensive, consumed by turmoil. I tried to imagine myself being hurled over the wall, narrowly missing the jagged rocks on the other side, landing in the water and then somehow crawling onto this very beach. It was as if the accident had befallen someone other than me. The cast on my leg was the only evidence to the contrary. The low stone wall at the side of the road was scarred upon close inspection – freshly cut jagged grooves and flecks of paint. "Do you think that was you?" asked Becky.

"I guess so," I confirmed reflectively. My brain was working overtime to try and stitch together the fragments of memory with what my eyes were seeing. "Let's go," I suggested finally, my mouth parched and stomach knotted. "This place gives me the creeps."

We retraced out steps through Glenridding and stopped at the White Lion in Patterdale, hopeful this may have been where we stopped. I recognised nothing familiar about the tall narrow black and white stone country inn, nestling between the road and the mountain, as we pulled into the car park. Inside the bar, I ordered drinks and some sandwiches. A few minutes later a barmaid approached the table with our food. I saw in her face a curious flicker of recognition. "I'm sorry," she called to me, placing the food down on the table, "I didn't recognise you before – what happened to your leg?"

She must have noticed my hesitation and appeared a little embarrassed. "Oh, sorry, I must have the wrong person."

"Have we met before? I'm having some difficulty remembering…I had an accident." I pointed at my leg.

"Oh," she said, appearing marginally flustered. "A few weeks ago," she paused. "I think you were here – on a motorbike, only with a different girl." She nodded in Becky's direction, causing a faint look of embarrassment on both hers and Becky's faces.

"Are you sure? This is very important." She must have taken pity at the look of desperation on my face.

"Give me a few minutes. I'll come over and have a chat, when the lunch time rush is over."

Fifteen minutes later she reappeared, with a man, whom I assumed was the landlord. He was in his mid-fifties with receding grey hair and broad shoulders.

"Hello again, I hear you had an accident." I moved to stand, but he urged me to stay seated. Instead he drew up a seat next to me, as did the barmaid.

"I know I was in this area a few weeks ago. I was hit by a drunk driver, a few miles up the road and knocked unconscious. I can't remember much…"

"I think you sat outside," he replied, turning to his daughter. "You remember?"

She nodded. "I fell over, landing on a load of glass. You and…"

"Tara?"

"I remember that day quite clearly," offered the landlord – his memory clearly jogged. "It was the day of the bomb in Manchester…" I shot a look at Becky who pursed her lips, but expressed no trace of emotion, despite the bomb reference.

"You and…Tara picked me up and cleared the glass up, before anyone else fell."

"I just don't remember," I replied, shaking my head.

"You both left here together, I'd say around 2pm," indicated the landlord, turning to his daughter. At that moment, the pub door swung open and a party of ramblers approached the bar. "Please excuse me," he said. "I must go and serve. I hope we have been some assistance." His daughter stood as well.

"Can I ask you one more question: did we seem happy, you know, like when we were together? Or did you sense tension – like we'd fallen out, or had a row?"

She contemplated my question, looking a trifle perplexed, unsure how to reply. Finally, she offered, with a degree of hesitation. "For what it's worth, you seemed pretty happy."

The café in a back street of Penrith was fairly dark and dingy, with peeling yellow walls, lined with tatty magnolia wallpaper, aged by years of nicotine and boiling fat. Even the fake veneer tables and wooden chairs appeared to have last seen a makeover when the Beatles were number one first time round. I scanned the punters, as I walked through the door, trying to figure out which of the sad old men nursing their chipped cups and saucers and toasted teacakes might be my nemesis? I picked a booth near the window, reflecting that Becky had made the correct decision to remain in the car. I had barely sat down, when a nervous voice said, "Mr Flemming?" I turned round to match a face to the voice. Whatever devilish image occupied my mind was instantly dispelled. He didn't resemble Satan incarnate, or the author of all my misfortune. Late thirties, with slightly thinning light brown hair and a long thin face – the kind of guy I passed each day in the street, without a second thought.

"Coffee?"

"Tea," he replied, without aggression, but perhaps a note of trepidation. "My solicitor told me not to come under any circumstances," he offered, with a hint of rebellion, as his lip curled up in the extreme corner in a nervous grimace.

"So why did you?" I replied curtly, fixing him with a frosty look.

He paused for a second. "Curiosity…" He rolled his eyes upwards. "Guilt – heaven knows." His misgivings were obvious. "What do you want anyway?"

I breathed deeply and launched into a narrative, which was becoming depressingly familiar. "I can't remember what happened…" I began tentatively. "The last few hours before…are non-existent."

"What makes you think I can remember? Clarity of thought was not exactly flowing in abundance. I was drunk remember."

He almost spat the words out, as if by getting the "D" word out, before I had the chance, he would extinguish its venomous potency. Partly I desired to embarrass him, watch him squirm with regret and remorse. I didn't anticipate I would be the one who was embarrassed. What the hell was I doing here?

"I remember leaving the lay-by – a rare moment of certainty in a world of confusion. I was going to confront her – my wife. Make her see that she had to come back to me. I had to make her see…" His voice trailed off, his hands turning the teaspoon in jittery apprehension. "And then, then I came around that corner, and…" His voice faltered. "There you were. I had no idea I was on the wrong side of the road. I remember trying to brake, to swerve." I could feel the emotion in his words as the pitch of his voice rose. His eyes narrowed, but didn't quite close. "The car, it didn't seem to want to respond. The wheel felt so heavy. I couldn't avoid you. It all happened so bloody fast. I could do nothing. Nothing at all…"

He must have sensed my not so well concealed scepticism and looked at me rather pitifully. "I'm not saying it wasn't my fault. I have no problem in admitting that," he confessed. "Is that what you wanted to know? Are you satisfied now? If you've come here to exact an apology: okay, I'm sorry." I ignored him. I was in no mood to be gracious.

"When you came around the corner and saw my bike, did you see anything else?"

"What are you getting at?"

"What did you see – describe it to me?" I was growing desperate for confirmation.

"You – on a motorbike."

"Anything else," I pressed more forcefully.

Perry appeared to draw into himself, a forlorn figure. "I'm not sure."

"Think man – this is important." I must have shouted, because I felt others in the café stop and look around at our table. He moved in his seat and stood to go.

"I thought I was doing you a favour. I need this like a fucking hole in the head. I've already apologised. I'm not sitting here whilst you take your pound of bleeding flesh." I placed my hand on his arm.

"Sorry. This is important to me. Please." Shit, now I was apologising to him. He sat down reluctantly. He was shaking. "Focus on what you saw as you approached the corner. Was there any other traffic?" A glazed look came over his pale washed out features. I could see him re-analysing those fateful seconds in his head.

Finally, after an age, he shifted his attention back to me. "I'm not sure," he offered, sighing. "It had just started to rain." Upon reflection, he added, "I don't think there were any other cars. The road was quiet." I longed to ask him if he had seen another bike. The question was on the edge of my tongue, gagging to explode out of my mouth. Never suggest the answer to the question you want to hear. This had to come from him. Nothing else would satisfy me that he wasn't just telling me what he presumed I wanted to hear; anything to get this crazy idiot out of his hair. "Nothing else?"

He held his head in his hands, elbows resting on the table, emitting a low groan. "I can't remember," he replied agitatedly.

"That makes two of us then," I replied brusquely.

"Look just tell me what the hell it is you want to know. I can't be doing with all this…" My expression was blank. If he didn't know, what could I do? It seemed I'd had a wasted trip.

"If you can't remember anything else, that's answered my question." I stood to leave, tossing the money for the drinks on the table. I limped slowly towards the door, suddenly feeling claustrophobic and in need of a good dose of fresh air.

"Wait." I manoeuvred round to face him. "It's just such a haze," Perry continued, in a grimace of frustration. I turned my attention back towards the door. I had my back to him as he spoke, with look of bewildered triumph. "I think…maybe there was…I have this image… of another motorbike passing me, just before I reached the corner."

"Are you sure?"

"Look mate, I'm sure of nothing." Don't call me mate, I'm not your bloody mate, alright pal.

"Is that what this is all about?" I hadn't the heart or the inclination to respond. "How's the leg?"

"It'll heal," I replied flatly, looking him coolly in the eye. "In time."

My cast was removed on 17th September 1996 – thirteen weeks and four days after the accident. The relief was akin to being released early for good behaviour. I required endless physiotherapy and the occasional use of a stick for a few months, so I was by no means back to normal, but I was able to scratch my leg for the first time in months and the elation was palpable. That week offered a release in other ways. Snippets of the accident, which had so stubbornly eluded me, began to flash into my consciousness. Suddenly, I could remember the white Montego appearing around the corner and was able to recall a faint feeling of panic in the water. Each was like a small piece of a jigsaw puzzle you try and piece together when you have lost the cover and you are unable to identify the image you are seeking to reproduce.

The ambulance log helped. What had puzzled me since obtaining the police report was the identity of the Good Samaritan who dialled 999? The first witness on the scene was a Mr Adrian Raynor and his teenage son Mark. When they found me I was apparently 'laid out cold' on the beach. Shortly thereafter, they heard the sound of sirens wailing and saw the arrival of the ambulance and a police car. The Raynors were the first at the scene. So who called the police? This left only one possibility, which occurred to me, once I realised that my mobile phone was missing. I was able to establish that the last call logged on my phone took place at around 2.16pm and the approximate location, by identifying the first radio mast the call had been routed through. The caller had dialled the emergency services. The ambulance computer log finally confirmed my suspicion. "*Anonymous female caller. Mobile phone – accident on the A592 approx 1½ miles north Glenridding. Motorcycle and car: 2 casualties. M/cyclist unconscious. Car driver intoxicated. Road blocked.*" All the evidence pointed to Tara calling for an ambulance before apparently vanishing into thin air. I was staggered that she felt able to abandon me in such circumstances.

Like an old companion, the dream that had haunted me after the accident had returned. I felt disorientated and alone, paradoxically not alarmed or isolated. I sat upright in bed dazed – my body cold with perspiration. I threw the covers back and lay there breathing deeply. The veil was ripped in two, an instant snapshot. I was back in the water. I was drowning. My head was heavy and my body lifeless. I felt her surrounding me, towing me relentlessly towards the shore. I sensed her panicked fear, as she battled with my weight, her nervous exertion and the fight against cold and fatigue. I was vaguely conscious as Tara struggled to half drag, half carry me up the beach. Over three months after the accident the enormity of her actions sank in. The words of the police officer rang deafeningly in my ears: *"I guess somebody is watching over you."* Tara had pulled me from the water – saved my life. But for what: to leave me without explanation on a lonely beach?

Chapter Sixteen

Friday 4th October 1996

I WAS CONVINCED I was still asleep, when I first heard the sound of splintering wood. Perhaps I had drunk too much the night before and this was my head leading the protest on behalf of the rest of my beleaguered body. It was after all, still before 6am. The sharp crack, as my front door gave way to the force of a police battering ram or was it an axe, cruelly wakened me from the innocence of my slumber. At the sound of the second thud and the violent stamping of feet on my stairs, I opened my eyes and tried to focus on the approaching alien invasion.

Before I had the opportunity to gather my thoughts, the bedroom door burst open with a force, which nearly removed it entirely from its hinges. "What the fuck," I began, as three uniformed police officers appeared around my bed, their firearms ominously pointing in my direction. There was no mistaking the fourth intruder as a plain-clothes officer. It was like a cliché from a bad TV show. Was it the moustache or the cheap looking shirt? His mouth was moving, but the sound was inaudible. Does not compute, screamed my brain. It was a nightmare I definitely wanted to end – like right now might be a really good time, please.

"Thomas Flemming?" the plain clothes officer began, in a callous tone, which sent a chill down my spine.

"What the bloody hell is going on?" My sense of bewilderment and disorientation increased by the minute as the surreal violent pantomime unfolded in my bedroom, although, curiously I did not panic. After all, I was still dreaming right? The moustache flashed his Special Branch warrant card in my direction, as if it was his most treasured possession.

"You are under arrest, upon suspicion of offences under the Prevention of Terrorism Act. You do not have to say anything, but it may harm your defence, if you do not mention when questioned, something which you later rely on in court. Anything you do say may be given in evidence. But I suppose you already know that," he hissed scornfully.

Never did I ever imagine in my wildest nightmares that the familiar words of the police caution would be regurgitated for my benefit, as I lay naked in my bed surrounded by police officers. "Get dressed," he ordered impatiently, casting his beady eyes around my bedroom. "We have a search warrant. We intend to search the premises. You have two minutes." With that he turned and walked out and one of the uniforms followed him. The other two stood impassively as I pulled on my jeans and grabbed a T shirt from the floor, before placing my hands in a pair of rigid handcuffs, that I could feel almost instantaneously digging into my wrists, constricting the blood supply. I felt totally nauseous and utterly petrified. I really needed to piss. They only took the cuffs off reluctantly. I guess it was that or one of them would have to undo my fly and disentangle me.

Having my clothes on at least gave me a veneer of confidence. "Look officer," I began, as I was led down the stairs. "I think there has been a terrible mistake here. If we can just sort it out…"

"Just shut the fuck up," he barked gruffly.

"Just remind me what it is exactly you are arresting me for," I asked, incensed at their violation of my sanctuary.

He laughed. "The brief wants to know what he's done," his colleague mocked, in a sarcastic upper class accent. I was unprepared for the foot he thrust in my direction as I approached the bottom of the stairs. I tripped and landed harshly on the wooden floor. With the cuffs on, I was unable to break my fall using my arms. I toppled sideways as I fell, more concerned about injuring my still fragile leg than receiving a bloody nose. The pain was excruciating, as anguished shock waves reverberated along the length of my body. The plainclothes officer appeared as I lay on the floor.

"Pick him up, and put him in the back of the van. Stupid arsehole," he added none too subtly in the uniform's direction. I always remember a face, and a warrant number. See you in court pal. You won't look so bleeding smug then. How the hell was I going to convince the boys in blue that they were making a mistake of career destroying proportions? It never actually struck me that they might have intended to arrest me.

I was placed in the back of a waiting police van. Heaven knows what my neighbours must have thought? I could feel the curtains twitching; good old Mrs Belcher from next door, confiding in the rest of the neighbourhood that she always suspected I was up to no good, what with motorbikes, loud music, and friends with long hair. I never believed he was a lawyer, I could hear her saying.

In subsequent hours, with nothing better to do than contemplate the bare institutional walls of my police cell, I began to wonder why the police hadn't just knocked on my door? Apparently, it retained an element of surprise. Oh yeah, because it is really subtle at 6am to destroy a hardwood door. In my state, if they had rung the bell I would have opened the door, thinking it was the postman. Did they really think I would attempt a dramatic escape out of the window stark bollock naked? Sat in my lonely cell, I came to the conclusion that they just got a kick out of knocking people's doors down. Haven't they got better things to do – like catch real criminals?

Travelling in the back of the police van, with blacked out windows, sat between two uniformed officers, siren blazing, I tried to rationalise my predicament. I felt the piercing eyes of the officers staring at me, with scarcely concealed hostility. It wasn't professional detachment: just doing our job, you understand. I had the distinct impression they were longing to give me a good hiding, begging me for an excuse to pounce. I just sat there utterly confused and lost. Hadn't the moustache mentioned the Prevention of Terrorism Act? Did they think I was a terrorist? I felt like vomiting – the need to retch rising like a volcano from my belly. I racked my brain. My thoughts turned automatically to the bombing, like twisting the dial on the radio to the same pre-determined station. I thought of Ben, and felt faint. I prayed this was some form of sick joke.

I commanded myself to relax. I needed to keep my wits about me. Breathe deeply. I was innocent of whatever it was they thought I had been involved in. I believed in our system of justice – truth will out. Not much of a comfort, as we had all become used to the Court of Appeal quashing convictions as unsafe after the poor appellant has spent twenty years in prison. Usually for terrorist offences: the Guildford Four and the Birmingham Six to name but two. I knew they could hold me for up to seven days without charge under the anti-terrorism legislation. Could I inform someone of my arrest: who would I tell anyway? I could hardly ring my father and tell him I had been arrested on suspicion of being a terrorist! The pain in my chest and side where I had fallen had now subsided to a dull ache, but even the slightest movement sent electric shock bolts of stabbing pain through my central nervous system and still tender ribs.

The tension reached fever pitch as the van drew to a halt and the back doors flew open – I was so nervous I could hardly breathe. The two uniforms sat either side of me almost lifted me up by the handcuffs and manhandled me out of the van and quickly inside the double doors to the police station. They didn't bother with booking me in with a custody sergeant. He'd clearly been expecting me. "Cell three lads," he called. "I have the paperwork ready." No one directed a word to me. I was about to protest my innocence, to plead with him there had been a simple misunderstanding – one we could speedily resolve. When I opened my mouth the words simply refused to emerge. A voice inside me counselled – retain your dignity. Don't speak unless spoken to. Only answer the questions they ask. Besides what was some crusty overweight custody sergeant going to do? Was he really going to write an entry on the log sheet: prisoner complained he had been arrested due to horrible mistake. I didn't have any valuables to take from me. I had not even had chance to pocket my keys. Not that getting back through the front door would present much of a problem. They did remove my shoelaces though. What did they think I was going to do with them? Use them to climb through the small grill in the top of my cell and escape through the ventilation system to the roof, where my comrades in arms were waiting with a stealth helicopter? Or end it all perhaps – well after seven nights in this shit hole?

The cell door closed behind me with a metallic clink. As the hours passed the four walls seemed to grow ever closer – like a cheap seventies horror movie. I had left my watch at home and had no idea how long I was incarcerated for – time appeared to stand still. They brought me some food at what I guess was about lunchtime – if you can call it food, that is. I asked to make a phone call, but they just fobbed me off.

"Later: after you've spoken to the gaffer." I guessed they would keep me locked up, before they interviewed me. Soften me up. Intimidate me. It was working. How exactly was I going to explain why I had not appeared at court that morning and seemingly had disappeared off the face of the planet? The wrath of my senior clerk, a disgruntled solicitor and a client without a barrister were however, the least of my worries.

Sometime mid evening, the key turned in the cell door. Finally, they have worked out that this was a big mistake. They will apologise. I will appear magnanimous, smile sweetly and then sue them for false imprisonment. Instead, I was led to an interview room. Don't let them see you're frightened; just being in this place made me feel guilty of something. Anything, just get me out of here, screamed my brain, which was scared witless.

"The time is now 7.05pm. My name is Detective Inspector Royles," said the moustache. "For the purposes of the tape recorder, present in the room are Detective Sergeant Deakins and PC Wood." It was the morons who had entered my bedroom earlier that morning. Royles undid the top button of his shirt and loosened his tie, like he was saying, we are going to be here a while, I'd better make myself comfortable. Psychological games, I told myself. Keep calm. "Do you understand what is happening?" he gestured towards me. I nodded. "Can you confirm it for the tape?"

"Yes," I acquiesced meekly.

"I am obliged to remind you that you are still under caution. Do you understand?" I nodded again. "Can you confirm your full name is Thomas Andrew Flemming?"

"Yes." I felt the eyes of everyone in the room bearing down on me. I wondered if there was one of those false mirrors like you see in the movies, with all the big wigs sat watching me, drawing up a profile – I searched the grey institutional walls in vain.

"Thomas, or is it Tom?"

I felt like saying, it's Mr Flemming to you, but resisted. "Tom will do."

"You filed a missing person report, on the..." He opened a brown folder in front of him and checked the paperwork. "...21st June of this year in respect of one Mrs Tara O'Neil. Is that correct?"

"Is that what this is all about, a missing person report from months ago? Is that really why you smashed my door down and arrested me in my own bedroom?" Deakins smiled. He was younger, cockier. He thought he was getting to me – that smug self-satisfied grin. This one will come quietly Guv. I'll have him eating out of my hands. Not bloody likely.

"I'll ask the questions. Your girlfriend was she?"

"Ex," I added.

"Oh, why is that?"

"Figure it out yourself. I filed a missing a person report over three months ago. I have not spoken to her since. It is hardly the basis for a meaningful and stable relationship." I paused, the cogs in my brain ticking ahead. "Have you found her?"

Royles leant forward, across the table. "Are you certain you have not seen her since you made that report, received a phone call, postcard, letter, email perhaps?"

"I just said so."

He waved his pen in my direction. "Just making sure I am clear what you are saying."

"So now that's clear, can I go?"

He ignored my question and obvious sarcasm. "How long had you known her?"

"Can I ask the relevance of this question?" I was feeling obstinate and a desire to be belligerent. I failed to see where these questions were leading.

"Humour us," Deakins replied, his arms folded firmly across his chest, his piercing gaze relentless.

With my fist, I wanted to say, but caved in. "We met in the summer of 1995. We went out a few times and you know one thing led to another. I thought we were doing okay…it was fairly steady until, well…until she left."

"I have here the details you gave when you reported her missing. Quite a tale you told him!" Royles sorted through his file and then read it out to Deakins, a sly sarcastic grin emerging at the corners of his thin lips. "Tom says he was involved in a motorcycle accident. He thinks Tara was at the scene on another motorcycle and that he was knocked unconscious. He has difficulties in remembering what happened. Thinks she might have been involved in the accident. No sign of her when he awoke in hospital. No trace of her since. She has not turned up for work. Worried as he has not seen her since…" Royles' mock sympathy really got under my skin – smug git. "Is that really what happened, Tom? How's your memory?"

"Are you accusing me of lying?"

He looked wounded, but shook his head. "I just wondered if your recollection had altered; that bang on the head affect your judgement?" Deakins sniggered. I glared back through clenched teeth.

"Some idiot drove on the wrong side of the road coming around a corner after consuming half a bottle of gin. When I came round in hospital she had disappeared. Check the police report and my medical notes, if you like. If you can read big words, that is," I sneered.

"Help me out here," queried Royles, leaning further across the table, his patience clearly wearing thin. "There is no mention of a phantom lady biker in the police report."

"I spoke to the drink driver a while ago. He said he remembers seeing her."

He was ready with the reply. "That's not in his interview."

"He was drunk remember."

The room was hot, stiflingly hot – the temperature rising with the pressure I felt. Whilst answering the questions, I was trying to think ahead – second guess them. Where was this leading? A thought suddenly struck me: did they suspect foul play? Was I the prime suspect?

"Is she dead: is that what this is all about?" I blurted the words out like a confused child. Royles and Deakins exchanged a glance, and I thought I detected a half smile. "Do you think I killed her?" I asked, losing my cool, raising my voice in pitch and volume.

Royles replaced the missing person report in the file and flitted through the file until he found the documents he was searching for. He removed a page in triumph and then cleared his throat. "2.35am on Sunday 16th June 1996. A security camera on the M6 near the junction with the M5 in Birmingham took this photograph." He handed me an enlarged black and white photograph. I could see the motorway, and the hazy outline of an MGB with Tara's registration number.

"4.16am, same vehicle different place. M25 clockwise, approaching Dartford Tunnel." He handed me the photograph. I glanced at it. I had no reason to disbelieve him.

He returned the photograph to the file and then paused for a second, allowing his revelation to sink in. "It took us five weeks to locate the car, abandoned in a quiet residential area of Dover. Surprise surprise, there was no sign of its owner. We are more interested in what the pair of you were up to before she disappeared in such a hurry? From our perspective, she's rather left you in the lurch. On the 17th June, according to Interpol your girlfriend caught a flight from Paris to Boston and disappeared. Los Angeles, Chicago New York – who knows?" He turned to Deakins. "Wasn't there a supposed sighting in Florida?"

"That's right Guv," Deakins responded enthusiastically. Now I was genuinely confused. My mind could not assimilate all these new facts being tossed in my direction, like fireworks against the early November night sky. For months, I had been starved of information regarding Tara – reliant upon speculation and guesswork. Scratching around for half clues and speculative hypotheses. Now I was being bombarded with detail. And I had still not figured out why.

"He's still not got it Guv," smirked Deakins, chuckling at my apparent slowness.

"Good actor?" suggested Royles flippantly.

"All that courtroom performing eh!"

"Having to pretend the little shit didn't do it." Royles studied me, noting my blank confusion. "Do I have to spell it out to you?"

"I'm all ears," I replied, racking my brains to try and figure out his next move, but I was all out of guesses.

"On Saturday 15th June, an IRA bomb destroys Manchester City Centre. Twelve hours later, your precious Irish girlfriend abandons her job, boyfriend, cottage, recently acquired motorcycle and most of her possessions and leaves the country and her car, Lord Lucan style, before hot footing it across the Channel to France. Does that not strike you as a trifle odd? See the connection yet?"

My entire body felt numb, a dead weight. It was absolute bullshit, of course. But the mere fact they could conceive that Tara was involved was enough to knock the wind out of me, like a heavy punch. After a few seconds, quasi-normal function returned as my brain began to amass the evidence in rebuttal. "It's good to see that bigotism is alive and well in the Greater Manchester Police. Don't they send you anti-terrorism guys on racial awareness training – equal opportunities and all that? Someone Irish leaves Manchester the day after a terrorist incident. Well it must have been her. Why the hell didn't I make that connection? I must be so bloody stupid," I replied disdainfully, incredulous at the very possibility. "I really hope you have got something else?"

Royles smiled slowly and spoke delicately, precisely, just loud enough for the tape – his face close enough for me to inhale his acrid sweat. "Oh I do, Thomas. I do."

"She was with me the night before. We spent the day the bomb went off in the Lakes together," I confessed in a panic.

"Is that your alibi?"

"My alibi? You think I need one? You'd better be taking the piss?" By now I was emotionally drained, shaking like a leaf, unable to think straight.

"I can assure you that we are deadly serious," Royles replied, placing his face only centimetres from mine, aiming to intimidate me. "You're playing with the big boys now. And boy, are you in some serious shit. So it's time to cut the smart remarks and the pretend ignorance." I sat in stunned silence, sensing the fear welling inside and fought back the tears, unwilling to let them see they had got to me. How could they say these things about Tara? How could they think I might have been involved? Didn't they realise that the only fatality was my brother? It was like a never ending nightmare that combined your worst fears and heaped the guilt of the world upon your shoulders. At that second Royles' pager sounded. He pulled it off his belt, looked at the number and grunted. "We'll continue this later." Deakins stopped the tape and I was escorted back to my cell.

I lay on the thin mattress and sobbed. A voice in my ear was whispering: what if they are right? It was the only credible reason anyone had so far come up with for Tara's disappearance. I replayed our time together. Looking for clues, searching for signs: odd words and strange coincidences. Tara's late husband's brother had come to stay from Belfast. An empty dark mass of fear welled inside me. Had I been duped all along? Had I really slept with a member of the IRA, been intimate with my brother's killer? I closed my eyes. I wanted the earth to open up and swallow me. Yet, I could not conceive these as the actions of the woman I had loved. Stripped of my friends, family and the familiar, I felt alone and vulnerable, pacing my cell, then curling up in the inadequate blanket, trying to rest and conserve my energy. Moments later I heard the key in the cell door.

I held the polystyrene cup of lukewarm instant coffee tightly, nursing it between my fingers. "You want a cigarette?" asked Royles, taking the pack of Silk Cut and removing one with his nicotine stained teeth. He appeared fresh, clean – maybe he'd changed his shirt. I felt dirty, sullied. He held the pack over towards me. I took one. I felt like I was in a movie, as I lent forward and he lit it. I inhaled deeply. Royles opened his folder with a flourish, withdrawing a photograph. He slid it across the table. "Recognise this?" he inquired. I could see them both studying me closely, watching my body language. I glanced down at the black and white security image. It was a lorry – a white Ford Cargo truck with a red cab. I noted the registration number C214 ACL. 'Jack Roberts Transport' was emblazoned down its side. It didn't take a degree in advanced detective skills to work out where they were coming from. "It doesn't ring any bells," I lied. I had seen it in the papers following the bomb.

Royles leant back in his chair, placing his hands in his suit pocket. "It was bought over the telephone from a dealer in Eye, Cambridgeshire, on the Friday before the bomb, by an anonymous Irishmen. It was then delivered to a parking compound near Peterborough. Keys were hidden in the cab. Payment of £2000 cash was received by the seller, by a taxi driver later that Friday afternoon. Isn't it amazing, how some people will turn a blind eye for a wad of cash? The vehicle was seen being driven out of the compound. No one it seems could describe the driver. It then disappears. Not a trace." He mimed the disappearance, with his right hand like a magician at a child's party, before replacing the photo in the folder. "Until Thursday the 13th June 1996 3am, when it was spotted filling up with diesel at Hilton Park Services on the M6. Driver paid cash. Wore a hooded top and turned away from the security camera, in an attempt to conceal himself." He took a sip of his coffee, building to his grand finale, like he was in the full flow of a closing speech to a jury.

"You will never guess where it turns up next?" I wasn't given an opportunity to reply to Royles' rhetorical question. "Recognise the address?" He read out Tara's address in Styal. "Ring any bells?" he spat sarcastically.

"You know it does," I answered quietly, with a reluctant sense of defeat.

"Next door neighbour, Mr Morton says, 'at first I thought it was removal truck. I heard it on the drive, in the early hours of Friday morning. It woke me up. I only caught a glimpse out of my window, as they closed the barn doors. There were two or three men. I thought nothing of it until I saw the name Jack Roberts Transport on the TV, you know after the bomb. I knew I had seen it somewhere before. It was the same lorry.' " I felt ill. I inhaled the final dregs of my cigarette and then stubbed it out in the ash tray. "Let me continue. The witness was asked about the Friday – the day before the bombing. He says… here we go," searching for his killer line. "'I don't remember much. I remember her boyfriend arriving on his motorcycle. Then they drove away. Last I saw of her.'" I thought of the conversations that I had with Morton since Tara had disappeared over rent and clearing some of Tara's belongings out of the cottage. The boxes that now lay in my garage piled up next to Tara's Zephyr. I was damned if I was going to let the old sod flog it. He never said a word to me about…I guess he thought I was one of them – nosy old git.

"Still sure that you don't recognise that truck? It blew away most of the city centre? Injured hundreds, one person dead – look again," Royles demanded, raising his voice and thrusting the picture back in front of me, his stubby index finger pointing to the CCTV image.

By now I was reeling. "I had no idea. Are you certain?" I spoke softly, shaking my head in disbelief – nearing the point of capitulation.

"Come off it Tom, you're a sympathiser. You hang around with enough Irish republicans, you get to see things their way." Amazingly, he sounded as if he actually believed it.

"You must be joking…" I almost laughed. It would have been comical but for the fact that we were discussing cold blooded murder. "You're not serious." I remember sitting in that hard chair thinking, are they talking to me? I had never even been to Northern Ireland. The only Irish person I knew was Tara, oh and Sean and Kathy.

"What is this – guilt by association?"

I saw Deakins reach down to a brown paper bag that was placed behind his chair. He opened it and spread out the contents. There, to my astonishment, placed on the table in front of me were the three books I had purchased months earlier on the IRA.

"Is this it?" I scorned. "You're accusing me of being a sympathiser with the Provisional IRA on the basis of three commonly available paperback books?"

Royles remained steadfast, Deakins stared impassively. "Hardly your average bedtime reading now is it?"

"Her way of inducing you into the organisation," Deakins surmised. "You had to take a history test on the Republican Movement?"

What planet did these people live on? "Have you tried Waterstones? Head for Political Science or History and look under Ireland. Are you suggesting anyone who reads books on the history of the IRA is automatically a sympathiser with a terrorist organisation?" Maybe they really did have nothing on me after all.

"Look Tom, we know O'Neil was involved. You were seen at her house the night before – the bomb was still there. That puts you in the proximity of the bomb. The two of you spend the night away from the house and conveniently spend the day together, where you have an accident. She then disappears and you have the perfect alibi. Put it all together, and what have you got?" Royles asked rhetorically, clapping his hands. "It doesn't look good Tom. What are you gonna tell the jury? You knew nothing about the bomb in the garage and have no explanation as to why your terrorist girlfriend did a runner?" He paused to light another cigarette, in a post coital fashion, now he'd revealed his hand. "What I don't understand is why someone with a highflying career would throw it all away? For what Tom: a conflict that's not yours?" He tossed in the rest as an after thought, twisting the knife a little further. "For a girl you barely knew. You're a bloody fool…"

As the interrogation progressed, it dawned on me that they had not made the connection between Ben and myself. It was time to turn the tables. "You have got it all worked out haven't you? A nice convenient circumstantial theory." It was my turn to lean towards Royles. "Apart from the fact, it's simply not true. Yes I bought the books, but not for the reasons, which you have alleged. I bought them in a vain attempt to understand – to rationalise why someone would want to decimate my city. And as for the bomb, how are you going to prove I was in any way involved? Like you said why would I? For her: I'd be a fool, particularly since she left me remember. We're hardly Bonnie and Clyde riding into the sunset together."

"Maybe she was just using you. Convenient alibi, you being a barrister," suggested Royles, shifting his ground somewhat. "Of course, you knew nothing," he said, with a generous dollop of cynicism. "But you do happen to have an unhealthy interest in Irish republicanism." He was challenging me to explain. So be it.

I paused and then squared up to Royles, studying the lines on his face, the puffiness beneath the eyes, the flaccid pallor. "I wanted to know what it was about the squalid conflict in the North of Ireland that my brother had died for?" I spoke calmly and firmly, watching his response. They had no idea. I saw Deakins' expression change from smug complacency to searing panic – the colour draining from his face. Royles just kept eye-balling me, like it was all part of the game. I had seized the initiative and was determined to keep up the momentum. "Do you really think I would have played a part in such an atrocity without ensuring that my brother and sister in law were miles away? Do you think I could be so fucking callous as not to warn them?" I turned to face Deakins. "And I really don't take kindly to being accused of having a hand in my own brother's death. As for Tara, if what you say is true, I shall have to live with that. Now, if you have anything to else to ask me, go ahead. Otherwise charge me, and we will deal with this in court." I was physically shaking with rage, righteous indignation and a burning sense of betrayal. With Royles and Deakins on the back foot, the interview was quickly terminated.

Alone in my cell, I tried to fathom the wealth of facts peppered at me like automatic gunfire. I picked at the lukewarm food. Had they spat in it, thinking I was a terrorist? Here I was in the middle of the night locked in this lonely damp cell – I tried to sleep, but my brain was swirling. In the darkness, my thoughts drifted to Ben, Becky and the child that was soon to enter this cruel world. Could Tara have really been involved? We had toasted Becky's pregnancy together. Did Tara know then what would happen? Did I lend her respectability? Had I been her stooge all along? Pretending to be in love, whilst planning to murder and maim? How was I supposed to feel about someone who had the capacity to both take and save lives? Thoughts swirled around like a tornado in my head. Round and round as exhaustion eventually got the better of me and I succumbed to a fitful sleep.

"How much do you actually know about Tara?" was Royles' opening gambit, early the following morning. There was a subtle change in emphasis. He was now pumping me for information. He was no longer accusing me of being an active participant with her in any illegal activities, or so I hoped.

"Depends what you mean. I'm not trying to be difficult, but I thought I knew her well. But sometimes a person only shows you what they want you to see." My voice trailed off.

"About her past Tom – what did she tell you?"

I shrugged my shoulders, having no reason not to come clean. "I knew about her husband – Patrick. He was a doctor, killed by a British army patrol at a checkpoint – least that's what she told me…"

"What about the rest of her family?"

"She didn't talk about it all that much," I replied honestly, beginning to loathe the sight of the same four walls.

"The RUC want to question her about a number of terrorist incidents, including the shooting of a police officer. She disappeared in January 1994, then turned up working in leafy Cheshire. She was a 'sleeper.' She makes a life and a home over here. Then when the moment is right, slips out of the woodwork and helps plant a bomb, then slinks back as if nothing happened, into domestic bliss."

"Except she didn't," I replied coldly. "She ran."

"Come on Tom, work with us. Give us something to go on. I want to believe you, but it just seems so implausible," Royles replied, scratching his head, casting a perplexed glance to both me and Deakins, who was remaining ominously quiet.

My patience was running thin. A growing sense of exasperation enveloped me. "I knew nothing about whatever that sick bitch was up to. And to be honest I don't give a shit what you believe. If you think you have enough to charge me, go ahead. Otherwise, can we please end this pointless charade?" I banged my clenched fist on the table.

"We are almost through," Royles replied calmly, switching tack again. "Don't you want to see your brother's killers caught and punished?"

I wondered how long it would take them to resort to this line of questioning. I ignored him. "What about the others? Tara didn't drive the truck. And she certainly didn't plant the bomb. The most you can prove is that she let them store the truck on her premises. Maybe she didn't know what was going on?"

"Come on Tom. You don't believe that any more that I do," said Royles, quietly, with a faint hint of incredulity. "We have a possible ID from the service station on the M6. Fraser Dennehy – wanted by the Garda for bank robbery, the RUC for questioning in relation to three shootings and an attack on a police station in South Armagh. Oh and the Met think he may have been involved in the Baltic Exchange bombing. You really think your pretty girlfriend had no idea what was going on?" His final words were loaded with scepticism.

I shook my head, weary with the weight of newly acquired knowledge. "How the hell am I supposed to know? How can you prove they even knew each other?"

Royles ignored my question and pressed on. "As for the others, we have very vague descriptions that could fit half of the male population of Newry. But rest assured, we will get them."

I debated saying nothing about what I knew, just in case Tara was innocent. However, my anger got the better of me. If they were right and I prayed they were not, then she deserved everything she got and more. So I capitulated and began to talk.

"I didn't see her much in the week before the bomb," I began.

"Go on," Deakins encouraged.

"She told me that Pat's brother was coming across from Ireland for a few days. She thought it might be awkward. He didn't know about us. She didn't want to upset him."

"Life goes on," Royles nodded sympathetically.

"That's what I said. Looking back, she was really quite insistent that I didn't come round to the house, whilst he was there. Maybe, a little too insistent...."

Deakins flicked through the brown file on the desk in front of him, before exclaiming with a vague hint of triumph, "Patrick O'Neil: two sisters – no brother."

They released me a couple of hours later on bail without charge. However, it was far too early to say that I was in the clear. Did they believe me? Perhaps they believed Ben had been a tragic mistake: a casualty of war? All I knew for the moment was I was free. It proved little consolation. I had no money, no keys, and only the clothes I was stood in. Deakins offered to arrange a lift home in a panda car. I politely declined. I needed fresh air and to stretch my legs. Royles' parting remark was, "be sure to get in touch if she contacts you." Some chance of that. Back home, I locked myself in the bathroom and vomited repeatedly.

Chapter Seventeen

THE FOLLOWING MONDAY I knocked on the door of my Head of Chambers. I couldn't bear the press broadcasting my arrest, before I had the opportunity to explain. Besides, I figured it prudent to get my defence in first. I had lied to my senior clerk. I rang him on the Saturday afternoon soon after my release. I'd told him I had blacked out – a side effect of my head injury.

"Come in." William Boston QC looked up from behind his imposing reproduction regency desk, crammed with papers. "Thomas. How are you? I hear you had something of a bad turn on Friday?" He took his glasses off, and lay them down in front of him.

"You could say that," I replied, closing the door behind me. He was a brilliant advocate and a real gentleman, but possessed a ruthless streak; he would do anything to preserve the carefully nurtured image of Chambers. He enjoyed a reputation second to none for persuading a jury to eat out of his hand, yet he smiled warmly and invited me to sit down. "What's on your mind?" he asked.

"Where to begin," I sighed, sitting down opposite him, conscious of the hundreds of briefs and shelf upon shelf of ageing law reports and studiously avoiding eye contact. "I'm afraid I've been less than honest regarding Friday." I kneaded my hands together nervously. "Physically I'm fine. That was just an excuse to explain my no show at court." I paused and breathed in deeply. "I was arrested on Friday morning."

"Good grief." He sat upright in his chair. "What happened?" I could see the lines appear on his furrowed brow, his temples tinged with grey distinction.

I ran my hands through my hair and tried to think of the simplest way to explain. Like there was one? "The police smashed my door down at 6am. I spent the next twenty four hours in a police cell and an interview room, whilst I was accused of everything from IRA membership to having orchestrated the murder of my own brother."

Bill clasped his hands together, incredulous. "That's insane. You'll make a formal complaint of course?"

"If only it was that simple."

Bill's expression changed to one of puzzlement. "I'm not sure I follow. There's no substance to the allegations?"

"Of course not, it's Tara they suspect, not me. My connection appears to be guilt by association." I stood and watched the traffic streaming by through the open window; people in suits hurrying along or looking idly in shop windows. I turned back to face him. "Tara's landlord identified the truck with the bomb in at her place. The neighbour says he saw me there on the Friday night – same time as the truck. Oh and they found a couple of books I bought on the IRA to get my head round Ben – can you believe they thought they were training manuals?"

"Perhaps they are clutching at straws?" offered Bill. "Irish girl disappears, shortly after bomb – following up every lead."

I rolled my eyes and looked up to the ceiling and groaned. "You have no idea how much I hope you are right. But they reckon she is wanted for questioning by the RUC." I flopped back into the chair, emotionally exhausted. "You never think this crap will happen to you."

"I assume they haven't charged you?"

"What with: having an Irish girlfriend? Being unwittingly in the vicinity of a truck loaded with fertiliser…" I stopped to catch my breath. "Can you believe they didn't know about Ben? They sat there and told me that someone had died, as if it was my fault," I offered in disbelief, still stunned by their accusations.

"These last few months haven't been easy, have they," offered Bill sympathetically, shifting uneasily in his chair.

"It just makes me so angry."

"Them or her?" His eyes focused on me, wondering if I was approaching some form of breakdown.

"How could she have done it?"

"Perhaps she didn't?" His words hung in the air, whilst we pondered the ramifications. "There could have been any number of reasons, why she might disappear," he reasoned unconvincingly.

"None of which are half as credible," I replied, shaking my head, desperately hoping it wasn't true, but deep down being painfully aware it was. His worried silence was the only confirmation I required.

"Have you told anyone else?" Bill asked, contemplating containment.

"No although half the neighbourhood heard my front door being demolished."

"Family?" he probed.

I shook my head. "How on earth can I tell my expectant sister in law that I was arrested on suspicion of involvement in her husband's death, or my parents for that matter?" I asked in a mixture of sorrow, fear and frustration.

Bill considered my words, before finally replying "If they decide to charge you...." There followed an almighty pregnant pause. Bill picked up his glasses and held them tightly in his hand, before clearing his throat, as he always did when he had to say something unpleasant. "You do understand the publicity would be terribly damaging. We'd have to ask you to resign – no, take a temporary leave of absence," he said, attempting to sweeten the pill. "Just till it all blows over. Other than that we will brave it out – together."

Should I be grateful that he had placed the reputation of Chambers above my innocence? I knew realistically that the prospects of being charged were remote. Understandably, however, I was concerned that my life now lay in the hands of a bunch of idiots who believed a few books on the Republican Movement meant I was a subversive dangerous terrorist or that I was liable to conspire to cause explosions all because I had dated the enemy. The prospect of waking up every morning with this sword of Damocles hanging over my head was daunting.

I reflected that in the space of a year, I had lost a brother and a lover, broken my leg, destroyed my Harley and now my career was on the line. I knew there would be no triumphant return – even if charged and acquitted. Innocent till proven guilty was a legal fiction. Not in this city. I would be ostracised – the end of a promising career. He escaped on a technicality: just because the jury found him not guilty does not mean he didn't do it, only that they couldn't prove it. Long memories and unbending prejudices. I needed a drink. And then another, and another, till the pain faded.

I sat in the bar, drowning my sorrow in Caffrey's. Within hours there would be crisis meetings in session. Senior members of Chambers would be informed. I doubted all and sundry would be told until it became absolutely necessary. I attempted to visualise the stunned silence in the Chambers meeting, as the facts were gravely unfolded. Then the factional huddles over the following few days, on the stairs, in the kitchen and behind closed doors; comparing notes, surprise and dismay, whilst composing individual damage limitation strategies. Ever noticed how the English love a crisis? We rise to it – Dunkirk spirit and all that. Well not this Englishman – there was only one spirit I was interested in.

The bar had been empty when I had first arrived. Now it gradually filled up as friends, colleagues and lovers filed out of their offices. I didn't pay much attention. I was far too preoccupied. I drained the dregs of my drink and watched the few remaining white bubbles sink to the bottom of the glass, gradually numbing my senses. I looked along the bar to try and catch the attention of the barman. After a couple of minutes, I thought I had finally caught his eye. However, instead of serving me, he approached the girl standing next to me. I hadn't even really been aware of her up until that second. Over the sound of Liam and Noel on the juke box, she ordered. "Tequila shot – make it a double."

"Ice?" he asked.

"Neat" came her emphatic response.

I watched in fascination as she handed him a £5 note and then raised her glass and knocked it back in one, her long fair hair dancing on her shoulders, as she threw her head back. She then slammed the glass back down on the bar. I watched her visibly relax as the warmth of the Tequila hit the back of her pale throat, mixed with the taste of the frosted salt. I was on the verge of ordering another beer as the barman returned with her change. Before I could open my mouth, she butted in and ordered another. "Bad day?"

She glanced at me indifferently. "You could say that," she replied, returning to her drink and then added, almost as an afterthought. "Do I know you, you look familiar?" She said it with a glint of recollection that indicated that wherever it was, it hadn't been too unpleasant an experience.

"Anything's possible." I searched my brain for recognition. "Here, let me pay," I added, handing over the money to the barman and ordering a beer. "It's about the only way I am gonna get served around here."

"Thanks."

She was attractive: blonde hair with a slight curl, deep blue eyes with long sensual lashes and long shapely legs protruding from her short skirt. She caught me watching her and returned the gesture, parting her full lips ever so slightly. "You don't look like you've won the lottery yourself?"

"Tell me about it," I replied, swigging on my beer, shifting subtly on the bar stool towards her.

"How long have you been sat here nursing your troubles?" she asked sympathetically, her eyes lighting up for a second, in a highly alluring manner.

"Is it that obvious?" I replied, flirtatiously. I raised my glass. "I've stopped counting. Here's to bad days, fucked careers and shitty lives."

"I'll drink to that," she smiled empathetically, clinking her glass with mine and then thrusting the rest of the tequila down her throat.

I held out my hand. "Tom."

"Natalie," she replied, extending her carefully manicured fingers in my direction. I took her hand and held it for longer than I should – just long enough to make my intentions clear.

"So Tom," she asked, pulling up a stool close to mine. "Tell me why your life is so shitty?"

"You don't really want to know," I said cagily, stalling to dream up a convenient lie.

Natalie caressed her empty glass on the bar, fixing her attention on me. "It can only make me feel better to know that someone else's life is as messed up as mine." Her face broke into a gentle, almost intimate smile. Catching the eye of the barman, she ordered two more tequilas. "Here," Natalie offered. "Trust me these were not designed for drinking alone."

"It looks like I'll be made redundant," I lied, clearly despondent.

"What do you do?"

"I'm a lawyer."

Natalie frowned. "I didn't know they made lawyers redundant?"

"Neither did I – bad patch apparently."

"After three," Natalie commanded, placing her hand momentarily on my shirt sleeve. "Let's knock them back together."

I needed no further invitation, the seduction of her gesture obvious. "One, two, three...." I threw the liquid to the back of my mouth and felt its sharp pepper taste slither violently down my throat burning my wind pipe. I sensed the alcohol reach my brain, dulling the pain of reality.

"Got it," said Natalie, licking the remains of the tequila from her glass with her index finger. "Castlefield gym, that's where I've seen you?"

"I've not been for a while." I pointed to my dicky leg. "Broke my leg a few months back in a bike crash – kind of limited my running potential. What about you," I enquired, placing my elbow on the bar, hand on my temple, closing us off from other drinkers. "What's so bad you've done this many tequila slammers on a Monday evening?"

Natalie snorted in disgust. "You're not the only one with employment issues – I was, how do they say it, deemed surplus to requirements."

"You were sacked?"

Natalie nodded, a slight hesitation in her voice, and lowered her voice, almost conspiratorially. "There was some money missing out of the till – I got the blame. The other two girls have to be innocent – right. One is best friends with the manager's daughter, the other is shagging him." She spoke with a feisty aggression that smouldered in my direction.

"Sounds like you need a lawyer," I whispered back – playing along, enjoying the ease of conversation.

"I thought I'd just found one."

"Seriously," I said. "You shouldn't let them get away with it."

Natalie's face hardened, wrinkling her brow, a faint dimple appearing on her left cheek. "Screw the job – it was a pile of crap. There'll be another." She tossed her hair back, where it fell loosely over her face. "Can we change the subject; it's not cheering me up any." Frankly, it mattered little to me what the subject of conversation was, just so long as Natalie kept talking and the drinks kept flowing.

An hour later I found myself in a taxi on the way back to Natalie's flat, one hand fondling her knee, the other caressing her breasts through her blouse, our lips entwined in a furious embrace. Thirty minutes and further generous measures of tequila later, I watched, as she slipped out of her bra, kissing me hard on the mouth, the enticing silky touch of her femininity, as her firm breasts pressed against my naked chest. I'd forgotten how beautiful, how stimulating it was to feel the delicious warmth of another, slowly melting the pain of my loneliness, even if only for a few sublime hours.

In the morning, amidst the hangovers and embarrassed awkwardness of the whole morning after thing, she scribbled down her telephone number and I made all the right noises about calling, but I never did place that call. I could tell you that my indiscretion was explained by alcohol. The truth is far more complex, if less attractive. It had been an age since I'd laughed and flirted with a girl. For one night, I was able to transcend the mundane. I actually forgot about Tara, the police, and all the other crap in my life. It was like a breath of fresh air to talk to someone normally, with no taboo subjects: brothers, former girlfriends, bombs and road accidents. On a deeper and more unattractive level, I slept with Natalie for revenge. I was saying to Tara, I don't need you. You were nothing special – I exorcise you from my life. However, life is never that simple. To the astonishment and horror of my conscious mind and despite the loathing I felt towards her, the ghostly face my subconscious wrestled with, as I made love to Natalie, was still Tara's.

I jealously guarded my secret. I knew, at least in part who had been responsible for the death of my brother but could not bring myself to disclose this to my family. I now even had a fairly good explanation for Tara's disappearance, yet I pleaded ignorance whenever asked if there was any up to date news. I would bite my tongue and conceal the awful truth that lay bubbling just under my veneer of normality.

Of course, the pretence could not last forever. One day my castle built of sand would be washed away. However, I never imagined I would be forced to confront those closest to me quite so soon. I thought I'd have time to prepare and psyche myself up to face the naked and brutal truth.

31st December 1996

In what is being seen as the IRA's final nail in the coffin, rejecting the latest peace proposals put forward by John Major for inclusive talks following a renewed cease-fire, a 1000lb bomb was abandoned at Belfast Castle, where 400 guests were attending a wedding reception. The RUC accused the IRA of attempted mass murder in luring security forces to the site before detonating the weapon. The site had to be cleared before the bomb was made safe.

John Major's latest moves in the peace process follow renewed discussions between Gerry Adams and John Hume the leader of the SDLP. They had submitted proposals to the British Government suggesting moves, which could be taken to bring about a renewed cease-fire. The stumbling block appears to have been the British Government's insistence on an open ended time lag or period of decontamination between the renewing of any cease-fire and the commencement of all party talks.

Part Three

*'People crushed by law have no hopes but from power.
If laws are their enemies they will be enemies to laws;
and those, who have much to hope and nothing to lose
will always be dangerous, more or less.'*

Edmund Burke 1729-1797—Irish Born Whig Politician and
Man of Letters (1790 Reflections on the Revolution in France)

Chapter Eighteen

I BECAME AN uncle on New Year's Eve, December 31st 1996. I suppose it is a little ironic, a year that had changed all our lives so much should end on such a high note. Hannah Louise Flemming arrived at 7.24pm, after Becky had endured twelve hours of labour. Afterwards she joked that if Ben had been here she would have killed him for putting her though the unappreciable pain of childbirth. Joking apart, it was never far from anyone's mind that Hannah would never know her daddy. As I paced up and down the maternity unit corridor waiting for news, it felt so very strange. In that parallel universe, Ben, not I paced the well-worn floor. Hannah weighed in at seven pounds six ounces – I know some people are interested in those kinds of details. I was just thankful that after all that had happened, Hannah was born with ten little fingers and toes. She was beautiful, innocent and utterly helpless. Her arrival catalysed the healing processes and prompted a celebration. My father danced round the room in delight, clutching his precious granddaughter – a link to his dead son, close to his chest. Becky and Hannah left the hospital on New Year's Day. I spent most of the afternoon finishing the decorating in the nursery.

I arrived home about 6pm. It was dark, raining and the wind had picked up. I felt its cold touch through my clothes as I parked the Alvis. I stank of paint and wood glue after building a chest of drawers for the numerous baby outfits Hannah had already acquired. I had just stepped out of the shower, when there was a sharp knock on the door. I pulled on my jeans and grabbed my T-shirt, shouting "coming," as I ran down the stairs. I yanked open the front door, whilst pulling the T-shirt over my head. I remember being transfixed by the figure that stood on my doorstep – surveying her in stunned disbelief. It took a second to register, as her hair was shorter and dyed blonde – her skin tanned. But her eyes remained the same – fierce green and penetrating. She was soaked to the skin, her hair matted to her face, shivering with cold. I stood rooted to the spot, unable to speak, as if someone had frozen my heart and my tongue.

In the early months following Tara's disappearance, I daydreamed about what I would say if she reappeared – rehearsed my big speech. It was therapy, helping lessen the pain of separation. As time passed, self-doubt crept in. Maybe she had left because of me? How come she didn't possess the common decency to tell me to my face it was over? The overriding question: why? After my arrest, I acquired an answer. My ignorance was replaced by burning anger at Tara's betrayal. To ease the pain, I ranted at an imaginary figure that would not answer back, or force me to be rational. Yet, when the dress rehearsals were over, and the opportunity to say my piece for real presented itself, my finely crafted oratory and vitriolic accusation amounted to nothing. Perhaps this was a scene nothing could prepare you for?

She stood at the front door like some ghostly apparition. "Tom." Her voice hadn't changed – the one I had heard a thousand times in my head since her departure. Hearing her seemed to spur me into action, as I tried to grapple with her presence, after all that had happened. I closed the door quietly leaving her standing in the rain. I felt my knees slacken and I slumped to the floor, head in hands, water dripping from my still damp hair. I felt numb. "Tom," she called, through the glass pane desperately. "I know you can hear me," she pleaded. I couldn't decide whether to tell her to go fuck herself or to return upstairs and pretend the last five minutes had never occurred. "We have to talk." I noticed the subtle increase in the pitch of her voice, the hint of despondency. "Please," she begged.

"We have nothing to talk about. Please just leave me alone," I shouted back through the door in fervent indignation.

There was a brief silence. "You at least owe me the opportunity to explain," she urged, crouching on the doorstep, her face against the frosted glass, her fingers pushing open the letterbox. I doubt she could have said anything more calculated to make me rise to the bait.

Anger enveloped me, as I sat on the hall floor, its ugly power surging through my veins. I jumped to my feet and violently wrenched open the door. Tara had backed off a few feet and now stood, soaking wet, hands in the pockets of her coat, her head bowed in submission, just waiting. The rain was pelting down outside, and if I had not been so furious, I would have seen that she was visibly shaking from cold. But my corrosive animosity was such that I was unable to perceive anything beyond my sense of injustice and wounded betrayal.

I stepped onto the drive in my bare feet. "I owe you?" I spat the words like an insult. "I owe you nothing." Tara was taken aback by my vehemence, but I continued my tirade. "See this," I shouted, pointing at the front door. "Look nice and new, does it? It's only a few months old. Shall I tell you why? A dozen armed police officers decided to destroy the other one, before arresting me in my own bedroom, and keeping me locked in a police cell for two days. You know why?" I yelled. "Because they thought I was an IRA sympathiser, who had a hand in the murder of my own brother!"

Tara's head remained resolutely bowed, absorbing my abuse, allowing my wrath to spew forth and mix with the raindrops that fell from her thin jacket and hair to the floor. "Imagine my surprise, to discover their only evidence was my involvement with you. How could you: my brother? I have a niece who will never know her father and a brother who will never hear his little girl's first words, or watch her take her first step. Who made you God, gave you the power to choose who lives and who dies? Are we equal now, your husband my brother?" The emotion overpowered me, memories of Ben and seeing Tara, the object of both loathing and desire. I could see the pain my accusations inflicted – or was it guilt? Frankly, I didn't care. I just wanted to vent my rage. I wanted to see her suffer, for vengeance eased the pain of the gaping black hole in the centre of my very being. Exhausted, I retreated inside, fully intending to close the door behind me.

My resolve lasted only seconds. I turned to face her, as tentatively Tara approached me, her arms open in meek surrender, unsure of her fate. "Tom, I don't know how much they told you. But I do know you don't know the truth – only I do. I've done some terrible things, and God knows I have to live with that. But I'm not the monster you make me out to be. I came here, because…." Her voice faltered before recovering her composure. "I'm going to the police. You deserve to hear what I am going to tell them. I don't want you to hear this on the radio or read it in the paper. I want you to listen to it from my lips.

And then I'll leave…" Tara kept her eyes fixed firmly on a spot on the hall floor. "…Afterwards, you'll never have to see me ever again."

The façade I had constructed crumbled. I was still unable to reconcile this familiar face with the evil I was told she was capable of. Isn't this what every victim of a crime desires? To face their tormentor and trace the uncomfortable shifting glance of the eyes, as they are confronted with the consequences of their actions. To try and make sense of the senseless act and to ascertain if there was any sign of remorse?

"You'd better come in," I finally relented frostily.

Tara was soaked through to the skin. She shivered, as she held her folded arms defensively across her chest. A strange mixture of emotions engulfed me. Make her sit there and say her piece and then leave me to my morbid solitude – to reflect in peace. Instead, I fetched her a towel and some dry clothes. I omitted all mention of the box of her clothes stored in my spare room, in case it revealed some distant bygone hint of affection. She changed in the bathroom. Minutes later, she emerged, towel in hand, rubbing her hair dry. I handed her a cup of tea. It had been something mundane to do to try and get my head together. Her new close cropped hairstyle added a certain starkness to her chiselled features. She looked tired and seemed to have gained a few more lines around her face. New dark patches under her eyes were visible through her tanned skin. Was there really a difference from when we had first met? Or was I looking at her with open eyes for the first time? Tara perched uncomfortably on the edge of the sofa. Her slender fingers were wrapped around the mug of steaming tea. When I had first met her she was full of confidence and vibrancy. Perhaps the vulnerability had always lurked under the surface; now it was transparently visible. There was something of the hunted animal about her. Alert to every sound and movement, paranoid it might represent a threat. And in that instant, I felt a tinge of pity for her, and for what she had become.

My pity was soon replaced with anger. I paced the room. "Tell me," the jilted lover in me began, firing questions at her. "Were we just an elaborate alibi for your nefarious activities? Did you earn extra kudos by fucking the English enemy? Did any of it mean anything at all to you? Did you all enjoy a good laugh at my expense?"

"Stop it, Tom. Please," she pleaded, shaking her head. Her eyes peered in earnest at me. "It wasn't like that. I didn't mean for any of this to happen."

"It's a bit bloody late for that, isn't it?"

Her head hung low. "You were the best thing to happen to me in an age. You won't believe me, but I loved you." She looked up, gathering strength from within. "I still do."

I shook my head, unwilling to listen. "Spare me, Tara please." I rolled my unreceptive eyes to the ceiling in disgust.

"I am so sorry," she offered hoarsely.

"That won't bring Ben back. And you're responsible," I shouted, from the far end of the living room.

"I had no idea what they were planning," she replied.

"Oh, come on," I spat with incredulity. "What kind of fool do you take me for? You are a member of the IRA, aren't you?"

"I used to be," Tara confirmed, averting her eyes from mine, placing her mug on the floor, "a long time ago." Her voice was muted, words spoken in guilt, under her breath.

"Why, Tara?" I asked, finally breaking the silence. "Why us? How do you live with yourself? What the hell do you think the death of my brother is going to achieve? Why did you leave me on a beach with a broken leg? I don't know…" I gesticulated with my arms, raised high above my head in despair and confusion. "I need to make some sense out of this unbelievable mess. Can you understand that?"

Chapter Nineteen

"WHAT IS YOUR earliest memory?" Tara asked, "as a kid?" I was about to tell her that my patience was running thin. I had not invited her into my home to reminisce about my childhood memories. Instead I repressed my cynical desire to be obstinate.

"I don't know," I lied, not even attempting to answer her question. Tara was indifferent, caught up with the images inside her head, oblivious to the world outside.

"I was five: 9th August 1971, the day Section 12 of the Northern Ireland Special Powers Act came into force – internment without trial. It was supposed to stop paramilitary action on all sides. But they only arrested suspected members of the IRA. The Protestant gunmen were left untouched, their arsenals intact. I was oblivious to the bombs, riots, burning cars, shootings and the daily abuse. I thought everyone lived this way. I woke up, sometime after 4am, to noise and commotion on the street, banging on the door. I was so scared – Mum was screaming. Marie, my sister and I crept out of bed to the top of the stairs and peered round the banister, as Dad was frog-marched out of the front door in handcuffs. Marie was a year older and tried to explain it to me. She didn't understand any more than I did. I was convinced they were coming for me next. Dad was calm and dignified, offering no resistance. He tried to soothe my mum's distress. 'It's all a mistake – they'll sort it out, I'll be back in no time. Go back to bed'. That was the last I saw of him for months."

Tara hesitated and lit a cigarette, struggling to hold her lighter steady. "The British army had confused him with an IRA activist with the same name: Joe McCabe. Incompetent fools got the wrong man. He was no threat to anyone, just a regular hard working family man. The other McCabe had been tipped off and had crossed the border into the Republic. Despite his protestations, they held him without charge for ten months in Long Kesh. They never even acknowledged their mistake." Tara smirked sarcastically, exhaling cigarette smoke in two blue columns. "They only released him because they arrested the other Joe McCabe in the South.

"Mum cried for most of the rest of the night, her head buried in her pillow so as not to alarm us kids. Eventually, we both climbed into bed with her. She attempted to reassure us, but I knew she was lying. The next few nights saw an endless stream of riots and pitch battles with the RUC and soldiers. We were not allowed to play out on the street. The street in West Belfast where we lived was in a mixed area – mainly Protestant, but with a significant minority Catholic population. I played out in the street with kids who were Protestant as well as other Catholics – the distinction was lost on me.

"The days following internment were like a powder keg waiting to be lit. The entire province seemed to be in flames. Rioting – with Protestant gangs on the rampage and Catholic youths fighting back, erecting barricades from burning vehicles to protect Catholic areas. Each morning you would look out onto the street to view the previous night's carnage. Broken glass from smashed windows and burned out cars and vans. Two nights after Dad was taken, there was a knock at the door – I ran down the stairs, hoping it was him. Mum ushered me back upstairs, before placing the chain on the door. Slowly, she edged open the door. 'McCabe?' He was nothing more than a spotty teenager. He thrust a note into her hand. I watched from the bedroom window, as a gang of about ten lads walked up the street, already knocking on the door of another Catholic family. Mum sat at the kitchen table, her head in her hands, sobbing quietly. I watched her crumple up the note and throw it in the bin. When I walked into the kitchen, she tried to hide her red eyes. In my childlike innocence I asked. 'Is Dad coming home?'

'Soon,' she answered. 'Soon.' They gave us twelve hours to leave, or else the house would be burned down. This was to be a Protestant street from now on. My mum was not easily intimidated and refused to be forced out of her house by a bunch of yobs. So we sat and waited, not daring to go out, waiting for nightfall. Neighbours called round to say goodbye. 'Think of the girls,' they urged her. After she put us to bed, she packed a suitcase. I woke to the sound of breaking glass. At first I was confused, disorientated. I started coughing, and couldn't stop. Orange flickering light, flames and smoke. Outside, I could hear angry chanting, shouts and screaming. My abiding memory shall be of the thick acrid smoke that only comes when chairs, curtains and carpets burn in a confined area. Mum swept me up in her arms, whilst desperately holding onto Marie's hand, thrusting us down the stairs, towards the front door, shouting at Marie, who wanted to fetch her doll, 'leave it. I'll get you another.'

"Flames danced around the curtains and sofa, with a greedy intensity, consuming everything in their path. Every intake of breath was painful. My lungs felt like they were about to explode. The wet cloth Mum placed over my face seemed wholly ineffective. My throat seared with pain and I just kept coughing. A jumping spark ignited Marie's nightdress. She shouted and screamed so loudly that I wanted to cover my ears. Mum opened the front door and picked Marie up and threw her outside. With me in her arms she smothered the flames. All three of us were hysterical. The street was full of people – all former neighbours. As I looked around, the whole street seemed to glow red, orange and yellow against the blackened sky."

Tara reached for another cigarette, before resuming. "When Mum jumped on Marie to douse the flames, a roar of laughter swept through the assembled throng. Every house in our street occupied by Catholics was either abandoned or burning. We left carrying only one small suitcase and a half-full bin liner. Not one photograph exists of me before I was four, or of my parent's wedding day – only our memories. The RUC and the British army stood on the street corner and watched it all happen. Not a single solider or police officer raised a finger to stop it."

Tara sneered sarcastically, inhaling deeply on the cigarette. "I suppose I should be grateful we all survived. We were homeless, with no possessions and a father in prison." She stubbed out her cigarette, sending glowing ashes spiralling into the air. "We were accommodated in a Catholic community centre, along with twenty other families. Eventually, they allocated us a flat previously occupied by a Protestant family in a Catholic area. They had moved out, worried about reprisals. At least they had a choice. Mum didn't have the heart to tell my Dad about the house. His powerlessness would have driven him insane with guilt. He eventually found out through one of the other internees, whose family had also been bombed out. When he was finally released, he was quieter, more restrained. He had lost the sparkle in his eyes." Tara ran her hands through her still damp hair. "Before, he would pick me up and dance whilst listening to the radio. I would giggle, as he sang along. High above his head he would twirl me, telling me I would be that tall one day soon. I don't remember ever seeing him dance after he came home.

"Northern Ireland is not like the rest of the UK – it was never a democracy. The system was skewed in favour of unionists. If you were a Catholic in the Protestant six counties, you were second class citizens. Dad tried to get work for three years after he was released. He would go to interviews, and would do well until they asked him whether he was a Catholic. All of a sudden the job vacancy no longer existed. In the end he stopped putting his address on the application forms and used his cousins who lived in a mixed area. It was the same with housing. Easy to get a council house if you were a Protestant – but Catholic families lived in overcrowded squalor."

"So it's okay to kill, as long as it's Protestants who are oppressing you?" I asked angrily, shaking my head in disgust.

"What the fuck do you know?" Tara's words emerged like poisonous venom. "This was never about Protestants and Catholics for me. It was never sectarian – which church you went to. It was about equality or the basic rights that you take for granted."

"And do bombs and murders make you more equal?" I enquired, avoiding her piercing facial expression.

"Of course not," she retorted angrily. "But for a little while I thought it was the only language the Brits spoke. God knows you practised it enough on us." Her voice was softer now, her eyes less fierce, replaced by a sense of deep sadness, which even I could see through the barrier of my rage.

"You say Brits, but I didn't discriminate against Irish Catholics. Many things have been done by the British Government that I never agreed with: sinking the General Belgrano, banning Unions at GCHQ and killing unarmed suspects in Gibraltar to name but three." Tara looked surprised at my last example. "Even terrorist suspects have the right to a fair trial."

"Does that include me?" she inquired quietly, her temper subsiding.

An awkward silence ensued.

"Dad was spared the worst of the 'In depth techniques,' once everyone bar the Northern Ireland office knew they had the wrong man. There were various tortures, mainly learnt from controlling colonial insurrections in Africa. They would make you stand spread-eagled against a wall and place a canvas hood over your head to achieve sensory depravation. You can breathe only with difficulty. You lose track of time, day and night – become confused and unhinged. Finally they blast you with white noise. It enhances your sense of isolation. You can hear nothing but this awful hissing noise, hours on end, until you think you will go mad. Is it any wonder they were never the same again?"

Tara stubbed out another cigarette. "You got anything to drink?" I walked to the kitchen, and splashed cold water on my face, if only to ensure that this was real and not some kind of waking dream. I returned, carrying a bottle of Talisker single malt and two glasses. She downed the measure I poured for her in one greedy gulp.

Tara continued with a new-found sense of determination. "The soldiers were the most tangible sign of the fear that pervaded both our home and the community we lived in. Living in a nationalist area meant that we were prime targets for random searches by the British army. It was their way of intimidating us – letting us know that nothing was sacred. The bastards would come into the house and literally turn everything upside down – furniture, bedding and carpets. They would trample up and down the stairs whilst we would all be cowered in the corner like frightened mice. It would take Mum hours to clean up. Is it any wonder that the British army came to be seen as the occupying force? I grew up wanting to ensure that my family could live in peace, without fear. I doubt you would have felt any different," she added, shifting from her perch on the arm of the chair, reclining back into the sofa, indicating it was going to be a long night.

I sighed, also sitting down, but on the other side of the room, in a dining chair. "It's a question of what you do with that anger." I replied cautiously. "There is always a choice."

"Maybe," Tara replied, her voice fading, as she clutched the now empty glass tightly between her fingers.

Chapter Twenty

"YOU ONCE TOLD me your father was a mechanic. Was that another part of your elaborate web of deceit?" I asked, attempting to rile Tara.

"It was the truth," she replied calmly, not rising to my provocation.

"I suppose I should be grateful, not everything in our relationship was a sham," I noted acidly.

Tara rubbed her eyes with her fingers, bowing her head slightly. "Don't do this Tom. I never wanted to deceive you."

I exhaled in disbelief. "Did you just conveniently forget to mention to me that you were hoping to bomb, maim and intimidate your way to a united Ireland? Perhaps you could have slipped it in as we made love. 'By the way Tom, I just forgot to tell you....' Inserted it in amongst the kisses and intimate pillow talk."

Tara shook her head defensively, almost in sorrow. She stood to face me and then fell back into the chair, pulling her legs up close to her chest. "Stop it now – please. Why must you torture us both so. I sure as hell hope it makes you feel better?"

"Nothing could make me feel better," I replied petulantly, relishing her unease.

"Dad drifted in and out of employment, working for garages on a casual basis. If he was in work he was always happy. We wouldn't have to tiptoe round the house watching out for his mood swings. On pay day he would always bring me and Marie a little present. We loved it while it lasted, but were always aware that it may be a different story the following week. In the 1830's, Belfast was the fastest growing city in the British Empire. By the turn of the century it was one of the most industrialised and advanced cities anywhere. In just seventy years, it had turned into a backwater, where you could not find work for love or money, if you were a working class Catholic." Tara was reflective. "They built the Titanic in Belfast. Highly appropriate – a sense of tragedy that has since proved very hard to shake…"

"Your father?" I interrupted, anxious not to hear a history class on great shipping tragedies of our time.

"In late 1980 he at last got regular employment – with DeLorean – building the DMC-12 Coupe."

"Back to the Future," I recalled fondly. "Pity it didn't manage to stay in production until the film came out in 85. They'd have shifted thousands.…but it doesn't help when the MD is caught with a suitcase full of cocaine."

Tara nodded solemnly. "They closed in 82. Dad always said they were the only British carmaker to turn a profit in 1981 with a full order book. They were short of operating capital – now we know they lost millions. It was supposed to be the car that would last forever – built from stainless steel. I'm only surprised an iceberg didn't hit it," she added, with a cynical smirk. "Dad got a redundancy payment and bought a van – set himself up as a mobile mechanic." Tara's focus appeared glazed, distant, as if in another world.

I was no longer in the mood for confrontation. A sense of foreboding caused me to calm my natural instinct to hurl the insults back. Perhaps I could sense the anguish in her eyes. Tara lit another cigarette, exhaling slowly, through pursed lips, filling the room with smoke. "15th April 1984. I was seventeen. Every Thursday Dad went out for a drink with a couple of old mates: Paul McGee and Eamon Murphy. I used to baby-sit whilst studying for my A levels.

"Dad and I had had a row, after I threatened to jack in school and find a job. I was sick of having no money. He had gone ballistic, telling me that he wished he had been given the opportunities that I had available. He resumed his theme as we drove towards Paul's house to drop me off: 'You thought any more about your future?'

" 'No,' I replied sullenly, anticipating another lecture.

"But his voice was calm, reassuring. 'Tara, you've got brains – more than me or your mother.' It wasn't true but it suited him to say it. 'Don't get trapped in this place,' he gestured towards the grim housing estate surrounding us. 'The world is so much bigger than the narrow horizons of the people round here.' He rotated his head to smile, as we slowed for a white van, which had pulled out in front of us. We braked for the traffic lights, but by then it was too late.

" 'I'll think about it,' I replied. In the split second that our eyes had been focused on each other, we failed to spot the doors of the van in front of us open."

Tara's voice trailed off – she screwed her eyes tightly closed. The intensity of the pain was too great. "Standing in the back of the van – dressed all in black, balaclava over his head, gun in his hand. I can't even begin to describe the sense of total and complete terror. I shouted, 'Dad.' I shall never forget the look of powerless realisation and utter horror on his face. He lunged towards me, attempting to protect me. My cries were drowned out by the gunfire and the shattering windscreen. The gunman fired twice and then the van accelerated away as the lights changed. I covered my face, diving down in my seat, trying to protect myself from the bullets and broken glass. I screamed myself hoarse. I lay there convinced I was dead, sobbing endlessly. My white T-shirt splattered with blood – thick deep crimson blood. Dad lay draped over the wheel. Once I stopped screaming, there was a strange eerie haunting silence. My arms felt too heavy to move. One of the bullets had ricocheted and caught my arm."

Tara pushed up her right sleeve and twisted her arm around towards me, revealing a once familiar faint red scar.

"It wasn't until I was being pulled out of the car by a paramedic that I realised he was dead. I saw where the bullet had penetrated his forehead; the trickle of blood that dribbled down his nose and across his cheek. My face had been cut by the glass fragments and the wounds were now beginning to pump blood out freely. Even now, I still wake at night and see his face in that split second before the gun fired. It haunts me – the total helplessness to affect your impending doom. How do you live with the memory of a dying man's face, an instant before the executioner's blow strikes him down?

"The UFF admitted responsibility a week or so later. As for why, I think everyone in Ireland would ask that question after every sectarian murder, Catholic or Protestant. He was an easy target. A Catholic former internee, with his name emblazoned over the side of his van. He worked in all areas of Belfast, nationalist and loyalist. The bottom line is he was a non-practising Catholic killed by a Prod gunman in a sectarian act of meaningless stupidity."

The pain in Tara's voice turned to anger. "For what purpose – to tell him to stay away from loyalist areas? To frighten and intimidate other Catholics?" She pushed the stub of her cigarette around the ashtray, in slow circles and whispered. "He was only forty six."

"I'm sorry."

Tara acknowledged my civility with grace, a solitary tear trickling across her cheek, which she wiped with her sleeve. "You're not the only one who knows the pain of losing someone."

"I knew that already."

I needed to stretch my legs. The atmosphere was too intense. I went into the kitchen, refilled the kettle and then stepped onto the patio. It was still raining. I let the blustering gusty wind sweep over me, until I could feel the chill of the night permeating through my T-shirt and my still bare feet could stand the wet concrete no longer. It was past 11pm. I felt no tiredness and had little desire to sleep – only to rationalise what I had heard. I returned to the now smoke-filled living room with two mugs of tea and handed one to Tara. She hadn't moved. I eased a little closer to the armchair and sat down.

"You're wet?" she observed.

"I needed some fresh air. How did you cope, seeing…?" I couldn't articulate the words.

Tara breathed heavily, her rib cage rising and falling. "These days, you get offered trauma counselling sessions – our local priest came round to pay his respects and that was that. You have no choice but to carry on, follow the same routines. People tried to help, but there is no consolation. Mum was absolutely devastated. Friends rallied round, but our household was sad and empty after…I can't begin to describe to you the pain and the anger I felt. I desired to lash out, to fight back, to let them know they couldn't just kill with impunity."

Tara sipped the hot tea, pressing the mug to her pale lips. "I had a Saturday job in a mobile burger stand. In July, the local Orange Order has a march. They walk down the street, proclaiming how the Prods gave us Papists a good pasting hundreds of years ago, lest we forget. It's hardly the safest place in world, but he was offering double time. Sometime after 10pm, worse for wear with booze, one guy took it too far. He alleged I had short-changed him from his £20 note: oldest trick in the book. I tried to calm him down, to defuse the situation. He wouldn't let it go, called me a 'fuckin' Fenian lying whore,' in a loud and obnoxious voice, to the delight of his mates. It's the standard insult – you learn to ignore it. But something in me snapped and the red mist descended. He was a big fella, with a ruddy complexion, podgy cheeks and a wide neck. I don't know where I summoned up the courage from. 'You're priceless you are. Men like you don't grow on trees. You fucking swing in them.' At the same time I mimicked an orang-utan, my hands curled under my arms, whooping with my lips. Then I decked him through the window of the van."

"You hit him?"

Tara was laughing now, a glimpse of her old self just ascertainable. "Sent him sprawling." She mimed the punch – a swift upper cut. "Clean hit to his lower jaw. God it hurt my wrist, but it was worth the pain. I thought I'd provoked a riot. They rocked the van from side to side a few times, but then lost interest. Unfortunately my boss didn't view my heroics in the same light and sacked me."

Tara reflected for a second. "I surprised myself, that I was capable of such aggression. The hostility, it just exploded. After Dad died I just lashed out at everyone around me. Random discharges of unfocused rage, like carrying shit around in a very thin bag. You never knew when it was going to split and the contents explode everywhere. I was aggressive in school, with the teachers, and friends alike. For a while they all indulged me in light of what had happened. I was consumed by a deep dark loathing of the men who could perpetrate such an act of senseless cruelty. I would wake at night, tears streaming down my face, with fury and resentment. Part of it was guilt. Why hadn't they shot me instead? Can you believe I felt guilty for simply surviving? When you are in that place, the world is very lonely. I needed a focus or I knew I would go insane – the festering pain eating away like acid. Marie's reaction was the opposite. She internalised everything and barely mentioned him. My poor mother, it must have been hell, trying to deal with her own grief and loneliness, as well as raising two dysfunctional teenagers.

"Eventually I realised my worst fear was being trapped in those streets. My father had been right. So I threw myself into passing my A-levels, obtaining a place at university, and then leaving the past behind me. At the first opportunity I was getting out and as far away as possible."

Chapter Twenty One

"SO HOW DID you end up at Queens?"

"Not all our dreams achieve fruition. The humdrum of practicality always intervenes. I couldn't leave Mum. Marie went to study in Dublin. I did what I thought I ought to do. Perhaps things would have been different if I had moved..." Tara stood to stretch her legs, her arms still determinedly folded across her chest, her body language still defensive. The T shirt clung to her frame – the outline of her rib cage visible, since she'd lost weight. "You know some of the rest. Patrick and I met at university and for a while the waters were smoothed."

"Some?" I enquired – my mistrust obvious.

"I haven't kept anything back from you," Tara said, holding her eyes firmly on mine.

"Ha," I snorted in disgust. "You told me Pat died in a car crash." I returned to pacing the floor, running my hands through my hair – in both anger and despair. "How am I supposed to discern between truth and deceit. Do you even remember what truth is?"

"Come on Tom, it's no great crime to tell a white lie about how your husband died," she interrupted. She stretched out her legs, then pulled her knees up to her chest, hands across her shins. I sank back into the sofa. "I never meant to lie," she said faintly.

"You don't appear to have tried very hard," I reproached her.

"It was a part of my life that I was trying to leave behind. Pat's death hit me hard and contributed to my involvement in the Republican Movement. Being in England, teaching, meeting you, it was like I was a normal human being again. I wasn't ready to talk about it...."

"When would you have been ready, if I hadn't forced it out of you?" Tara offered no reply. "Everything, it was all built upon lies. I don't even recognise you. Don't you see – you're a lie." Tara contemplated the floor impassively, unwilling or unable to look up at me.

"The British army just got away with it, no justice and no retribution. They were saying that Pat was of no importance – one more civilian casualty that we can ignore. Patronise the family and try and blame the dead man who can't defend himself. The soldier carries on with his life and career, earns a good living, has a family and someone to come home to, whilst..." Tara's voice faltered. "Pat was only twenty-seven. He had so much life to live, so many plans. I had been cheated of the promise of the life we were to share together. Cruelly deprived of a love that I believed was my right." Tara spoke eloquently, passionately of her loss – and that was something I could identify with.

"Sometimes, I wish I had never met Pat." Tara threw her hair back and reached for a cigarette. She didn't light it though, just twirled it in between her fidgeting fingers. "The loss was just too great to bear. Like a child given a present who plays with it gleefully, only to have it snatched back minutes later. That's enough happiness for you. No more. When my dad died I had a future to aim for, a life to live, a goal to work for. Now, it all seemed so meaningless. The rage and animosity I had repressed resurfaced with vengeance. The dam exploded and I am afraid I succumbed to the basest of all emotions – revenge".

Tara hesitated and then approached the bottle of Scotch. "May I?" I gestured for her to continue and thrust my glass in her direction. She poured two large measures and then sat back down on the sofa. Choosing her words with obvious care she began, "Francis Bacon wrote, *'Revenge is a kind of wild justice; which the more man's nature runs to, the more ought law to weed it out.'*[2] I am afraid that I am living proof of the truth of those words," she confessed.

"Are you saying you joined the Provisionals for vengeance?"

Tara raised her eyebrows, a hint of exasperation apparent. "If only life was that simple." Tara finally lit the cigarette she had been twisting between her fingers. I took one as well, finding blessed relief in the ensuing nicotine rush. "After my dad's death I began to ask questions. Who would want to kill him? What motivated these people? Why

---

2   Francis Bacon, 1st Baron Verulam, Viscount St Albans (1561-1626) Essays: Of Revenge

was no one ever arrested or convicted for his murder? And in that way I was receptive to the message: there was a conspiracy between the loyalist paramilitaries, the RUC, and the British Government; a coalition of forces responsible for the way in which Catholics and nationalists were treated. It was easy to see the British army as an occupying force and the answer to Ireland's (and hence my) problems was persuading the British to leave, making way for a united Ireland. Although I shared some sympathy with the republican view of what was wrong in the North, I never subscribed to physical force republicanism."

"What changed?"

"Patrick was the straw that broke the camel's back. The whole system seemed to conspire together to ensure justice was never done. No one seemed to care: army, police or politicians. They would just ignore it, wash their hands and walk away. It rankled so deep…"

"Enough to kill?"

Tara thought for a moment, leaning her head slightly to one side. "In a war there are always casualties. Anyone who knows the political situation in the North of Ireland knew a war was being fought. In a war people die on both sides. But that was then – I would make no attempt to justify any of my actions today." Tara's body language corroborated her words. Her shoulders tensed, head bowed, her hair falling loosely over her face, obscuring her facial features, as she wrung her hands together, cupping them under her chin. "It was a war foisted upon us, upon me. I saw myself as a defender, standing against a vicious enemy who occupied my land at the barrel of the gun."

Tara flicked ash, rotating the cigarette delicately on the edge of the ashtray. "I wanted to play my part, ensure that another son or daughter, husband or wife didn't lose a father or a husband the way I did."

"So you kill someone else's instead?" Tara glared at me frostily and with perhaps a tinge of guilt.

"The more British politicians asked: why are we wasting soldiers' lives for a country that isn't our own, the quicker they would leave. It was an armed struggle because the enemy is armed."

"And your life?" I enquired thoughtfully.

Tara's frostiness melted slightly. "That's the risk you take to live in a free country. No one decides overnight to join a paramilitary organisation. It's a gradual process, which involves luck, turmoil, fear and yes, excitement. I weighed the risks and the consequences. What did I have left? There is no romance. It's a creed which appeals only to the basest instinct of hate, unbridled power and bigotism. But I wasn't to discover that until later – much later."

A part of me was drawn in, anxious to understand. At the same time I was repulsed, like a child covering my eyes at the frightening scenes unfolding on the TV screen. "Does the IRA have a recruiting office?" I jibed cynically.

Tara ignored my barbed remark. "Many people I had never met attended Patrick's funeral. It was a solidarity thing. People who wanted to stand up and say what had happened to Pat was not right. One of them was rumoured to be a senior republican. He shook my hand and embraced me, like he was sharing my pain. 'If you ever need anything, call me,' he said. He handed me a scrap of paper with his telephone number on. Two months later I called and told him I wanted to assist. I heard nothing for a few months. I guess he figured it was my irrational grief speaking. Give her a few months and she will drop these crazed delusions. Then one day out of the blue I received a call. No pleasantries, just, 'you still want to help?' He told me some fellas needed a place to stay and lie low for a night or two."

"You mean IRA men?" I asked.

Tara nodded a confirmation. "One night there was a knock at my door. Three men appeared. They were polite and courteous. I knew they must have been on a job. I didn't enquire any further. It was not my position to do so. They kept their heads down and disappeared the next morning. It was only as I listened to the radio the following morning and heard about the shooting of a part time UDR man that I realised that his killers had spent the night in my home."

"How did that make you feel?" I enquired, almost dispassionately.

"Strange at first. It turned my stomach. In part for self-preservation; the fear that they might trace the gunmen back to me." Tara looked reflective. "At the time, I shed no tears over the death of a UDR man." Her voice hardened. "He knew the risk he took…

"Every couple of weeks I would have visitors – each looking for a safe place to crash. Jimmy Kelley arrived at my door, one September evening with two other operatives. It was obvious they had been involved in an operation. His eyes look glazed – like when you're drunk or high. It's the adrenaline. Kelley was the OC of one of the

Belfast units. He had an arrogance I hadn't detected in others. I showed them to the spare room. You wouldn't accommodate IRA men in the living room. You would be surprised how many neighbours would sell you out to the RUC for a few quid. About 10pm I began to hear raised voices. I was intrigued. Eventually I tiptoed up the stairs. I winced each time the stairs creaked.

"I overheard them talking about the job. They had been waiting – parked up across the street from a bakery in a stolen car. They watched him arrive and checked his identity: Captain Stuart O'Brien, part time member of the UDR and a civilian working at a nearby RUC station. O'Brien was lazy. He forgot to take a different route each day; failed to vary the times he left. If you stick to the same pattern, one day you will become a target. That's just the way it is."

Tara spoke as if it was his fault for making an attempt to lead a normal life. Was that the quid pro quo? If I can't have a normal life, then neither can anyone else? I felt a burning desire to confront her warped morality.

"O'Brien emerged from the bakery and stood in the autumn sunshine. Kelley waited till his back was to him and then fired off three shots in succession out of the car window. 'Go, go, go' shouted Kelley, slapping the dashboard. They abandoned the getaway car a mile away. It was doused in petrol and lit – the forensic evidence quite literally went up in smoke. I ought to have been shocked, appalled that the men in my house had taken part in a brutal cold-blooded murder of a man in broad daylight. I was scared but I also felt excited."

I felt sick. What appalled me was how anyone could not be disgusted by the scenes Tara recounted – the fact that someone I had been so close to could have supported the actions of such men.

What follows in the next chapters is the rest of the story Tara told me that night, although not necessarily in exactly the same chronological sequence as she recounted it. She jumped around in response to my cross-examination of her motives and perception of events, so I have placed her words in chronological order.

How can I be sure that this account is accurate? In the pain of Ben's death, I of all people retain the right to be sceptical. I abhor violence, from the school playground to the football stadium, state repression to acts of terror. Force is the argument of last resort for those who cannot win the battle of hearts and minds by rational debate. However, that does not mean that in extreme circumstances, I would not be capable of acts and deeds which in the normal course of events I would find both horrific and morally reprehensible.

Not that this in any way absolves Tara of responsibility for her actions. She never sought to argue that she was a product solely of her circumstances, that violence was somehow the natural consequence of the perceived injustice surrounding her. She chose to bear arms in circumstances where many others didn't. That is a decision she came to regret, every day for the rest of her life.

Chapter Twenty Two

Autumn 1991: *Belfast*

EVERY FEW WEEKS, I would receive a phone call telling me that such and such a person required a place to stay. Occasionally, I would be asked to convey messages across the city. I was inconspicuous as a woman. Usually there would be instructions to go to this house or that pub at a certain time, and I would surreptitiously pass on the information. You never knew whose phone was tapped or home was under electronic surveillance. Using trusted third parties, who were unknown to the police, was in reality the only way to keep effective secure lines of communication. The reply to the message might be a hurried scribble on a scrap of paper or on a ripped up cigarette pack. In this way, I got to meet a fair smattering of IRA men in both Belfast and from further afield. With an album of suspects, I could have done significant damage, should I have chosen to reveal what I knew to the RUC. My loft also became popular for storing equipment: guns or ammunition, even explosives or detonators. Initially, I was a little uneasy. How would I explain the presence of a handgun or semiautomatic ammunition next to my Christmas decorations? But, gradually I just accepted the risk as part of the territory.

On the outside I was a regular teacher – competent but unassuming. By night, I had entered a whole new world. I used to get grief occasionally from my Year 11 students. They would answer back, swear or once in a while attempt to physically assault me. I often wondered how they would have reacted had they known about some of my extra-curricular activities.

I became used to running all over the city at the drop of a hat. So when the telephone rang one Sunday afternoon, asking me to meet a contact at a particular churchyard, it did not strike me as being out of the ordinary.

The weather had definitely turned from what had been late summer sun only a few weeks previously. Now there was a biting edge to the wind. The leaves danced around my feet as I entered the graveyard. I hurried through the gate and made my way to the rear of the church. As I approached the rendezvous point, I saw Eamon Magee was waiting. The man who had attended Pat's funeral and the facilitator of my inexorable slide into the arms of the IRA. He smiled in a fatherly manner. He offered me a cigarette. His features had a harshness that I had not noticed previously. The lines on his face told their own story. I had learnt to recognise the small tell tale signs of those who had chosen to live a life inseparable from the political violence that came to define their identity. No small talk, just an indifferent, "are you still interested?" He observed me in silence, as if weighing up whether to dissuade me. Did he remember the day he had been asked the same question? Did he regret all the things that he would never have, that normal people take for granted: stable home and family, security and the ability to sleep at night, without one ear open for every noise in the street outside? He withdrew his hand from his grey overcoat and pressed into my hand the piece of paper he had been caressing between his fingers. I took it from him – my fingers briefly intertwined with his in a moment of confusion that I thought would see the wind blow the scrap of paper away. 7.30pm Tuesday night, along with an address.

It was just another two up two down terrace house. The bell didn't work. A gentle rap, then louder. After a couple of anxious seconds, I heard the muffled bark of the dog and footsteps in the hallway. It seemed like an age before the door was opened, and a late middle-aged man peered at me from behind a locked chain and greying stubble. I recognised him: Rory Brady, one of the Training Officers for Belfast. He appeared shocked. "Well screw me."

I could hear a child's voice in the background, but it was quiet in the front room. He pointed to the cheap sofa then sat in the armchair opposite me, drawing it close. So close, I began to feel uncomfortable, on edge – vulnerable. "A woman," he muttered to himself, in mild disgust, as if taken by surprise, but it soon became clear he knew all about me. Maybe it was part of the intimidation. He spoke almost menacingly. "We both know why you're here." My mouth was dry and I was lost for words. "There are only two certainties in this organisation. One, you will be killed. Two, you will go to prison. It's too late when you're in the dock to say that you never wanted this. You make that decision now." His voice increased a notch, as did the intensity of his stare. "Only if you're prepared to accept the fact of prison or death can you become a volunteer. Many people have joined Óglaigh na hÉireann for all the wrong reasons. Okay, so your old man was killed and your husband as well. But if that's your motivation walk away – now. You have your life ahead of you. Do you want to spend it in prison, molested by some butch lesbian every night for the next twenty five years?" If it was his job to try and make me think twice he succeeded. Prison was not an appealing concept. But I was way beyond changing my mind. The empty desperate void inside me pushed me relentlessly on.

Brady drew ever closer – I could feel his breath in my ear, as he spoke. "There are many men who get this far and then walk away. They decide their families are more important. There are even fewer women who have what it takes. What makes you think you are so different?" There was a sneering misogynist overtone to his voice. The atmosphere was stifling. Suddenly I felt a wave of claustrophobia. "Go home; think about dying, bleeding in the street, gunned down by a bullet from a British gun. Don't dream that you'll be made a martyr. There is no glory in death. It's a fucking lonely world, as your life slips away. If you walk away no one will criticise you. You wouldn't be the first – and you sure as hell won't be the last."

I was haunted by the image of Pat lying bleeding, his life ebbing away as his blood stained the cream car upholstery a deep burgundy. It hadn't occurred to me previously that his overwhelming emotion might have been loneliness. I regretted more than ever that I hadn't been there in those final gasping moments of consciousness. Nothing Brady could have said would have dissuaded me.

My initiation began the next day. The IRA uses a training manual called the Green Book. It's a constitution, disciplinary code, handbook and training manual in one. Once the Education Officer was satisfied I knew the manual backwards – I pledged an oath of allegiance to Óglaigh na hÉireann.

Thereafter, I was sent to a block of flats in the south of the city. I had no idea what to expect, but anticipated another round of lectures. I was quite surprised then, when a well dressed woman in her early forties, with luxurious dark shoulder length hair, opened the door. She smiled warmly, instantly putting me at ease.

"They will try and break you," she lectured me, as we sat around her kitchen table. "They will think because you are a woman you are weak. Under the prevention of terrorism legislation you can be held for seven days. Believe me girl it's a long time. They will use very minute of it to their advantage. If you give them a way in, they'll squeeze you like an orange. Suck all the information they can out: names, places, dates, details of operations, your cell members, anything they can use. Understand?" I nodded. "Don't even think about answering questions, even the apparently innocent ones. Once you have told them you take sugar in your tea it's too late."

She sensed my scepticism and frowned angrily. "In a few weeks, months, maybe years, you will be desperately trying to remember every word – cursing your sorry arse that you didn't pay more attention." I was about to remonstrate with her but she continued before I had an opportunity to argue. "They arrived at my front door at 4am – forced me to dress with female officers watching my every move. When they try and hurry you up – refuse. Take your time. Don't let them know they have you rattled. It's psychology," she taught, touching her forehead with her finger, whilst her cigarette ash burned down to a fine delicate powder. Put on nice clothes and make up. Do your hair and wear perfume; show them you care about your appearance – that you're fixing to walk out in however many days.

"They banged me up and then made me wait for five hours before they pounced. You must keep your head together. Keep calm – this is a battle you can win. They're clean, fresh and relaxed. I felt dirty, tired and tense. Then they started asking questions. They need a confession from you. If they have anything on you, it will be a rumour or a tip off from an informer. If you tell them nothing, eventually they will have to let you walk. Seven days is nothing compared with a life sentence.

"Stare at them intently. It freaks them out. Turn the tables. It humanises them, a face beyond the uniform. You're marking them out, recording every detail of their features. Hair colour, eyes, nose, jaw, and the clothes they wear. Make them start to worry that one day the position will be reversed. Their biggest fear is being targeted and eliminated by the Provisionals. Man, I put the fear of God into them. Piss before every interview. The bastards won't let you go once they have started. Try and make you feel uncomfortable, so you get so desperate you'll say anything. I peed all over the floor – made a bloody great big puddle in the interview room. Fucks your dignity, but it's a small price to pay for freedom. That was day two. They never made me wait again. Eat whatever food is given to you. The idiots who think they are being hard by refusing food are the first ones to break. Try and exercise and sleep at every opportunity." She lit another cigarette. "The RUC is a male dominated police force. They told me they were also holding a rapist in the building and if I didn't co-operate with them they would let him out for the night. The Sergeant playing the bad cop routine told me that he would watch the fun, whilst the good cop told me everything was getting out of hand and that he could only protect me if I helped him. It was all bullshit, but at 3am when a man was brought to my cell in handcuffs and two officers began to uncuff him, I screamed blue murder. I made so much noise that the whole building knew something was going down. If you draw attention, they will back off. The next morning I was back in the interview room like nothing had happened. They released me soon afterwards…"

It was after 10pm when I finally arrived home. I had not long kicked off my shoes and sat down in front of the television, when the doorbell rang. I dragged myself to the door. It was Marie. We'd spent a lot of time together in the immediate aftermath of Pat's death. I needed company and desperately didn't want to be alone. But in the ensuing months we'd grown apart. She was a high flyer, having graduating from Trinity College in Dublin. She was working in advertising and looking for a one way ticket to a new life. The final straw came when she discovered I had been to a couple of Sinn Féin rallies. They symbolised the paramilitaries that she despised. I had seen her less and less. The tension between us had been palpable. "Grief you're hard to get hold of – you need an answer phone." She brushed past me, throwing her leather jacket effortlessly on the banister. "Thought I would pop round and see if my lesser spotted sister still existed."

"Very funny."

"I've been offered a position in Dublin," she confided. "I'll be there for a few months. There's a possibility they will to send me to the States for a while – New York probably… "

"Congratulations," I said, embracing her. "That is fantastic. When are you off?"

"Next week."

"So soon?"

"There is nothing to stay around here for."

"Thanks," I replied, defensively. There was an awkward pause.

"I don't mean it like that Tara," she said apologetically. Her voice was earnest and full of emotion. "This place contains too many memories. Every time I put the TV on, I hear of another shooting, another killing." Marie was never honest about her emotions. Even as teenagers she would never let on if she had a boyfriend. She always guarded her privacy jealously. We had barely talked about our father. It struck me as strange she chose this moment to open up. Perhaps it was her way of justifying the fact she was leaving. Marie pulled away, dabbing her eyes with a tissue. "Tara, promise me one thing?" An edge of tension crept into her voice, as if she knew she was asking something which might not be within my gift. She placed her hand on top of mine, squeezing affectionately. "Promise me you will not get involved?" I was about to feign ignorance, but it would have been a pointless façade.

"What makes you think I would?"

"I'm not stupid. You're being sucked in. I couldn't bear to turn on my radio to discover that you have been shot or blown up. Please," she begged.

I could have lied, told her what she wanted to hear and sent her on her way with meaningless reassurances and platitudes. Which would have been crueller? I felt compelled to make a stand. My words seemed like a dagger in her side. The pain was obvious in her face, and my guilt manifest. "For crying out loud, haven't enough people died Tara?"

"The only way to stop this nightmare is to fight back."

"You can't see it can you," Marie replied, with an air of desperate resignation. She shook her head with regret, her shoulders sinking low under a weight of sadness. "Have they really brainwashed you to believe that if you do force the British to leave the unionists will make peace?" She glared at me, more in pity than anger before retrieving her jacket. "You're not the solution, you're the problem."

I made no attempt to follow her. So deep had my involvement become that I could no longer listen to rational argument, even from a member of my own family. So convinced was I of the cause which I now espoused, I chose it over my own sister.

Chapter Twenty Three

A FEW WEEKS later, I was sent to the South to County Mayo where I handled a gun for the first time during basic military training. It was bloody uncomfortable – not to mention cold – trying to sleep on the floor with only a sleeping bag and four blokes in late January. On the Saturday afternoon we hiked into the hills. The Training Officer stripped a gun down and put it back together whilst we watched. He talked us through ammunition, the safety catch, how to oil and clean it, load, aim and shoot. It takes time just getting used to the weight and feel of a weapon. We practised on mock up targets, using a 9mm handgun and a semi-automatic rifle. Handguns are like gold. The IRA was awash with Kalashnikovs and AK47's courtesy of Colonel Gaddafi, but we had a limited supply of small arms.

Since the mid-eighties the IRA has been organised on the basis of cells. Too many super-grasses had infiltrated the organisation and devastated it from the inside. If you only knew the specific members of your cell then the amount of damage you could do was limited. A woman is less noticeable than a man. A couple can walk down the street without attracting the attention of a potential target or the security services.

My unit comprised five others plus myself. We met every week or so at a safe house – only occasionally at each other's homes, but there was always a fear about electronic surveillance. We only ever spoke in whispers. My first cell meeting was held on a Wednesday night in late September. We all crammed into the back room of a sympathiser's house. Ours was a new unit that had been put together with only one or two more experienced operatives. The idea was simple: the security forces have a fair idea through intelligence and informers of the identities of a hefty number of volunteers. If one of those individuals is spotted away from his home patch it arouses suspicion. That increases the presence of the security forces in that area. The operation then gets postponed or abandoned because the risk is too great.

The officer in command of my cell was a guy nicknamed Spender – Sean 'Spender' Burns. A massive guy: well over six foot, with a hell of a beer gut. Someone remembered that Shirley Bassey track 'Hey Big Spender' and the name stuck. A veteran at twenty-nine, he joined the IRA at seventeen. He'd killed at least three members of the RUC and come close to ending the careers of heaven knows how many others. If killing in general, was his passion, shooting soldiers or RUC officers was a fixation – the mere thought of it made his eyes sparkle with delight. I swear it gave him a hard on. He could be the life and soul of the party, particularly after a few pints, but possessed a ruthless streak. He was one guy you didn't want as an enemy. I heard he kneecapped a guy allegedly for thieving – republican justice. Rumour was the guy was having an affair with Spender's wife. Damn near bled to death before the ambulance reached him.

A guy called Hugh – the rest of his previous cell had blown themselves up attaching a UCBT in Ballymurphy. Hugh talked about explosives the way that some men talk about sex or football – always bragging about prior jobs, particularly to us raw recruits.

Kieran MacKenna was the other experienced volunteer. He was tall, with longish curly black hair and narrow eyes. Originally from Newry in South Armagh, I was left with the distinct impression he looked down on the Belfast Provies compared with the South Armagh volunteers. Every time things didn't go according to plan, or someone screwed up, he would comment that it ought to have been left to the professionals. To some extent he had a point, almost all of the spectaculars on the mainland were conceived, planned and executed by the South Armagh brigade – Baltic Exchange and Docklands to name but two.

Then there were the new recruits: Dave, Mickey and I. Dave was only twenty. Being a member of the IRA gave him street cred with easily impressed girls, who had romantic notions of republican heroes.

A Bold Deceiver • James Hurd

A beanpole covered in adolescent spots, he had little formal education, but he could fix almost any piece of electrical equipment. Great for rigging detonators or cloning mobile phones. He reminded me of the guy from Thunderbirds – Brains I think it was.

Mickey and I were the only two members with regular jobs. As a volunteer you are supposed to be 100% committed to the cause. That was incompatible with holding down a full time job. The IRA pay full time volunteers a small weekly allowance. They survive on what can be begged, borrowed, stolen or taken in DSS payments from the enemy they are trying to defeat. Mickey's job, as a postman, however, provided a valuable source of intelligence information. When there was a target to check out, Mickey would simply cycle down the street with his post-bag and check to see whether the target's car was visible, whether he parked it in the garage or on the drive, what time he left for work etc. As for me, I had the perfect cover, a respectable taxpayer, not the sort of person upon whom suspicion was likely to fall.

After we had all been introduced, Spender gave us a welcome lecture. With his leadership and guidance, this unit would become the most effective and successful in Belfast. Remember, he concluded, the more successful we were, the quicker the Brits would see the futility of continuing to occupy our country and bugger off. This provoked nods of approval from around the room. A wave of excitement flowed through my body. I actually believed this was a war that could be won. It just took dedication, commitment and time.

Spender then moved on to discuss prospective operations. The IRA had received intelligence to the effect that a part time UDR or by now RIR officer called O'Grady, who drove a blue Renault, lived on a particular housing estate in North Belfast. The car had been seen going back and forth on a number of occasions. We needed to pin his address down. "I can cycle home from work that way," offered Mickey. "Do you have the registration number?"

Hugh looked blank. "Err, I think so," he offered in an unconvincing manner. "It will be stashed safely at home."

Spender was less than impressed. "Mickey – keep an eye out, we need that address." He finished speaking and looked around the room before moving on to the next operation.

It was Kieran who provided the idea for our first operation. "My cousin's lad works in this greasy spoon café. Regular crowd – sees the same faces most days. I was round at their place the other night. Jimmy tells me there are three fellas who come in most mornings – reckons they're RUC." Spender's eyes lit up – a perfect opportunity to put himself and his unit on the map.

"How's he know that?" asked Hugh sceptically. "He's having you on."

Kieran shook his head. "Last week one of the fellas goes up to the counter to pay. Pulls his wallet out of his pocket and his warrant card falls on the counter. So Jimmy, cool as a cucumber, acts normal, as the guy quickly pushes it back in his pocket."

"Nearest RUC station?" asked Spender.

"Half a mile away."

"Have they been in since?" Spender pondered the possibilities, biting his tongue.

"Yesterday – I guess they reasoned Jimmy hadn't noticed. I say get them there and then. We wait outside till they come out and then open the door – bang, bang, bang." Kieran mimed the actions with obvious relish.

And so it was that at 7.30 the following morning, Dave and I found ourselves drinking strong sweet tea out of dirty mugs in a grotty little café in North Belfast. We sat at a table in the far corner and tried to look innocuous, whilst attempting to study the faces of the patrons. "Do you think that's Jimmy?" Dave whispered, spying the pimpled youth stirring a large teapot before filling two mugs.

"Could be," I replied, without conviction, my eyes glued firmly on the door. From the banter, it was obvious most punters were regulars. I was paranoid that we didn't fit in. I had to repeatedly reassure myself that I was simply another member of the class that had to earn a living, having a quiet brew before trudging on to the monotony of paid employment. I glanced at my watch – 7.55am, silently cursing Kieran, when the bell over the door clattered and three middle aged men entered, sitting themselves down at an empty table by the window. "Usual, Billy?" shouted the café owner, looking up from his griddle, the sweat pouring off his forehead, as he wiped his hand on his already stained white T-shirt.

He nodded in reply. "You're looking well Johnny," he teased. I studied their features. They appeared sure-footed, a sense they were in control. One of them looked up from their conversation and gave the café a cursory once-over – our eyes met for the briefest second and my heart missed a beat. But all he did was smile in a flirtatious kind of way. They felt secure in this environment – safe. That would cost them dearly.

The IRA is regarded as the most dangerous of modern urban terrorists. Dedicated and ruthless – efficient and deadly. But for every spectacular success, another ten ended in dismal failure. Some through poor planning, others through incompetence and yet more through sheer bad luck. I suppose the intended victims would probably refer to it as divine providence – so it was to be with this job.

Spender and Kieran would be the shooters. Hugh and Dave would hijack a van. Mickey was to call in sick and then he and I would hijack a getaway car. When the RUC men exited the café, Hugh would pull out and drive slowly down the road. Kieran and Spender would then open the side door and let them have it, before accelerating away to the rendezvous point – some waste ground about a mile away. Mickey would be waiting with the hijacked car. As Spender went through the plan, it became obvious that there was no role for me, once we had secured a car for the getaway. "Why am I not involved?" My bristles rose in annoyance, assuming it was chauvinism, but there was a plausible explanation – albeit one I was reluctant to accept.

"If they recognise there is a woman in the unit, whose face do you think will spring to mind first? I'm not taking that risk."

"What about Dave? He was there too," I insisted.

"Even with a mask on – you're still obviously female." I was really pissed off at the time, but in the final reckoning, I was relieved not to be associated with the job.

Hugh had been scouting a guy who brought his work's van home every night. Mickey located the car to hijack a few streets away. It had to be a four-door. Valuable get away time would be lost if Spender had to clamber into the back of a two-door hatchback. I have never felt so nervous, as Mickey and I approached the front door. Mickey checked his combat knife. "You got the gun?" My mouth was too dry to respond – I just nodded a confirmation. At every step along the pavement I was watching out in case there was a RUC patrol. I'd have difficulties talking my way out of this one, I reflected, fingering the cold metal in my jacket pocket in trepidation. My fingers touched it for reassurance, constantly checking to ensure that the safety catch was on. "You ready?" We exchanged a final look of encouragement, before pulling the black balaclavas down over our heads. It was 6.30am and by now the morning was light. After repeated knocks, at last we heard footsteps and a woman's voice. I remember the nervous anticipation as the bolts on the door were slung back – the adrenaline surging through my veins. The second she twisted the latch, we both shoved the door hard, sending the woman staggering back a few paces.

"Provisional IRA" I shouted from my diaphragm. It didn't sound like my voice: so harsh and shrill.

"Oh dear God no," she shouted. I thought she was going to faint.

"What the hell is going on," a man's voice shouted from upstairs.

"No one is going to get hurt. All we want is the car keys." The bloke appeared at the top of the stairs, dressed in just a pair of trousers, still clutching his shirt. "You're not having my fucking car, you miserable bastards."

I thrust the gun in his direction and looked as if I was intent on using it. "Don't be a fucking hero. You'll live longer." Inside I was shaking like a leaf. I could barely hold the gun steady.

His wife began sobbing. "Oh no…Bob, it's only a bloody car." Seeing sense at last, he admitted defeat.

He appeared seconds later with the keys, muttering "thieving bastards," under his breath.

Mickey snatched the keys out of his hand. "Don't report this car stolen for six hours – or we'll be back!" It was a lie, but they had no means of ascertaining that and it would be a brave man who called the IRA's bluff.

"Don't forget this is for your benefit," I added, as we pulled the door closed behind us.

―――

I visited Spender that evening when I had heard no word on the job. He was in a foul mood, reclining back into the threadbare armchair. "Of all the bleeding screw ups – this bunch of useless tossers couldn't organise a piss up in a brewery."

"What on earth happened?" I asked impatiently.

"I'll tell you what went wrong – Hugh. Kieran and I were here with the shooters. All ready to go. The daft bastard didn't turn up until seven minutes to eight. By the time we got there, they'd gone." The van had a flat battery. Hugh had to find a pair of jump leads; took him over twenty minutes to get the thing started. There was something vaguely amusing about the thought of Kieran and Spender anxiously waiting for the pick up, automatic weapons at the ready, whilst Hugh ran round like a headless chicken trying to jump start a van with a flat battery.

"No wonder the shit gave him the van keys so easily," Spender mused, breaking into a rye smile. It taught us a valuable lesson: never check the vehicle at the same time every day and just assume it's been used.

Later in the corner of a quiet bar, sat around a rickety table in the corner, thick with the smell of smuggled cigarettes, Spender and Kieran took it in turns, in hushed tones, to impress Dave with their war stories. Each one becoming more and more outlandish as the glasses emptied. After Kieran boasted he'd shot an SAS man between the eyes, Mickey turned to me and smiled. "Is he full of it or what?"

"I think we are supposed to be awed by his credentials."

Mickey laughed at my irreverence. "You go to college?" he asked, lighting a cigarette.

I nodded. "Queens."

"Must be better that being a Postie. I thought about going to college…but my girlfriend Bridie got pregnant. I have to work to support the baby. "

"Boy or girl?"

"Laoise – she's almost one."

"Bridie – does she know?" I enquired tentatively.

"It didn't take her long to work it out. At first she said nothing. But I think her curiosity just got the better of her. She asked me outright. I didn't deny it. What's the point?" he replied, a little defensively. "We have no secrets. She is as committed to the cause as I am."

Monday morning dawned with the spring sun shining brightly, before being replaced with endless drizzle. This time Kieran was tasked to hijack the van. Hugh and I hijacked the getaway car. The second time was easier. I knew the routine and knew I just had to keep cool. Like sex, you know, never quite so nerve-racking second time around.

I left Hugh at Spender's place where everyone was waiting for Kieran to arrive with the van. Spender was anxiously pacing the floor and checking his watch, the two semiautomatics now retrieved from the arms dump, located in a sympathiser's under-stairs cupboard.

It was with mixed feelings that I hurried to my car during the morning break. I fumbled with the keys, dropping them and cursing myself that I would miss the news headlines. *In what is being widely seen as a sectarian attack, armed gunmen opened fire on a quiet Protestant café in North Belfast from a moving vehicle, shattering the glass and firing indiscriminately inside. Two people have been taken to hospital with gunshot wounds. A number of others are said to have cuts and lacerations caused by the shattering glass. Police sources would not comment on a rumour that the café was a regular haunt of off duty RUC officers. No organisation has yet claimed responsibility for the attack, but it is believed to be the work of the Provisional IRA."*

Once the initial euphoria had subsided, it was replaced with anger – firstly directed at the media for portraying this as a sectarian attack, later re-directed towards Kieran and Spender. They were supposed to fire as the RUC men left the café, not randomly through the window. I didn't care about the RUC men – that was the risk they took in wearing the uniform, but innocent people were different. And besides it was a great propaganda coup for the Brits and unionists. It allowed them to portray us as a bunch of wholesale murdering bigots.

I had still not managed to calm down by the time I arrived for the hastily convened debrief meeting later that evening. Naively, I expected the mood to be sombre, with an inquest into what went wrong. The jovial atmosphere that greeted me was somewhat surprising. "We showed them hey!" Spender emerged into the room with a look of triumph on his face. "They have just confirmed that the two in the hospital are RUC officers."

"Pity we didn't finish them off" growled Kieran, to general grunts of approval.

Mickey was the first to pour cold water on the party. "How come you didn't wait till they came out – you'd have finished them off then?"

"We had to improvise," Hugh replied. "There was nowhere to park where we were close enough to have a full view of the café. I drove round the block a couple of times, any more and someone would have got suspicious. It would only take one of the RUC men to see us drive past twice and the bastards would have darted out the back door."

"So I made the decision," asserted Spender, "if there was nowhere to pull in on the next bypass we'd open fire. Hughie slowed as we drove past and Dave threw the door open…"

"Then I let rip," interrupted Kieran, peppering the room in imaginary gunfire. "I got one in the leg, as he dived under the table. He won't walk again."

"Smooth getaway. Arms back in the dump. Good job lads,"

concluded Spender.

"And we scared a few Prods into the bargain," smiled Kieran. "Not a bad day's work."

Deep within my sub-conscious, this was the moment when the first doubts were sown. For me, this war had never been about killing or maiming Protestants, because they happened to attend a different church. I saw only the uniform, the loyalist mobs that operated with the covert support of the security forces, or the occupying forces of the British army who paid only lip service to impartiality. I had no axe to grind against innocent civilians. The thought of the IRA as a sectarian Catholic army as opposed to republican freedom fighters, I found deeply disturbing. However, I was so busy I had no opportunity to philosophise over the fine technical distinctions I drew in order to justify the killing of some Protestants, but not others.

Chapter Twenty Four

OVER THE FOLLOWING weeks, Spender started putting increasing pressure on Mickey to find the blue Renault belonging to the RIR man. Hugh had been unable to locate the registration number. Spender eventually decided that Dave and I would walk through the housing estate pretending to be a couple, looking for the car. We walked tens of miles to no avail. Eventually, the whole project was abandoned. It was the way that things worked – plans were conceived and then dropped; initial enthusiasm often waned once the practical implications were considered.

Hugh provided us with the information for our next major job in the summer of 1992. He sat quietly during the cell meeting, whilst others discussed proposals which were either impractical or simply too grandiose. We were stunned at the audacity of his plan. The idea was to hijack any old shed of a vehicle. The owners would be instructed to wait thirty minutes before ringing the police and reporting it stolen by the IRA. A couple of hours later, the car would be driven onto a nearby building site where Corporation houses were undergoing renovation. Hugh would place a bomb in the car. The detonator wire would be buried under the piles of sand and rubble, running to one of the nearby empty houses. An anonymous tip off would be made to the local RUC station, reporting a suspicious vehicle being abandoned by a group of masked men. The registration number would be given. The RUC would send out a patrol, knowing it had been hijacked only hours before by the IRA. Maybe they would get lucky with a stray fingerprint or other forensics. As they examined the car, the bomb would be detonated.

The following evening Spender, Kieran, Hugh and I checked out the site. There were about fifty post war houses undergoing renovation. The contractors had left at 5.30pm, leaving the site open. Like most building contractors in this area of Belfast, they hedged their bets and paid tax to both the British Government and the local Provies. We chose the detonation point and the spot where we would park the car. The getaway car would be positioned three hundred yards away over some waste ground and through a gap in a hedge. Kieran chose a spot on the other side of the street where he could have a pop with the semiautomatic at anyone left standing.

One evening, a few days later, Hugh and Kieran arrived on my doorstep carrying a rucksack. Once the door was closed behind him, Hugh asked. "Can I borrow your bathroom?" Fifteen minutes later I ventured upstairs. Hugh was crouched on the floor, a fag hanging out of the side of his mouth. Spread out around him was everything you need to make a bomb: detonator, battery, wire and Semtex.

"What the hell are you doing?"

Kieran grinned. "It's for the job. Here have a feel." Wearing bright yellow marigold washing up gloves, he held out a lump of Semtex.

"What's wrong with your bathroom?" I asked Hugh incredulously.

"I thought that the wife and kids were going to her mother's. I was just about to start building when she arrived. It would have given the old biddy a heart attack." I had to laugh. The best laid plans sent awry by the actions of one mother in law? I grasped the yellow looking plasticine like substance between my thumb and forefinger, after donning a pair of gloves. Semtex is such a sod to remove from skin. It had a putty like consistency. The yellow surface was mottled with brown and orange specks, like a rare bird's eggshell. I was amazed at how light it was given its destructive power.

"Not much to it?"

"This is just the primer for the fertiliser in the boot." When he'd finished, he presented the device, like a proud father displaying his new born offspring. "What do you think?"

"Great," I replied, handing it back to him as quickly as possible. Explosives scared the shit out of me. After much persuasion, I agreed that they could leave the bomb hidden in my loft until the following afternoon. Hugh disappeared quite quickly, but Kieran hung around, drinking my whisky. He invited me down the pub, but by then it was late. I made some excuse about having to finish some marking for the following day. I suspect that explosives were not the only subject on Kieran's mind that night – and that was one road I had no intention of travelling.

―――

Spender delved into a canvas bag, lying on the floor of the car and removed a couple of two-way radios. "You know what to do?"

"I phone the peelers once everyone is in place and warn you when they're approaching. We all drive off into the sunset together."

"Very fucking romantic, I'm sure," added Kieran, a broad grin on his face.

"Dave's holding the owner of the car; gonna make sure they say the right thing to the peelers."

At that moment there was a squeal of brakes, as Dave pulled up in a stolen Nissan. "Here we go people," ordered Spender.

Everything appeared to be proceeding as clockwork. Spender and Hugh were concealed, ready to activate the detonator. I dialled the local RUC station from the phone box and did my good neighbour impression. And then, we waited. I sat on the wall at a bus stop. The nearest RUC station was approximately one and a half miles to the east, but we had no idea from which direction the patrol would appear. Minutes later, instead of the familiar shape of an RUC Land Rover, a British army Saracen trundled in my direction. As surreptitiously as I was able, I hissed into the radio, "Army Saracen approaching – ETA less than a minute." I turned my head away as the large green military vehicle thundered past me and then waited.

"Jackpot," bellowed Spender into the radio. Five minutes later the ground shook with the explosion and a plume of smoke billowed up behind the part renovated houses. My first instincts were pride and elation. However, I soon realised the explosion had been no way near large enough. Something had gone wrong. I panicked at the vision of Spender, Kieran and Hugh confronting a Saracen armed with only a semiautomatic rifle and a pair of handguns. I quickened my pace towards where Mickey had parked. As I turned the corner, I could hear shouting. Mickey was revving the engine. Spender and Hugh emerged running from my left, ripping their balaclavas off, as they sprinted towards the car, sweating like pigs. Spender spied me out of the corner of his eye. He pulled the radio to his mouth. "Get the hell out of here. We're splitting up."

Spender headed for the cover of the nearby housing estate. Hugh piled into the passenger seat, and Mickey sped away, wheels spinning. Seconds later, soldiers emerged over the brow of the hill, pouring through the gap in the hedge. Now might be a good time to leave, I reasoned, heading in the opposite direction. I discarded the radio in the hedge. I'd walked no more than ten paces when I was confronted by an authoritative bark, "Stop – put your hands where I can see them." A sickening feeling hit the base of my stomach – it was like being struck with a baseball bat. Had they seen me throw the radio in the hedge? It had my fingerprints on it? Shit – why hadn't I worn gloves? I turned to face two soldiers in full camouflage khakis each carrying a SLR.

"Name?" the nervous soldier demanded, gripping his rifle ever tighter. I replied in the same sullen manner adopted by all civilians in Catholic areas. It was a good job he couldn't see the rate at which my heart was beating. "Where are you going?"

"I've been visiting a friend. I'm waiting for a bus. Is that a crime now with you fellas?" I responded, with controlled hostility.

"Three men came running this way – did you see anything?"

I shook my head, "I was in my friend's house. We heard a bang." The solider studied my face. Our eyes interlocked for a brief instant. I returned his smile, flirtatiously, before gingerly walking away, swinging my hips to ensure he remembered me with his dick, not his brain. I could feel the beads of perspiration trickling down my back, hugging the contours of my spine. For the first time since I had joined the IRA, I felt real unadulterated fear. It turned out that the Semtex primer had exploded but had failed to detonate the main charge. The result being that instead of wiping out half a dozen soldiers, they fanned out and began scanning the area. Even Kieran, usually keen to shoot anything wearing a British army uniform was more circumspect, knowing when he was seriously outgunned; unprepared to die for the cause that day.

If commitment won wars we were guaranteed success. Unfortunately poor training, inferior equipment and sheer incompetence play a major part in how the Provies operate. Often the ammunition doesn't fit the guns or the weapon is new to the shooter. Unlike the British army who train to a very high standard on a standard handgun or rifle, sometimes we were swapping weapons on a regular basis, depending on availability.

Intelligence was our other key vulnerability. Take Hugh's registration number fiasco: can you imagine Special Branch walking around Belfast looking for an IRA suspect, having lost the registration number? Our unit had been set up with the specific aim of allowing unknown volunteers to enter areas that other more prominent volunteers could not access in safety: Protestant middle-class housing estates in the suburbs, where RUC officers lived. Take the war to their back yard, where they felt safe. The IRA has a network of spies every bit as sophisticated as that operated by Special Branch. Everyone from the chemist's assistant who memorised the number plates of vehicles entering the fortified police station across the street, to the neighbour with a grudge. A good deal of this kind of information began to be channelled in our direction.

On one occasion we received information about a green Rover, supposedly driven by a prison officer giving inmates in the Provie H-block in the Maze a hard time. We knew that the guy lived somewhere in North Belfast and the registration started with an "NZ". Whilst carrying out surveillance on a RIR solider as he drank in a Pub outside Belfast, I saw an NZ-plated green Rover pull up in the car park. I even got a good look at the guy. The trouble was we had no description, so I had no means of verifying if he was our man or not.

We discussed the problem at a cell meeting. Spender was impatient that all the intelligence work we were doing was proving unproductive. He was anxious to raise the profile of our unit by undertaking successful jobs. There was a good degree of grumbling from both Mickey and Dave. They felt that they were getting all the laborious surveillance tasks. Hours of sitting in the cold just watching and waiting, whilst Kieran and Hugh sat on their arses, and then got the opportunity for glory. Spender was about to tell them that surveillance was the very rationale for our existence, when I intervened. "We are letting them out-smart us."

"What do you mean?" demanded Spender, sensitive to any criticism of his leadership.

"We should have a database for all this information. We could then cross-reference the leads. That's what the RUC do. We'd know the registration plate for that Renault driven by O'Grady, for instance," I said, with a nod to Hugh's inept filing system. The subject matter of the conversation then moved on, new jobs, old jobs, potential jobs, dream jobs and pie in the sky jobs.

A Bold Deceiver • James Hurd

I later discovered that my idea was not original – a computer database did exist. A solid and respectable member of the community behind closed doors spent many lonely hours inputting IRA data. He had been required to begin again from scratch, as the previous incumbent's house had been burgled and the computer was stolen. The computer was discovered by the RUC, when the thieves tried to sell it to an undercover officer in a pub. You can only imagine the delight and surprise of the Special Branch when the hard drive was booted up and its secrets revealed. There was a suspicion within the IRA ranks that the burglary was a cover story. Who nicks second hand computers: no resale value and too bulky for an opportunistic thief? It was some coincidence that the kid tried to sell it to an undercover peeler? Rumour has it there was a tip off from an informer. That had been two years previously, and the impact was still a gaping wound, with many jobs abandoned that had been meticulously conceived and planned.

I learnt all this from Dermot McDonnell head of Internal Affairs or the Civil Administration Unit in early January 1993. He also had some responsibility for security and intelligence in Belfast. He and his team hunted out informers and touts. Most of those suspected of working for the police either disappeared or their corpses reappeared –if you get my drift, usually shot through the back of the head. You have to be a certain kind of character to work in internal affairs, whichever side you're on. Spying on your own colleagues wins you few favours in the popularity stakes. McDonnell had a reputation that far surpassed those who worked nominally under the control of the rule of law. A head case that got his kicks torturing hapless victims until they confessed. So the evening he arrived unannounced at my door, I admit to feeling a little apprehensive. He was short and skinny, with closely cropped black hair and small cold blue eyes. They seemed to penetrate my skull and rummage around in my brain searching for a weakness he might exploit. I once heard him described as the sort of person who can kill a good party just by turning up.

"I'm told you're interested in computers," he commented without emotion.

I racked my brains, before eventually recalling my comments from months before. "I merely indicated we ought to beat the Brits at their own game."

"What if we already were?" he enquired, raising his eyebrows and staring in a manner which made me feel uncomfortable.

"Not seen much evidence of it." I reiterated the fiasco over O'Grady's registration number that had us running round Belfast like headless chickens, checking out endless blue Renaults.

McDonnell smiled diplomatically. "We have a problem. The fella who is presently entrusted with maintaining our modest database is due to retire. We need a replacement." His eyes fixed chillingly upon me, before commencing the aptitude test. "How would you learn from past security failings?"

I hesitated for a moment, having been put on the spot. "You can never eliminate risk but you can reduce it to within manageable precautions."

"Give me practicalities?" growled McDonnell, with an unnerving focus on me, undressing my mind rather than my body."

"Use a notebook. It's easier to conceal and it's portable."

"It's also easier to steal," he countered, with a touch of arrogance.

"That proved no deterrent." Touché. "Use a detachable second hard drive. You keep the database on the second drive. If you treat the detachable hard drive with the same degree of security we treat weapons, there shouldn't be any problems. Thirdly, build security into the hardware and the software. Encrypt the data. It is not 100% tamper proof – but it can take months to decode. It buys us time. Programme the system, so that in the event that the wrong code is entered the data becomes irretrievable to all apart from the serious techno-geek. Worst comes to the worst, you lose the data – but at least it doesn't fall into their hands. The biggest security risk though would be…the operator."

McDonnell nodded, showing a modicum of respect for my answer. "You retain the advantage for the moment of being unknown. It may well be in due course you become more valuable to us outside an ASU."

"Please don't patronise me," I retorted, furious that there was a sexist motive. "Keep the women away from the guns."

McDonnell did not rise to my bait, and aside from a terse grin, he expressed no emotion. "There is more than one way to win a war Tara." He stood and re-buttoned his coat. "I'll have the equipment transferred in the next couple of weeks." It was a statement not a request.

Within a month, I had taken delivery of a 166 Pentium notebook, quite powerful for 1993 with two interchangeable hard drives with encryption software from the Czech Republic. The hardware solution utilised a security card, which kicked in before the operating system was booted, blocking unauthorised access. As the New Year progressed, I gradually began receiving surveillance information. There were notes of meetings or debriefs of jobs where intelligence information had been collated and discussed. Information derived from each of the cells that Spender, Kieran and Hugh had previously belonged to. A sort of working brief of planned operations and the titbits of information they had obtained. I then went through the slow laborious process of entering the information onto the computer. At the same time, I was deliberately given a slightly more back seat role in being assigned tasks in our unit. It soon became apparent that it was no way near as interesting as actually carrying out a job – but I realised that I was playing a crucial role, which I was confident, given time, would translate into positive results.

The breakthrough took place in the spring of 1993. For months we had been trying to hit a particularly notorious RUC officer: Detective Inspector William McCleash. He had a reputation as a vicious sod who had an interrogation technique, which had made him very unpopular. So unpopular that when the police released a senior IRA man, the order was given that all efforts were to be made to eliminate him. McCleash often sanctioned beatings on detainees, punching you where it would hurt but where the bruising would be kept to a minimum. Playing on the worst insecurities of prisoners, he would suggest that he had intelligence information that the prisoner might be interested in, such as photographs of his Mrs with another man. "Did you know she was having an affair with a mate of yours – he's an IRA man as well? Go for a pint with him – done jobs together. Now he's screwing your wife...." On the table would be a large brown envelope allegedly containing the photographs, which he would tap from time to time, before suggesting a trade: the photos of the phantom lover, in exchange for information on known IRA men. The identity of the IRA man would be cleverly suggested through subtle hints, in the hope that the prisoner would in his rage drop that individual in the proverbial.

Some months earlier our unit had recruited an informer who lived in a flat overlooking a RUC station. She provided us with basic information about the comings and goings at the base, including details as to the civilian vehicles regularly entering the police station. I had a list of about twenty vehicles, which were regularly seen going in and out of the tight security of the main gates. Her window was at an angle from the heavily fortified gates of the RUC station. She was able to see the side of the vehicles but had a limited view of the registration numbers. From the men who had been interrogated by McCleash, we had been able to build up a very good description of our man: five foot eight, broad shoulders and slightly overweight, with large jowls, which hung down off his cheekbones and dark hair loosely parted down the middle. The final piece of the jigsaw was matching McCleash to his car and then finding the best place to take him out.

It never ceased to amaze me the variety of people who would provide information to the IRA and their reasons were not always motivated by politics. A scruffy one bedroom flat situated on the second floor of a 1960's modernist block; ten flats with little concrete stairs and a communal hall, which stank of stale urine, rotting vegetables and flat beer. However, that smell was considerably more pleasing than the insipid odour inside Flat Nine. Laura, a young girl in her early twenties ushered me inside. Almost immediately I was hit by the nauseating smell of soiled nappies left to fester.

"Sorry," she apologised. "It's difficult keeping on top of things when you have two young ones and no man around." The living room was strewn with wet clothes drying on airers, dirty plates and discarded toys. To her, providing information to the Provos added a little glamour to her dull existence. She also earned a few extra quid, which helped when the length of the week exceeded the meagre state handouts. I handed McCleash's description to Laura, emphasising how important it was we discovered what vehicle he drove. I flattered her, telling her how important the work she did for the cause was. She positively basked in the praise. I handed her a crisp new £10 as I left. I felt sorry for her, as she resumed her vigil at the lounge window.

I returned the following week. Laura looked pale and tired. She had been unable to get out to the phone box in the last couple of days, as the baby, Liam, had been unwell. The doctor had told her to keep him indoors. "But I have what you're looking for," she said with a glint of pride. "Black Sierra – I've seen it three times this week. Description fits your man – as best as I can see side on – always different times. I'm pretty sure it's him."

Whilst sitting on Laura's toilet, it occurred to me that her bathroom window might afford a better view of the main gates to the RUC station. Standing on the toilet, I carefully pushed the upper section of the frosted glass window open. I watched as a police Land Rover pulled through the gates, its registration number clearly identifiable. At the next cell meeting, Spender assigned Dave and Hugh to watch from the bathroom window. I must have neglected to mention the nauseating nappy smell. They'd discover in their own good time.

Hugh and Dave spent the entirety of the next meeting bitching about having to crouch on Laura's toilet seat amidst the smell of nappies. Spender and Kieran though thought the whole thing was hilarious and roared in laughter. At least the mission had not been wasted. We now knew that McCleash drove a 1991 Black Ford Sierra 2 litre and the registration number: JTZ 5921. McCleash was a professional, never leaving the base at the same time. He varied his route, sometimes driving in from the left, other times from the right. It meant it was almost impossible to track him unless we had a car positioned ready to follow him. However, a car dawdling outside a heavily armed police station was bound to arouse suspicion. We needed to attack him on neutral ground.

As I finished entering twenty or so pieces of information into the database about suspected loyalists, former UDR or RIR men and the routes of routine British army patrols, for some reason McCleash came to mind. Most intelligence work comes from the detail – what if there was a clue there all along that had been overlooked? A database search using the registration number drew a blank. I next tried a search on all black vehicles. Two new references caught my attention. Months earlier Mickey claimed to have seen an RUC officer in a black saloon car on his post round. He had been cycling past him at a junction at about 7am. As Mickey approached on his inside, he swore he saw the flash of metal, as the driver moved to conceal a police issue handgun on the passenger seat. Mickey surmised that the driver had been sloppy getting into the car and had not hidden his weapon. Mickey noted part of the car registration – JBZ 59. He had only the briefest glance at the driver and could not provide any description. What if the driver had been McCleash? I was momentarily foxed by the fact that the registration plates were slightly different. What if he changed his plates? As a high profile RUC officer who was known by sight to a number of IRA men, it was a reasonable precaution to take? It fitted the profile, security conscious, always taking different routes and times. And if Mickey had been right, it also narrowed the search considerably. If Mickey was the first person, who could potentially see into the car, it meant he probably lived in the vicinity.

The second reference was to a black Ford saloon car and had been provided by a member of Kieran's previous unit. There'd been a crazy early morning operation to hit an RUC patrol. The plan was to spray a Police Land Rover with a batch of armour piercing bullets when it stopped at a set of traffic lights. In fact, the lights were on green and the Land Rover slowed only momentarily as a pedestrian crossed the street. The shooters got off as many rounds as they could, but the Land Rover sped away to safety. However, within minutes the area was flooded with police and a British army Saracen. The shooter was situated on the roof of a block of flats. He remained concealed on the roof, just out of sight of a helicopter circling above, watching the clear up operation. He noted that the first car on the scene within minutes of the attack was a black Ford driven by a plainclothes RUC officer.

I rummaged in my desk for a Belfast A-Z, marking the location where Mickey had seen the saloon and traced my finger to the position of the failed job. I gloated in triumph: less than three-quarters of a mile between them. If McCleash lived locally, he may have been the first to respond. Ten minutes later I banged on Mickey's door. In my haste, I'd forgotten he had to get up at 4am. I cursed my insensitivity, as the light was switched on in the upstairs bedroom. Mickey looking seriously miffed, peering at me through sleepy eyes. "Bloody hell Tara: do you have any idea what time I have to get up?" he said wearily, running his hand through his dishevelled hair. "I'm not doing a job now. Spender can bloody do it himself."

A shout echoed from upstairs. "Who is it? Get rid of them – calling at this time of night." I suddenly felt very guilty.

"It's no one. Go back to bed. I'll be up in a minute."

"Did no one bang on the bleeding door then? Was that a woman's voice?" Mickey rolled his eyes to the roof. "We've only just got Laoise off to sleep."

"Sorry. This'll only take a minute." I opened the A-Z on the table. "Remember the guy you saw with a gun on the passenger seat?"

He nodded. "And?" as if to say is this what you have dragged me out of bed for?

"It was McCleash. Show me your round," I demanded, pointing at the map. It looked very probable that McCleash lived on a housing estate adjacent to Mickey's round. The most direct route to the RUC

A Bold Deceiver • James Hurd

station would take him past the junction where Mickey had seen the black Ford. It was also within minutes of the location of the Land Rover ambush.

I drove around the middle class neighbourhood, consisting of modern neat detached houses separated seemingly only by inches. I parked the car and scouted the area on foot. Pedestrians make less noise. It was at times like this I wished I owned a dog- it would be the perfect cover for late night walks. I crossed off roads in the A-Z under streetlights, before I finally stumbled upon number 43 Barley Field Road, situated right at the end of the development, overlooking a park and some waste ground, at the end of a cul-de-sac. A black Ford Sierra sat in the driveway, registration number JTZ 5291. I contemplated the closed curtains of the master bedroom and wondered if he was sleeping soundly? Enjoy it while you can.

I ought to have reported straight back to Spender, but I was conscious I would have looked a bloody fool if the car belonged to an unsuspecting civilian. Besides, I was not ready to lose control. This was my discovery. Two days later I returned at 6am and concealed myself in some undergrowth at the far side of the park facing the house. With powerful binoculars, I observed our man emerge, carrying a briefcase. He fitted the description perfectly. To the world, he was a civil servant, middle manager or bean counter. I watched him kiss his petite blonde wife on the doorstep and then check surreptitiously for a UCBT under his car. I wondered if he told his wife what he did at work, when she asked if he'd had a good day? A frightening thought emerged from somewhere deep within. If I had a partner, how would I answer that question? Great day darling: very successful. I have plotted and planned the death of another human being. Was I any different – really? Just on the other side of the great divide? I ruthlessly suppressed my doubts – mine was a just war. Looking back, it scares me that I had become so involved, so preoccupied with fighting my war that I hardly spared a minute to consider his wife, who would be widowed.

Spender's plan was for shooters to be concealed in a stolen British Telecom van at the telephone exchange box, a couple of streets from McCleash's home. This avoided the need to have to drive a vehicle in and out of the cul-de-sac and turn round. As McCleash approached, the back doors of the van would swing open and they would shoot him through the windscreen. Kieran had wanted to take a shot from the park with a telescopic rifle and then simply melt away. Spender was concerned there was a lot of open ground to cover before he could reach a get away car.

McCleash turned into Dawlish Road at 6.01pm. It was far enough away from his home that in the event the job didn't come off, it wouldn't appear that his home address had been compromised. Dave, acting as the lookout man, spotted him thirty seconds later and lifted the radio to his lips, behind his newspaper. In the van, Kieran held the Armalite and waited. Spender had his hand on the door catch ready to swing it open, when he appeared in Hugh's side mirror. To this day no one knows what went wrong. Instead of driving past the parked BT van, McCleash veered tightly to the right and ducked down a side street before Spender had time to release the door catch. For a moment, they stared at the empty road before the self-preservation instinct kicked in. "Get us out of here – he must be onto us," bellowed Spender to Hugh, who thrust the van into first and accelerated away.

Our anger and bewilderment soon degenerated into recrimination. Spender immediately pounced on Dave. "He must have seen you." He stabbed his chubby finger menacingly towards Dave, his face red with anger.

Kieran was also fuming but his explanation was more sinister. He sat tapping his fingers, as the arguments went back and forth. "It's simple," he began acrimoniously. "McCleash saw or knew something, which caused him to alter his route at the last minute. He was on the lookout. That must have come from one of us." He scanned the room, meeting each of our eyes, as if he could determine our innocence or guilt in a single suspicious leer. At this point Spender stepped in. If he didn't quell this now, it would spell the end for this unit. We were required to place trust in each other during operations. Division spelt disaster. "No more talk of touts. The guy got suspicious and took an alternate route – perhaps the BT van was reported missing. We'll try again next week."

Seven days later, we went with Kieran's plan. He was concealed in the undergrowth, on the far side of the park, armed with a rifle and a telescopic sight. McCleash emerged out of the house shortly before 7.30am. Kieran fired off two shots, as he reached for the driver's door, striking him in both the shoulder and the stomach, before making a clean getaway. His wife witnessed the entire event. He spent six weeks in hospital and was eventually retired on medical grounds.

McCleash marked the high watermark of my involvement with the IRA. I had become a deadly pawn in a war machine. And if the events of the following weeks had been different, maybe I would still be there today. What followed shook my belief in a cause I had been willing to sacrifice everything for and awoke the humanity inside me.

Chapter Twenty Five

IN EARLY NOVEMBER 1993, my mother was rushed into hospital after collapsing at home. The corridors reeked with the familiar odour of hospital disinfectant. The same smell that clung to Patrick's clothes, hours after he returned home. Now, as I breathed in, I fought to keep my mind from remembering and travelling back to places still too painful to visit.

My mother lay sedated, an intravenous drip in her arm, free from the fears of the reality that surrounded her. She looked pale and tired, her greying hair and the worry lines on her forehead, conspiring to make her look older than her fifty-five years. The constant fight to raise two children single-handed had taken its toll. I intertwined my hand in hers and softly squeezed. I guessed it was cancer before the doctor confirmed the grim truth. The doctor's words hung in the air, floating around the room, so that their meaning remained tantalisingly just out of reach. I remained by her bedside for an hour before leaving her to the peace of sleep. I wiped away the tears from the corners of my eyes, dabbing them gently with a tissue, as I walked down the corridor to the car park. I felt anger in my sadness. This would not have happened if my father had still been alive. The struggle she had fought, the grief and the loneliness had thrown her headfirst towards an early grave. The UVF had as good as pulled the trigger. It had just taken nine years for the bullet to hit the second target.

As I shuffled lethargically along the corridor, my eyes to the ground, I felt instinctively compelled to look up. Approaching me,

A Bold Deceiver • James Hurd

in the opposite direction was a woman in her late thirties. Her neat blonde hair was tied back loosely. She pulled her coat open a little as she stepped into the warmth of the hospital reception. Our eyes alighted upon each other momentarily. She smiled and I attempted to return her polite gesture. She too had been crying, her makeup smudged with tears of pain. Although we were physically dissimilar, I was unable to shake the feeling we were a mirror image of each other, that we shared an affinity in our anguish. Yet, I also retained a nagging perception of familiarity. My brain flicked through its subconscious memory banks, searching for a match. As so often happens, as you turn your mind to an unconnected subject, the answer snaps into focus. I was fumbling in my handbag, trying to locate my car keys. The image appeared in a heart-wrenching explosion: an ugly guilty flash that caused me to momentarily hyperventilate. I did know the identity of those chiselled features – and I knew whom she was visiting. The last time I had seen her, it was through the lens of my binoculars, as she kissed her husband goodbye – a husband, who now lay in agonising pain, fighting for every breath in an adjacent ward – Mrs McCleash.

I felt dizzy, weak at the knees, as I sat shivering in the car, my head buried in the steering wheel. Was there a deeper significance in my assumption that our grief was the same? It was the emotion of knowing my mother was terminally ill. I should feel no pity for McCleash or his family. I absolved myself of any guilt. He was the author of his own pain and his family's – not Kieran who pulled the trigger, not the IRA and not me.

I was haunted by her innocent unsuspecting smile. If only she had known she was smiling into the face of one of her husband's attackers. She pervaded my dreams, each nightmare a variation on a theme. As McCleash's wife and I pass in the corridor, her smile changes to vitriolic accusation. She peers straight into my head and absorbs my guilty secret. She remains silent, as if the look of horror on her face represents condemnation enough. When I wake, the sheets are wet with perspiration. In a second variant, she smiles and then opens her coat to reveal a rifle, which she points at me. Laughing with revenge she opens fire. I wake before the first bullet hits.

My mother died two weeks later. Marie and I barely exchanged pleasantries. We both stood silent at her bedside, as the glowing embers of her life faded into the blackness of night. We spoke only of practicalities: wills, flowers, priests and headstones. Though both of us wished to be reconciled in our mutual loss, a chasm now lay in our midst. A chasm that neither of us was prepared to contemplate crossing.

The run up to Christmas was traditionally a busy time for the IRA. The ability to strike economic targets was high, as the city centre swelled with Christmas shoppers. My unit was involved in the placing of incendiary devices in high street shops. Spender phoned adequate warnings and no one was injured. It raised our profile, before we announced a seventy-two hour cessation over Christmas. No one other than the top Sinn Féin strategists considered seriously the possibility of a longer cease-fire.

The Christmas spirit passed me by. I had only just buried my mother. Mickey called round to offer his condolences, a couple of days after the funeral. I was glad of the company. We had become close over previous months and if there was anyone I wanted covering my back in a firefight, it was Mickey. I'd been to the pub with him and Bridie on a couple of occasions. He'd lost his job, because of his poor attendance record. Spender was forever putting pressure on him to do jobs late at night or early in the morning. Mickey was testimony to the fact it is almost impossible to serve two masters. I reflected sombrely that the quality of my teaching had also probably plummeted. I felt partly responsible, being out of action with attending the hospital and with the database. Mickey and Bridie were having a rough time since he lost his job. They had been rowing constantly, mainly about money. Bridie accused Mickey of having an affair. He told me Bridie had taken to spending lots of time at her mother's house. Mickey in turn had taken to drinking heavily and planning a New Year treat with Hugh – blowing up the Sorting Office.

Mickey and I had both been invited to a Christmas party at a local republican bar. Mickey said Bridie had agreed to attend. He was hoping for a reconciliation. I declined the invitation, but he persisted until I no longer had the will to resist. I sat at my dressing table, putting on makeup, deciding what to wear – the same pattern repeated by thousands across the country. I looked back at the reflection in the mirror: was it all worth it? I could have dated, but then, my life was complicated enough. Where would I have found time for a relationship? With the guilt of McCleash's wife fresh in my conscience, my resolve wasn't so firm. I banished such nebulous thoughts with two stiff gulps of Black Bush.

The party atmosphere was dense with heaving bodies, dancing to the band blasting out jigs and reels from the far end of the hall. Everyone cheered as the fiddle player sank to his knees, whilst the drummer kept the beat and the audience clapped, their feet stomping. Glancing across the gyrating bodies on the dance floor and the backs of heads nodding in time to the music, I recognised many familiar faces: a who's who of local IRA operatives. I had no appetite for a party, acutely aware of that desperate feeling of being alone in a crowded room, even when forced to dance with the few who refused to take no for an answer. Spender, Hugh, Kieran, Dave and Mickey were all there. Each one had the wife or girlfriend of the moment in tow. Jimmy Kelley, OC of a rival unit was stood at the bar. He was still furious that we had found McCleash before his boys. Our entire unit swaggered with a new found kudos – except me. Each time I allowed myself a hint of pride, Mrs McCleash put in another unwelcome appearance.

I sat with Mickey and Bridie. I watched them dance – I noted they were close but not too close. A woman notices these things. How much of it was alcohol or bravado in front of comrades? She was an attractive woman. Five foot six with a slender figure, long brown hair which curled slightly over her bare shoulders and ample breasts that had all the men on the dance floor throwing surreptitious looks in her direction whenever their wives weren't watching. She revelled in the attention, flirting back. Mickey was too drunk to care, happy they appeared reconciled. I headed towards the bar. When I returned Mickey was sitting alone, mournfully inspecting his half-empty pint glass. He offered me a cigarette. "I really thought we had put everything behind us." His eyes were glazed with drink, but his sadness seemed genuine. "One minute we were there on the dance floor, the next she was gone." His voice trailed into his beer glass as he lifted it to his mouth. "I've never seen her move so quickly, like…she'd seen a ghost…" He shook his head, downing the remnants of his beer. "Bloody women."

"You can hardly expect me to sympathise with that sentiment." That brought a half-hearted smile to his face. "I'll check the toilets. I have to go anyway."

What was I supposed to do if I found Bridie? I was in no position to provide relationship counselling to anyone. Besides, I doubted I would prove her ideal confidante. It was probably me she had accused

Mickey of having an affair with. I stood at the wash basin, washing my hands, inspecting the peeling paint and faded tiles through the dirty mirror. There was only one cubicle occupied at the far end of the block. I turned off the water tap and listened. What the hell was I doing standing listening for imagined sounds in a toilet after midnight? I heard a quiet sob and I backtracked towards the cubicle door. "Bridie, is that you?" There was no indication that anyone had heard me. What more could I do? "It's…err Tara," I began hesitantly.

"What do you want?" She sounded angry, but on reflection I think it was just suspicion.

"Mickey was worried."

"He sent you?"

"Not exactly. This was the only place he had not checked. I'll leave you in peace."

There was a metallic clink as the bolt on the door slid back. Bridie stood, hiding in the shadow of the half open door. Her spotless makeup was now stained with dark streaks. The sparkle in her eyes had faded to a dull pain. "I can't go back," she insisted forcefully, her eyes constantly darting towards the door. She appeared lost, given the pathetic look she cast in my direction. "Please get me out of here."

"Take a walk?" She nodded, relieved at the prospect of escape, terrified of the run across exposed ground to safety. "I'll meet you by the door in a minute. Okay?"

She nodded. "Don't tell Mickey you found me. I really can't face him right now." She needn't have worried. Mickey had drunk himself into oblivion. I slid her coat out from underneath him, wincing at the drunken renditions being performed with the aid of a Karaoke machine.

Bridie relaxed as we walked, placing some distance between us and the party. We sat on a park bench – she withdrew a cheap bottle of vodka from her bag and held it to her lips. Her body shuddered, as the liquid kick hit the back of her throat. She held out the bottle. What the hell – anything to fight back the freezing cold. "I've been refilling my glass from this all evening – cheaper that way."

"Feeling better?"

She bent forwards and placed her head into her hands despairingly. "You in the RA with Mickey?" Not many people had asked me the question directly before and I had become so accustomed to lying, I didn't know how to respond. I hesitated, which clearly confirmed my guilt. "Don't worry. I'm used to keeping my mouth shut. I spend my life waiting for the knock on the door informing me of his arrest or death. I pretend to be asleep when he comes home in the early hours. But I never sleep till I'm sure he's safe. Instead, I spend my time driven out of my mind with worry, whilst we keep up this crazy pretence – that somehow I'm better off not knowing. But not knowing is worse, so much worse." What could I say? I was as guilty as Mickey, except I had no one waiting at home and for once I was glad.

It was freezing now – the wind was bitterly cold. I pulled my jacket tighter around me, and made signs as if to move. The vodka helped, but not enough. Bridie sat motionless, lost in a world of her own. "Tonight must have been about more than Mickey?" The vodka had loosened her tongue and she longed to confide in someone. Often it's easier to tell your inner most fears and secrets to a virtual stranger – it's less complicated, less judgmental.

"If I tell you," she began, "you have to swear not to tell anyone." She reminded me of a child with a secret. But she was deadly serious. "You have to promise." There was an earnestness to her voice which left me with a foreboding as to what she might reveal.

"Okay. I promise." She breathed in deeply and took refuge in another gulp of vodka. "I've never had the courage to tell Mickey. Too terrified he would leave me." Her words were hard to decipher between her muffled sobs. "What would we do without him? I couldn't raise my baby on my own. It was only supposed to be once – extra money for Christmas, what with Mickey being out of work. I thought I had got away with it, but he was there tonight – what if he tells Mickey?"

"Tells him what?

"I…." She hesitated. "I am, or was a call girl."

I don't know what I had expected her to tell me. An affair, spiralling debt or an unwanted pregnancy – anything other than she'd been working as a prostitute. Nor at that stage, did I realise just how profound the implications of what she had just told me were going to be. "You're shocked right?" she noted, burying her head back in her hands.

What was I supposed to say? "It's not the sort of thing people tell me everyday. What do you mean though about seeing someone tonight – a punter?"

The story that she unfolded was both devastating and tragic. As a desperate seventeen-year-old Bridie had run away from home, after she had been raped at a birthday party. She wept as she told me, her tears flowing uncontrollably. She didn't tell anyone. The pain was too intense and the shame too great. It would mean admitting she was drunk. The thought of her father's face was too much to contemplate. Her ordeal only escalated a week later when her period didn't start. The pregnancy test confirmed the awful truth. She ran away to Belfast. What little savings she had been able to take with her were soon frittered away. She survived on the streets for a couple of weeks, begging and stealing food, before meeting a couple of the girls who worked the streets. They took her under their wing. Helped her get a place to live and obtain an illegal abortion for a price. The first time had been an ordeal, but she reassured me it got easier. She told me that you kind of become dead to what is happening to your own body. A mental switch flips inside your head. You learn to ignore the gropes and groans and imagine yourself some place far away: a tropical island or the top of a mountain on a sunny day. Anywhere but the seedy bed sit, the smell of cheap perfume, used condoms and dysfunctional men who treated her like a lump of meat, satisfying their own dreams and desires, whilst slowly but surely sucking the life and hope out of hers.

Bridie gulped the dregs of the vodka and threw the bottle towards the nearby rubbish bin. "My clients ranged from plumbers to office types – businessmen, even a couple of policemen. God they were shit lays," she joked. "Mind you it's nothing out of the ordinary around these parts to say you've been fucked by a peeler!" She smiled for the first time since she had left the dance floor. "One night we were out for one of the girl's birthdays. That's how I met Mickey. He thought I was a barmaid. I had to tell him it was a Prod bar so that he wouldn't come and look for me." Her eyes came alive as she recalled happier times. "Things became more serious. I never expected them to – else I might have told him the truth from the outset. But once you start lying, how do you admit your deception? We moved in together when I fell pregnant. I just gave up working. For the first time, I actually felt happy. We were managing okay until Mickey lost his job. Do you have any idea how many bills there are to be paid? Almost everything is on credit: the sofa, TV, washing machine, even the pram. What the hell are we to do when they repossess them?"

"So you...?" I didn't need to finish the sentence.

"It just happened." I closed my eyes to shield the pain of watching her cry and shiver through her inadequately thin coat.

"It's cold. Come back to my place." I placed my arm around her as we walked to the taxi rank.

In the relative warmth of my kitchen she continued. "This bar was advertising for extra staff. I went up there, but they had already filled the position. I hadn't noticed him at the end of the bar, as I talked with the landlord. A client from the old days called Pete. He followed me onto the street, called out my name. He offered me a £100 – a lot more than usual. He caught me at a bad moment. The money was simply too tempting."

I pulled the last two cigarettes from the pack on the kitchen table. Bridie declined, sticking to her hot tea. "It was cheap, nasty and uncomfortable in the back of his Volvo estate and I felt like a piece of shit. I had forgotten how mind-numbingly grim it could be, lying there whilst he pawed and grunted. All I could think of was my precious baby. I was doing it for her. You always hope you will get away with it. But we never do, our dirty little secrets always come back to haunt us. We did it in the far corner of a multi-storey car park. It was dark and the car was parked against a concrete pillar. Afterwards, as I adjusted my bra, I had the feeling we were being watched. I looked out of the car window – there was this guy stood by his car, about two car's length away on the next aisle. The boot was open, like he was pretending to load the shopping in. He was staring in our direction. I pressed myself into the back seat. I figured he just stumbled across us, a free live sex show. I took the money and fled. I shielded my face as I headed for the stairs and didn't give him a second thought – until tonight. I was on the dance floor. As we turned, I looked up towards the bar and did a double take on a face, like a bolt from the blue. He was stood at the bar drinking. It sent a frightening chill down my entire body. I had to get out of there."

"Did he see you?"

"He could have. What if he knows Mickey and recognises me – what if he tells him?" She was hysterical again now, crying and shaking uncontrollably.

"Are you sure it was him. It was rather dark in there?"

She shook her head vehemently. "You think I would be in this state if I wasn't sure?"

I was left in no doubt that she believed she had seen the car park spy. "Describe him?"

"Err...I can't think straight. Tall, dark, black hair – I can see his face. It's hard to put it into words..."

She gave up a few minutes later, without adding to her sparse description. It could have been half the men at the party. Privately, I wondered if she was over-reacting. Guilt and alcohol can sometimes play tricks on the mind.

Chapter Twenty Six

I WOKE WITH the mother of all hangovers. Bridie had already left. I swallowed two Aspirin, washing them down with strong coffee, hoping the caffeine buzz would energise my still screaming head. I had an appointment with my mother's solicitors. Afterwards, I didn't feel like going home. I wandered round the shops, trying on more clothes than I could possibly carry or afford. It felt good to be normal, if only for a few hours.

Soon after I arrived home, Spender and Kieran appeared. They seemed agitated. "Where the hell have you been?" asked Spender. "I've been trying to reach you all day."

"Out," I replied, deliberately being obstinate. "What's the urgency?"

"Need to use the computer," Kieran volunteered impatiently.

Spender sensed my unease. "We're all part of the same damn unit. Everyone knows that's how you found McCleash. I'll square it with McDonnell," he advised, asserting his authority.

"What's so important – you discovered Paisley's alarm code?"

"You're funny."

From halfway down the loft ladder, grasping the hard drive in its plastic dust covering, I heard Spender talking to Kieran. "For heaven's sake sit down. You make the place look untidy. Better still make yourself useful, put the kettle on – you're like a dog on heat." I booted up the database, as Kieran emerged from the kitchen with three mugs of tea. I entered the security password. December's was 'MARKIEVICZ'.

"What you after?" I enquired, removing the mug from Kieran's outstretched hand.

Kieran pulled a piece of crinkled paper from the back pocket of his jeans. "MDZ 1317 – it's a Special Branch car. We were undertaking surveillance – followed him into a car park, but then we lost him in traffic. He was driving a Volvo estate, metallic silver."

A search on the number plate was a long shot and drew a blank. If he was Special Branch then his plates would be changed every few weeks, unless he simply rotated them, and then we might be lucky. I refined the search, entering Volvo and silver. One hit – our contact in the chemist's shop, who faithfully noted down the cars seen entering the adjacent RUC station: 4th October 1993. *'Volvo estate silver – seen entering station at 9.32am – civilian clothes.'*

"You got a name?" Kieran shook his head rather ponderously. "That's it then."

"It must be him," blurted Kieran in triumph. "It's too much of a coincidence. It must be a Branch car." I thought he was being a little presumptuous – we had nothing to link the Volvo Kieran had seen to the car seen entering the RUC station.

"What's the plan then?"

"Not sure yet," mused Spender. "Wanted to make sure it was him first."

"Then why the hurry?"

"Tip off," offered Kieran. "Suspicious source, I wondered if I was being set up."

I was spending Christmas Eve alone. Neither of the invites I had appealed: drinks with some of my fellow teachers or a local republican bar. It didn't strike me as odd that I felt equally comfortable in each setting, dependent upon which character I was playing that day. The knock on the door soon after 7pm revealed a teenage girl, with a message for me to attend at a safe house later that evening. I guessed it was McDonnell. The reason for my summons I was less sure of.

The safe house belonged to sympathisers who had made themselves scarce for a small price. McDonnell was one of the relatively senior men in the shadows of the IRA, always on the move. The risk of loyalist attack or RUC arrest was ever present. The front of the house was quiet and in darkness. He stood in the kitchen, digging into a large pizza, still in its cardboard box. He ate with his hands, noisily sucking the red tomato sauce off his fingers after each slice, catching the sliding mozzarella cheese with his open mouth. After he had finished eating, he commenced talking. Despite being dressed in scruffy jeans and an old T-shirt, there was something authoritative, even menacing in the intense stare from his cold eyes. "Good job finding McCleash." Praise indeed from a man who was not renowned for compliments. "You have proved the value of the database. You're too important to risk on ASU jobs. We can't afford for you to be picked up and have your house searched. I want you to consider standing down and devoting all your efforts to the database."

"I joined to…" I began to protest.

"You belong to this organisation to further its objectives. Bomb planters, shooters, they're ten a penny. We have to deploy our assets wisely. This is your strength. But if you don't feel…"

"I didn't say that," I replied, frustrated, yet flattered.

"Then it's settled." McDonnell was not used to taking no for an answer. By one means or another. "One more thing," he added before dismissing me. "You'll need assistance. No one is indispensable Tara," he added coldly, as if I needed reminding who was in charge. His harsh features eased a little. "Besides, it would drive you insane sitting in front of that screen every bloody night. Spread the workload a little…" he added, in a patronising tone that made my blood boil.

"Who?" I asked, resigned to the fact it was an order. I was not being consulted.

"I'll let you know. See yourself out."

"Arsehole," I whispered to myself, perhaps a little too audibly. I was determined not to be drawn into the game of sycophancy played by so many others.

"Oh, by the way," he called down the hall in a tone that made it clear he had heard my insult but chose to ignore it, "take this – I may need to contact you at short notice." He tossed a mobile phone in my direction. "A box of hand written files will arrive on Boxing-day. Appropriate eh!" he joked, laughing at his own attempted wit. The hall was in darkness, as I buttoned my coat. A muffled noise from upstairs caused me to stop. I listened, but discerned nothing further. I must have imagined it. The cold winter frost hit me as I walked the streets, admiring the Christmas trees, bright with fairy lights and tinsel visible through the windows.

I spent Christmas Day with my only remaining relatives living in Ireland. It was good to be with a family. To watch the wonder and excitement on young innocent faces, as they ripped the paper from their brightly wrapped gifts. I detested Christmas for all the painful family memories. The temporary happiness of the two Christmases Patrick and I spent together were the cruel taunts of some sadistic being, reminding me of the extent of my loss.

I returned home after 7pm. I was asleep on the sofa in front of the TV, when I was awakened by a frantic knocking. I slid back the thick bolts I had installed in the event of a police raid. I had reasoned they might buy me an extra few seconds whilst I made my escape through the rear. Mickey stood on the doorstep, his hair was unkempt, his clothes looked creased and dirty, dishevelled and rough. His face conveyed raw fear. My initial reaction was that Bridie had told him the truth and he had gone on the mother of all benders. "Have you seen Bridie?" He spoke quickly, impatient to get his words out, gasping in deep breaths. It was obvious he had run all the way.

"I haven't seen her since…"

"She's disappeared," he blurted in desperation.

"Come in."

He stepped inside. "Only for a minute, I have to keep looking."

"When did you see her last?"

"Yesterday afternoon. She said she had a couple of last minute things to buy for Christmas." He fell silent, wringing his hands together. "She never came home."

"Was Laoise with her?"

He shook his head. "No, I was looking after her. She's with my mum."

There had to be a rational explanation? I scoured my brain searching for a connection with her earlier revelation. "Have you tried the hospitals?"

He nodded. "All of them. No word. I wondered if she had come back here. We had a long talk. I told her I'd find a job, spend more time at home. Maybe do less RA business. We were looking forward to Christmas. It was our first with Laoise." In the pit of my stomach I harboured a deep feeling of unease – a voice warning that something horrible was imminent.

"You ought to sleep. There's little further you can do tonight."

"How can I sleep? She could be anywhere – injured…I have to

go." He stood, his body reinvigorated by fear. The adrenaline pushed him onwards. Before I could offer my assistance, he'd disappeared – a shadow patrolling the streets, searching in the night. I tossed and turned in bed but uninterrupted peaceful sleep proved to be a guest who'd checked out of this hotel leaving no forwarding address.

The following morning I called at Mickey's place. His mother opened the door looking disappointed. "I thought you might be Michael," she replied, frostily.

"I'm Tara, friends with both of them." She relented and shook my hand. "I saw Mickey last night," I explained. "Has he been back?"

There was a cry from an upstairs room. "Excuse me." She returned a minute later carrying Laoise. She quietened down as she rocked gently in her grandmother's arms, oblivious to the tension in her voice and the worry that consumed her. "Mickey said not to ring the police."

"I'm sure he had a good reason."

"We both know the reason. I've little time for the RUC myself. But this is different." There was an intensity in her expression that left me in no doubt of her intentions. Anyway what harm could it do? A missing person hardly connected me with terrorist activity. Equally, I had no desire to have my anonymity compromised. "Can you look after Laoise? I'm going to call the RUC."

"I have plans," I began to say, but changed my mind. "I'll have to take her home." I scribbled the address and telephone number down. "You can pick her up later." She handed me the child and picked her coat up from off the hook. "You'll find her things upstairs."

Locating the pushchair brought her mother's plight sharply back into focus and provoked an irrepressible fear. What if she had decided to see one more client? What if she had been attacked or abducted?

Back at my place, Laoise drifted off to sleep after an hour of crying. Minutes later, Dave appeared on the doorstep. "Be quiet. Baby is sleeping."

"I didn't know you…" he began, looking slightly puzzled.

"I don't, stupid. It's Mickey's daughter," I replied, wondering just which planet he inhabited. I showed Dave into the lounge. "Bit early for you isn't it?"

"I'm your back up on the computer…" He looked a little uncomfortable as he spied Laoise, but I thought nothing further of it. Soon after lunch, three large crates were delivered. Packed inside each one were notepads, files, exercise-books and loose pieces of paper.

Where the hell had all this materialised from? They must have been hoarding intelligence information in individual cells for months. Each contained valuable data gathered from units from across the city. Dave groaned as we began to extract its contents. "This will take for bleeding ever." Bloody McDonnell, whose bright idea was this anyway?

We took it in turns – one hour sessions. I would read out entries and he would type them, then we would swap. We spent most of the next two days doing exactly the same. It was boring and monotonous. We tried working separately after the first day, taking it in turns to work for a couple of hours, then relax or sleep. By day three, we had reverted to working together. It was more productive. You didn't lose your place or miss a line so easily. We ended up looking after Laoise for twenty-four hours before her grandmother collected her. There was no sign of either Bridie or Mickey.

Even though it was mind-numbingly tedious, I knew that once the back of the work had been broken, we would have a formidable intelligence resource, which would enable us to become so much more efficient. It also kept me occupied. The moment my focus shifted from what I was reading or typing, my mind wandered back to Bridie. The longer time dragged on, the worse my fear; the statistical chances of finding her alive decreasing with every hour. By 5pm on the third day my head was pounding and I felt like collapsing with fatigue. It was like someone had held open my eyes and poured salt straight in. Every time I pulled another notebook out, there was another underneath, like constantly sailing towards the shifting horizon.

"Had enough?" asked Dave. "Let's finish and then I can go down the pub. I'm dying for a drink." Reluctantly I retrieved a small notebook from the bottom of the crate. I began to read. "February 1993: metallic silver Volvo, registration number MCZ 1327. Suspected SB officer… Drummond." I scanned the rest of the entry without it registering. I had read so many of the damn things, the contents had ceased to have any real significance. Five minutes later, the penny dropped. "Shit – stop." I rifled through the pile of discarded pages and studied the entry in more detail.

"What is it?" asked Dave, annoyed that I had interrupted his typing rhythm.

Drummond – thought to be Special Branch. Been seen curb crawling. Possible operation – volunteer dressed as hooker. "Run that name." Dave appeared reluctant, but sensed my impatience. Apart from the entry we had just typed, there was one additional reference. A volunteer had been arrested a few months earlier. The arresting officer, as recounted by the volunteer was called Sgt Peter Drummond.

Was Peter Drummond the SB guy Kieran had been following? All of a sudden I was confronted with a scary clarity. Bridie said that her client had been called Pete and that a couple of her old clients had been police officers. She was handed £100 by Pete for sex in the back of a car. How many men frequented prostitutes in Belfast? How many police officers? How many men called Peter? How many with Volvos? The registration number was only two digits different to that given to me by Kieran, which would fit with a high profile RUC officer. Rotating his number plates, but keeping them similar would draw less attention in his locality – amongst his neighbours. I pulled up the earlier reference from the chemist's shop – the car had been an estate – isn't that what Bride had referred to – doing it in the back of Volvo estate? She was seen in a car park by someone who attended a republican party. I racked my brain for the description Bridie had given me. It fitted many people, including Kieran, who had said he was undertaking surveillance in a car park. That linked Bridie with Kieran – possibly. It would also explain Kieran's earlier impatience, given there was a sufficient nexus in time between the sordid car park sex and the party. No wonder he was on my doorstep the next day. It was a crazy jumble up of coincidences, which I longed to believe were the product of my warped exhausted imagination. My sense of foreboding grew, as I recalled Kieran's accusation that there was an informer in our unit. Did he think Bridie was a tout – had he seen the money changing hands? Dave guessed from my expression that I was scared witless. He asked too quickly, guilt smeared all over his face that he was unable to camouflage. "What do you know about this?"

"About what?" His pretence at innocence was transparently thin.

"Don't bloody lie to me, or I'll swear I'll kill you. Spender, Kieran and Drummond?" I shouted, shaking with apprehension. "I'd be more worried about me than them, if I was you." He was caught in a dilemma, between his vow of silence to Spender and a confrontation with me.

"They didn't tell me much…" His attempt at stone walling lasted only seconds.

"Lives may depend on your next answer. Think carefully." I successfully intimidated him – he was in no mood for a fight. His body language altered; his shoulders relaxing in defeat.

"I met them in the pub on Christmas Eve. I heard them speaking in hushed tones. They stopped when I joined them. I heard Kieran mention Drummond. He said that they would get him and his bleeding touts. I had no idea who they were talking about until you told me about Bridie. I realised it was Mickey. Kieran said there was an informer. I reasoned she had probably left him after she'd discovered his secret – grassing little fucker."

"You stupid little shit," I slapped him across the face, more in frustration, than any sense of protecting Mickey's reputation. I had supposed Mickey was still out looking for Bridie, or drinking himself into oblivion. It hadn't occurred to me that they might think Bridie was acting as a conduit for Mickey and that he was in danger.

"What the fuck was that for," he squealed, rubbing his reddened cheek and retreating to the other side of the room.

"Why the hell didn't you say anything?" I asked, incredulous at his silence.

"I…" His voice faltered, stammering to justify his actions. "I thought it best to keep my head down. If there's a tout, it won't be long before the peelers are knocking on my door. I don't want to go to prison."

"You naïve selfish little twat. You'd better finish this lot off," I snapped, reaching for my coat and car keys.

"Where are you going?"

"To do the decent thing – to demonstrate the backbone you so obviously lack."

I had no idea what I was going to do when I got there. I was banking on McDonnell listening to me. I hoped my hunch proved accurate. McDonnell was head of the Civil Administration Unit. He was in the safe house over Christmas. The muffled noises I had heard – what if that had been Bridie? I felt sick. I pressed the accelerator down harder, taking my aggression out on the car, as I threw it round a bend and listened to the tyres screech. I just prayed I wasn't too late.

I banged the door and rang the bell. No reply. Come on, open up you bastards. A neighbour appeared to inform me what I already knew. The occupants had gone south on holiday and wouldn't be back until after the New Year. There was only one other place to head: Spender's. No sooner had he opened the door than I was at him. "Where are they?" I snapped.

"Who?" he asked, a genuinely innocent look of surprise on his face.
"Don't play games. Bridie and Mickey," I replied, pushing past him.

He was quiet for a moment, as if trying to figure out which was the best tactic to use on me – pull rank or a quiet friendly word in my ear? His reply was measured and with authority. "This is not your business Tara. Go home. There is nothing you can do. I am telling you this as a friend and a colleague." He appeared both serious and saddened – the colour had drained from his face. He looked tired and gaunt. I hadn't considered the consequences of this sorry mess for him. A unit commander, who had failed to spot an informer.

"You must stop this," I pleaded. "Whatever Kieran thought he saw in that car park between Drummond and Bridie, it was not a pay off for informing on this unit. It was Kieran, right?"

When Spender recovered from the shock of realising I knew information which was restricted to only half a dozen people all far more senior to me, he ushered me into the living room. I relayed the whole sorry saga. I felt uneasy about betraying the confidence placed in me, but I had little choice. After I finished, he sat back in his chair, closed his eyes, tipped his head back slightly and breathed in deeply. "Sweet Jesus, I hope you're fucking right. Wait here," he commanded. He picked up his jacket and closed the front door behind him. I watched him run to his car and drive off.

Spender returned an hour later. It proved the longest hour in my entire life. I rose from the chair, at the sound of the key in the door. The slow precise movement in removing his jacket, replacing it on the hook. I knew then. I met him at the door, our eyes intertwined – his face pale, his cheeks sallow, as if the life had been sucked out of him. "Tell me it's not true."

He collapsed back in the chair, closing his eyes, and spoke faintly. "I was too late." He covered his face with his hands and for a moment I thought he might actually break down.

"Please tell me she is alive." The tears I'd been saving, in the hope they would be tears of relief, now flooded in sorrow, regret and anger.

"Bridie signed a confession last night. She was executed this morning." Spender spoke from behind the hands that covered his mouth.

I felt so empty. His words echoed hollowly around my head. "No – it can't be. There must be some mistake."

Spender finally removed his hands, shock engulfing his face. "I wish there was. I'm sorry."

"Confession? How many fucking cigarettes did McDonnell and his cronies have to burn into her to get her to sign?" I was angry now and approached him, remonstrating with my hands. Later the sorrow would return. But for the moment fire and fury reigned. "If you break enough of my sodding fingers, I'll sign anything you bloody want. What are we: the KGB?" I was walking around the room, shouting at Spender, who sat unresponsively, his head absorbed in his hands.

He let me rant and rave for a couple of minutes, until I was tired and heavy with exhaustion. "The body will be dumped tomorrow. A press statement from the Army Council will state she was a paid Special Branch informer and was sentenced to death for her crime. That's the line the entire movement will take, including you. This conversation never took place and no mention will ever be made of it again. Do I make myself clear?" I knew they had to try and cover their own backs. Bridie just happened to be the sacrificial lamb for their desperate incompetence and paranoia. Almost as an afterthought, he added: "Mickey is alive. He will be released and then dishonourably discharged. He will be required to leave Belfast."

"You're not going to tell him the truth? You'll let him walk around believing that his girlfriend was selling IRA secrets to the Special Branch – you can't do that!"

"Is it any worse than the truth? The bitch was whoring to the RUC – one way or another."

I was sick to death of the lies. "So we brush the sordid truth under the carpet like it never happened?"

Spender attempted to appear like a soldier – his shoulders stiffened and he thrust his chest outwards in a show of authority. "Let's not give the enemy a propaganda coup. It's life and shit happens."

I didn't ask him the burning question. What if I was unable to put it behind me?

I had reached a crossroads where I would have to make a decision. But like a super-tanker it takes time to change direction. The momentum of each day carries you forward, from one job to the next – onwards and downwards in a never-ending spiral of violence.

I was haunted by the image of Bridie. What a raw deal fate had dealt her. I hated Drummond with all the ferocity I could mobilise. As a woman, I hated him for exploiting vulnerable young women with the power of his money. That he could stoop to buy sex like it was just another commodity. Like it didn't matter – only this time it did. It cost Bridie her life for £100 and a quick fumble – a cheap orgasm for which she paid dearly. My loathing wasn't restricted to Drummond. He might have sealed her fate, but he didn't pull the trigger. I had never had the romantic view of the IRA that they were incapable of doing wrong. But I believed in the cause I was fighting for. Yet in a British court of law Bridie would have been acquitted. Guilt or innocence, words McDonnell and his henchman didn't understand. The truth didn't matter. What Kieran thought he had seen was evidence enough.

I thought of her in a blacked out bedroom. I tortured myself that the noises I had heard in the safe house, were the whimpers of pain after a beating. I knew she wouldn't have signed a confession without the use of force. She had been a prisoner for four days before she was killed. My stomach turned at the thought of her head being held under the water of a filled bath – the helpless writhing and impending sense of drowning, then the gasps of air as her body sucked life back into her lungs and the questions would start again. Had they forced her to stand naked? Blindfolded her, whilst they took it in turns to punch, kick and beat her?

In my nightmares, this evil barbaric vision haunted me. I saw Bridie reach the point where she would say anything to stop the pain. Sobbing as she signed the confession – leaning on the bare wooden floor, contaminated with traces of blood. Dressed in simple overalls she would be carried in the early hours to the boot of the car. The boot would be lined with plastic sheeting, later disposed of to ensure no forensic evidence remained. She would then be driven to a remote spot, her hands tied tightly behind her back, and then forced roughly to the ground, onto her knees. Still sobbing and pleading her innocence, a hood would be placed over her head. Her final view of this world would be the soil she knelt upon. Two shots would then be fired into the back of her head. I would wake at this point, sweating and crying, exhausted with emotion.

The following day, the partially clad body of a woman was found on waste ground just across the border near Dundalk. A statement issued by the Provisional IRA later confirmed that they had carried out the shooting. The statement alleged that Miss Bridie McDonagh was a paid informer for the RUC.

Until they found the body, there was a little part of me that hoped there had been a mistake; a lie to ease the pain. Whatever subterfuge it had provided was now ripped away. I turned to the only thing I knew that could dull the pain. I got exceedingly drunk. And cried tears for Bridie, Mickey, Laoise and for me and what I had become.

Chapter Twenty Seven

IT WASN'T AS if Bridie was the first person accused of informing on the IRA. There was however, something about this killing which sickened people across Northern Ireland, regardless of their tradition or allegiance. The rumour mill was strong – within hours, the RUC was briefing that the young woman had been totally unknown to them. The killing aroused significant publicity because of the Christmas timing. It made a mockery of the seventy-two hour Christmas ceasefire, announced with great fanfare only a few days previously. Good will to all men – perhaps that didn't apply to women, reasoned one newspaper?

The first and most immediate head to roll was McDonnell's. Amongst nationalists there was a feeling he had gone too far. Sinn Féin activists were furious. How were they supposed to deal with this one on the doorsteps? McDonnell became a semi-public scapegoat to those in the know. However, McDonnell was an effective and competent operator – no one wanted to lose him altogether. He was seconded to the English department and relocated south to the Republic.

Against the specific orders of Spender, I met Mickey. He was a broken man, devastated by the events that had befallen him and his family. He sat opposite me in the café, stirring the sugar in his tea, almost in a trance. Two of McDonnell's henchman had picked him up, indicating they had news of Bridie. He'd had no idea that the IRA held Bridie until he was informed she had signed a confession. His hands were shaking. He blew his nose and attempted to put on a brave face, but there was no disguising his anguish. The cowards hadn't even had the guts to tell him a death sentence had been passed. He only discovered Bridie's fate along with the rest of the world, when her body was found. Unable to comprehend how his beautiful innocent girlfriend, mother of his child had been executed by the organisation he had dedicated his life to, he had more questions than I could answer.

I debated long and hard what I should tell him. Which was crueller, to believe that Bridie was an informer, or a desperate woman trying to make ends meet? He tapped his fingers on the edge of the table – a slow repetitive beat. "It makes no sense – she hated peelers. She had too much pride to demean herself for their scabby money: why?" One minute he would shout and I would think he was going to hurl the crockery against the wall in anger. The next moment his mood would swing, and he would succumb to morbid introspection. "If I hadn't become involved with the IRA – I killed her…." He wept uncontrollably.

"I know what happened." He lifted his eyes from the half-empty mug and the tea ring stains on the veneer table. "I shouldn't even be speaking to you." Deference was a word I had learnt to despise over recent days.

Mickey appeared suspicious. "They sent you to make sure I keep my mouth shut. Well fuck you." His hands shook as he tried to light a smoke. It took all his concentration, but he couldn't hold his hand steady. I lit it for him.

I reached my hand out across the table towards his, but he recoiled. "I'm telling you this because you need to know it was a terrible mistake. That's why they want you out of the way. Not to remind them of what a bunch of useless pricks they are. Drummond was drunk and had come on to her in the car park. He pestered her, until she had threatened him that her boyfriend was in the Provies. He'd panicked and tried to buy her silence with money. She'd refused his cheap bribes. Unfortunately, they'd been spotted in the car park by a reconnaissance unit. They'd seen the wallet and knew what Drummond did for a living. Bridie had felt frightened and intimidated, but had resisted telling you, in case you did something stupid. That was what she was upset about at the party." I bowed my head in shame, as I confessed that Spender had tried to stop McDonnell, but it was too late. I left Mickey in the café. My final view of him was through the window, as the sales shoppers streamed by – a broken disconsolate figure.

A Bold Deceiver • James Hurd

I walked down the familiar streets – roads I had walked a thousand times seemed strangely alien. I had been transported to a parallel dimension where the physical geography remained unchanged but the old certainties had been blown away – literally, with two bullets.

When later that evening, I received an order to attend Kieran's house, I felt less than inclined. Kieran was the last individual on the planet I wanted to see – apart from perhaps McDonnell. But in times of stress, the brain reverts to familiar patterns. A soldier falls back on his training. The Green Book was clear. Obey orders and attend meetings.

"Tara," spoke a voice from my left on the sofa. To my surprise it was Jimmy Kelley, who had spent the night in my spare room, over two years earlier. When I'd last seen him, it had been at the Christmas party. "Sit down." I edged towards the armchair. Kieran and Spender were ensconced on the sofa. I wondered how much Kieran knew of my involvement in Mickey's release?

"How are you?" inquired Kieran, attempting to soften his usual growl.

"I'm fine. Why shouldn't I be?"

"Well, I know you were close to…" He couldn't even bring himself to speak his name. "Well, morale is bound to be low at the moment. It's been a difficult time for all of us," counselled Kelley. "Touts are bad news. Better it was sorted now, before any real damage was done." Spender studiously ignored my obvious incredulity.

Until that moment, it hadn't occurred to me that neither Kieran nor Kelley actually knew the truth. They actually believed Bridie and, by association, Mickey were guilty – stupid ignorant fools. I didn't know whether to loathe them or pity them.

"We have a job planned for tomorrow. Some of my people were picked up by the RUC last night at a checkpoint. We need your help." Kelley said, with a degree of humility that struck me as being out of character.

"Bad luck." I replied indifferently.

"With them out of circulation – job's screwed. This sweet mother is too good to miss – taking out a SB man. The plan calls for a woman's touch." If his words were delicate, the implication was clear: a honey trap. Using my sexuality to lure a man to his death was not why I had joined the IRA. If they were deluding themselves for one minute that I was about to prostitute myself for the cause, after the events of the last few days, they could go screw themselves. It was the antithesis of all I believed in. Mascara and pouty lips, whilst the 'real' volunteers waited round the corner with a gun. I despised the very idea.

I shook my head firmly, rising from the threadbare armchair. "Rethink the job boys or find yourself a different whore!" I made ready to leave. The meeting was over.

"It's an order Tara," Spender demanded sharply, although he appeared uneasy pulling rank.

I turned to face Spender, smouldering with rage. "I don't care if the order came direct from Adams and McGuinness – no."

"Oh," said Kelley, in surprise, from the other side of the room. "What with you being close to Mickey, I thought it might have a personal dimension? Guess we'll have to call the whole thing off – pity." In a flamboyant gesture he raised his arms in despair and then brought them down onto his thighs. My brain must have been working slowly, because it took a second to make the connection. Once it was made, they had me hook, line and sinker. "Drummond?" I gasped, sinking back into the chair.

Now the feminists will scream hypocrisy. Whatever happened to your noble ideas of equality – of not demeaning your sexuality in such a fashion? Every time I closed my eyes I saw Bridie's tortured face. "I'm not saying yes, but…where?" I asked wearily, resigned to the inevitable.

"He'll be in Crystal's nightclub tomorrow, New Year's Eve. He's good mates with the owner Billy Magee. He's holding a private party."

My instinct for self-preservation kicked in. "Magee – he's UVF?"

"He's a gangster with fingers in lots of pies, including bankrolling some loyalist tossers if they do the odd favour for him."

"What's Drummond's take?" I asked reluctantly.

Kelley continued with the briefing. "He and Magee watch each others' backs. The Branch doesn't look too hard at Magee's business affairs and Drummond collects the odd favour and gets passed the odd bit of information along with some free booze. The event is strictly invitation only. "

"The place is going to be crawling with loyalist thugs and the bleeding RUC," I observed warily, distinctly uneasy with what was being proposed.

Kelley smiled. "One of our people is the head barman – got us an invite." He slid a brown manila envelope in my direction. "Kenny will introduce you. The rest is up to you...." Kelley paused before continuing his briefing. "Drummond will be relaxed. It's his home turf..."

"Do we need to draw you a map?" Kieran added sarcastically, observing my all too apparent unease.

I ignored his jibe. "The plan – or am I supposed to stiff him on the dance floor?"

Kelley spread out a rough sketch plan of the club. "Fire exit is here." He pointed to the plan with his stubby finger. "Near the bogs – door has been rigged so we can open it from the outside."

"Think you're up to it?" asked Spender anxiously, lighting a cigarette. I nodded towards him, making my expression as unaffected as possible, suppressing the anger and mournful tears I still felt over Bridie.

"You might need this." Kelley handed me a black and white photograph, which was slightly grainy, shot with a long lens. "I'd hate you to miss him," he smiled sweetly.

I hardly slept that night. I could feel the tension building in my stomach. My brain was racing, planning strategies and worrying. In retrospect, it was little short of suicide. If there were UVF boys there and something went wrong, it would not be pleasant. There was no Plan B – if I was exposed...? When sleep finally overtook me in the early hours, it provided me with little solace. Bridie, McCleash's wife and my mother, all crawling around in my head, while I lay helpless to respond.

I tried on virtually every piece of clothing I owned before returning to the first outfit. The contents of my wardrobe lay scattered in discarded piles across the bedroom, bathroom and landing. My hair had been up, down and in at least three different styles before I left the house just after quarter to nine, complete with blonde wig and more make up than I had worn since I was a teenager. I was wearing a little black dress, cut low enough at the front to attract his attention, but just high enough to keep him guessing.

Crystal's catered for those who wanted a late licence and a guaranteed pickup without being too particular. I stood in line with the New Year revellers before handing my ticket in to the seven-foot doorman. It felt strange being surrounded by couples, groups of girls and lads, all on a high for the celebrations to come – laughing, joking and flirting. I hesitated by the double doors, whilst people streamed past, like a diver bouncing at the end of the high board. "You coming in or what?" shouted a lad in front.

"She's put off knowing you're going in, you ugly fucker," shouted one of his mates, to the general amusement of his cohorts.

"Fancy a dance?" the first guy joked, as I pushed past him.

"Maybe later, when I'm pissed and can't focus on your face," I responded, entering the spirit of the occasion, sparking further hilarity.

Bodies seemed to be pressed into every corner. The dance floor was heaving. Already there was the smell of hot bodies, intertwined with cigarette fumes and dry ice. I pushed through the crowds visible only in the flashing half-light. "Kenny here?" I shouted at the barman, over the constant thump of the bass woofers. "Tell him it's Stacey."

A minute later I felt a vice like grip encompass my arm and a broad dark figure pulled me towards an alcove. "Who the bloody hell are you?" he hissed in my ear. "Where the hell is Annie?" he scowled – clearly perturbed at the last minute switch.

"She was picked up. I'm the understudy. I'm no more enamoured with this than you. So just point out our man and let's get on with it," I remarked coldly, wrenching my arm free.

I sat on a stool, near the bar, taking in the layout. I sipped vodka. I was dying for a cigarette. I only resisted in case he was a health Nazi. I spied Drummond as I drained the final drops from my glass. He swaggered towards the bar, like he owned the joint. He looked better in real life than the grainy black and white photograph: tall, with thinning hair and a full square jaw. He obviously worked out but was still a few pounds overweight. I could see his well-developed upper body physique through his shirt. A surge of relief washed over me as I saw him stub out a cigarette. As I fumbled to pull a smoke out of the packet, Kenny appeared by my side. "Stacey," he called. "I'd like you to meet a friend of mine." My heart thumped and I could feel the nervous energy starting to coarse through my veins. "This is Stacey," he said. "We go way back."

"Nice to meet you," Drummond replied, stretching out his hand. "I'm Pete." He smiled warmly, his eyes drifting towards my chest, where he lingered, down to my waist, legs and then back up. *Subtle.* His eyes on me sent a sickening chill down my spine. Had those eyes smiled at Bridie? Even if the circumstances had been different, he wasn't my type: too many smart remarks and an unshakeable belief in his own self-importance.

I shook his hand. He had a firm grip, with a heavy gold signet ring on his right ring finger. *Those hands.* I noticed a narrow depression on his left-hand ring finger. He'd removed his wedding ring. *Poor woman.* "Kenny." There was a shout from the bar. "Lager's off. I think it's knackered."

"Excuse me for a moment," apologised Kenny. "If you want a job doing, you have to do it yourself." It was now or never.

"You here alone?" he shouted over the music. *Original chat up line.*

"I'm waiting for some friends." I glanced at my watch. *You might meet them later, if you're lucky...*

"Get you another drink?" *Don't appear easy.* He sensed my uneasiness. "Hey, it's only a drink. I promise," he laughed, placing his hand on my shoulder. *Yeah right pal.*

"Vodka tonic thanks." He took my empty glass, his fingers brushing the side of my hand. *Oh God what am I doing?*

"So how do you know Kenny?" Drummond asked, handing me a replacement.

"He used to go out with one of my girlfriends," I lied.

"So what do you do Stacey?" He inched closer towards me, which in normal circumstances would have caused the alarm bells to ring at a deafening volume. I in turn edged a little closer. *Remember positive body language.*

"I'm a teacher." What was the point in lying? He wouldn't be telling anyone.

"Do you enjoy it?" *Like you give a shit about anything other than getting inside my knickers.*

"It pays the rent," I replied, inhaling on my cigarette. I changed the subject to his favourite. "What about you?"

"Salesman" *How many times have you pedalled that lie?* "Not seen you here before. I know most of the regulars." *Screwed them you mean.* "I'm here with some mates." He waved towards a distant table on the other side of the dance floor. "Always nice to meet new people though." *Oh please.* He lent in a little closer as he spoke, so that I could smell the aroma of his breath: beer and spicy food. *You are such a turn on.*

Drummond insisted on buying the drinks – I guess he reasoned I too was for sale. I needed a straight head, but it was New Year's Eve. I couldn't appear too prudish. I can't recall with any clarity what we discussed. There's just this blank space – a missing segment in time.

My focus was so intense, everyone else slowly disappeared: the dancers and loiterers, music and lights, punters and DJ, until there was just Drummond and me. He talked and I tried to listen. He told me what car he drove and invited me to his villa in Spain. As the empty pint glasses grew, so his inhibitions diminished. We sat down, and I felt his hand on my knee and then his arm half round my waist. *Those hands, those same hands – I know where they have been.* It took every ounce of my will power to allow him touch me, to appear interested in his conceited bigotry, to create the impression, however unlikely, that I might just be begging him to screw me before the year was out.

When he got up to visit the toilets my heart rate increased. What if he was no longer interested? On the other hand, he would be near the fire exit? I glanced at my watch. 11pm: too early. Closer to midnight would be better, as everyone would be a little more inebriated. *Just keep him interested.* It would do Kieran no harm to sweat in the cold a little longer. "Pete," I called, as he stood. He leaned over me and moved his head towards my ear. "Hurry back soon." I placed my left hand on his face and planted a kiss full on his lips. *Only an appetiser baby.*

"You bet," he smiled, stroking my thigh with a triumphant glint. As soon as he disappeared I ordered another round. I laced his beer with a double vodka. That ought to slow him down a little. Despite the booze, he would at some point appreciate the danger. Then his instinct and training would kick in. I downed one final drink and watched Drummond stagger back, zipping his fly as he emerged into view. The smug satisfied expression told me all I needed to know. Tonight was going to be his lucky night. *Dream on baby.*

"Let's dance," I begged, offering him my outstretched hands, swaying side to side, as provocatively as I was able, attempting to conceal just how self-conscious I felt.

"I have to warn you though I'm a bit of a mover," he joked, wiggling his hips from side to side. *So sophisticated. How could a girl say no?* The dance floor was heaving as the countdown headed towards midnight. The DJ whipped up the anticipation. The music grew louder, frantic as the classic eighties tunes rocketed out of the speakers and the dry ice machine worked overtime. Walking on Sunshine, Tainted Love, Come on Eileen, 1999. As we danced, he kept trying to slobber over me. Each time I would tease him, blow him a kiss, laugh and pull away, remaining tantalisingly close enough that it was obvious what was on the menu. *Enjoy it while you can – scum.* He sensed I was just playing hard to get and joined in – in drunken expectation. After a few minutes he seemed to tire of my teasing, and when the opportunity arose he placed his arms around me. I felt his hands slide firmly down my back. Touching, caressing, until he reached my arse which he pinched with a mischievous grin, before taking up position on my waist. *Those hands again. I know the price you paid.* I reciprocated, burying my head into his sweaty shoulder, as we rolled together with the rhythm of the song. I glanced surreptitiously at my watch: five minutes – time to move up a gear. *Are you ready for some action baby?* I moved my head slowly backwards until our lips were only millimetres apart, before kissing him hard on the mouth. Drummond pulled me towards him, caressing my waist. As we danced, I ensured we edged almost imperceptibly towards the fire doors. *This way baby. Not long now.*

"One more tune and then let the celebrations really begin," crooned the DJ. I kissed him more forcefully. He was lost in a drunken frenzy and the excitement of the moment. As we embraced, he pressed himself against me – I could feel his erection, rubbing against my groin. *Enjoy it. You won't use it again. Your back seat screwing career is about to end pal.*

"Oh God Pete, I want you now," I murmured, with as much false passion as I could muster. Inserting my hand between our intertwined bodies, I unbuttoned the top button on his shirt and inserted my hand, running it across his chest. He glistened with anticipation. He thought all his Christmases had come at once. *Guess who's fucking who baby?*

Drummond groaned as we moved seamlessly off the dance floor towards the darkened recesses. The lights were dimmed for the countdown: "20 seconds…19…18…17." The crowd roared out the final seconds of the year. Drummond pushed me against the darkened wall. I felt the bitter taste of his passion as he forced his probing tongue into my mouth. His left hand gripped me tightly as he rubbed his hand across my breast – softly at first and then harder as his momentum grew – caressing, squeezing and pinching. *Those hands again.* I closed my eyes and fought to restrain the tears. I felt so damn cheap. Only adrenaline and my desire for revenge enabled me to keep acting my part in this deadly charade. "10…9…8…" He pushed my dress upwards, his left hand stroking my thigh, his fingers reaching the top of my stockings. *Almost there baby. Lights on amber.*

"Not here," I said. He mistook my anguished whimper for desire. "Too many people."

"5...4...3..." His probing fingers crawled higher, whilst the other cupped my breast roughly grasping for my nipple. *Red light pal.*

"Out back." I pointed in the direction of the fire doors.

"2...1..." Before he had a chance to object, I thrust my hand into his and enticed him towards the doors. My back was against the door and I was ready to resume my sick seduction. *Full time baby – the referee's gonna blow the whistle.* "Happy New Year," bellowed the DJ, followed by a tumultuous cheer from the assembled hoard. A tidal wave of cheers, party poppers and drunken clapping. For one horrible second, I wondered if there was actually anyone on the other side of the door? As Drummond's hand again reached for my thigh, I arched my back and leaned forward, pulling him closer and then slammed back on the door, summoning every ounce of strength I possessed. *"Should auld acquaintance be forgot and never brought to mind? Should auld acquaintance be forgot for the sake of auld lang syne?"* The sound of the singing filled my ears, as I tumbled backwards into fresh air. The two or three seconds before I hit the ground seemed like a lifetime. I was trapped in a kind of limbo, half standing, half sprawling, half inside, half out, half hot, half cold, half human and half machine. I closed my eyes and prayed I would not be alone with Drummond – ever again.

I curled myself hard into a ball and rolled, landing awkwardly on the cold concrete. The last thing I wanted was Drummond landing on top of me, particularly if there was no welcoming committee. *"For auld lang syne my dear, for auld lang syne, we'll take a cup o' kindness yet for auld lang syne...."* The cold air hit me like a brick. I could feel my body shivering. A helping hand lifted me – it was Kieran. Drummond lay sprawled on the floor behind me. He was still conscious – good. I wanted to watch his reaction, staring down the gun barrel, knowing he was about to breathe his last. And I wanted to whisper in his ear, just so he knew why. The change in atmosphere took a second to register: from erotic encounter to the imminence of death. His eyes opened wide, his pupils dilated, darting around, assessing the danger. In the dim light and the shock of the fall, it took him a split second to focus on the hooded Kieran and the silenced Colt .45. I could almost see his prick droop in sheer unbridled terror. *Not so tough now pal?* His initial instinct was to run. The fall and the alcohol slowed him. Kieran stamped on his hand – hard. "Arrr shit. You fucking bastards," he screamed, grabbing his hand and wincing in pain.

"Now let's not be too hasty, shall we," replied Kieran, pressing the silencer against his temple "Move." He dragged him a couple of feet to the left. Just enough so I could push the door closed. We didn't want any additional guests. For some reason, it wouldn't fully shut. Everyone inside was far too pre-occupied in any event. "You bloody whoring bitch," he swore in my general direction.

I nuzzled my face to his ear. "In your dreams pal." I ripped a section of tape and pressed it across his mouth, squeezing the flesh on his cheek between my thumb and forefinger. I gestured to Kieran. "Get on with it. I've had enough of this place for one night."

He grunted his approval. Drummond was shaking like a leaf. I could ascertain little whimpers behind his gag. "Give the Almighty my regards," snarled Kieran, as he thrust the gun into his ribs. Drummond winced. He was shaking his head in a desperate plea for a last minute reprieve. He ought to have known better.

"Hang on a second," I gestured. I bent down, close to Drummond's ear. "Let me acquaint you with the facts. I want your last regret to be that poor girl you screwed for £100 in a car park. She is dead – all because you couldn't keep your tiny prick to yourself. And now so will you be." His eyes opened wide, whether in understanding or incomprehension. No time for questions pal, time out. "Go on," I urged Kieran.

He lifted the gun again. The fire door opened slightly in a gust of wind and the opening bars of 'New York New York' drifted out, as the muted bark of the revolver was masked by the music, the silencer imparting a metallic thud as the bullet entered Drummond's chest. Kieran pulled the trigger again – three shots in quick succession. At the sound of the silenced gunfire I froze on the spot. Kieran was tugging my sleeve. "Let's get the hell out of here."

Neither heaven nor hell could have persuaded me to run. For I had seen an apparition in the second before Drummond's head jerked forward, his hands gripping his chest where the bullets invaded his rib cage, and he finally succumbed to his grizzly fate. I had seen my dad. In his last few gasping breaths, Drummond's eyes were focused upon me. Yet I didn't see Drummond's pained terrified expression, but instead the serene vision of my father. The same expression I'd seen all those years before, in the passenger seat of his van, powerless to act – just before he was shot. Dad didn't speak, but I could still hear his words, whether telepathy or intuition, asking me over and over again in a soothing voice. 'Why Tara – why?' In the time it took to fire those three shots, I saw the truth: every life lost regardless of religion, politics or uniform. Each and every one was my father. I was shaken violently out of my trance, by the sound of the music, as the fire doors swung open. A bouncer appeared. "Hey, these aren't supposed to be open. What the hell's going on?"

Kieran beckoned. "Come on." I took one last look at Drummond and ran, kicking my heels off and running with them in my hands.

I didn't look back. Even when I heard the cries of: "He's dead." I pushed my legs forward mechanically – ignoring the approaching footsteps and clambering almost headfirst into the back seat of the waiting car.

Inside the safety of my own front door, I fell to my knees, burst into tears and wept uncontrollably. I felt such a vivid plethora of emotions: I felt cheap and humiliated. I shook with a deep sense of self-loathing. I managed to climb the stairs and remove my dress, throwing my underwear off, desperate to step into the shower and wash away the dirt. Drummond clung to my clothes like cheap perfume, infiltrating my nostrils and making me feel nauseous – but I was also trying to wash away the memories. I broke down and sobbed like an orphan child, lost and alone. Even though I had not pulled the trigger, I may as well have done. My lies and false seduction hung heavy upon me, causing me to double up under the hot water, weeping and despising what I had done. I realised for the first time the ugly nature of my vengeance. Far from asserting Ireland's destiny, I was caught up in an endless spiral of violence repeated through generations. Did Drummond have children? What if after his death he or she joined the UVF and the cycle commenced all over again?

Imagine how Columbus would have felt if he had sailed off the edge of a flat earth and the grim reality hit him: his life had been a totally useless waste. I felt like that, only worse. For my actions were more than benign stupidity. I felt a black all consuming void of guilt, which encircled me like leaden chains, making every movement almost more effort than I could bear. As the hot water cascaded over my head, trickling through my hair, over my face, enveloping me in a cloud of steam, I cursed my stupidity. Watching Kieran fire into Drummond's quivering pathetic body, I discovered that nothing was worth the death of another human being – even one I despised.

Cowering, I glimpsed at the razor blades on the shelf and did contemplate the final solution. I got as far as opening the packet before I realised I lacked the courage even to take my own life. A part of me wouldn't let me – the voice that whispered that I had to suffer for my actions, death was too easy. Two other considerations weighed heavily upon me. The first was very practical. Numerous people in the club would have seen me with Drummond. A description of me was inevitable. What reassurance I could summons – that it was dark, everyone was drunk and that I was just another face in a crowd – provided little consolation. The other was more nebulous. Whether a dream or a hallucination, I was sure my father was sending me a message. Maybe, just maybe, if I got out now, things would work out. My decision was made before I stepped onto the bathroom floor, draping a towel around my shoulders. To where and to do what I had not even the semblance of an idea; I just knew I had to get away and quickly.

Chapter Twenty Eight

I DON'T KNOW what possessed me to be so devious. Hidden in my sub-conscious existed a plan to undo at least some of the damage of previous months, even if little more than a token gesture of defiance. Before I left the house, I booted up the database. I did what I had done with every new month, I changed the password. I packed a rucksack, wrote a resignation letter, citing personal difficulties and tried to sleep, waiting for the sound of the RUC pulling up outside. At 6am, as the rest of the city slept off their New Year hangover, I slipped quietly into the back seat of a cab bound for the ferry terminal and Liverpool.

I'd used McDonnell's mobile phone only once or twice. I wasn't even aware that it was switched on. So when I heard the dull ring, muffled from within my rucksack, I assumed it belonged to someone else, but the upper rear deck of the ferry was deserted, as we slowly manoeuvred away from the dock. Leaning on the handrail, the wind blowing through my hair, I retrieved the call. "I thought we agreed you would keep a low profile," McDonnell lectured coldly. "Every news broadcast is full of your exploits. Who authorised the job?"

"Kieran and I stood in for Kelley's people. Spender informed me it was an order."

There followed a brief pause. "You should know better than letting a job become personal."

"I did as I was told, but two hundred people in that club must have seen me with Drummond."

McDonnell sensed the tension in my voice. "Where are you now?"

A Bold Deceiver • James Hurd

"I'm going to disappear. Lie low." I saw little point in lying.

"Don't come back for a while. If you're in England ring this number." I noted down the digits mechanically. "He'll let you know if it's safe. Don't attempt to contact me direct." He gave me a code, which I noted down, although I had no intention of ever using it.

"Ring Dave. Tell him to collect the computer."

The line went dead. Did you pull the trigger? Did you enjoy the power? Did it get you off – you sick piece of shit?

As the landmass of Ireland grew smaller on the horizon, I punched the rubber keys. It rang for what seemed like an age, before it was finally answered. A woman's voice shouted. "You must be bleeding joking. Do you have any idea what time we got to bed?"

I was in no mood to be played with. "Tell Dave to get his lazy arse on the phone now or the Provie nutting squad will be round to recreate his sodding knee caps."

Seconds later, Dave picked up. "This better be good. Do you know when I got to sleep?"

"Before me, no doubt. Get a pen." I could hear him fumbling at the other end. "You've to collect the computer. I've got to lie low for a while."

"Why…? Shit – Drummond. Was that you?" he asked, his brain churning through his hangover.

"No time to chat now Dave. It's a new month, we have a new password. Note this down. We don't want to lock the system. Cost a fortune to resurrect that data."

"Relax will you – what's the code."

"HFTCUW3189"

"Say again."

"HFTCUW3189."

"Slowly," he shouted into the phone.

"Hotel, Foxtrot, Tango…"

"You're breaking up."

I breathed in deeply and the die was cast: "Hotel, Foxtrot, Tango, Uniform, Charlie, Whisky, Tree, Ait, Wun, Niner."

He read it back to me until I was content he had accurately recorded the incorrect sequence. My gesture of defiance to the movement I had come to despise. If it prevented one more death, then I took some consolation. The coast of Ireland was fast disappearing into the mist of the Irish Sea. My final act of rebellion was to throw McDonnell's precious mobile phone overboard. I watched it splash and sink amidst the wake of the ship until it finally disappeared from view.

I travelled across Europe, North Africa, Egypt and Algeria, and the back packer's route through the Far East. I hoped time and distance would replenish what I had lost. Never settling down means you never have to open up – no one probes beyond the superficial. By the end of the summer though, I began to reassess my position. I was homesick. Not for what I had left behind – but the life I longed to lead. Yet the fear persisted that I would be arrested on arrival in the UK. I contemplated ringing the number McDonnell had given me. I sat on the idea for days – too scared of the consequences, too cowardly to seize the moment. I made a final decision after the intense euphoria of the cease-fire. There was no war to go back to – or so I dared to believe.

2nd January 1997: 3.45am: *Manchester*

"Why Manchester?" I asked Tara.

"I met a couple of girls from Manchester in Hong Kong. They invited me to stay." Tara lit another cigarette, the tip glowing bright against the subdued lighting. "There was no conspiracy or hidden hand, just another decision made in the heat of the moment and repented at length…I finally placed the call. 'I'm ringing to enquire about the advert for the Volkswagen Golf.'

"'I have two available, do you prefer green or red?' replied the softly spoken voice, without the slightest hesitation.

"'Which has the lowest mileage?'

"'Let me check. Can you call back we're rather busy at the moment.'

"I rang back two hours later. 'The green Volkswagen has only done eighteen thousand.' It was the green light. 'Would you like to take the vehicle for a test drive? Where are you coming from?'

"'Manchester.'

"'I'll telephone you if it's sold before you get here. If you leave me a contact number.'

"I suppose that's how they found me," replied Tara philosophically, drawing a final drag from the cigarette, before flicking it into the ashtray.

"It's an amazing coincidence that you just happened to rent a house with a very large garage. Very bloody convenient."

"Believe what you want, Tom." A touch of weariness entered Tara's voice. "If there was any such forethought, it certainly didn't emanate from me. The operational significance of where I lived was entirely lost upon me. I didn't set out to look for a home to conceal a van loaded with explosives, if that is what you are suggesting."

"Yeah right."

Tara ignored my sarcasm. "In Manchester, I gradually began to relax and ghosts of the past began to fade. It came home to me during a lesson when one of the kids told me that his dad was a police officer. I shudder at the thought of what I may have done with that information had I still been in Ireland. I was appalled by what had happened to Sean. I didn't expect to encounter such anti-Irish sentiments. I suppose a bombing campaign on the mainland changes everyone's perceptions. Kathy could not understand why someone would want to hurt Sean. What could make a man hate someone with a different accent so much? It wasn't so difficult for me. That was when it struck me that there might be a connection with the Warrington bomb. I was lucky enough to stumble on that article in the paper. And then of course, I met you…"

How many times had I been back in that conference room as Tara handed me that newspaper cutting? The double-edged sword of emotion still glinted as sharply.

"In an odd way I felt sorry for Higgs. Our weaknesses were the same. Only my descent from victim to aggressor was swifter and more heinous." Tara stood and stretched her legs. "I never believed I'd be close to anyone else. I didn't deliberately avoid relationships, just that – like I said, my life was complicated." Tara looked faintly embarrassed.

"Spare me Tara please," I replied swiftly, gesticulating with my open palms. "I don't need your meaningless platitudes, and I will not be patronised." I stormed to the far side of the living room and stared aimlessly out of the window, watching her reflection draw slowly nearer. "I'm not here to bullshit you Tom, appease you or even justify what I have done. If you want the truth…"

"The truth?" I turned to confront her. "The truth is that if you had had one scintilla of genuine feeling for me…" I emphasised my words making a tiny gap between my thumb and forefinger, "…you wouldn't have assisted in the murder of my brother and then disappeared. I hate you." I wanted her to be angry, to provoke her, so that I could justify striking her. I wanted nothing more than to slap her hard across the face, to watch her recoil in pain, as if this would quell my grief. I was shouting and crying at the same time. Tara absorbed my insults. Why didn't she retaliate? After a couple of minutes of pacing and shouting, accusing and vilifying, I collapsed back into the chair.

Once my raging torrents had slowed to a pitiful trickle, she pressed on, tentatively. "You gave me a second chance – a world apart from my previous existence," she stumbled nervously, determined to force the words out. "I regret the deceit more than anything," she implored. "But how could I have been honest? Once I'd found you... I couldn't bear the thought of losing you."

"Perhaps you should have thought of that before..." I retorted coldly, at her honesty.

"I realised too late I couldn't build a life upon a foundation that simply didn't exist. No matter how far I ran, I could never escape. I would always have to pay a price." Tara looked pensive, her lips trembling, contemplating how to explain. I began to interrupt her but she pressed on regardless. "I wish we'd met under different circumstances. The guilt of what happened to Ben will always be with me." I felt solid impenetrable cold rock inside my heart, just hearing her speak his name.

"Your dead uncle, was that another lie?"

Tara nodded defensively, rubbing her eyes with her long slender fingers. "It was McDonnell – his cool, 'hello Tara.' It was as if we had only seen each other the other day. Until that moment, I retained this illusion of control, then the hopelessness flooded back. I could have said thanks but no thanks, that I was no longer interested, told him I had cold feet and a new life. Somehow the words wouldn't form. I wanted to scream no, but had no voice. All the old hates and fears, memories I had tried to suppress, flooded back.

"'Some lads need a place next week and the use of that garage of yours.' It wasn't a request. It was an order.

"I had become a classic sleeper agent. This was a plan that had obviously been on the drawing board for some time. Planned and prepared during the cease-fire. Only a handful of people would know the full details of the operation. Sleeper agents are told nothing. Then they cannot be compromised."

"You could have called the police," I reasoned somewhat naively.

"And said what, excuse me I am a former IRA activist, and some of my former colleagues are coming to pay me a visit. That would have been me for twenty-five years. My instinct for self preservation took over."

"How did they know to trust you?" I persisted. "You had buggered their software?"

"Two members of my family had died in the Troubles. They blamed Dave for the database. McDonnell trusted me. I'd kept my mouth shut over Mickey and Bridie and had only left after being implicated in a killing. I'd lain low and made contact when it was safe.

"Of course, I knew when they arrived they must have been planning a job." Tara was contrite – the shame visible on her face. "It has tormented my every waking minute since. But I had no idea what the target was."

"And that makes you less responsible?"

"No, of course not…" Tara said guiltily, wiping her eyes again and sniffing. "All I am saying is that there was no way of stopping whatever it was they had planned without exposing my past."

"So Ben died to keep your grubby little secrets. I hope it was worth it!"

"From the second that Kieran arrived at my door with Fraser Dennehy, I was paralysed with fear and inaction. In my worst nightmare, I never expected it to be Kieran. His broad grin sickened me as my mind flashed back to that New Year's Eve, when he emptied the revolver into Drummond's chest. It felt like another lifetime…" Tara's voice trailed off, as she nervously bit her fingernails. "Dennehy's a hard nut from outside Newry – a good tactician, proficient with firearms and explosives. The third member of the unit was another sleeper. I only knew his nickname: Charlie. It is standard procedure that we would be unaware of each other's identity, so in the event we were arrested we could not compromise each other. They drove the wagon into the barn under the cover of darkness. I never even ventured near the damn thing. I had no inkling that a bomb was being planned. My impression was that they were simply killing time. It could have been a dress rehearsal."

Tara closed her eyes momentarily, acknowledging her culpability, before pulling the final cigarette from the pack. "Perhaps I could have tampered with the detonators – done something. Anything.…"

Tara closed her eyes, her clenched knuckles turning white. "I stood in the bar, whilst you were in the toilets. Out of the corner of my eye, the TV captions grabbed my attention. 'BBC Live – Bomb in Manchester.' I can't begin to describe the depths of despair into which I plummeted." Tara wept uncontrollably. "If I'd stayed, it would only have made things worse."

"Tell me just exactly how you think my situation could have been any worse?" I demanded coldly. "You might have had the decency to have finished it," I said in disgust, "told me you didn't give a damn and walked away. I could have rationalised that, chalked it up to experience and moved on. Instead I woke up in a hospital bed alone. I spent months wondering what had happened – not knowing if you were dead or alive – searching constantly for what I'd done to drive you away, only to find out across a windowless interview room, from the smug shit that'd arrested me on suspicion of the murder of my own brother."

"All my life I've run away. I fled to the IRA, away from the life destroyed by the soldier's bullet. I fled from Ireland, unable to confront what I had become and take responsibility for my actions. I planned to slip away that night. As it happened, fate intervened."

"You told me once that drunken drivers were not fate – just stupid people, as I recall."

Tara's face broke into a coy, but short lived smile, her eyes narrowing slightly. "It's good to see that not everything I told you was wasted. I remember leaning the Zephyr slightly round the bend. The Montego appeared from nowhere, cutting me up as he slew onto our side of the road." Tara buried her head in her hands. "I heard this sickening sound, metal and squealing rubber, glass and bone. God, it was dreadful." She paused to wipe her eyes. "It all happened so fast, you both swerved at the last moment, the bike pirouetting – somersaulting in mid air." It felt strange to hear another perspective on the accident. For so long, it had been my own private nightmare. "I'm haunted by the image of you in my mirrors sailing through the air, arms and legs flailing, like a leaf buffeted by the wind. In the aftermath, there was just silence. It was eerie," she added. "Standing in the road – I felt cheated that you'd been hit and not me...."

Tara closed her eyes. "I have this vivid recollection of the blood stained face of the driver, sprawled awkwardly over the wheel, visible through the shattered windscreen, blood on the dashboard, inter-mixed with fragments of glass. I screamed at him. 'You bastard, you bastard

– I hope you're dead,' at the top my voice, until my chest hurt."

"Was I in the water?" Tara shook her head. I knew she was lying and I appreciated why, but was in no mood to be gracious and so let it pass.

"You were on the beach, out cold. I delicately removed your helmet and felt for your pulse."

"And then you just left me?" I accused her. "So long farewell – abandoned, injured by the side of the bloody road."

"It wasn't like that Tom. It took every ounce of energy I possessed to reach you and call 999. They kept asking my name and where we were and I couldn't remember. I was speaking gibberish. I lay by your side to wait, holding you close, closing my eyes and wishing this was just a nightmare. We'd wake up – no accident, no bomb and no pain. A couple of minutes later, engine noise nudged me back to reality. If I'd hung around, there would have been police and ambulances and questions and I don't think I could have coped. But you weren't alone. As the car slowed, I hid in the nearby trees. I watched as they lifted you onto a stretcher... I waited until everyone had gone, curled up into a ball ...I rode back to Manchester that night..."

"Picked up the MG and drove to Dover, took a ferry to France and 747 to JFK" I completed her sentence, sternly relaying the account I'd been given.

"Police told you?" I nodded. "I rang the hospital from Calais. I only found out about Ben on the TV." She closed her eyes tightly and put her hand across her mouth, squeezing her nose between her thumb and forefinger, her eyes red and swollen. "In a dingy hotel in downtown New York, around 4am, I swallowed a bottle of Paracetamol and drank a bottle of Jack Daniels, before cutting my wrists with a razor blade. The maid found me, a few hours later in a pool of blood." She offered me the evidence of her brutally scarred left wrist – a trophy of her remorse, but I couldn't look.

"If the maid had been an hour later, I'd be dead. I spent months cursing the efficiency of her cleaning schedule. I hadn't the courage to try again when they finally discharged me. I waited tables, switching off from life. The routine preserved my sanity." Tara ran her hands through her now dry blonde hair and held them at the back of her neck. "But I could never rest. Forever haunted by images of the accident and the bomb, consumed with guilt and remorse. Sitting in a dingy apartment in the dark, listening to the traffic and trains roll by whilst the neighbours quarrelled and their hapless kids dealt crack on the stairwells, I reached the end of the line. I reasoned life couldn't get any worse. I couldn't sink any lower." Tara lifted her head and fixed her rigid determined gaze upon me. "My first task was facing you." She allowed a hint of a smile. "I don't think the police, courts or prison can be any more difficult."

I glanced at my watch. It was almost 5am. "You'd better get some sleep." I fetched Tara a couple of blankets. I turned to leave the room, my head pounding and my brain whirling, my heart almost too heavy to support my movements. I watched her pull the blankets over herself and turned out the light. "I'm so sorry," she said.

I stood in the half open door as the first rays of dawn struggled to break free. "Words, Tara. You can repeat them all you like. It doesn't change anything."

Part Four

Chapter Twenty Nine

I BURIED MY head in the steering wheel, the engine still ticking over, minutes after Tara strolled confidently into the police station, with no apparent hint of nerves. After the faintest of smiles from her sleepless reddened eyes and a subdued, "goodbye Tom," she disappeared. Exhaustion hit me shortly thereafter. It was 9am. Tara had re-entered my life for just over twelve hours and vanished again like a ghostly apparition. Throwing one last glance towards the depressingly forlorn police station entrance, I nudged the Alvis into gear and pulled away.

By the time evening arrived, I had resolved to do three things. One – sleep. Two – I needed distance and perspective – space to get my head straight. I phoned Chambers, indicating there had been a family crisis, which wasn't far from the truth in light of the third thing I felt compelled to do – I had to tell Becky. After all, Tara had at least done me the courtesy of a face to face confession. I debated putting off the inevitable, but the longer I prevaricated, the worse the consequences would be.

Becky peered round her front door in surprise. My tired face gave away the seriousness of the situation. "You look terrible, like you've seen a ghost," she joked, beckoning me in, but motioning for me to keep quiet – she had just got Hannah off to sleep.

"You're not far wrong," I swallowed hard. "Last night, Tara reappeared." She ceased drinking her cup of tea mid gulp. "What happened? Where is she?" Becky's face was a mixture of curiosity and disapproval.

"She's gone again," I replied cagily, grasping for the appropriate words. "I escorted her to the police station this morning." I breathed deeply and then dived in head first. "Tara's wanted in connection with the bomb." There I'd said it. Becky's face was expressionless for a moment, then a picture of confusion and disbelief.

"Your Tara – not the Manchester bomb?" I nodded silently, and closed my eyes.

Becky was absolutely no different to me: craving answers, scanning the papers for scraps of information. You survive on a starvation diet of half rumours and intuition. All of a sudden you are force-fed with a mass of detail – impossible to digest in one sitting. Becky pulled up a seat – a look of complete desolation on her face. I saw myself reflected in her features. "I don't understand, how Tom why?"

I explained to the best of my abilities, attempting to convey what I had gleaned from Tara. Perhaps I was too harsh? After all, I'd had much longer to come to terms with the brutal truth. I might have heard it from her lips only the night before, but I'd known the stark headlines since my arrest. I remembered only too clearly my frame of mind incarcerated in that bare cell, overwhelmed with anger, sorrow and bewildering incomprehension.

After a few minutes, Becky stopped asking questions and began lashing out in vitriolic accusation and recrimination, shouting that Tara was a "sick murdering bitch." I longed to escape, unable to cope with watching Becky's anguish spill forth like black oil on a cream carpet. What could I say? I had flung precisely the same allegations back at Tara. Yet in a bizarre twist, the advocate in me, almost sought to defend her intent, reasoning her involvement in Ben's death was minimal compared with the evil of MacKenna, Dennehy and McDonnell.

I placed my arms around Becky, attempting to comfort her in our shared grief. For a minute, we swayed together, smarting in our mutual betrayal. Shortly thereafter Becky's mood changed. She berated me, pounding my chest with clenched fists, licking her reopened sores. My efforts to rationalise the situation were rebuked. "You shit," she screamed. "How can you defend her? Have you no shame?" Upstairs, Hannah stirred and began to cry.

"Let's just calm down." I didn't notice the palm of her hand until it was too late. Becky slapped me viciously across the face. I reeled backwards at the ferocity of the impact, only slowly regaining my balance. My cheek smarted with pain. Becky seethed with anger, her hair matted over her reddened cheeks, flushed with emotion.

"I'll calm down when you stop pissing on your brother's grave," she retorted. I picked up my jacket and left the house.

Had she hit a raw nerve? Was I vulnerable to the allegation that the mere act of questioning the degree of Tara's involvement was a betrayal of Ben? The lawyer in me could rationalise – mitigate on Tara's behalf. The brother and the jilted lover desired only to lash out. Later I rang my father, but he seemed more concerned about my betrayal, than his own grief. The pretence of parental concern masked their desperate pain. Did it mark a turning point that someone had finally been arrested? Perhaps justice could be done? But justice is a system, not a concept. No system would ever bring Ben back. When sleep finally descended, it was a blessed relief, my brain unable to cope with the swirling unresolved conflict of emotion.

I left Manchester early the following morning for Tenerife. Mainly I just sat on the beach, watching the orange sun set across the shimmering waves or drinking at anonymous bars, scanning the readily available English newspapers, for the inevitable story about the arrest of an IRA suspect in Manchester. Time to consider the thoughts crawling around in my head – from my dead brother to my terrorist girlfriend: ex-girlfriend, ex-terrorist? My stomach turned. Tara had the opportunity to prevent that bomb ever reaching its destination. A flat tyre might have been enough. I struggled so hard to reconcile the gentle, funny woman I had fallen in love with, with the twisted vengeful violent character that emerged from Tara's catalogue of horror.

After trials of the most heinous criminals, the culprit is frequently portrayed as an evil monster or a wicked inhuman animal. In order to work up the tabloid's sneering outrage, the perpetrator has to be utterly vilified, demonised and de-humanised. By stripping them of their humanity, we caricature them as distant from our moral respectability. Herman Hesse once wrote that if you hate an individual, you really hate something in that person that is part of yourself – it's seeing that trait in ourselves that frightens us.[3] Could I ever de-humanise Tara in this way, reduce her to a hate figure? I'd slept with her – loved her. Did that heighten my sense of betrayal or assist in understanding her actions? I was repulsed by the violence, consumed with animosity for the one visible face of my late brother's killer. Still, a haunting voice whispered in my ear: hadn't I ever been weak or lied in the interest of

---

3   Herman Hesse. German Novelist 1877-1962 Demain Ch.6

self-preservation? Not on that scale. Tara crossed a line into violence I doubt I would ever have followed. Perhaps her remorse was genuine? Sometimes that wasn't enough though. With all my heart I tried to hate her – and for a while I succeeded. By the time I sat sipping my gin and tonic on the plane home, I resolved to put the whole experience behind me and start afresh.

Saturday 11th January 1997

The Kippax stand was as packed and lively as ever; Maine Road hummed with anticipation, for the visit of Crystal Palace. It was a scrappy football game with few real chances. At half time, my mate Nick left the stand to grab a couple of coffees. I was leafing through the programme notes, contemplating how much colder it was in Manchester than Tenerife, when someone sat down beside me. I was about to ask Nick how he had managed to elbow his way to the front of the tea hatch so quickly, when I realised that it wasn't Nick. "Sorry mate. You got the wrong seat…"

"Your pal won't need it for a few minutes, Mr Flemming." I turned to see the face of the stranger who appeared to know my name. Not your typical football fan – expensive three-quarter length black leather coat. He had a strong firm jaw line, closely cropped dark hair and a very serious face. "You're a difficult man to locate," he commented, focusing unwaveringly ahead on the pitch through his silver rimmed glasses.

"Who's looking and why?" The conversation was becoming increasingly bizarre.

He spoke quietly, conspiratorially. "I've spent the last few days with your girlfriend. Or should that be ex…"

Things were becoming yet more surreal. "Why not try my bedroom," I growled sarcastically. "That's where you boys usually find me."

He ignored my obvious sarcasm. "Tara said we'd find you here. We were going to pick her up at the airport. Curiosity got the better of me. Touching she came to you first!"

"What's with the cloak and dagger shit?" I replied, growing a little impatient.

He leant forward, ensuring no one else could hear. "I'm responsible for a liaison task force between the Greater Manchester Police Special Branch, the Met's Anti-Terrorism Branch and the SIS."

"SIS?" The penny dropped. Secret Intelligence Services – MI5 had been given the leading role in co-ordinating intelligence against terrorism in Northern Ireland a couple of years previously. They had to give them something to do to justify the swanky offices, once it became clear that the Russians really weren't coming. "I didn't think you boys went in for inter-agency co-operation?"

A bemused smirk engulfed his face, along with a discernable tut. "You really shouldn't believe everything you read in trashy paperbacks. Let's cut the crap," he replied impatiently. "Plausible deniability. If you repeat one word of what I am about to say, I will personally ensure you're discredited as a grief stricken twat – understand?" I nodded, suddenly feeling just the slightest bit intimidated, like a pupil in the headmaster's study. "I'm offering you a once in a life time deal: National Lottery bonanza rollover jackpot. An opportunity to nail the others – you know whom I mean," he lectured curtly, removing his glasses. "We need your co-operation." He had a degree of earnestness, which pierced his offhand sobriety.

I was speechless. Mainly because I had absolutely no concept of to what he may have been referring. He reached into his wallet and pulled out a cream business card. I turned it slowly between my thumb and forefinger. "If you're interested, we'll talk some more. Don't wait too long Tom. Time is precious. Enjoy the game…"

Moments later Nick returned. "I don't bloody believe it," he cursed angrily, handing me the coffee. "Some moron told the plod I was carrying a knife. Not bloody funny."

"He was after your seat."

"What?"

"Never mind." For some strange reason, I struggled to concentrate on the second half. It's not every day that MI5, or whoever they were, comes to visit. I was still contemplating what it all could possibly mean when Tuttle scored an own goal on sixty-four minutes to put City ahead. But in typical Blues style, depression was the order of the day for the 27,395 fans that watched Ndah equalise on eighty three minutes.

Chapter Thirty

I DELIBERATED AT length that night – unable to sleep, my mind awash with the possibilities and pitfalls. Eventually, curiosity got the better of me, but I decided to hedge my bets, discover what was on the table and then take stock. After lunch, I dialled the number on the calling card. "What are you doing now?" asked the voice from the previous day. "There's a Little Chef on the A556 near junction nineteen of the M6. Be there in an hour."

"How will I find you?"

"We'll find you."

I waited only a couple of minutes before the black BMW pulled into the car park. The passenger door swung open and a thickset man emerged who wouldn't have looked out of place in the England rugby squad. "Mr Flemming?" He gestured for me to follow. I felt increasingly like I was trapped in a movie, where the hero gets taken in a black limousine to see the gangster boss in his luxury hideaway only to be shot, beaten up and left for dead.

The impressive eighteenth-century country house was not quite what I had expected. A young woman wearing jeans and a T-shirt opened the front door. "Hello." I didn't quite dare add *Miss Moneypenny*. She acknowledged my greeting without really responding, leading me down an exquisitely decorated corridor into a large kitchen. Finely polished copper pans hung around the ceiling, over the Aga, reflecting the dying embers of the sunset. The guy from the previous day was sat at the large oak table. He offered his outstretched right hand – his grip firm and masculine. He grinned broadly. *M, I presume*? "Haydon Powell. Good game?"

"I lost concentration during the second half."

"Sorry for the interruption. You want coffee?" he asked, pouring the steaming liquid into two mugs. His relaxed manner was quite disarming, compared with the day before.

"So this is where my taxes go," I commented, glancing around. "Not your average nick."

He continued to smile. "A haven from the storm made available for us at times like this."

"Is Tara here?" I asked, curious as to her location and involvement in whatever was being planned.

"You can see her shortly if you want. Your call…"

I confess to a degree of exasperation. "First, you accost me at a football game, then I am driven to the middle of nowhere by two guys on their way to audition for a Steven Seagal movie. Will you please tell me what the hell is going on?"

Powell cleared his throat, as he sat across the kitchen table. "Most pundits predict Major will call the election for the first of May. He's conned himself that the longer he leaves it, the better his prospects. Within months, we will have a Labour Government."

"Never trust opinion polls," I replied, but he'd already moved on.

"The peace process in Ireland is stalled. Major's majority is wafer thin. He needs the UUP's permission to wipe his own arse. There's no prospect of a new cease-fire before the election. There is no incentive for anyone to do jack shit. Instead they are jockeying for position and for what follows."

"Which is what?" I asked, intrigued by his musings.

"Sinn Féin will call a renewed cease-fire over the summer, if Labour gets in: long enough to show some steely defiance to their own supporters; short enough so Blair can claim a breakthrough. Then they finally get down to talking instead of shooting."

"Are you pissing in the wind or is this based on genuine intelligence?" I enquired, suspicious of his agenda.

His serious countenance dropped for a second at my irreverence. "It's an educated guess. The IRA will not renew their cease-fire until a day is set for substantive all party talks to commence. The Americans will push for Sinn Féin's inclusion. The IRA will announce a cease-fire a few weeks before the talks are due to commence to allow for a so called "de-contamination" period before the others will agree to suspend their moral distaste and negotiate. In public anyway – everyone knows we've been talking to them for years."

"If they really want peace, why blow up Docklands or Manchester?" I asked innocently.

"All political violence serves a political motive. Docklands concentrated the minds of the politicians. You play the game our way or else. The Government is coerced into action and the grass roots supporters are kept happy."

"What about decommissioning? They'll never hand over the guns – surrender and all that?"

"They'll fudge it. Blair will do just enough to stop the unionists walking away, and enough to keep Sinn Féin at the table."

The sceptic in me was not convinced. "You'll understand if I don't hold my breath for peace. Paisley will never make peace with Adams."

"They'll ignore him, if they have to. Do a deal with the more moderate UUP."

"And the chances of peace?"

Powell considered my question, sipping his coffee. "If they don't do it this time – that will be it for a generation. Another twenty years of a war that neither side can win."

"Where is all this going?" I asked, slightly impatiently.

"The politicians will deny this until they are blue in the face. We all have to make compromises. They declare a cease-fire – then nominally so do we. Imagine the peace talks reach crunch point. Crucial negotiations are in progress with both sides threatening to walk away. We do a midnight raid and arrest a known terrorist gang – not conducive to compromise. The delicate house of cards you have patiently constructed crumbles."

"Are you saying you won't arrest the Manchester bombers, if there's a cease-fire?" I spluttered, stunned by his apparent admission to complicity in doing bugger all.

Powell ignored my obvious disbelief, pressing on regardless. "There is a small window of opportunity. If we act quickly, we can apprehend the ASU who planted the Manchester bomb."

Powell led me out of the kitchen and back down the corridor into a study of sorts, lined with full bookcases, and a reproduction desk – the top inlaid with green leather. There was a French window, which looked out over the extensive and well maintained gardens. He fiddled with the lock on the desk and extracted a number of brown files. "Kieran MacKenna aged thirty four. Joined the South Armagh IRA at seventeen. Responsible for numerous shootings and bombings including the murder of Sergeant Peter Drummond." He paused for effect. "You've probably heard about DI McCleash?" I nodded silently. "MacKenna moved to the English Department during the course of the first cease-fire. He was a member of the unit that bought the truck in Lincolnshire, packed it full of fertiliser and drove into Manchester City Centre. From the security camera images, we have a probable identification of him as one of the men who abandoned the truck in St Mary's Gate." He tossed the file back on the desk, and picked up another. "Fraser Dennehy – gifted explosives expert. Approximately one third of the large explosive devices built in South Armagh in the last ten years have this guy's prints on. Also involved in three armed robberies in the Republic of Ireland. The RUC reckon he was responsible for killing three off duty soldiers with a booby trap bomb under their car after a fishing trip."

He tossed the file aside. "Dermot McDonnell, thirty five. Former head of the IRA Civil Administration Unit. Spent his time kneecapping and torturing informers." He mimed the shooting of a gun in the back of the head with this left hand. "Real nasty piece of work; moved after a botched execution of an alleged informer. He now operates from Dublin. He is one of the team that co-ordinates the English Department."

"Yet you let known terrorists walk the streets with impunity?"

"There's a huge difference between what I know to be true, and what can be proved to the satisfaction of a judge and jury. I wouldn't do anything to compromise the safety of an intelligence agent."

"Where does Tara fit in?" I asked.

Powell approached the cabinet in the corner and pulled it open revealing a bottle of Scotch. "Drink?" he asked pouring two small but equal measures into the cut glasses, before reclining in the armchair. "Intelligence sources predict a major escalation of the bombing campaign in the run up to the election. Put pressure on the British Government, to try and ensure concessions later on. We expect another spectacular, such as Manchester – a major propaganda coup prior to the election. Tara's agreed to help us."

"She's going to give evidence against them?" I guessed naively.

"One IRA member's word against three others? Now asking a jury to believe that despite her previous involvement, she wanted nothing to do with the bomb? She just happened to live in a place with a significant sized garage, but was unaware of the target. Even now, you're not entirely convinced that she is telling the truth?"

I contemplated this for a second. "What do you plan to do?" I enquired.

"In a few days she'll be quietly released."

"What?" I replied, in astonishment, nearly choking on my Scotch. I had never actually considered they might let her go. "Why?" My brain finally caught up with my mouth. "She's going back isn't she? Only this time working for you?" Powell nodded. "Where do I fit in?"

"Perhaps Tara had better explain."

Tara was seated on the far side of the sitting room. She rose as the door opened. It was ironic I had spent so long convincing myself I would never see her again. Yet here she was, walking towards me. How should I react? Resent her trying to involve me in her games or give her the benefit of the doubt? I did the latter simply by virtue of being tongue-tied. "Tom." In the old days there had been such warmth. Now she hung back, thrusting her hands uneasily into the pockets of her jeans, averting her eyes to the floor, casting nervous looks around the room, anywhere but in my direction. I felt like an awkward teenager. "Nice cell," I quipped petulantly.

Tara edged forward, ignoring my sarcasm. "I didn't know whether you'd come?"

I stood resolute in the middle of the room. "I'd convinced myself I'd never have to see you again." I didn't notice if she smarted at my brutal honesty and frankly I didn't care, such was the turmoil my brain had been plunged into.

"This is something I have to do," Tara said. I could tell she was both serious and earnest.

"Rejoin the IRA as a British agent?" Hearing it from Tara's lips didn't temper my sense of shock. I recognised the fiery stubborn determination in her eyes that I had once come to both love and loathe in equal measure.

Her voice was now frantic, but practical. "There's nothing left for me. I'm going to get ten to twenty years. Time to reflect – it's not enough to be sorry Tom, is it? I can't abdicate responsibility, stand by and watch another person die. If I help save the life of one person, maybe, it won't bring them back, but…at least I'm trying in some small way to make amends…." She stopped for breath and tried to gauge my reaction. "I turned a blind eye to what was going on, in the hope that it would all go away. That led to the death of a person I knew and hurt those I loved most in this world."

"It doesn't matter that Ben was my brother," I retorted coolly, my feet advancing, propelling me towards her. "You can personally castrate the fuckers with a spoon – guess what," I hissed like a coiled cobra. "It won't bring Ben back."

Tara closed her eyes, blocking out my hostility, leaning against the low window sill on the far side of the room, to the right of the grand fireplace. "Don't you think I know that? Not a day will pass when I will not regret my actions and the sequence of events that brought me to this place." She placed her hand on my upper arm, just beneath my shoulder and my will to argue was diminished. "Don't you want to see them brought to justice?"

"You're preaching to the converted," I insisted. "But Tara, he's gone and that's that. This is no game. If they discover what you are up to…"

Tara attempted to convey the impression that she was relaxed about the danger she was placing herself in, but I could sense her tension – she appeared edgy, her body rigid, as she tightened her grip, pressing her fingers into the flesh of my arm. "I've lost everyone I ever cared for: my dad, Patrick and you. Frankly, I don't give a shit." There was a brutal harshness in her words that I found chilling.

"You don't get it do you," I retorted, placing my hand on my chest. "It is all very well you playing the martyr, but what about me? I have already lost one person I loved to the IRA. Am I supposed to sit back and wait to view more gruesome pictures on my TV? Afraid to turn on the radio for fear of hearing the inevitable, whilst you run around playing secret agent to appease your own miserable guilt?"

Tara was offended at my questioning of the purity of her motives and slunk backwards, leaning against the fireplace. "Your call Tom: which is worse?" She fired the question back at me, her eyes ablaze. "Waking up to hear that some other poor sod is coping with the grief of another senseless death?"

I buried my head in my hands, sinking into an adjacent armchair. My head hurt. "They're using you, you know?"

Tara's frown dissolved, as she sensed a breakthrough – the faintest hint of a cynical smile beginning at the corners of her lips. "Of course they are. The police and security services don't give a shit about me. I'm expendable. Here's the rub, the antipathy is mutual. I'm using them too."

She misjudged me. I backed away, treading a path towards the door. "You do what you have to do – just don't expect me to stand by and watch." Suddenly, I felt very weary. My strength sapped. "You're asking too much. Whatever it is, do it alone. I hope it helps you sleep at night. God knows, you'll be the only one." With that I exited, pulling the door closed firmly. I didn't mean to slam it, but it was heavier than I supposed and clanked noisily behind me.

I wanted to run, but felt compelled to remain and stood with my back to the closed door. The wounded hot head in me would not entertain Tara, her clandestine activities, or her insidious new bedfellows. Yet a calmer wiser counsel emerged. If you walk away, you'll forever be haunted by the possibilities of what might have been. I didn't want another person to go through what Becky, my parents or I had been through. "Damn," I relented, opening the door again.

Tara was sitting with her arms folded. She looked up as I re-entered the room, an expression of either surprise or satisfaction observable on her face. Gone was the fear, the hunted animal, I had observed only days previously. It had been replaced by a weary sadness, like the wild animal that eventually becomes resigned to the confines of the cage. "Okay," I nodded wearily. "No promises. Just tell me where do I fit in?"

We drew two chairs close together. Tara leaned forward and began nervously. "I have to convince McDonnell I can be trusted, that I'm not suspected by the security services. I have maintained a low profile, respectable job and a steady relationship with someone above suspicion."

"Me?" I answered, already resigned to what I figured she had planned, shaking my head at the audacity of what was being proposed.

She nodded. "If he thinks that we are together…"

"It enhances your cover story. Our cohabitation makes you appear a loyal but safe pair of hands. Let's say you get enough information to put them away. What's the end game Tara?"

She raised her voice slightly, and I felt her stiffen at the implied criticism of her precious plan: "I have no crystal ball. The future is uncertain, but it's my only future."

I glanced out of the window into the black night outside. I could hear the wind howling around the gutters and a cold breeze blowing through, where the sash had been left ajar. "Well?" she asked, with a degree of subdued impatience.

"I'll think about it."

"So?" asked Powell, as he led me back down the corridor lined with paintings of long dead nobles, walking over highly polished, but well worn hardwood floor tiles – they exuded a patina which only comes with age. How many secrets and shady deals had these portraits been privy to, whilst hung on these walls?

"I want to see them tried, convicted and sentenced" I confirmed.

"So do I, but I won't risk undermining agents' covers to do that." We returned to his office and sat down.

"Meaning as long as Tara is providing useful intelligence titbits, you'll use her to your own advantage?"

"You make it sound so mercenary." Powell appeared a tad wounded. "We're talking about saving lives. Do you have any idea how valuable an intelligence asset Tara could be?"

"What if her cover is blown?"

"We always look after our own," he replied sternly. "It's in our best interest," he added.

"Assume she gets out alive. Then what?" I enquired more forcefully.

"If you are looking for immunity from prosecution, you can whistle. It's out of the question." He spoke slowly, emphasising its non-negotiability. "Anyway is that really what you want – Tara to walk away from all of this?"

I bit my tongue and thought for a moment. "You'll forgive me but my feelings about Mrs O'Neil are rather ambiguous. The prospect of her living under my roof is nauseating. A simple guarantee is all I ask. In the event that she ends up in court, the judge will be made aware before sentence is passed of anything that she's done to assist – a full and honest account."

"Is that your price Tom?"

"I don't have a price, as I can't be bought and don't really give a shit about you or her. Just indulge my sense of fair play."

"I'm wounded that you don't think we would," he replied seriously, but leaving me with the impression that he was being duplicitous.

I leaned forwards and was probably more aggressive than I intended. "I don't really give a shit how long she goes down for. I've not signed the

Official Secrets Act. You leave her high and dry – I might be tempted to go to the press. You can stick plausible deniability up your arse." I paused. "After all, my brother died. I don't care if the media brand me a crackpot. I could still kick up enough fuss to have you boys scurrying back into the dark corners you occupy."

Powell sat behind his desk, contemplating me, slowly rubbing the tips of his fingers together: "And if I agree, are you in?"

"Looks like I really don't have much choice."

"There's always a choice Tom."

The following Monday I attended at the offices of Stuart Barton & Associates, Solicitors – a small high street firm, with one solicitor. The associates amounted to one legal executive and a secretary. Stuart Barton operated out of an office above a row of shops in West Didsbury. It was all a far cry from the days we sat together in undergraduate law lectures daydreaming of fast cars, beautiful women and changing the world. Now I sat in his cramped office and slid the thin brown envelope across the table. "Bought a new bike yet?"

"Soon," I smiled. Stuart had sorted out the legal mess following the accident, including the money for the trashed Harley. "I need you to swear an affidavit and witness my will. You'd better read it Stu." He ripped open the brown envelope and pulled out the two documents I had drawn up. The first was an affidavit. I had studiously written a full description of my encounters with Mr Powell. I included a summary of everything Tara had told me, as well as all I had gleaned from the police on my arrest.

Stuart Barton, drinking partner and legal advisor, looked up from his reading glasses a couple of times, speechless, as I read the pin board in his office, stuffed with yellowing notes of legal events, which had long since past. When he had finished, I handed him a sealed letter. "In the event that anything happens to me, you are to follow the instructions in there."

"Do you have any idea what you are getting yourself into?" he cautioned me, as a friend and a client, his face a vision of gobsmacked disbelief.

I reflected on his question, giving it due gravity before speaking. "The truth: no. At least this way, my back is covered."

I had to tell one other person – my head of Chambers. Sitting in his room, trying to explain the impossible was no easier second time around. "Tara is alive. To all intents and purposes for the outside world's consumption, apart from my family, we will have the appearance of cohabiting." His desk had listened to some stories over the years – some genuine, others comprising the most elaborate and sophisticated deceit imaginable. None I'd wager were as bizarre as the account I revealed.

Bill paused to compose his response, counselling caution. "It's not your battle Tom."

"What would you do in my position?" I asked. "Would you really walk away?" For once, Bill had no answer. "This is without a doubt the toughest decision I've ever had to make. I don't see an alternative though. Not really."

Chapter Thirty One

THE MESSAGE ON the answer phone was curt and functional: I could expect a houseguest that night. I was unbelievably tense, nervously chain-smoking cigarettes I had in theory long since given up – pacing the floor like an expectant father in the maternity ward. Resentful for being dragged into a deadly game, with a woman I despised, yet reluctant for events to transpire without my involvement. I must be insane. Not only was I proposing to let my ex-girlfriend move in, but she happened to be a self-confessed terrorist and now, a double agent.

After numerous false alarms, Tara's MG pulled into view, freshly released from some anonymous police compound. Its arrival stirred echoes of the past, back to the Friday night before the bomb and the unpalatable chain of events that led me to this point. The sick thought ripped across my subconscious horizon like a jet fighter and then vanished from view. Tara stood on the doorstep, a holdall loosely over the shoulder, dressed casually in jeans and a T-shirt. Neither of us spoke until the door was firmly shut behind us. "I didn't know what time to expect you."

"They let me out this morning," Tara replied, dropping her bag to the floor. "I didn't want to come straight here – just sitting and waiting, listening for every creak on the stairs – I went into town. I haven't seen the city centre since…" Her voice trailed off. Neither of us particularly wanted to mention the 'b' word. "I had to buy some clothes anyway…"

"Some of your things are in the spare room. I rescued them from the cottage – it's all yours," I indicated awkwardly, laying down the parameters without emotion. "Put the MG in the garage. I don't want Becky discovering your car."

We sat at the kitchen table that evening – the dirty plates pushed to one side, comparing notes. "McDonnell's bound to be suspicious that you disappeared so suddenly after the bomb."

Tara spoke with grim determination. "I dread encountering them, immersing myself back into that world. Getting in will be no problem. I have a good cover story. It's staying sane afterwards that concerns me," she replied, somewhat distracted, twisting her hair around her index finger. There was a pregnant pause as we both contemplated what that might mean, before Tara asked hungrily. "Got any fags?"

"When will it end?" I asked, tossing the packet across the table.

"Either when I get them or they get me."

"Them? Is that the whole damn lot of them, or just the ones it's personal with?"

Tara deliberated. "As many as it takes. Every operation stopped is potentially another person free to live a normal life." In the fading light, her resolve burned ferociously and it disturbed me. Mistakes are made when the goal becomes more important than the risks taken to achieve it.

"And you? Let's say it all goes according to plan. Immunity for services rendered?" I asked, attempting to discern any difference between what we had been told.

"No Tom," she replied, not in anger, but melancholic introspection. "What's a couple of years remission off two life sentences?" It was difficult to conceal my cynicism, which bubbled to the surface. Giving Tara a hard time appeased my conscience, at least in part.

Tara retired to bed. I sat in the emptiness of my own kitchen reflecting on her physical closeness, contrasted against the overwhelming chasm that now existed between us. It was a strange twist of irony that I had longed for months in vain for her return, only to now have her sleeping under the same roof in these most peculiar and undesirable of circumstances.

There was a sense of unreality about the following days. Both of us were on edge, like soldiers anxious for the battle, apprehensive for the unknown. I tended to work late, staying out of her way. When we did communicate it was in monosyllables, a noticeable atmosphere of tension between us, each distinctly uncomfortable in the other's presence. In retrospect, I must bear the responsibility. When Tara finally left Manchester for Dublin we were barely on speaking terms.

The previous evening there had been a repeated knock at the door. We both nearly jumped out of our skins, consumed with nervous exhaustion in light of the strange environment in which we were immersed. It was Becky. My relief soon turned to panic. The consequences of her finding the two of us together made my blood run cold. Tara appeared next to me, her eyes darting nervously between me and the front door.

"Becky," I mouthed silently. I gestured for her to hide. I had neglected to consider how I would explain to my family that Tara had been released without charge, let alone why we were apparently cohabiting. I could hardly explain Tara was a double agent. Becky, looking somewhat uncomfortable, stood on the doorstep. Excellent timing, why couldn't she have waited until tomorrow?

"I was out of order the other night," she began, walking into the kitchen and laying her handbag on the table. "It was just such a shock. I got to figure it must be worse for you – the total betrayal…why the hell did you beat yourself up over that sick bitch?" I wanted to level with Becky. Yet no more than a few feet away, Tara was eavesdropping on our entire conversation. Why should that bother me? After all, I had not concealed my views from Tara. Still I hesitated awkwardly. "Becky," I began. "I know how you must be feeling…"

She interrupted me. "I shouldn't have taken it out on you." She sat down and appeared deflated. "I go a few days convincing myself I'll be okay. I immerse myself in looking after Hannah and work." She clenched her fist as she spoke. "Then suddenly I'll hear someone speak on the radio or I'll be reading a book, or look into Hannah's tiny face and they all scream Ben. The façade of normality crashes. I feel like a rubber band that's been twisted and twisted inside until I'm so knotted up that I want to explode." I suddenly felt very guilty, the sorrow all too obvious on her face.

"I know how hard this is for you," I said. "But trust me you're not the only one."

Becky nodded an acknowledgment. "Yeah." I stuck to the comparatively safe ground of banality, pouring her a cup of tea. We sipped in silence, sealing our reconciliation. If you could call it that, in light of who was hiding in the spare room.

"What I can't understand," queried Becky, placing her mug down on the coffee table, her brow deeply furrowed, "is that there has been nothing in the news about her arrest?"

I was now trapped between a rock and a hard place. I hated the deception. "You hear about these kinds of things all the time," I lied. "It will take days, maybe weeks to debrief her. The RUC people will have to come over to interview her. And they will want to keep it quiet – her compatriots will do a runner if they hear she has been arrested." It was a flash of inspiration, and not a million miles from the truth.

"Have you heard anything further?" she enquired, searching for further snippets to help her comprehend, to deal with the enduring grief.

"I haven't heard anything and neither do I expect to. Tara came here, seeking I don't know what – confession or absolution?" I replied, abandoning any pretence I could walk a tight rope between both Becky and Tara. "I listened to her story and then politely showed her the door. She left me remember – walked away, and now I am glad she did. She can reflect on that from behind bars. I never expect to see her again."

After Becky had left, Tara ventured into the kitchen. "Is the coast clear?"

"Yeah," I handed her a beer from the fridge. I sure as hell needed one.

Tara shook her head. "No more alcohol. I'm going to need a clear head."

She poured a glass of water and twisted it pensively in her hand, musing on what she had overheard. "Was all of that true?"

"You wouldn't be standing here if it was." Had I wanted to hurt Tara as well as reassure Becky?

"You sounded very convincing," Tara said, clearly smarting – wounded, but not surprised.

"I could hardly tell her the truth," I replied, defensively, sensing her unease.

"I guess not," she agreed reluctantly. "Did you have an argument?"

"You could say that," I replied, taking a long cold swig from the bottle.

"What happened?"

"Trust me you really don't want to know." I tried to close the conversation, knowing where we were heading, but to no avail.

"I do, if it concerned me."

"Don't push it Tara." I finished the beer and placed the empty bottle firmly on the kitchen worktop. "She called you a sick murdering bitch. I tried, for a reason, which now escapes me to defend you, at which point she accused me of pissing all over my brother's grave. And the sad fact is she wasn't far wrong." I let my cruel jibe hang in the air, and walked out of the room. Twisting the knife in Tara's direction seemed to appease the guilt I felt for my involvement in this entire escapade.

By the following evening the house was empty, although the MG was still hidden in the garage. This is going to sound strange, but after her departure an uneasy feeling of regret remained. The following weeks can aptly be described as amongst the slowest in my entire existence. A week after her departure, I began to fear the worst. I imagined unspeakable horrors in those lonely hours, unable to share my fears. Despite my outward animosity, my grief and bitterness became less important than her physical safety. Was that the first milestone?

The call came in Chambers, late one Thursday evening. "Tom. It's me." A wave of relief enveloped me. Whatever else I felt, I was glad she was alive. It was impossible to discern from the tone of her voice whether she had been successful, over the background noise from the public phone. "I'm in Dublin. I'm catching the ferry back to Holyhead. I'll catch a train back. Thought I ought to warn you…" Her tone was abrupt, apprehensive, clearly anticipating I would be less than enthralled at the prospect of her return. The opposite was in fact true.

"I'll pick you up" I insisted. In contrast to my previous reluctance to be in her presence, now I was offering to spend three hours in a car with her. Tara didn't object.

The wind seemed to blow relentlessly off the Irish Sea, ushering in a chill that blew straight through my T shirt, shirt and thick coat, as if they comprised little more than a string vest. Riding a bike in January was warmer than this. I bought a coffee at the passenger terminal and waited for the early morning ferry to dock. I sipped the insipid liquid, listening to the squawk of seagulls and watching the dot on the horizon grow into a monster car ferry.

My eyes scanned the faces as they emerged from the ferry, looking for Tara. I failed to recognise her at first – the upturned collar of her overcoat obscured the lower portion of her face. Her pace quickened once she spotted me – her steps were more assured. In an exaggerated gesture, she slipped her bag from her shoulder and flung her arms around my neck, pressing her cheek against my chest. I confess surprise and apprehension at her apparent enthusiasm, given the terms of our parting. "Kiss me, now!" she hissed. When I hesitated, she put her hands on my cheeks and moved to kiss me and whispered innocuously. "And look like you're enjoying it. We're being watched." Taking the cue, I tightened my grip around her waist and kissed her hard on the mouth. There was a strange familiarity in her feel and taste, accompanied by a disturbing repulsion and a sense of violation. I played along. "Darling, it's so good to see you," I said, squeezing her hand.

She smiled back warmly as we exited towards the car park, grimacing through clenched teeth. "Don't overdo it."

Once out of earshot, I complained. "What the hell was all that about?" I unlocked the door of the Alvis, desperate for the inadequate heater to warm up.

"I was followed," she replied, yawning and slipping into the passenger seat. "IRA guy called Collins, just keeping tabs. Making sure my actions conformed to the lies I've been pedalling." Before I could probe any further, Tara's eyelids became heavy and it was obvious she was struggling to stay awake. Long before we exited Anglesey and picked up the A55, she was fast asleep. I dropped her at the house after exacting the promise she would reveal all that evening. Right after she had reported in to her new paymasters.

Once accustomed to the idea Tara was alive, my repugnance towards her, which had faded over past weeks, reared up again like an ugly serpent that tied my tongue and froze my ability to think of anything other than Ben. A constant wrestle ensued between guilt, and reassurance that what I was doing was right. It was Tara who broke the ice, as we were clearing away after dinner. "I was surprised you volunteered to collect me – thanks anyway." She looked better for some sleep, if moderately jaded. She had lost weight, her clothes appearing to hang more loosely off her slight frame than previously. The confidence and self belief that had once attracted me to her now appeared tarnished and weathered with fatigue.

I tried to convey the impression it was no big deal. "No problem – the least I could do." Her doubtful probing expression made me feel distinctly uncomfortable. Tara lifted the saucepan off the draining board and wiped it dry, before replacing the tea towel on its hook.

"I know having me around isn't easy. I'll stay out of your way as much as possible," she replied, as we moved though to the living room. "I've tried to be honest. You know things about me that no one else alive knows. It would make this a hell of a lot easier, if you would level with me occasionally, no matter how painful."

The devil on my left shoulder desired to rant and rave, wave my pitchfork and lecture her that she had no right to request anything. The angel on my right shoulder was more conciliatory. I ran my hands through my hair and sighed internally, bowing my head and closing my eyes tightly. "The truth is I am consumed with guilt that I am even speaking to you, let alone pretending to be cohabiting. I have only to think of Becky and my parents and the resentment wells up. I convinced myself that I hated you. But in the last few weeks I have lain awake worrying – tortured by horrible scenarios of your demise. If I hated you, I'd take a perverse pleasure in that – wouldn't I? Instead, I willed you to survive. Now I even feel guilty about that," I added, shaking my head. "The last few weeks have given me nothing if plenty of time to think. Not that I have reached many definitive conclusions. I do however, owe you an apology."

Her curiosity aroused, Tara stopped fidgeting with the TV remove control and blinked, her eyes opening wide in surprise. "You say this isn't easy for me, what I failed to appreciate is how bloody difficult this is for you. Coming back here and having to face me. Let alone having to go out and face them. I had the opportunity to walk away from this – I didn't. I agreed to this charade, now I have to live with it."

Tara looked away, a subdued expression on her face – tinged with guilt. "I should never have put you in this position. I hadn't really thought through the implications."

"I made the decision remember."

"I made it difficult for you to refuse," she confessed. Now who was being honest?

"The fact is our interests coincide," I reasoned. We sat in silence until I poured a couple of Jamesons. "Here's to success and civility then." For the first time, there was just the slightest hint of warmth between us.

"Truce?" I replied.

"Truce."

I sat there for a moment, contemplating the golden liquid, and her, the embodiment of my guilt, grief and now hope. "Are you going to tell me what happened then?"

Chapter Thirty Two

ONCE IN DUBLIN, Tara had checked into a cheap hotel just north of the city – a five minute walk from the heart of city centre, Temple Bar and the shops on Grafton Street. Rising early, she forced down a piece of fruit and two cups of strong coffee at an anonymous café. From there she walked across the city to the Sinn Féin office, where she handed in a letter to the receptionist. "Make sure that Dermot McDonnell receives this."

"Who?" replied the woman without any real conviction, "I'll be waiting." How long before he would receive her simple note. *'Meet me outside the Post Office, O'Connell Street. Any day 1pm: Tara O'Neil.'*

For the next three days, Tara browsed in shop windows along O'Connell Street, as 1pm approached, sauntering past the rendezvous point, keeping in step with the lunchtime crowds, ambling past tourists snapping photographs by the memorial to Pearse, Connolly and others. She hadn't expected McDonnell to show for the first few days. He was nothing if not a consummate professional. Anyone could have left a message as part of a set up, to lure him into the open. She waited until 1.30pm each day before slipping quietly away.

On day four, the switch was flicked from pause and the action began. A figure emerged from a side street and fell into step a couple of paces or so behind her. He was just a little too eager. The hairs on the nape of Tara's neck stood erect and the adrenaline kicked in. Her heart rate increased. It wasn't McDonnell – he was too tall. He was young and inexperienced. Quickening her pace slightly, Tara veered towards the shop window, pretending to glance at the display, ignoring her own reflection and concentrating on the shadow behind her. She turned left down a side street and quickly darted left again into a back alley, back firmly against a fire escape. It took a split second for him to appear into view. *"History teaches us that the tactical use of surprise can outwit an enemy who believes he is prepared or whose guard is down, as in the German invasion of France in 1940 via Belgium, the Netherlands and the Ardennes Forrest by-passing the Maginot Line…"* How many times had she given that class? Before he had an opportunity to orientate himself, Tara thrust her knee forcefully into his groin. He gave a muffled cry, and doubled over, wincing in pain. Tara lunged, pushing him firmly against the wall, digging her elbow into the left side of his ribs. "Know what this is?" she hissed, gesturing with her eyes towards the bulge in her jacket pocket and its familiar threatening shape. "Piss me off and I'll use it." He nodded, anxious not to antagonise this apparently armed, but unpredictable psychotic bitch. "Why are you following me? No bullshit," she cautioned him, with a quick flick of bulky pocket in his general direction, which contained nothing more than a plastic imitation.

"Dermot got your message," he squealed, blurting the words out through his throbbing ribs.

"Why didn't he come himself?" she retorted, refusing to ease her grip.

"I don't fucking know. Ask him yourself."

"What did the tosser tell you to do?" To emphasise the question, she prodded the replica towards his belly.

"Alright, I was supposed to find out where you were staying and report back."

Tara pondered a response. "Okay, errand boy – give the useless cocksucker a message: Robbie O'Shea's place tomorrow night. No address till at least the second date. I'm not that kind of girl. Oh, and anyone else tries following me, I won't ask questions." Tara waved her coat pocket in his general direction. With that she relaxed her grip and he scampered away, shaking his head incessantly.

Robbie O'Shea's place was not the most salubrious of public houses in Dublin. It was situated in a basement, which you entered via a set of steep steps, descending into the darkness, before entering the warmth of slopped beer and ageing tobacco smoke. The décor was simple but

A Bold Deceiver • James Hurd

authentic – not mass-produced in Burton upon Trent. Tara ordered a drink. Sipping Guinness she waited, eyes glued to the door at the far side of the room. She watched the young couple flirting at the adjacent table. It aroused a distant yearning for better times. No time for sentimentality – focus on the job at hand. It was nearly 11pm before McDonnell arrived. Tara recognised the swagger – slow and deliberate. The same closely cropped dark hair and skinny frame supporting those same cold penetrating eyes, protected by thin framed glasses. McDonnell surveyed the room, as he waited for the thick black liquid to settle at the bar, before sauntering in her direction, dressed in black jeans and a dark shirt. He placed his leather jacket on the adjacent chair and sat down opposite her, withdrawing a cigarette. He breathed in and slowly exhaled, before breaking into a conceited meticulous grin. "I knew you were for real when Davey said you had called me a cocksucker. You scared the fucking crap out of him."

Tara felt no need to respond and smiled, concealing the cold nausea, which hearing his voice induced. "Good to see you Dermot, been a long time."

"Where the hell have you been? There was a rumour you'd ended up in a training camp in the Bekka Valley?"

"Let's just say, I've seen a bit of the world," she replied, doing nothing to dispel the rumour. McDonnell sipped his beer, watching her every move closely.

"You wanted to see me?"

Tara nodded discretely, without apparent emotion. "It's the right time, now the heat's off." She spoke in a carefree throwaway manner, as if asking a stranger the time.

"Let's take a walk." They left their drinks unfinished. Away from the risk of being overheard, against the backdrop of passing traffic, McDonnell cautioned her. "Perhaps you've forgotten the rules. General Order Number One: *Membership of the Army is only possible through being an active member of an army unit or directly attached to HQ. Any person who ceases to be an active member of a unit or working with General HQ automatically ceases to be a member of the Army. There is no reserve in the Army. All volunteers must be active.* You've been away a long time."

"Don't bullshit me, Dermot. I know the bloody rules," Tara argued, as they passed under the shadow of a street lamp, her collar turned upwards against the cold. "The first duty of every volunteer is not to be apprehended by the enemy. I left Ireland because Kelley and Spender screwed the Drummond job, making me the most wanted woman in Ireland 1994. I did as instructed, by you, if I recall correctly." Tara paused, casting a sideways glance, her breath visible as she exhaled. McDonnell remained impassive and emotionless. "I disappeared and laid low. At your suggestion, I chose to settle in England and got myself set up well there. No one suspected I was anything other than Miss Goody Two-Shoes teacher. First major operation, your boys botched it."

"The operation was a perfect success," he replied flatly, without emotion, as they waited to cross at a set of traffic lights.

"The bloody idiots drove a seven and half tonne truck through the village and up my drive with Jack Roberts Transport splashed across the side. All it would have taken is a quick coat of paint."

McDonnell grunted. "It was the middle of the night, as I recall. Anyway, you're here aren't you, what's the big fucking deal?"

"The big fucking deal, as you put it, is that the truck was seen by my next door neighbour, who was woken by the noise," Tara remonstrated, reaching for a cigarette. "Couple of days after the bomb he started making noises about seeing a wagon matching the description. I was tipped off by one of the other neighbours who thought the old bigot had just had too much to drink. Great job boys." Tara mimed mock applause, cigarette in hand, sending smoke up in waves like a bonfire night sparkler. "What if the old sod went to the police? Every peeler in Manchester would have descended on me."

"What happened," McDonnell asked, with only a passing interest, his eyes resolutely focused on the pavement ahead, searching for prying eyes.

Tara took a deep breath and hoped her lies appeared convincing. "I had no choice. If I had stayed the risk was just too great."

"Where'd you go?"

"Got myself on a teacher exchange programme and taught in Boston for six months. I arrived back just before Christmas."

"You've been back?" McDonnell asked – his curiosity aroused at the possibilities opening in front of him.

"Back – I live there. I managed to salvage the situation. My cover remains firmly intact."

"You flew back into Manchester?" he asked incredulously, watching her intently, his interest stirred.

"I tell you its sweet. No one is the remotest bit interested in me. Well almost no one."

"Meaning?"

"Meaning, I have the perfect cover story. Not only am I teaching nice middle class English kids, the guy I'm living with is a respectable lawyer. I tell you I'm above suspicion." Tara laughed, fabricating pride in her accomplishments.

"Same guy as before?" McDonnell enquired.

Tara nodded a confirmation with a hint of coyness. "He has no idea I left for any other reason than to teach abroad for a while – opportunity of a lifetime."

"What do you want from me?"

Tara selected her words with caution, leaning towards McDonnell, her eyes glistening with determination. "I've always let others make the operational decisions, accepted orders and did what I was told. Drummond, Manchester, even Bridie McDonagh. Twice that has almost cost me everything. Now I have the advantage of a brilliant set up in England. There's an election coming. Let's send the Brits a message: if they want peace they can stare at it, down the barrel of my rifle."

McDonnell weighed her words, careful not to reveal any indication of his views. If he was unnerved by the reference to Bridie he concealed it well. He clasped his hands together in the cool evening air. "It's not my decision. You would need the approval of the Army Council."

Tara commanded herself to refrain from appearing desperate – making a conscious effort to remain forthright but calm. "Bullshit. General Order Number Three only applies in the case of a dismissal or resignation. Enforced absence does not count. I know the territory and have a perfect cover. And your boys owe me after last year's cock up." Her final words lingered in the air like a noxious odour.

"I'll be in touch," McDonnell replied, apparently unmoved, over the backdrop of the passing traffic.

"How?"

It was his turn to smile triumphantly. "Davey followed you yesterday. He even knows your room number."

A week later, Tara drove her hire car into an industrial part of town, once dominated by factories, now falling into disrepair. She replayed the story she told McDonnell, re-checking there were no obvious blunders. Satisfied, she left the car unlocked. In the event of a hasty retreat, she reasoned it might save a few vital seconds, mindful of the numerous movies where the dumb blonde fumbles and drops the car keys, as her assailant approaches. The gate was unlocked as per instructions. Tara examined the cracked panes of glass in the small windows and cracking brickwork. Close up, the warehouse yielded its secret: an empty shell, exposed on one side to the elements. Tara trod carefully across the tumbledown pile of bricks into the large empty floor space, strewn with rusting hulks of iron that echoed the desolate ghosts of activity past. The wind blew through the empty space, whistling softly. A stagnant pool of water dominated one corner, trickling from a leaking pipe, polluted with the unmistakable floating sheen of waste oil and industrial effluent. At the base of a set of wooden steps, Tara placed her foot on the first riser. It cracked, rotten with age, the noise reverberating through the exposed rafters. "You'll have to use the ladder," called a hauntingly familiar voice. Kieran MacKenna stood some ten feet above her, looking down. "Stairs are bust."

"Whose bright idea was this shit hole?"

Kieran twisted his nose into the air. "Didn't think we'd be seeing you again," he taunted, with enough rancour to rile, without being openly confrontational.

"What the hell does that mean?" Tara snapped, rising to the bait, placing her foot on the first rung of the rusting ladder.

"I thought after the last job you'd gone native," Kieran retorted, with obvious sarcasm. Tara squared up for battle like some medieval ritual. "You've got a bleeding cheek. If you hadn't ballsed it up in the first place."

"What the fuck are you on about?" he asked defensively, grabbing her arm as she stepped off the top of the ladder.

"You may as well have painted, 'IRA Active Service Unit Tour 1996,' down the side of the truck. You could have cost me thirty years."

"Bollocks O'Neil, you panicked because you can't stand the heat. Just like Drummond. I practically had to drag you away."

"Selective memory Kieran," Tara replied sharply. "They were supposed to use someone anonymous. Instead every bloody clubber was busy giving detailed descriptions of me to the peelers – I took the risk, not you."

"Alright children." McDonnell emerged from the shadow of the dim light below them. "Glad to see you've reacquainted yourselves."

Tara nodded an acknowledgement to Fraser Dennehy, his slender five foot seven frame slouching a few feet behind McDonnell, his hands shoved deep in the pockets of his leather jacket. Dennehy stroked his three day stubble, spat out his chewing gum and shook his head. "Always the bloody same, you pair. You're both alive – what more do you want?"

McDonnell grunted in agreement, as he clambered up the wrought iron ladder, up to the first floor landing into what would once have passed for an office, now contaminated with rotting plaster and stale urine. "You never mentioned working with him," Tara harangued McDonnell, thrusting her accusation in Kieran's direction – hoping her controlled hostility would enhance her credibility.

"You want in – my terms. Otherwise you know where the door is. Either bugger off or deal with it," McDonnell growled at the pair of them. He placed his palms flat on the table, ensuring he had their attention before commencing the briefing. "Northern Command is holding a de facto cease-fire. Sinn Féin can do well in this election. McGuinness can unseat Rev McCrea and Adams can regain Hendron's seat in West Belfast. Too many fuck-ups back home cost votes – hence the de facto cease-fire."

"Politics is bullshit," grunted Fraser, lighting a cigarette. "The British only understand one thing." He mimed firing a gun with his first and second fingers. "What did we get last time?"

"Eighteen months of inaction," added Tara. "The British aren't serious about disengaging. Let's not fall into another trap." There followed a general nod of approval around the table. "There will be no new cease-fire," cautioned McDonnell. "Not unless there are some major bloody concessions. Like the withdrawal of all occupying forces."

"I'd rather bomb the buggers out," smiled Kieran chillingly, leaving those gathered in no doubt of his sincerity.

"Here's your chance," replied McDonnell. "The Army Council have authorised a major offensive in England prior to the election." He made eye contact with each of them. "You have been entrusted to carry out this operation. So put your petty differences behind you. Fraser, Kieran." He glanced to each in turn. "I'll say this, so there is no misunderstanding. Not painting out the lettering on the truck from the Manchester job was sloppy." The two men averted their faces from his stinging criticism while Tara gloated with satisfaction. "However, there were mitigating circumstances. The truck should have been parked at

Charlie's place where the fertiliser was loaded, until the day of the job. However, the premises was fingered in some trumped up stolen vehicle racket, by some squealing little grass, anxious to ingratiate himself with the police. The truck had to be moved at very short notice." McDonnell turned to lecture Tara. "I authorised the truck to be moved. If you have a problem, take it up with me – not them." McDonnell nodded towards Kieran and Fraser. "You played it by the book and used your initiative to disappear. In doing so you preserved your covert identity." There was a moment of contemplation as each licked their wounds, concealing their obvious satisfaction at the others' dressing down.

"The British will not be allowed to ignore the situation in the six counties. Our objective is to make Ireland the number one issue – to remind them every day there is unfinished business. There will be no screw-ups: maximum disruption, minimum embarrassment. In a war there will always be casualties. Let's just not hand the enemy any propaganda coups. Understood?"

There was a reluctant acceptance around the room, amid unease that the Armalite appeared to be subservient to the ballot box – at least for the moment. "Targets?" asked Kieran, anxious to get back to plotting mayhem.

"Motorways, railway stations, shopping centres and other high profile events. We'll spice it up as polling day gets closer," he added, with a hint of pleasure. "Let's make election day go with a bang."

"What about equipment? They will be watching Stranraer, Holyhead and Liverpool like hawks." Fraser injected a dose of sombre practicality.

"The British cling to a mind set that sees the threat only across the Irish Sea – a lesson for all of us. The gear will arrive from the continent, via Dover or Folkestone and go to Charlie's place." McDonnell spoke with unbridled triumph at the thought of outwitting the enemy. He rounded on Tara. "You select the preliminary targets, undertake the reconnaissance. You," he nodded at the other two, "will rendezvous in England in six weeks and make the final selections. Then you wait for authorisation from the Army Council."

"Are we the only unit on the mainland?" asked Tara, attempting to glean useful information.

"There's a secondary unit in London." McDonnell looked pensive before adding, "but you will be the primary unit. Security is not quite so tight in the North."

A Bold Deceiver • James Hurd

They stood to leave – the meeting finished. "Still sleeping with the enemy Tara?" probed Kieran, barely concealing his glee at her discomfort.

"Leave Tom out of this," she replied, her cheeks flushing red with anger.

"Heaven help the poor sod who crosses you," he laughed sarcastically.

"What the hell are you going on about?" asked McDonnell in ignorance.

"She's shacked up with this guy right," laughed Kieran, "who has no idea who blew up his brother!" With that they all begin to smirk, as the penny dropped. Tara forced a smile, desperate to retain her shaken composure, as her stomach turned.

Back in her hotel room, Tara was gripped by the twin emotions of euphoria and exhaustion, as the adrenaline that had sustained her, ebbed away. She slept for a few hours in the late afternoon. When she awoke, loneliness and desperate isolation had replaced her initial relief at survival. Checking out of the hotel, she drove north out of Dublin. One benefit of the former cease-fire was comparatively relaxed security on border crossings. Emotion consumed Tara as she slipped unnoticed into Northern Ireland soon after midnight. Driving familiar roads, she watched her speedometer nervously, anxious not to draw unwanted attention to herself.

It was almost 1am, by the time she pulled to a halt. Cold air infiltrated the open door. The temperature was below freezing. Tara exhaled clouds of vapour as she approached the churchyard of St Mary's Parish Church. A place of mixed emotions: having both been married to and buried her husband within the confines of these walls. The spire of the church was black and impenetrable, against the dark night.

Finding the wrought iron gate closed, she clambered over the low wall, dropping effortlessly to the other side, clutching the flowers purchased from the all night service station. Tara navigated a route between the headstones by the moonlight. At the graveside, she carefully arranged the flowers on the hard stone, slippery to the touch, as the night dew froze. She traced her finger over the fine grooves, one letter after another: Dr Patrick O'Neil 1964-1991. She tried to conjure up his smiling face, but the only image she recalled was the pale, lifeless corpse lain out in the mortuary. "I'm so sorry," she whispered in the darkness, gently stroking the headstone.

On the other side of the churchyard, her parents lay – reunited side by side. In front of her father's grave, Tara recalled her vision of the dying Drummond. "Is this what you wanted?" she asked. Huddled against the gravestone, she felt peace through the numbing cold. Her resolve not to run away, however great the temptation, bolstered. As the first rays of dawn appeared on the horizon, she slipped away, nursing the car south, through the freezing mist, towards the ferry terminal.

Chapter Thirty Three

I CONFESS DEEP unease regarding the state of affairs confronting me during the spring of 1997. Fearful of giving succour to terrorism, under my very roof, a plot was being hatched to wreak havoc on an unsuspecting public. The fact that information was relayed to a covert police task force didn't appease my sense of distaste. When Tara had first told me that she had been assigned the task of choosing and scouting out targets, I went ballistic. Informing on the IRA was one thing, playing an active role in their nasty little plans was another altogether. The former offended my moral sensibilities less. It had never occurred to me that Tara would be required to immerse herself into active terrorism, planting bombs and firing guns. It was both perverse and macabre. I refrained from indicating my feelings in the interests of our newly forged truce. Tara however, sensed my negative vibes. "It's not really me making decisions about targets," she reassured me.

"Oh?"

"The initial list is being drawn up with a little help from Haydon and others."

"Let me get this straight. Our own security services are going to assist you in picking targets for the IRA?" I asked incredulously, shaking my head in disbelief. "The whole world has gone absolutely insane."

"It allows us to select targets with a reduced risk of civilian casualties and where there is a possibility that covert surveillance could be used," she replied, with a bemused smile.

"You're going to film them in action?"

"It's one option under discussion – think that would stand up in court?" Tara asked, with a glint of satisfaction, at the prospect of such an elaborate sting.

For the next few weeks, we trod water in a phoney war, waiting for the real battle to commence. True to both of our words, we remained civil. As the days passed, I gradually came to terms with the necessity of her presence and the atmosphere of recrimination, imperceptibly at first, began to subside. Tara also relaxed her guard, as I no longer sulked around the house, picking a fight at every available opportunity. We were thrown together in collective alienation, isolated from the world outside, living in a constant pressure cooker.

We knew MacKenna and Dennehy might arrive unannounced any day, champing at the bit to resume their campaign of terror. One night in mid-February, unable to sleep, my mind churning like a washing machine on overload, I headed for the kitchen in the dark. My mouth was dry and in desperate need of water, the pale moonlight illuminating my path. "Can't sleep either huh?" Tara sat at the table, glass of water in hand, my old bathrobe pulled around her, as I swigged from a bottle straight from the fridge.

"I didn't see you there," I replied, in surprise, spilling water down my T-shirt.

"A case or this?" she asked.

"Sorry?"

"Keeping you awake."

"A mixture of everything – I hate all this uncertainty. You?"

"I'm stuck between a rock and a hard place: torn between Powell and his cronies and maintaining my credibility within my unit," Tara complained, draining her glass thirstily. "I'm trying to ride two horses at the same time. Haydon is advocating a strategy of not planting any actual explosive devices. He thinks it's enough to make a hoax call and then sit back and wait."

"Maximum disruption, but minimum casualties, right?"

"No bomb, no casualties. But it will never work. If you cry wolf too often, people stop listening. Once the authorities think the IRA is not serious, then they have lost their most potent weapon. After a couple of hoax calls, they'd scale down the security alert. Kieran and Fraser would never buy it. It would be seen as a sign of weakness."

"Are they pressurising you?"

"Trying, but it is my call. I'm the one taking all the risks."

"There is a third option," I said, thinking out loud. "Compromise, in a way that keeps everyone happy: you plant a bomb or device on day one. You communicate a warning. The area is sealed off and people evacuated. The police find the device and know you maintain the ultimate threat. On day two, you make the threat and they evacuate the site and find no device. Day three arrives: you're the police officer. It's your call when the warning is phoned in. Do you call their bluff or not? If a bomb explodes and people are hurt, the shit hits the fan big time. As long as the threat remains credible, they take no chances."

"So, what are you suggesting?" asked Tara curiously.

"Mix it up a little. Phone a false warning, say every third operation?" Tara pondered this for a moment, the cogs in her brain ticking away. "I can't believe I am sat here having this conversation," I said. "If it wasn't so scary, I might laugh."

"You'll get used to it."

"I sincerely hope not," I replied, standing, with the firm intention of returning to bed. A sudden thought crossed my mind. "If this is a set up why do you need to do more than one job – if you manage to get the evidence on videotape?"

"It's not quite that simple."

My brain raced through the possibilities, recalling McDonnell's explanation for moving the Manchester truck. "It's not about MacKenna and Dennehy. It's about the other sleeper in the unit – Charlie was it?"

"Kieran and Fraser are the icing on the cake," Tara sighed, emptying her glass. "They want the location of the arms dump and Charlie. If they get him, they will destroy the infrastructure and break the IRA's capacity to act on the mainland."

"Charlie – is that his real name?" I mused.

Tara shook her head. "Highly unlikely – it's just a code name."

"Why haven't they told you?"

"The English Department is the most security conscious of all IRA units. Quite often one operative in the UK will be unaware of the identity of the other. Hence if I betray them, their entire infrastructure is not compromised."

"Titanic theory," I reasoned. "Ship floats even when three compartments are compromised."

"Let's hope the theory is as successful shall we."

As I walked across the kitchen, leaving Tara behind, a chilling thought occurred to me. "It could mean they simply don't trust you?"

"Why do you think I can't sleep?" Tara replied, replacing her glass in the sink.

From the day I had collected Tara from Holyhead, we had planned for the unexpected. We had rehearsed numerous scenarios, for example MacKenna and Dennehy turning up at the house unannounced. We considered Tara might be held against her will and might need to communicate a message to prevent me re-entering the house. The agreed danger signal was that the curtains would be drawn at the study window, which was at the front of the house. In all other circumstances, they were to remain strictly open.

Yet when our meticulous preparations were tested, a week or so later, I was found wanting. As I approached the front door, I was left with a nagging, if vague awareness of a subtle change in the environment. My uneasiness remained, as I inserted my front door key. As the door swung open, my mental checklist reached for the red alert button. I could hear voices in the kitchen. Stepping back outside, I cursed my shoddiness and inattention to detail, as my eyes alighted on the hastily drawn curtains. I re-entered the hallway and was faced with a split second decision – to stay or go? The decision was removed from my hands, when the kitchen door swung ajar, driven by a gust of wind from the open front door. I observed a figure with his back to me in the kitchen. A cold blast of air brushed the nape of his neck. Our eyes connected, each weighing up the other, entertaining the same thought process. So that's what he looks like.

"Hello," I called, desperately trying to remain calm, even though my heart was racing. If I blew this, it would jeopardise the entire operation, placing both our lives at risk – so no pressure then. I masked the hatred I felt inside – steeling myself to face Ben's murderers. Striding purposefully into the kitchen, loosening my tie, I beamed at Tara. "Hi darling." Tara reclined casually on the kitchen units, arms loosely folded across her chest, as I slipped my arm around her waist, pressing a kiss onto her cheek. She unflinchingly returned my gesture.

"Good day?"

"Not bad." Dennehy sat at the kitchen table studying an ordnance survey map, which he made a half-hearted attempt to conceal. He looked shorter than I had imagined him.

"Tom, this is Fraser," Tara gestured in his direction. "We go way back."

"Tom," I said, thrusting out my hand. Dennehy shook it apprehensively – his grip firm.

"Kieran," called the voice from behind me.

"Pleasure," I answered, shaking his outstretched hand. "It's good to meet Tara's friends. Can I offer you a drink?" I placed my hand behind my back, thrusting the other deep into my trouser pocket to stop it shaking. Despite my deep-seated loathing, I was taken aback by the ordinariness of their appearance. I suppose I ought not to have been surprised, Tara's physical appearance hadn't altered with her change of conviction.

"That's very hospitable, but no thank you," replied Kieran thoughtfully. "We were just on our way actually." His words were precise and measured, as cold as the eyes that were fixed alternately on Tara and then me.

Tara interrupted the awkward silence. "Fraser and Kieran are working locally."

"Aye," affirmed Dennehy, looking over to where MacKenna loitered uncomfortably by the fridge.

"Doing what?"

"Construction," they chorused almost instantaneously. "The second runway at the airport."

"Come on Fraser, let's leave these good people to their evening," interrupted Kieran, removing his denim jacket from the back of the door.

"Some other time perhaps?" added Tara.

"We should meet up for a pint or two," I added.

"We'd like that," replied MacKenna, shooting a sly uncomfortable glance across at Dennehy.

The front door closed with a dull thud. I shut my eyes and breathed a sigh of relief, like a diver gasping for air, emerging from the water. Had it been a grotesque dream? I couldn't reconcile their presence – in my home. Tara sank into the chair vacated by Dennehy, rubbing her eyes with her index fingers. "I guess there's no need to ask what the map was for?" Tara opened her mouth to speak, as if about to reel off a target list, but I interrupted her. "There are some things that I think it is best I remain in ignorance of." I was curious though. "I assume the equipment has been delivered?"

"Arrived at Charlie's last weekend."

"The infamous Charlie," I groaned. "Assure me the vehicle was tracked from Dover or wherever?" I probed, more in hope than certainty.

"Do you know how many containers arrive in British ports every day?"

"No. Do you?"

"A hell of a lot," Tara responded, lighting a cigarette. "Besides, if the authorities start checking every truck, it only increases suspicion. The aim is to lull them into relaxing – not make them so uptight they can't shit."

"So – stashed somewhere, unbeknown to the police and whoever else is on this taskforce," I reasoned, "is an armoury: explosives, guns, ammunition and detonators...?" Tara nodded soberly. "You have no idea, how much I didn't want to know that."

Later that evening, Tara appeared at the study door holding two tumblers of Scotch. Previously, I would have been irritated, antagonised by her very presence. That night, she provided a tonic. "I fixed you a drink," she said, standing in the doorway, unsure whether to stay. "Don't force me to drink alone." Tara handed me the glass and then curled into the leather easy chair in the far corner of the room. "Sorry about earlier – they turned up unannounced. It must have been weird, eyeballing Kieran and Fraser."

"Abomination now has a face," I grimaced, swirling the golden liquid in the tumbler – watching the light bounce off the crystal cut glass. "You reckon they planned to drop by unannounced. Like a test? Were we convincing?" I asked.

"It's possible, I guess."

"I almost believed it, for a brief interlude...." In the glistening half-light, reflected through the whisky glass, my brain was momentarily deluged with how things had once been. We exchanged awkward glances, before I was overcome with guilt.

18th March 1997

The Prime Minister, John Major today announced what we have long suspected – there will be a general election on the 1st May. He left Downing Street at 11.26am for Buckingham Palace for an audience with the Queen, and was granted the dissolution of Parliament on

A Bold Deceiver • James Hurd

8th April. The decision paves the way for the longest general election campaign in recent British history, giving the Conservatives 6 weeks to try and reverse their dire showings in the polls, which have consistently shown that Mr Blair is heading for Downing Street. The party leaders took no time to leave Westminster behind to meet "the people". John Major got out his soap-box and went to Luton, Tony Blair went to South London before heading for Gloucester. Paddy Ashdown headed to Taunton and the Liberal Democrats South West stronghold.

Chapter Thirty Four

25th March 1997

"Wilmslow, for heaven's sake?" I shook my head in bewilderment, dragging up the most exotic expletives I could assemble. Hours earlier, the IRA Army Council had approved the first operation.

"Tomorrow morning, an explosive device will detonate at Wilmslow station," Tara had said calmly – like announcing train timetable alterations, not the destruction of a busy commuter station. I was caught in a tantalising quandary: the same old contradictions, tension between the competing moral obligations of guilty knowledge and the desire for the ultimate success.

"Relax," Tara counselled. "Don't be so neurotic. The police are well aware of the operation. The railway station will be closed while the device is defused. We sever the West Coast Main Line for a few hours. The same will happen at Doncaster on the East Coast Main Line. The IRA scores political propaganda in severing north-south rail links and we move a step closer to ending this nightmare, which is the bloody objective after all." Tara was clearly fraught, her turmoil obvious. I could deal with this duplicitous carnage on an academic level: ideas, plans and reconnaissance. Now it appeared ominously chilling and I felt inadequate in the extreme.

"What if something goes wrong?"

"It won't."

"Yeah, right, because every IRA operation always proceeds precisely according to plan!"

"It's a simple device. Haydon has all the necessary information to defuse it." Tara's annoyance grew with my unrepentant belligerence. "Do you think I want to see anyone get injured? You have to trust me Tom." Her words echoed around my head, as I searched to comprehend. "Tom?"

"I can't cope with this," I finally explained in desperation, defeated by the enormity of events about to unfold.

Grabbing her jacket from the back of the chair, Tara replied in nervous frustration. "Great time to get cold feet. They turn up the heat and you bottle it. Thanks for all your bloody support," before she marched out, slamming the door behind her. Her stinging rebuke echoed around the four walls, long after the vibrations from the door had ceased.

Shortly after 2am the navy-blue Austin Metro indicated right, performed a U-turn and pulled into the kerb. The normally teaming city centre artery was quiet, save for the odd private hire vehicle whisking clubbers back to the silence of the suburbs, whilst the beat continued to pound inside their heads in an alcohol induced haze. Tara was concealed in the recess of a shop entrance, ten metres away from the illumination of the adjacent streetlight, dressed in black combat trousers and a black jacket, her collar turned upwards to conceal her lower face, the upper part hidden with a wide brimmed baseball cap. She moved stealthily, sliding effortlessly into the front seat. "You took your bleeding time," Tara rebuked MacKenna, pulling off the cap and running her hands through her hair.

Kieran grimaced as he fought with the gearbox to push the stick into fourth gear. "I got delayed collecting the kit."

"Fetching it from the dump?" Tara probed to no avail.

"Traffic jam on the motorway," he replied, concentrating on the rear view mirror.

"Problem?"

He shook his head. "Just paranoia." They rode in silence, as the city gave way to the southern suburbs, along the newly opened A34 by-pass. The only sound was the constant rattle and hum of the cranky 1100 engine.

"Good choice of motor – should be great for a quick getaway."

"You can nick the car next time then," Kieran retorted, slowing for the roundabout. The sign pointing to central Wilmslow dampened any further conversation.

If preparation was the key to success, the omens were good. They had spent hours walking the nearby streets, window-shopping and catching trains. They knew the surrounding streets like the back of their hands. The location of every CCTV camera and surveillance video was indelibly etched in their brains.

Turning right off the by-pass towards Wilmslow town centre, MacKenna dropped Tara a few hundred metres beyond the station, near Wilmslow Leisure Centre. She eased out of the car without conversation, positioning the cap low over her forehead and tucking her hair behind the collar of her jacket. Tara watched the Metro pull away, before she turned and began walking back towards the station.

Allowing the car to drift to a halt, Kieran parked close to Wilmslow High School. He yanked the hood of his black fleece up over his head and pulled the drawstring tight, before grabbing the large Adidas holdall from the back seat. He jogged across the deserted school playing fields, keeping low under the cover of a hedgerow and then disappeared into the darkness, as he approached the metal security fencing. Bending down, he withdrew a hessian sack out of the top of the holdall and carefully placed it on top of the sharpened metal poles, slid on his leather gloves and scaled the fence, dropping easily onto the path on the far side. Catching his breath, he advanced to where the steps of the pedestrian footbridge rose upwards and then waited – cursing the clear sky and pale moonlight. He checked his watch. Late again: third time this week. The temptation to believe in disaster was alleviated by the now familiar distant rumble. Beginning as a slow grumble, as the train drew closer the lines hissed and vibrated, until the growing crescendo peaked. The diesel engine thundered past, pulling a cargo of shipping containers, heading south for Dover, Felixstowe or Southampton.

One, two. three: MacKenna dropped the holdall over the low brick wall and leapfrogged through the undergrowth – the thud of boots landing on the gravel drowned by the passing train. He had no time to feel the pain from the bramble scratching its disapproval on his cheek. Pushing it firmly to one side, he walked forward, as the final container wagons still trundled by. Retrieving the holdall, he crouched on the railway embankment. To his left was the glow of the station platform forty yards along the track. He checked both ways before darting forward across the railway lines, treading softly on the stone ballast, bent low to avoid detection, until he reached the safety of darkness on the far side of the tracks and waited.

Slipping through the station car park, Tara pulled her cap a little lower over her forehead – just to be safe. She climbed the steps up to the platform and searched both ways, avoiding the one or two lights still switched on. Satisfied there were no staff still on duty, she walked south along the platform. After a final check at the end of the platform, she descended onto the stone ballast, passing the warning sign: *"Railway personnel only permitted beyond this point."* The station lights cast only a dim shadow beyond the end of the platform. Pressing herself into the darkness of the undergrowth, she proceeded slowly along the tracks, under the pedestrian bridge. Ahead was the signalling equipment – two grey boxes and a series of cables sat on a concrete plinth, linked to a signal further down the track, now glowing red. Down the line, MacKenna waited for Tara to approach, listening for the soft crunch of feet on the ballast. He placed his hand to the back of his jeans, feeling for his weapon, until he observed her slender form emerge from behind the upright for the overhead power gantry. He could just distinguish the shape of her breasts against her figure hugging top. "Psssttt." Tara stopped abruptly – listening intently. MacKenna emerged from his place of concealment and placed his hand upon her shoulder.

Tara jumped. "Shit, you scared me," her voice alternated between surprise and relief. "All clear?" he asked impatiently.

"Relax – there's no one about."

MacKenna approached the relay switch. Working quickly and professionally he removed a package from the holdall, approximately the size of a family biscuit tin, with an overhanging lip, a little like a chimney pot. He took the device from its protective cloth covering, sliding the small metal box out. Painted in a dull grey metallic paint, to the casual observer it superficially resembled the relay switch-gear it was subsequently situated adjacent to, albeit on a smaller scale. Tara scanned the surrounding area. "Hurry up. This place makes me nervous."

"Chill," he replied, "there's no train due for forty minutes." Tara assisted in brushing away the stray ballast which had invaded the concrete plinth, creating a flat space on which to plant the device – its location invisible to the untrained eye, but obvious to railway personnel, if they happened to stray this close. Once in situ, Kieran slid the top open to reveal the heart of the explosive device: a yellow/green strip of Semtex moulded to the shape of the tin – resembling the marzipan on a Christmas cake; wires attached to a battery; a detonator; and a centrally mounted electronic timing device. A final check to ensure the device was operational.

"Let's get the hell out of here," whispered Tara. MacKenna motioned towards the open holdall. It took a second before there was a sickening thud in the pit of her stomach. "What the hell?" she screamed under her breath at him, but he ignored her obvious fury. Instead, he pointed further up the track and motioned for her to follow. A light clicked on in a rear window, as a householder emptied his or her bladder on the other side of the by-pass. Too far away to be seen, but still, like foxes caught in headlamps, they both came to an instant halt. There was an audible sigh of relief, as the light clicked off and the world dozed back off to sleep. A hundred yards or so further up the lines, they repeated the same process, as a second device was withdrawn from the bag and positioned by the side of the track on freshly prepared ballast, which Tara had flattened with her gloved hands.

They left together, along the pre-planned exit route through the school grounds. The Metro started only with excruciating difficulty, accompanied by liberal chants of "come on you miserable bitch" from MacKenna.

"Our orders were for one device," shouted Tara, once they were safely moving.

Kieran smiled smugly. "Just a wake up call – to let them know we mean business."

Reaching into his inside pocket, one hand gripping the wheel, MacKenna extracted a mobile phone and pressed the call button three times. The screen now mirrored the timers at the track side. "How long between them?"

"See for yourself." MacKenna tossed the phone in the direction of the passenger seat.

"6.30 and 7.05 am," Tara read from the screen, watching in horror as the digits continued their relentless countdown.

MacKenna drove to Manchester Airport, parking the Metro into the Long Stay Car Park. They abandoned it on the third floor, once again pulling their caps down low across their faces. Opening the boot, Tara removed a suitcase stuffed with nothing more than crumpled up newspapers to create the impression of bulkiness and a small rucksack similarly packed. At terminal level, they removed their outer clothing and melted into a crowd of arriving passengers, before exiting the short stay car park in a burgundy Vauxhall Carlton motor vehicle, parked in anticipation hours earlier.

Forty minutes later, the key turned in the lock. Climbing out of bed, I slipped quietly towards the living room and stopped halfway. I had no desire to confront her, but was equally curious. I could hear heavy breathing – panting, she had been running. Tara's mobile phone bleeped as she switched it on. I recognised the creak of the floorboards – she was pacing up and down. I edged a few inches closer. "Come on, come on," she called, with definite anxiety. Finally he picked up. "There's a second device. Thirty-five minutes apart. Forty yards south of the station adjacent to a signal relay box in a camouflaged metal container similar to the switching gear. The second device is one hundred and fifty yards further south. You have to warn the local police…"

As an afterthought, Tara suggested that perhaps MacKenna used the Metro to collect the explosives? He'd been caught in a motorway jam. They could check the motorway cameras. He had driven north towards the city and then performed a U-turn, when picking Tara up. Was Charlie located south of Manchester?

At 5.32am, MacKenna placed a call from a public telephone box, warning an elderly female resident of Wilmslow. Waking her up from a deep sleep, she picked up the phone and was informed that there was a bomb at Wilmslow Police Station. She dialled 999 and passed the message onto the police telephone operator. An immediate emergency call was put out on all frequencies, telling all available units to evacuate the police station and nearby residents.

At 5.36am, I was wakened by the sound of the telephone ringing. I reached for the phone by the side of my bed. "Tara?"

"No it's Tom."

"Get her now." No polite introductions or hellos. This was business and he was serious. Darting out of bed, I ran with the cordless phone. Tara met me on the landing. I stood beside her as she listened, and watched her face turn from concern to indignation. "Damn," she almost screamed down the phone. Her brain was working overtime. "Tom, get the phone book – now." I grabbed the directory dressed in just my boxer shorts. "Look for a Wilmslow number and quickly." That was easier said than done, as numbers are arranged alphabetically by name not town. I scrambled through the pages, running my finger up and down the columns, desperate to locate a number. "Any number will do…"

"Altrincham – the hospital. That's not too far away," I said, glancing at the page. "At least someone will be there and awake." I realised this must relate to the warning.

Tara terminated the call with Haydon – I called out the number to her.

She dialled six digits before slamming the phone down. "Not from this number. It will be traced back here. The mobile – it's registered to a non-existent company based in the Turks & Cacaos Islands and an UK registered office that doesn't exist. The number?"

I called out the digits.

"Come on," she begged, as the phone rang. I heard the receptionist on the switchboard pick up. "Listen very carefully. This is not a hoax. There is a bomb at Wilmslow RAILWAY Station." She spoke slowly and emphasised the location. "It will detonate at 6.30am." She gave a recognised code and then hung up.

26th March 1997

The IRA scored a propaganda coup in the run up to the general election, as two bombs exploded in Wilmslow, Cheshire early this morning separated by 35 minutes. The first planted beside a relay switch box 40 yards south of the platforms at the town's railway station, exploded with a dull thud at 6.30am, which was heard over a mile away. Security services believe that the first bomb was intended to lure the emergency services into the path of the second, thus causing the maximum possible loss of life. Thankfully there were no reported injuries, even though the second, louder blast went off near where police and fire-fighters were erecting a security cordon. Police began evacuations after an elderly woman living on a nearby estate received a telephone warning at 5.32am. A man with an Irish accent told her that the bomb was at the police station. Eight minutes later a second call was made to a nearby hospital warning of a bomb at the railway station. The confused warnings caused potential tragedy, as at one point the police were evacuating people from the area around the police station to Wilmslow Leisure Centre, which is only 100 yards from the railway line.

A Bold Deceiver • James Hurd

The bomb blasts brought havoc to the West Coast Main Line. In a separate incident a man claiming to be from the IRA telephoned a warning of a bomb at Doncaster railway station, using a recognised code word. The station was subsequently evacuated and the East Coast Main Line also closed. The IRA tactic appears to have worked, if that was to disrupt commuters and rail travellers across the country, as for a while there were no trains running between the North and London. MI5 and police sources indicated this was not the "long awaited IRA spectacular" and the threat of further attacks was said to be "very high".

I called it quits early, unable to concentrate. My inside knowledge was a burden – a millstone around my neck. My guilt was eased only by relief that no one was injured. Rationally, it was not my responsibility. But I had chosen to co-operate with this hair-brained scheme. I found Tara in the living room, nursing a bottle of vodka. Curled up on the sofa, her eyes were red and angry. "Does it make you feel better?"

"I'll be sure to let you know when I've finished the bottle." She thrust the bottle in my direction. "On second thoughts, find out for yourself."

Loosening my tie, I fetched a glass from the kitchen and poured a generous measure.

Tara had withdrawn into herself – internalising her anxiety, to the exclusion of the outside world. Finally, with a heavy sigh, she placed her empty glass on the coffee table. "I thought I could handle this. I feel like a pawn, manipulated and used – utterly powerless. I am at the mercy of Kieran, the psychotic terror machine, who plants a second bomb in the hope of maximising the loss of life, and telephones a misleading warning. I did my bit – disclosing their locations, and details of how to defuse the bombs, avoiding the booby traps. I put my life on the line to ensure that there was an accurate warning: what do they do? Absolutely nothing. They just let them explode. You know why?" I shook my head. "To protect me – the pen pushers appear to believe that protecting my identity is more valuable than the risk to innocent lives."

Chapter Thirty Five

Wednesday 2nd April 1997

IN A CURIOUS mixture of natural beauty and manmade disfigurement, the orange glow of the setting spring sun silhouetted the hulks of railway wagons, sidings and overhead power cables, at Bescot Freight Depot. Not that the view was one restricted to railway employees or train-spotters. It was a view afforded to anyone with the misfortune to travel on the M6 north of Birmingham. Elevated sections of motorway towered on huge concrete pillars – a modern day Temple of Artemis, paying homage to the great god of the internal combustion engine. The nearby RAC Control Headquarters of blue/grey steel and glass, providing ever more informative ways of communicating the all too apparent congestion. Beyond was a curious mixture of the old and new: old industries long past their prime, cooling towers, factories, workshops, storage facilities, and new businesses encouraged into the re-landscaped remains of the once proud heart of British manufacturing.

By 10pm the traffic had eased. Commuters were all safely in the pub or in front of their television screens. A seven-year-old black Citroen BX travelling south past junction nine flicked on its hazard light switch. Tara shifted down into third gear, pulling onto the hard shoulder. Dennehy lifted the bonnet and poked his head underneath, before he emerged, shaking his head in bafflement. With a slight grin at Fraser's mock exasperation, Tara lifted the mobile phone cradled in her lap and punched in the now familiar number. "In position."

Dennehy returned to the passenger seat with the distributor cap, just in case. MacKenna returned his mobile phone to the passenger seat and twisted the ignition key.

Minutes later, a RAC recovery vehicle with false plates slowed to a neat halt only feet behind the ailing Citroen. The headlights from passing traffic cast shadows over the stationary vehicles, compounded by the RAC vehicle's rotating emergency beacon and the out of sequence pulsing of the Citroen's hazard lights.

MacKenna stepped onto the hard shoulder wearing a luminous orange jacket with RAC emblazoned across his back and chest. He and Tara gathered in front of the Citroen as the audacious charade commenced, in a stolen RAC patrol vehicle, less than a mile from their headquarters. MacKenna indicated for Tara to attempt to start the engine. MacKenna shook his head and buried his upper torso under the bonnet.

Wedged between the recovery truck and the crash barrier, Dennehy crouched by the open roller-shutter of the side compartment. Attached securely to the crash barrier behind them was a professional climbing rope. Dennehy secured the harness around his waist, pulling the thick straps tight. Tara removed a canvas bag from the tool compartment and extracted the compact device – her gloved fingers slipped the plastic explosives into a pouch Dennehy had already fastened to his chest. It fitted snugly. Tara tapped his chest twice in confirmation. Dennehy clipped his screw gate carabiner through the rope, locked it and gingerly climbed backwards, over the exposed concrete elevation. Slackening the rope, he lowered himself to a horizontal position and then commenced his slow descent down the sixty-foot concrete pillar. After twenty feet, he secured the descent rope, giving it a rigorous jerk to ensure it would hold. Reassured, dangling in mid air, he extracted the bomb and attached it to the pillar. Once satisfied that it was in position, Dennehy radioed confirmation.

Above, leaning over the barrier, craning her neck, Tara activated the device by remote control. Dennehy watched the LCD display illuminate, before commencing his descent. Pushing off from the column he took bigger and bigger jumps, the adrenaline surging through his veins. Once on the ground, he scanned the area for possible threats. Satisfied, he communicated the all clear to the carriageway above. Dennehy collected the fallen rope, looping it, whilst hiding in the shadows of the concrete monster above.

Kieran dropped the Citroen's bonnet and returned to the patrol vehicle, where Tara waited in the passenger seat. He had to wait for a few seconds, as two wagons trundled past at fifty-six mph, before he could pull out and accelerate past the parked Citroen – moving back onto the hard shoulder and reversing. He then proceeded to lower the rear wheel brace and secured the Citroen – ready to be towed. They trundled forwards, gathering speed along the hard shoulder. MacKenna reached second gear, before easing off the accelerator and bringing both vehicles to a halt. Alighting from the stolen recovery vehicle, he checked the front wheels of the Citroen, as if the canvas clamps securing the wheels had loosened.

At the side of the patrol vehicle, Tara repeated the earlier procedure, fastening the abseiling harness around her waist and double-checking her equipment – ropes and carabiner, in a mental routine which had become second nature. After a few seconds, Kieran joined her. "Ready?" Tara felt the tension in the rope, as she stepped backwards over the crash barrier. MacKenna watched her careful descent. Tara was nervous – strapped to her chest was enough plastic explosive, if not to destroy the motorway, then to blow her into a thousand little pieces. Tara had insisted the explosions ought to be large enough to make a very loud bang, but insufficient to do any real structural damage. The risk of major civilian casualties would be vastly counter-productive. McDonnell had thankfully agreed – at least someone had the barest semblance of sanity. Hanging suspended in mid air, she was convinced she was the most insane one of them all.

Tara scanned the pillar in the distance, trying to identify the device left by Dennehy, but visibility was too restricted in the dark. This will do, she thought. Tara secured her stop descender and hung suspended in mid-air. In the process of removing the explosives from the marsupial pouch, to her horror she accidentally knocked the handle in on the descender which jolted her downwards, free falling. "Shit." Hurtling towards the fast approaching ground, Tara reached out for the rope below the descender, grabbed and missed – excruciatingly it slipped through her fingers. Her heart beat raced. "Not like this – please," she screamed internally. Summoning all the reserves of her energy, she grasped the rope as the stop device on the descender held. Her grip was firm and she juddered to a halt. After the deafening wind and her pounding heart, all was suddenly silent. Gasping for breath, Tara tilted her head back and inhaled deeply. That was close. Way too close. She glanced up and then down. She had only dropped ten feet – it felt a lot more. She tried again. It took only a couple of seconds to remove and secure the bomb – the strong magnet attracted to the steel rods reinforcing the concrete pillar.

Tara relayed the okay to MacKenna and watched the red LCD display glow with life. She released the rope for her final descent, overwhelmed by a desire to place her feet on solid ground. Kieran abandoned the RAC patrol vehicle in a deserted lay by, swapping the Citroen at Keele Services on the M6 for a Ford Mondeo left there earlier that day. He placed two calls, giving coded bomb warnings to two hotels within a few miles of the M6. For good measure, he also phoned a phoney warning for a device on the M1 in Northamptonshire, *"just to make sure there was the mother of all traffic jams,"* as he recounted it later over a cold beer.

3rd April 1997

Switching from rail to road, the IRA have struck again, this time plunging the whole of the West Midlands motorway network into gridlock and chaos. Two explosive devices were discovered on the M6 near Birmingham, closing the busiest section of motorway in Europe. Not the fastest moving stretch of road in England at the best of times, the devices left 200,000 lorries and 60,000 cars stranded for hours. Police closed vast swathes of the motorway network after an Irish caller telephoned two hotels in the Walsall area, telling them that there were bombs which would explode under the elevated sections of the M6 by 9am this morning.

Hundreds of people were evacuated from their homes. Motoring organisations have estimated that the closures have cost British business a figure in the region of £20 million. Police went to work straight after the warnings were given, scouring the lengthy elevated sections of the motorway just north of Birmingham. During the search, two small explosions were heard, yet it proved impossible at the time to locate the source of the devices. However, late this afternoon, officers from the West Midlands Police located a bomb attached to a 60-foot control column near Bescot, near junction 9, better known to locals as the IKEA exit. The device was made safe, via two controlled explosions. A second device was discovered approximately 100 yards away. In Northamptonshire, the M1 was closed for 8 hours after warnings of a device. Police sources believe that this latest incident, along with the rail chaos caused last week in Wilmslow is part of a concerted campaign by the IRA in the run up to the general election to cause massive inconvenience to ordinary commuters and road users.

Earler that afternoon Tara had sat opposite Haydon, situated in an office nominally let to a firm of recruitment consultants. She wore a navy blue business suit, in a passable attempt to look like a client. Her cover, in the event she was followed, was her search for a teaching position. "Have they found the devices yet?" Tara asked.

"No – but there's no problem now they've gone off." Haydon rose from the desk.

"It just makes me nervous – that's all."

"How many times have we been through this," he replied, in exasperation. "If the bombs had been found and defused at 8am, what would have happened? Say it." He banged his hand on the desk.

"I'd have been under suspicion," Tara repeated wearily, but patently unconvinced.

Haydon stood opposite Tara, berating her. "No. By now, you'd probably be dead." He let that unpalatable thought sink in for a second. "My job is to protect the public, but it's also to protect you. If this whole operation is to be a success, we have to keep you inside long enough to destroy their infrastructure."

Tara offered no reply, tired of raking over familiar ground. She knew the argument was not hers for the winning and changed the subject. "Did you check the cameras?"

"Bingo," Haydon smiled. "We've obtained footage of the Metro on the M6. It looks like your hunch was right. Charlie is based somewhere in the Midlands."

"West Midlands – Birmingham area."

"What makes you so sure?"

"Something Fraser let slip last night. I was concerned that the police might be watching out for the stolen RAC truck. He said not to worry, as Charlie had made false plates and Kieran didn't have that far to travel wearing the originals."

"Where was the RAC vehicle stolen from?"

"Walsall"

"How long is not far?"

"Twenty to thirty miles – who knows?" Tara offered with a weary sigh, recognising the imponderable.

"Any idea how many garages or similar premises exist in a twenty to thirty mile radius of Walsall?" They sat in silence, contemplating both how far they had come and how far they still had to travel. "Any further fall out over the second warning at Wilmslow?"

Tara crossed her legs, mentally rechecking the conversations with Fraser and Kieran over the previous twenty four hours, to ensure that her contemporaneous interpretation had been accurate. "No. I think my explanation that I thought it was me who was to telephone the warning appears to have been taken at face value. Fingers crossed." She mimed the sign. "Kieran loved the confusion – reckons it gave us the excuse to blame incompetent policing if there were casualties. He wants us to do it again." Tara ran her fingers through her hair, resting on her elbows, nervous at a prospect, which if it materialised, might have deadly consequences.

"All set for Saturday?"

"Not a lot to do really is there?"

"It riles the hell out of me that I have to sit here and let this just happen." The frustration was obvious in his voice.

"Now you know how I feel."

Chapter Thirty Six

THERE ARE TIMES when you can know more than is good for your sanity. I spent Saturday 5th April 1997 at The Valley, watching Charlton Athletic play Manchester City with Stuart, attempting to place as much physical distance as possible between myself and Aintree. Even here, however, escape proved illusive. Shortly before the second half commenced, sketchy reports began to emerge that the race meeting had been officially abandoned and the course was being evacuated amid scenes of confusion, following a bomb threat from the IRA. Stuart was waiting for me to down my pint, as the news came through. "Good grief." His ashen expression turned from complete disbelief to accusation, in light of the contents of his office safe. "You knew about this?"

I nodded silently, pulling his arm. "Come on, we'll miss the start of the second half." I had to physically drag him away from the television screen.

"Aren't you interested?" he asked.

"Definitely not," I replied firmly.

Saturday 5th April 1997

In a cruel hoax, one of Britain's best loved sports events was today destroyed by the IRA, as the 150th Grand National had to be abandoned. More than 70,000 people had to be evacuated from the racecourse after a bomb warning to the Fazackerley Hospital in Liverpool. No details were provided as to the whereabouts of the device, leaving the police with little alternative but to evacuate the massive crowd. Thousands were left stranded, as they were unable to return to their vehicles, until they had been painstakingly searched for explosives.

An emergency plan was put in operation, as hotels were fully booked months in advance. People are being housed overnight in churches, leisure centres and sports arenas. Taxi services have been inundated with calls from thousands in the hope of arranging lifts home. The BBC, however, were not to be defeated and resumed broadcasting from the car park where jockeys, trainers and horse owners were interviewed about the day's events.

This latest IRA attack follows the chaos brought to both road and rail in recent days, causing massive disruption to the lives of ordinary people in the run up to the election.

Neither Tara nor Dennehy provided any details as to where the explosive device was located when they left telephone warnings. There was a very good reason for this, aside from a desire to be deliberately obtuse. There wasn't an ounce of explosive anywhere near Aintree racecourse. It was just a hoax, designed to cause the maximum disruption with the minimum risk. The really galling aspect was that I was partly culpable. On this the third job, the ASU called the bluff of the police and they were forced to respond in light of Wilmslow and Bescot. The only crumb of consolation was that whatever happened, despite the confusion and inconvenience caused, no one's life would be endangered that day.

I was still nursing the effects of a hangover, from my excursion to London, when I returned home. It was a lovely spring afternoon. Tara was sitting on the patio, staring into nothing, the collar on her jacket turned up, her eyes shielded by dark glasses. She sat with her feet resting on one of the other garden chairs, which she had moved into position in front of her.

"Hi," I called, but could elicit no response. If her eyes showed a flicker of recognition, it was concealed behind her sunglasses. I sensed a change in atmosphere: bad blood brewing. The mellowing of overt tension over recent weeks had been replaced by a brutal coldness. "See the news?" I tried again. "Those poor sods."

Tara was a picture of contemptuous disdain, her lips pursed firmly together. "I'm trying to avoid listening to the news. It's not exactly an achievement I wish to celebrate," she replied, returning her unfocused attention to the distant horizon, indicating this conversation was heading nowhere.

"Kinda hard to do."

"Not really. You just sit alone and don't go out. You don't put the TV or radio on and don't answer the phone. Simple really," she offered sardonically, cocking her head slightly to the left, before glaring a false smile and lighting a cigarette.

"Practical as well," I joked, commencing a tactical retreat back into the house.

"Just leave it Tom," she said angrily.

"Hey, what did I do?" I needed conflict like a hole in the head, with my hangover. However, my innocent protestations seemed only to rile her.

"Stop acting so bloody innocent," Tara barked, finally removing her glasses – her puffy darkened eyes smarting with animosity.

"I had a heavy night and frankly I'm in no mood for games. If you have something to say, I'm all ears." I raised my voice more out of frustration than any other emotion.

With that, Tara stormed past me into the hall with a purposeful stride that commanded me to follow, racking my brains as to what on earth had rattled her so. Tara reappeared from the study, her fist stuffed with a sheath of papers. "Here." She thrust them towards me, with a look of triumphant expectation – checkmate. I glanced at the crumpled pages. I recognised the text instantly – the latest entry, a rough summary of the events of the previous couple of days.

"So what's the problem?" I asked tentatively. Tara glared at me with the incandescent fury of a betrayed woman. She raised her arm in the air, releasing the papers, whereupon they separated and scattered onto the hall floor. "Why the hell are you spying on me?"

"Spying?" This was paranoia off the end of the scale.

"Why else would you write all this crap down?" Tara was livid. Suddenly an idea seemed to grip her. "Are you feeding this back to Haydon? Was that part of the deal? I know you don't trust me, but really Tom, I didn't think you'd stoop to the benevolent snitching jailer."

"For heaven's sake calm down." I confess to assuming that recent pressure had taken its toll, pushed her over the edge of mental stability, into a sanity free fall.

"Don't you dare tell me to calm down." Advancing towards me in a raging tantrum, arms flailing wildly, Tara pounded her clenched fists onto my chest and upper body, like a JCB on amphetamines. "Are you planning to claim the reward for the Manchester bomb? Or sell my story to the press. Is that why you agreed to have me here: compensation for my crimes – prostituting yourself and me. Well I hope your fucking blood money eases your guilt – Judas."

Tara's tirade was the final straw. I fended off her punches and tried to grab her arms, to restrain her, but she was way too quick. I'm not proud of it now – I snapped. It was brutal instinct. I slapped her hard across the face, hitting her square on the cheek, sending her staggering backward, recoiling and falling awkwardly, striking her head on the banister. With the dull thud of bone on wood, I regained my senses – too late.

"You bastard," she screamed. "Don't you ever come near me again." Her cheek glowed red with pain. She nursed it with her hand, regarding me with contempt before storming into the bedroom and closing the door behind her.

I sat down – dumbfounded by her accusations. I could hear Tara opening and slamming the wardrobe door. Where would she go – the police or the IRA? Part of me confessed relief. Perhaps if she did bale out, life would return to some kind of normality. After a few minutes, I ventured up the stairs. Cautiously I rapped on Tara's door. "Leave me alone." I turned the handle and gingerly entered the darkened room. Tara lay curled up on the bed, in a foetal position adjacent to her half-packed rucksack. "I'm leaving, just as soon as I figure out where the hell to go."

"You once told me that I owed you the opportunity of an explanation. All I ask of you is the same courtesy."

Tara was backed into a corner, but I remained the least unpleasant of her options. "I'm listening." Tara's face was flushed red, her scepticism nakedly apparent.

I stood hesitantly, at the end of the bed, desiring not to invade too far. "You may find this hard to believe," I began, "but I was trying to act in your best interests." I was met with an icy silence. "In Stuart's office safe is a written account, to the best of my recollection, of every snippet regarding this dangerous charade."

"Why Tom?" she asked, still perplexed and suspicious.

"Someone has to watch out for you. Who else will?"

"I can look after myself," Tara snapped, in red hot defiance.

I sat down next to her on the bed. "Sure, with a gun or planting a bomb, even abseiling down motorway columns. But when all this is over? Then what: a golden handshake and the keys to Buckingham Palace? More likely handcuffs and a cell in Parkhurst. That's when you find out who is the real whore." I threw her jibe back like a primed hand grenade. "And it ain't me babe. I told Powell at the outset what I would do. I'm your guarantee that they play fair. An affidavit each week at Stu's office, sealed and the date marked. I made it clear to Powell that if he doesn't keep his side of this Faustian bargain, I'll go public." Tara pulled the pillow closer to her, as if her very survival depended upon it, although there was no sign of regret for her accusations. "I wanted to ensure when this crap was over, you got a fair deal in court…" My words trailed off. Tara lay on the bed, rocking back and forth in the half-light, her features partially obscured by shadows, ostracised from both the worlds she inhabited. "So, if you still want to leave, be my guest…"

It was sometime after ten before Tara emerged from her self-imposed hibernation, edging slowly into the study, where I had a forthcoming brief spread out across my desk. Her eyes were still bloodshot with the afterglow of emotion, but without the heat of her earlier wrath. She lingered in the doorway, her arms folded defensively across the chest. I looked up, suddenly aware of her presence. "Looks interesting," she observed softly.

"Not really," I replied, "but refuge in even the dullest of subjects can be a blessing."

"Why didn't you tell me?" The softness of her tone belied the steel in the question. "Do you realise how much danger you put both of us in? What if Kieran and Fraser had decided to have a gander in here?"

"I wasn't aware they were frequent visitors to my study?" I remarked, with a degree of indignation. "I thought you deserved a fair deal for putting your neck on the line. At its inception, I couldn't tell you. There was so much baggage between us." Tara's arms slipped from their tight defensive position and came to rest loosely by her side.

"And now?" Her voice was gentler, almost timid – her anger dissipating.

"Now you know." When I reopened my eyes, Tara had approached. I could smell her fragrance. For the first time in an age, I glimpsed the vaguest hint of a smile, revealing the additional lines on her face, scattered like sunbeams from her eyes, across her upper cheeks.

"Hold me, Tom." Tara expanded her yearning arms and I felt an inclination to be close to her. I felt the touch of her hands as we embraced. In that one transient caress, I was more alive than I had been in months. It wasn't that the past didn't matter, it would always be momentous. Ben mattered, as did Becky and Hannah. But at that moment, the pain of the present seemed to temporarily drown out the cries of the past. I closed my eyes tightly, lest it should be over too soon. I memorised the smell of her hair, her hands resting on my back. It wasn't a sexual encounter, foreplay or a prelude to ecstasy. This was the totality. A kindling of human spirit, fired in adversity, in the intoxicating pressure of the frankly bizarre world we both inhabited and could not share outside these four walls. In one embrace we forgot how desperately alone we both felt and shared an intimacy seldom equalled.

Tara sobbed, her soft tears trickling onto my shirt, where they were absorbed into the cotton. "Someone to watch over me," she repeated. "I like that...."

7th April 1997

In defiance of the IRA the 150th re-scheduled Martel Grand National was run today in front of 20,000 spectators. At 2pm the Ghurkhas, who had played their way out of the racecourse on Saturday as they were being evacuated, struck up again in an attempt to recreate the atmosphere. The race will go down in history as not only the only Grand National to be run on a Monday but also probably the largest number of armed police ever to attend a sporting event in the UK. With helicopter blades whirring above, Lord Gyllene gave two hoofs to the IRA, as he led from the front to win the race some 25 lengths clear of Sunny Bay.

Over the course of the weekend, the police have searched every inch of the 250 acre Aintree racecourse and some 7000 cars. Thousands of race goers expressed their gratitude to the people of Merseyside. 2000 people slept in sports halls and over a 1000 in private homes. As many as 5000 people were fed breakfast by the good Samaritans of Liverpool on Sunday morning.

The following week saw the longest election campaign in modern history shift up a gear, but also a lull in the IRA campaign. A number of factors contributed to this, following the frenetic activity of Walsall and Aintree. The police were mounting additional patrols on motorways and the British Transport Police were in force on main line railway stations. The consensus appeared to be it would be too dangerous to attempt a similar operation the following week. In tandem with that, there was a perception that the oxygen of publicity would burn out if overloaded. If an event becomes common place, people lose interest no matter how horrific it is and the impact is diminished. Mass murder in Northern Ireland had become such a common occurrence in the seventies and eighties, it barely registered any more on the collective consciousness of those not directly involved. In the meantime, MacKenna had returned to Ireland, seeking final approval from the Army Council for the long awaited 'spectacular', at the climax of the election campaign.

I returned home one evening shortly after 9pm to the sound of loud music, as Pink Floyd thundered from the stereo – 'Dark Side of the Moon' reverberating around the entire house. The living room was shrouded in darkness. Before I could lower the volume, Tara placed her index finger over her lips and ushered me to silence. She motioned to me to follow her. Once in the garage, leaning over the Bonnie, Tara relaxed, Gilmour and Waters still discernible in the background. "What the hell is going on?"

"The house," she hissed disdainfully, "is bugged." Tara edged slightly further inside the garage, almost as if the very bricks and mortar were contaminated and slipped her hands into her jeans pockets. I furrowed my brow in disbelief. "Electronic surveillance, eavesdropping, spying, invasion of privacy, wire tap – you catching on yet," Tara reeled off her list impatiently, snapping her fingers before my face.

I mounted the Bonnie, trying to unravel Tara's riddles. "So our Recruitment Consultant friends told you?"

"Not deliberately." She pulled a cigarette out of the pack and struck a match. She cupped her hands against the evening breeze to protect the flickering flame. Waving the match in the wind, it flickered and died.

"Why would the IRA bug the house? MacKenna would have personally delivered your goodbye tout bullet by now? Anyway, how the hell would Powell know that?" I was all out of rhetorical questions.

Tara watched on in amusement, as she observed my cogitation. "Who blamed the IRA?" Tara noted my obvious lack of comprehension before ploughing on. "The significance didn't hit me till this afternoon. Haydon and I never discuss our personal lives. I have never revealed how we survive living under the same roof. He knows things must have been agonisingly uncomfortable – after everything…" Her voice trailed off. What a euphemism 'everything' was. It covered a multitude of sins, still too painful to voice. "He's never enquired about the atmosphere between us. I guess he assumed I'd made my own bed and I could lie in it. Same applies to you. So today, out of the blue, Powell asks me. 'How is domesticity with Tom: everything okay?'"

"Just making conversation?" I observed.

"No." Tara shook her head. "He appeared relaxed, but there was a definite, if well concealed, hint of tension. He knew we had the mother of all arguments the other night and why."

I loosened my grip on the handlebars finally catching her drift. I was incredulous. "Relax," I concluded dismissively. "You're paranoid."

"True, but wrong." She stubbed out her cigarette, as sparks danced across the floor glowing bright red against the darkening sky. "As I was leaving, Powell started chatting – at first, I thought it was just small talk.

"'Tom's approval means a lot? Let me give you some friendly advice.' I was too stunned to decline his patronising gesture. 'The less Tom knows the better. Let's not make him a target, if they can't get to you.'"

"I appreciate his concern for my welfare," I commented, leaning back on the bike.

Tara snorted. "He's watching his arse – not yours. You're no more of a security risk today, than at Maine Road." A look of weary triumph appeared on her face. Finally I had grasped her simple logic. "It's the only explanation."

The music drifted from the house in waves, as 'Money' gave way to 'Us and Them'. "This used to be my favourite album to get stoned to," I recalled fondly.

"I haven't smoked any since…" Tara couldn't complete the sentence.

"Amsterdam." The memory hung in the air like stale tobacco the morning after the night before.

"Want some?"

"Perhaps," Tara nodded coyly.

We sat on the patio in the dark. It was a clear night, cool as the temperature dropped. Drawing on a spliff, the stars seemed that much brighter, suspended in a three-dimensional expanse we call sky. The stars whirled in a pattern of celestial join the dots: a dragon or a smiling face. I passed the joint to Tara, already lost in a world of her own.

"Why," I asked, still puzzled.

"Why what?" came Tara's dreamy reply.

"Why would they want to eavesdrop?" Tara giggled uncontrollably. "What?" I asked indignantly. Her laughter was infectious, as she was convulsed in a coughing fit trying to laugh and inhale simultaneously.

"You're so naïve. They trust me to put my life at risk. But they're paranoid they might not squeeze every last ounce of useful intelligence out of me. They listen because they can. The IRA are the new communists. MI5 have to do something to protect their very existence from the Whitehall bean counters. So they spend your tax money on listening to what we talk about. Just in case…"

"Tom?" I was lying back in the chair in an intoxicated half-daze staring vacantly into the colours of the universe, but somehow obtaining formidable inspiration from so doing. "Tomorrow is Saturday. I need to get out. Come with me?" I hesitated, even though I was stoned. Since Tara's return we had not left the house together once. What would I say if confronted by a friend or colleague aware of Tara's disappearance? Worse still, the prospect of running into Becky was enough to make my blood run cold as ice. Besides, in the weeks that had passed, I left the house to escape Tara's haunting presence, not to court the relics of a long gone romance. But that night my demons appeared to have relinquished some of their potency. I looked across at her figure, silhouetted against the kitchen light, tracing the outline of her features. Tara seemed a million miles removed from the repugnant hate figure I had shown such antipathy towards months previously. Maybe like that hunting horn, the pain of the past was dying, as the wind carried it away. Alternatively, it could have been the euphoria of being high. "I'm not sure it's such a good idea."

Tara noted my obvious reluctance. "The only time I get out of this place is to converse with the psychotic and the paranoid."

"Which is which – the psychotic and paranoid: the police or the IRA?"

"Make you own mind up."

A Bold Deceiver • James Hurd

The sun shone bright in a blue sky, punctuated only by wispy cotton wool clouds and the white streaks left in the wake of jet airliners, as they climbed to cruising altitude on their way to distant and exotic destinations. I hadn't ridden for ten months, and now it felt both exhilarating and terrifying. I caught up with Tara on the A6 south of Stockport, before we broke free of the urban conurbation, heading into the Peak District. As the miles passed, I relaxed. The nervousness subsided and the phantom itch in my leg diminished with the exultation of freedom. With the wind in my face, I had a feeling of intoxicating gratification as I pulled open the throttle. I probably wouldn't have been revelling in such bliss, had I known that as we had idled at the traffic lights some miles back, a pair of eyes was taking a special interest in the two motorcycles situated three vehicles in front. A Triumph Bonneville sporting a registration number she was only too familiar with, and a Kawasaki that rang a distant bell – eyes that blinked in disbelief and horror at the obvious female rider, to ensure the vision was not a hallucination, or a case of mistaken identity.

We rode through Kettleshulme and into the Goyt Valley, where the reflecting sun shone on the reservoir causing the water to shimmer like tin foil. We stood perched on top of the dam, peering downwards, watching the water calmly lap on the smooth concrete beach below. Afterwards, we abandoned the bikes and headed up the rough mountain track, climbing upwards to the summit of Shining Tor, whose peak rose majestically to 1834 feet above our heads. Once away from other day-trippers and tourists, Tara became less inhibited. No relentless worried glances in all directions. "Race you to the fence," Tara shouted, already sprinting towards the other side of the field, inhabited only by the odd sheep who didn't seem particularly perturbed by our presence. "I let you win," I laughed, as she arrived first with a sense of smug satisfaction. Sitting on a dry stone wall half way up the hillside we basked in the sunshine. "This is fantastic, but...." Tara's smile appeared to darken.

"What?"

"But, it's not reality, is it?" Her enjoyment of the moment gave way to morbid contemplation; her eyes seemed to lose their sparkle, like dousing flames with water. "It's just that this isn't how I envisaged it would be." Tara wrung her hands together in obvious dejection. "I'm not stupid or blind. I live under the same roof as you. I see what's going on. You...your whole life is on hold. Like someone pressed the pause button. Or rather, I pressed the pause button. You hardly see your friends any more…"

I interrupted her mid sentence. "I went…"

"You only went to the game with Stuart because you couldn't bear to sit around and watch the mess at Aintree. You've stopped giving a shit about your career or your friends. I'm contaminating your life. The guilt – ever fearful in case Becky decides to pop round or I pick up the phone without first engaging my brain. Let alone the moral responsibility burdening you like a millstone, for this whole damn escapade. Having me around only rubs salt in your wounds."

"It's not like that," I reasoned with little conviction.

"Let's walk – I'm getting cold. You know the worst of it?" Tara continued despairingly, stopping in the middle of field to face me, our faces positioned only inches apart. "I could live with all that, if I believed something productive would emerge. All that has happened is that I have lent the benefit of my ideas, brain and even body to the IRA. I've not exactly thrown a spanner in the works so far." Tara gritted her teeth in frustration, tapping her index finger between her breasts. "I'm supposed to be undermining them, not collaborating in their lunacy."

"But you're feeding every ounce of intelligence back to the authorities."

Tara contemplated this. "What do they do? I mean actually do, other than compile files or dossiers? We haven't stopped one explosion, or arrested anyone. We're no closer to discovering the whereabouts of the explosives dump and to crown it all, they are spying on us. Is it any wonder I'm disillusioned?"

"Don't worry," I consoled her, once we had commenced our descent. "I'll sue the snooping reprobates for trespass and invasion of privacy, when all this is over."

That brought a rye grin of satisfaction to Tara's face. "Now that I would like to see."

"Race you down the hill," I called, sprinting off, before Tara had a chance to react.

"You cheating sod," she replied, gathering speed behind me.

The Cat and Fiddle, at Goyt's Moss is the second highest pub in England and a Mecca to bikers, given its position on the infamous A537 Buxton to Macclesfield road. At a solitary table in the far corner, sipping beer, chasing the white froth around the glass, Tara confessed her fears. "What happens if we fail Tom? Fraser, McDonnell, Kieran, Charlie they all slip through the net – become anonymous faces in the crowd. What if they succeed on the thirty-first? What will all this have been for?"

"Don't torture yourself with 'what ifs'. What have we lost?" I argued, growing a little impatient. "At least we will not be haunted for the rest of our lives, always wondering whether we could have stopped them."

"I'll be haunted whatever happens. My ghosts will just taunt me a little more vociferously if we fail. You, however, will be left with the indignity of knowing that I have screwed up your life twice to achieve nothing."

"Not nothing," I said, without further elaboration as we headed for the exit.

Chapter Thirty Seven

IMAGINE IF YOU enjoyed the power to foretell the future. Before you throw back the duvet, you are aware of the events that will unfold throughout the day. Sound attractive? If you knew your boss would be in a foul mood, would discover your partner was having an illicit affair, or your car would be stolen – would you bother getting up? What's my point? It's the evening of Thursday the 17th April. I had a trial listed in the Stoke on Trent County Court the following morning, which I knew would never be effective. The Provos were back in business. Friday 18th April 1997 would turn out to be one of the most nightmarish days ever to contemplate travelling anywhere in Northern England. It would enter travel mythology, as an urban legend. "Did I ever tell you about the time it took me fifteen hours to drive from Leeds to Birmingham?" Of course, when other commuters left the house, they had no idea what lay ahead. Me, I knew only too well and desired only to stay in bed. After all, I had the perfect excuse – I could foresee the future.

On the other side of the Pennines, dressed in a navy pin stripe business suit, Tara skirted across the darkened car park, only a few hundred yards south of Leeds railway station. With a black leather pilot case in her hand, Tara blended easily into the crowd – another anonymous employee – as she edged through the shadows, passing the few remaining vehicles, to where Dennehy was waiting in an Escort van. She slid surreptitiously into the front passenger seat. There would have been surprise, not to mention hysteria, if fellow car park users had known that the pilot case contained more than papers and a trashy novel. Equally, Dennehy would have been horrified had he known that in the six hours since he had deposited the cargo in her safe keeping, the police and security services had both thoroughly examined and photographed the device. "Begun to think you'd stood me up," he grunted.

"A good looking fella like you?" Tara smiled. "Where's Kieran?" she asked frostily, glancing behind her into the rear of the vehicle.

Fraser shook his head. "It's you and me."

"This has been planned for three," Tara replied impatiently. "Don't tell me he's still back home?"

Fraser leant across from the driver's seat, taking the pilot case from her. "The plan stays the same. You'll just have to improvise. We can do it with just the two of us."

"Where is he?" she said, with obvious annoyance.

"He had to go to Charlie's place, something about the positioning of the steel tubes for next week."

"I thought McDonnell had sent the team from 93 to carry out the construction work?"

"Me too." Fraser nodded calmly, without elaboration.

"So he's in the Midlands then?"

Fraser shook his head. "It's taking shape in Cambridgeshire." In the subdued rear of the van, aided by a flashlight, Dennehy extracted the package from the pilot case and carried out one final check, before inserting the device carefully into a shabby rucksack.

Tara watched Fraser slide the rucksack onto his shoulder and walk away, tracing his movement with her eyes, until he disappeared out of view, before easing out of the passenger seat and into the rear of the van. Once there, she quickly changed her clothes, swapping her two piece suit and blouse for tight black jeans, a figure-hugging low cut silk blouse, leather jacket and three inch high heels. In a compact mirror, with the flashlight suspended from the roof of the van, she fitted a jet black shoulder length wig and applied pale foundation, black eyeliner and bright red lipstick.

A quick glance at her watch started the countdown. Tara closed her eyes and breathed deeply to calm her nerves, but failed to ease the butterflies churning in her stomach. No matter how many jobs, she reflected, you never lose the nerves. It was the public nature of her role. She preferred operating in the shadows, waiting to pounce, not being in the spotlight. Leaving the car, she crossed Neville Street and walked underneath the railway line and into the station concourse. She paid cash for a return train ticket she had no intention of using. "Platform Three" nodded the uniformed employee behind the glass counter.

"Is it on time?"

She glanced down at a computer screen. "It was a couple of minutes late leaving York, but I think it's made up the time."

The platform was quite busy, filled with the usual mix of late working commuters, intercity travellers and those just out for the evening. At the opposite end of the platform, Dennehy stood clutching a note pad with a pair of binoculars round his neck, wearing a fake beard and glasses – looking the epitome of a train spotter and barely meriting a second glance from the waiting passengers.

This operation had been over a month in the planning. The relay-box situated near the end of platform three was the ideal location for a bomb. The lights at the end of the platform were dim and few passengers ventured that far. The crucial difficulty was people milling around. Not an insurmountable difficulty, however, if you turn it to your advantage – people provided camouflage. Planting the device at 3am would have been useless, as they would have stuck out like sore thumbs. At 9.45pm they blended into the melee, anonymous and unseen – except for the ever watching CCTV camera, situated high in the station roof. Concealed in the arching canopy overhead, the camera moved in a three hundred and sixty degree arc from left to right, taking a broad sweep of the platform in around thirty seconds.

No matter how many times they had attended the station and rehearsed the plan, MacKenna or Dennehy simply could not disembark from the platform, install the device and slip back into the crowd within the thirty-second time frame. The only solution then was to disguise their identity from the CCTV footage that would later be examined in meticulous and forensic detail.

Upon seeing Tara, in character, strolling confidently down the platform, Dennehy smiled to himself at the transformation in her appearance: business professional to gothic goddess in fifteen minutes. Taking this as his cue, he ambled into the gent's toilets. Locking the cubicle door, he removed the binoculars and donned a fluorescent orange Railtrack jacket and a navy baseball cap.

The other problem, they had correctly foreseen, given the nature of their campaign thus far, was the increased presence of the British

Transport Police – ever watchful for suspicious packages or activity – hence the clear need for a diversion.

The number of people on the platform swelled, as the station announcer indicated that the train was approaching. Tara picked out what she surmised was a student, with longish hair and baggy jeans in his early twenties, head buried studiously in a paperback book, and edged towards him. He was standing less than six feet away from where two British Transport Police Officers surveyed the waiting throng – eyes alert for anything out of the ordinary.

With a deep intake of breath, as the train ground to a halt, she forced the muscles in her legs to relax and keeled forward, clattering to the ground only inches from his feet. Once on the platform, Tara lay perfectly still, gritting her teeth against the pain in her forehead where she had collided with the unforgiving concrete. Why don't they make platforms softer screamed her brain – its instinct for self-preservation intact. The student was startled away from his novel, as he noticed the attractive young woman collapse in front of him. "Are you alright? Help," he shouted, alerting other would be passengers. "I think she's fainted." He shook Tara gently on the arm. "Hello."

Upon seeing Tara's collapse, the police officers hurriedly approached and took control. The female officer, short but broad, with closely cropped hair under her uniform hat, brushed the student nonchalantly aside. "Let me through – I'm trained in first aid," she informed him, in a business like fashion, feeling for Tara's pulse. Tara counted in her head how long she needed to wait to give Dennehy sufficient time. After a suitable interval, she judged it was time to stage a moderate recovery. Tara turned over and tried to sit up. "Take it easy love," the WPC counselled, patting the back of Tara's hand with her open palm. Tara feigned confusion, as she attempted to straighten her ruffled clothes, adjusting her blouse where it had fallen open to partially reveal her bra and praying that her wig remained secure. "You had a fall. You ok?" All around her, passengers pushed past impatiently, fighting to get on or off the train.

"Just a little embarrassed – that's all."

The WPC smiled back in a homely fashion. "You fainted before? You should see a doctor. You may have low blood pressure."

"I'm fine – I've just not eaten much today. Thank you – you're very kind." Tara pulled herself back onto her feet warily.

"Here have a drink," offered the student, withdrawing a bottle of mineral water from his bag. He smiled flirtatiously, allowing his interest to be just a little too obvious. Tara took a sip and handed it back, as they simultaneously boarded the train. She returned the smile, slightly flustered, but flattered, enjoying the innocent normality for the briefest of instants, before consulting her ticket and then turning back towards the door.

"You not getting this train?" called the student, with obvious disappointment.

"I misread my ticket," Tara lied, with faked embarrassment. "My seat's in coach F." She pointed towards the rear carriages. "Thanks once again."

Tara eased her way past passengers busy stowing their luggage, through into the next carriage, before exiting the train.

Dennehy had observed the street theatre just long enough to see the police officers turn their focus to the stricken female. He had pulled the baseball cap low over his forehead. If by chance anyone had spied him tampering with the relay box, given his appearance, they would have assumed he was on official Railtrack business. Once satisfied the police officers were suitably distracted, he had dropped lithely off the edge of the platform. Crouching forward, after a quick glance around, he had walked quickly, but not so fast as to draw attention to himself, the ten feet to the relay cabinet where he had pulled open the rucksack and placed the small device inside. Dennehy had activated the timing device, before closing the cabinet door behind him. Keeping low, he then waited until he heard the sound of the guard's whistle, before leaping back up onto the platform, under the cover of the slow moving train. In the toilets, he squeezed the fluorescent jacket back into his rucksack.

Outside the station, Tara wandered back down the ramp towards the city centre and entered a public phone box. Pushing a twenty pence piece into the slot, she dialled the number of the phone in the adjacent booth, just as Dennehy pulled the booth door closed behind him. The beard really did not suit him, Tara thought to herself. "Good night?" she asked.

"Everything went according to plan. I'll be home soon."

"Not too late darling."

Dennehy replaced the receiver and slid out of the phone box. Tara dawdled, pretending to talk on the phone for a further minute before hanging up, marvelling at Fraser's brazen audacity, as he calmly sauntered to the back of the nearby kebab queue.

Dennehy telephoned Leeds General Infirmary shortly after 7am, warning of a bomb at the railway station. A few minutes later, he placed a second hoax call, warning of devices at Doncaster railway station and on the M6 in Lancashire. Tara, meanwhile, phoned random members of the public listed in the telephone directory in Stoke on Trent, warning of devices at Crewe and Stoke on Trent railway stations, as well as on the M6 in Staffordshire.

Given the close proximity of the Leeds device to the station, with the possibility of civilian casualties, Tara pressed Powell to take evasive action. For once, he concurred with her assessment. However, a final decision was imposed over Powell's head. The official view was that defusing the device would alert the Provos to the fact that the security services were breathing down their neck. It would later emerge that GMP were reluctant to reveal to the British Transport Police that an agent had penetrated the mainland IRA operation – the fewer aware of Tara's existence the better. Instead, after a thorough examination of the device, a judgement was made that the modest quantity of plastic explosives would cause only symbolic damage. In a classic bureaucratic bungle, Powell assumed that the British Transport Police would actually act on the warning calls and close the station. Instead, they called the Provos' bluff and didn't evacuate until after the bomb had exploded. The exact scenario that shutting the stable door after the horse has bolted was invented to describe.

18th April 1997

Hundreds of thousands of road and rail users raised a collective groan of disapproval once again today, as the IRA struck for the fourth time during the general election campaign, bringing chaos and gridlock to large parts of Northern England. The terrorists forced the closure of 4 mainline stations and huge swathes of the M6 motorway. The most serious incident was at Leeds railway station, where a device exploded in a relay cabinet containing signalling equipment at approximately 9am. No one was injured, but the station remained closed most of the day. A warning was left at 7am at Leeds General Infirmary about a device at the mainline station. Telephone warnings of devices at Crewe and Stoke on Trent as well as Doncaster, turned out to be yet further hoaxes in the on going cat and mouse game between police and the

James Hurd • *A Bold Deceiver*

terrorists. Approximately 12,000 passengers were affected on both sides of the Pennines by the co-ordinated action.

On the roads, the alert began at 7.20am, when a member of the public received a telephone warning that there was a bomb between junctions 14-15 of the M6. Police closed the motorway from Junctions 13-18. There was further chaos, as warnings were also received regarding devices at junctions 28-29 in Lancashire, forcing additional closures.

British Transport Police defended their decision not to evacuate Leeds station until after the device had exploded. A spokesman said "If we evacuated every time, the terrorists would never have to plant another bomb and they would have won. We are never going to be 100% certain but in the end it's a judgement we have to make and we stand by this one."

Perhaps it was an act of defiance to the Provos that I would not let them control my life. They may have scored a propaganda coup, but they were not going to get the better of me. Tara was bemused by my defiance, as I insisted on attempting to reach Stoke on the Bonnie, sailing past hundreds of angry and frustrated motorists, stack parked to infinity. My opponent, however, was stuck on a train, and my client gridlocked on the M6. All of which gave me plenty of time to mull over the case, I was supposed to be arguing. It was a straightforward commercial dispute between a road haulage company and a plastics manufacturer, which was alleging a consignment had been damaged en route to Lyon and was now refusing to pay the carriage charges. Now, the delights of international carriage of goods law are far from exciting bedtime reading, but somewhere deep inside my brain there was a stirring – a sense that what I was reading had a wider significance.

Tara spent most of the afternoon being debriefed on the day's events. It sounded as if the meeting was more of a vitriolic spleen venting than a sober appraisal of strategic decision making, as recriminations flew. Tara ranted at Powell over his wanton disregard for life. In return, he took her invective with remarkable patience, before Tara stormed out demanding to know how she was ever supposed to trust him again?

You can imagine the darkness of Tara's mood that evening. She sat at the kitchen table and buried her head in her hands. "If I believed in the cause, I'd be whooping for joy. Instead I am burdened by this massive guilt trip, as I watch the pictures on the TV – knowing I have power, yet I am being forced to exercise it in a way which I despise."

"I thought they were going to close Leeds station?"

"Don't even ask." Tara rolled her eyes in frustration. "Powell said he was overruled."

"He's trying to ease himself off the hook," I replied, turning up the volume of the radio, given the ever present prying ears, whilst placing the salad in a bowl.

Tara flicked through the newspaper, without reading it, her eyes glazed and her mood resigned, as I stirred the pasta sauce on the hob. "We can't ride luck like this forever. Someone's bound to get hurt." She massaged her pained temples with her index fingers. "I feel so bloody useless. No, worse – a positive menace. Powell is scared crapless about the end of the month. But what else can I do?"

Tara played with the tagliatelle, twisting it round her fork, musing in a distant world. "I had a thought today," I said, disturbing her waking slumber.

Tara looked up only reluctantly. "Sorry?"

"I said I had an idea today."

"Hold the front page," she called sarcastically, returning her attention to her food.

"Do you want to hear it or not?" I was a growing a little impatient.

Tara lifted her eyes from the plate, regarding me in an inquisitive fashion, checking whether I was really pissed or whether my irritation was skin deep. "Go on then," she consented wearily.

"What makes you think Charlie operates garage premises?"

I had aroused her curiosity. "McDonnell told me in Dublin."

"What exactly did he say?"

"Is this idle speculation or do you have a point?" Tara shot me that look which said anything for a quiet life. "They had to move the truck containing the Manchester bomb from Charlie's place, as some ex-employee had bad mouthed him to the police in a stolen vehicle scam. They decided to move the truck at short notice, in case the police turned up with a warrant."

"Did the police attend?"

"Ah," she smiled weakly. "You're three steps behind – Powell's boys have gone over police records from East Anglia and Cambridgeshire with a fine tooth-comb and drawn a total blank."

"Because that was where the truck was from?"

Tara nodded. "Originally registered in Suffolk by Jack Roberts

Transport Limited..." Tara reeled off the information like a well-rehearsed sales technique: "...Great Blakenham. Just outside Ipswich. It was sold to Arthur Loveridge after he had advertised vehicles in Exchange and Mart."

"They check anywhere else?"

"West Midlands, after Fraser let it drop that Kieran didn't drive the stolen RAC van too far to Charlie's place to change the plates."

"What's the theory?"

Tara emptied her leftovers into the bin, before returning to the table. "Maybe the police didn't actually carry out the raid. Maybe McDonnell was wrong or Charlie overreacted. Hence we're still acting out this appalling charade. "

I pushed my empty plate to one side. "Did McDonnell ever use the word 'garage'?"

Tara furrowed her brow, trying to recall the precise words. "No, but it was perceived as the most likely permutation, although we are talking more commercial vehicle workshop than your local garage – as they had a paint shop for the Manchester bomb truck that would have been used to conceal the Jack Roberts sign, had they had more time, although they have checked other options too. Also, the scam was supposedly stolen vehicles – not to mention the modification of the van for the airport job, which requires some serious gear. Where exactly is all this leading?"

"My case today involved a haulage company. There were photographs of their depot and storage facility. Where better to hide a stolen truck than amongst other trucks? Who better to buy a truck from a dealer, even if anonymously, than a haulage company? What if Charlie runs a haulage company? One of his drivers gets pissed off and goes to the police. There in the yard, amongst all the other HGV's sits your Jack Roberts wagon stuffed with fertiliser."

Tara eyes lit up for the first time that evening as she assessed the implications. "He could have brought in the explosives himself. Regular haulage trips from...say Calais or Cork or even Dublin. The truck was bought just outside Peterborough. Why risk driving any distance, if they were in Birmingham they'd have bought locally...?"

"So we could be looking for a haulage company, with a base in Cambridgeshire and a depot in the West Midlands. And regular runs to the continent."

"Could be hundreds Tom," cautioned Tara, dampening my

enthusiasm.

"I wonder how many had a police tip off about stolen wagons in June 1996?" I asked rhetorically.

The strategy adopted by the IRA during the election campaign was a clever one. The risk to personnel had been low and the disruption to ordinary people's lives had been massive. The IRA had delivered the message that whichever party was elected, the most pressing problem on the incoming Government's agenda would be Northern Ireland. The Government would have to deal with Sinn Féin, regardless of their weasel words of mock revulsion.

Strategists had an alternative theory. The security forces had been so successful in disrupting operations on the mainland that spectaculars such as Docklands or Manchester could not be repeated. The ring of steel around the city of London is often cited as an example of this much tighter security. Hence the combination of small devices and hoax calls – the IRA were reduced to striking soft targets.

The IRA, however, was sensitive to the suggestion that it was, in any way, militarily weakened. If there was to be a renewed cease-fire, the Provies wanted to negotiate from a position of strength, not weakness. There was to be no surrender. That demanded a final reminder that they retained the ability to strike anywhere, at any time, at any target, be it large or small.

The operation planned for the eve of the election would certainly fall into the category of an 'IRA spectacular'. Whilst hardly breaking new ground, it was still a daring plan, which had served them well on two previous occasions. On the 7th February 1991, a Transit van had been driven to the junction of Whitehall and Horse Guards Parade. A hole had been cut into the roof and a wooden frame built inside to house three steel mortar tubes. The driver activated a timing device, before escaping on a motorcycle. Minutes later the mortar fired a home-made shell, which exploded in the rear garden of No.10 Downing Street, where John Major's War Cabinet was sitting during the First Gulf War. The IRA had shown its ability to penetrate the very heart of the British establishment, seemingly at will, bypassing rigid security precautions.

Three years later, on the 9th March 1994, the IRA fired mortars over half a mile through the rear window of a stolen Nissan Micra, over Heathrow police station, where three landed on the runway. The car had been stripped out and a metal plate welded to the floor for the tubes to be attached to. All three mortars failed to explode. An additional tube contained a device designed to explode and engulf the car. The audacious character of the attack was underlined by the fact the IRA struck again on both the 11th and 13th of March, sending mortars onto the south runway from tubes that had been buried on waste ground and activated by timers set days before.

The current plan involved a renewal of the mortar attack strategy. By the 30th April 1997, after a gruelling six-week election campaign, the final push would be on in the marginal seats. Tony Blair's final day of campaigning would take him from an 8am press conference in London to his home constituency of Sedgefield. On the way, he would pay a flying visit to the North West, attending rallies, meetings and walkabouts in Huddersfield, Wigan and Chester. He was scheduled to fly from Manchester Airport to Newcastle upon Tyne soon after 4.30pm. The IRA planned to fire mortars onto the runway at Manchester Airport that afternoon.

Personally, I don't believe that the IRA had any real intention of murdering Mr Blair. A tactical near miss would be sufficient to make their point, while keeping their hands relatively clean for the rapprochement that would surely follow the election. The history books are, however, strewn with examples of military operations that failed to proceed according to plan. What would happen if, despite their best endeavours, a device exploded on the runway, when an aircraft was either about to take off or land? Leaving aside Mr Blair, the risk of loss of life was immense.

Two weeks previously, a maroon Manchester City Council Direct Works Department Leyland Daff van had been appropriated to the IRA cause in Levenshulme by MacKenna. In an anonymously rented lock-up garage, the van had been temporarily spray-painted to conceal its identity while travelling south. The number plates had been replaced with fakes and the disguised vehicle had been driven to Charlie's premises. Once there, a two-man team from the Newry/South Armagh IRA had cut open the roof and installed a trap door and mortar tubes. The trajectory had been carefully planned from ordnance survey maps and video footage taken by Dennehy, whilst pretending to be a plane spotter. As at the 18th April, the security services had no idea of the present location of the van or its current state of readiness. They were well aware that the operation was planned for twelve days time, but the fear remained that the attack might be brought forward, as senior politicians of all parties were using the airport on a regular basis.

The pressure to forestall this final operation, and to do so expeditiously grew in the proceeding days, particularly after the Army Council sanctioned the mortar attack, following Dennehy's and Tara's final reconnaissance at the airport.

Standing at the junction of West Ringway and Shadow Moss Road, only a few feet from the end of runway, they scoured the scene with high-powered binoculars. The sky was overcast in late afternoon and the glowing approach lights burnt strong against the darkening sky. Neither looked remotely out of place amongst a group of about ten gathered to watch the descent of aircraft from all over the world into Manchester International Airport. The location of the launch site had been carefully chosen. Two hundred yards up the road, at the edge of the nearby housing estate, there was a piece of waste ground, backing onto the rear gardens of nearby homes. A relatively substantial hedge concealed the field from the casual observer. The other lesson, borne of experience, was that if you cannot hide something, make it look ordinary. What could be more ordinary than a Council van, restored to its original livery, parked on open land, perhaps with a lawnmower at the ready?

Dennehy scanned the horizon for any sign that security procedures had been tightened. He passed the binoculars to Tara. "Let's get out of here, before we start to look too much like plane spotters," Tara urged Dennehy, handing him back the high powered glasses. Once in the passenger seat of Tara's MG, Dennehy appeared thoughtful, contemplating the task at hand. Tara lifted her foot off the accelerator, letting the car slow slightly as they passed the rusty gate that formed the entrance to the launch site. "You look worried Fraser. See a problem?"

"Why do you think they never evacuated at Leeds?"

If Tara was nervous at the question, she concealed it with skill and professionalism – fast learning to take such scrutiny in her stride, no matter how quickly her heart raced. She shrugged her shoulders. "Maybe they concluded it was a hoax? Did you use the right code word?"

"Course I bloody did," he replied, irate at having his actions queried before relenting. "Every other call, including hoaxes, they've evacuated. Look at the mess we caused at Aintree."

"So maybe they're getting wise?" Tara reasoned.

Dennehy wasn't convinced. "It just doesn't feel right. Why take the chance?"

"You know how often they ignore warnings or fail to act promptly. Some incompetent Sergeant still wet behind the ears who's peeing his pants at what to do."

"Yeah, I know. It's just...." Dennehy stared out of the passenger window.

"Just what?"

"Ah nothing," he replied, waving to indicate its insignificance. "Just Kieran and his wild theories. You know what he's like," he told her dismissively, waving his hand. "He's convinced Leeds didn't evacuate because they had intelligence."

The traffic lights ahead changed to red. Tara engaged the handbrake and gripped it tightly to prevent her hands shaking. "How on earth does he arrive at such lunacy?"

"Don't ask me," Dennehy sighed. "If they knew how small the device was, maybe they would take the risk."

Tara felt her heart miss a beat. She wondered if this was the inevitable moment that she'd been dreading, before she quickly composed herself. A car sounded its horn. The traffic lights had changed to green. Thrusting the car into first she pulled away. "If they had any idea what was going on, you and I would have been arrested at Leeds. Anyway, what is he suggesting – we are all under surveillance and they saw the device being planted or someone told them – you or me I suppose?" Her voice was louder now, as she channelled her tension into abusing MacKenna. "Tell me you don't buy it?"

"No one is accusing anyone. I told him not to be so bloody paranoid. If there was a security breach, there would have been a cock up – instead it went exactly to plan."

"Quite," Tara replied, relaxing slightly. "Man is he one suspicious son of a bitch. Dennehy nodded silently, returning his focus to the windscreen. "He's just nervous about next week."

"He's not the only one. But we don't go around accusing him of touting do we?"

The irony was not lost on either of us. There was no evacuation at Leeds, in order to avoid suspicion falling on Tara. Yet that very inactivity had in itself precipitated the exact opposite effect. Despite her exterior bravado, the encounter clearly freaked her. Tara was unsure about Dennehy. Did he buy MacKenna's theory? Had they conspired together to evaluate her response when the subject was raised? Or was he forewarning her? Either way, it raised the stakes another notch, as the clock slipped closer to election-day. Tara had an inkling that the sands of time were trickling out, both for the operation and her personally. An unfortunate coincidence, I rationalised, in a fruitless attempt to allay her fears. But there was an apprehensive knot in the pit of my stomach, which told me otherwise.

Chapter Thirty Eight

THERE WERE APPROXIMATELY 112,000 HGV licence operators in the UK at the time. Between them they operated almost 400,000 vehicles. There were half a million HGV drivers employed throughout the industry, with approximately the same number employed in ancillary services such as warehouses, workshops and offices. Nevertheless by the 24th April, some six days before the scheduled date for the Manchester Airport mortar attack, the field had been narrowed significantly. Of the countless operators with depots in the West Midlands, less than fifty also had facilities in Cambridgeshire or East Anglia, transporting goods to the continent out of Felixstowe and Harwich. Of these, twenty-three also had depots of varying sizes in the Republic of Ireland and were all based within a twenty five mile radius from Walsall, north of Birmingham.

Posing as Ministry of Transport Officials, a sweep was carried out over a three-day period, covering all twenty three operators within the East Anglia/Cambridgeshire area. The decision to limit the search geographically was taken both due to time considerations and available manpower. The crucial consideration was to restrict knowledge of the operation to an absolute minimum. The wider the net was drawn, the greater the risk of an inadvertent security compromise. A simple tip off to a mate with a few crates of smuggled cigarettes would soon enter the gossip network and encourage everyone to tidy up their act.

In addition, a memo was circulated to all officers in the West Midlands and Cambridgeshire Police areas inquiring whether anyone could recall a tip off regarding stolen goods/vehicles and a haulier in May/June 1996. It was a final desperate measure, as there were seemingly no records of any arrests or convictions on the Police National Computer.

By 6pm on Saturday 26th April, each of the suspect premises had received a personal visit from two officers – a team of eight in total. They in turn met together with Powell and other senior officers from the Anti-Terrorism Squad led by Superintendent Ian Wallington – a veteran of recent IRA attacks in South East of England. Four firms were scrubbed from the list almost immediately, removing those operating exclusively domestic or local services, despite having franchise depots further afield. Small firms, who traded out of premises simply not large enough to have their own repair/welding capacity, let alone paint facilities, were equally eliminated. That narrowed the field to eleven haulage companies. As for the others, I was never informed as to the reason for their exclusion. However, by 5am on Sunday 27th April, seven haulage depots in East Anglia and Cambridgeshire were under twenty four hour surveillance, along with their counterparts in the West Midlands, just in case the re-sprayed Manchester City Council van had been transferred there on its way north.

Monday 28th April 1997

It was after 3am before Detective Inspector Gareth Radcliffe's night shift had begun to quieten down. A stabbing incident at a city centre night club in Peterborough, shortly after midnight, had kept him and his team occupied, taking statements from witnesses, visiting the complainant in the Accident and Emergency department and scouring the streets with the uniform patrol. They had arrested a suspect, but he wouldn't be sober enough to be interviewed until the following morning. Pouring a cup of strong coffee, Radcliffe contemplated the depressing amount of paperwork the last three nights had generated. He was still rifling through the files piled on his desk in despair, when he managed to lose the co-ordination in his left hand for just long enough to tilt his mug to the left, sending a stream of hot coffee all over the desk. "Shit". He stood to avoid the trickle of liquid about to incriminate his trousers and reached for a pack of tissues. Lifting a pile of memos from his desk that were the most heavily contaminated, his attention was drawn to one, with half visible text: "**IMPORTANT–**

James Hurd • *A Bold Deceiver*

Information is urgently required with regard to any officer who had a complaint made to him or her in June 1996, regarding possible criminal activity in the course of the complainant's employment working for a local haulage company or similar undertaking."

A distant bell rang, there was a familiarity, but nothing he could quite put his finger upon. Bean counters and bureaucrats were ensuring his life had degenerated into a constant paper chase. He almost deposited the damp stained memo straight in the bin. There was just this nagging doubt at the back of his mind. Just in case, he scribbled the phone number down on a scrap of paper before depositing the memo in the bin, along with the rest of the brown soggy mush. Ten hours later, lying in bed, listening to the distant sound of lawns been mowed and a radio playing up the street, Radcliffe contemplated abandoning any further attempt at sleep. Reluctantly pulling himself out of bed, he headed towards the shower. Whilst his mind glided in neutral, suddenly out of the blue a distant memory was triggered. By the time he left the shower and shaved, the image was focused and sharp. Leafing through an old notebook at the start of his next shift, confirmed his recollection. He retrieved the scrap of paper from the night before and dialled the number. "This is DI Radcliffe from Peterborough…"

"Superintendent Ian Wallington, what can I do for you Detective Inspector?"

"Your memo landed on my desk. I don't know if this is what you're after, but I was given some cock and bull story from a guy about his boss during the first week of June 1996. He claimed he worked for a local haulage contractor, who he alleged was part of a smuggling scam, importing booze, fags and possibly illegal drugs."

"Got a name?"

Radcliffe thumbed his notebook. "Darren Harris."

"Haulage Company?"

"Err… JB Waterson (Transport) Limited."

"You follow it up?"

Radcliffe let out a grunt. "Yeah, till I found out he'd been sacked for having his hand in the till. We reckoned he was trying to get back at his boss by shopping him."

"Any truth in it?"

"Anything's possible. We'd never have proved anything though. The little shit was sent down a couple of weeks later – seems he was part of some car ringing scam."

"Any idea where he is now?"

"Not my case, but he may still be in the system. What's the score?"

"No big deal, it may fit into a current investigation. Peterborough nick, if I need to come back to you?"

"Yeah." The phone went dead, without so much as thanks for taking the time to call.

It took just two phone calls and ten minutes for Wallington to identify that Harris was currently serving a four year sentence for offences of theft and handling stolen goods, and to locate his current place of incarceration as HM Prison Blunderston, four and a half miles north of Lowestoft. Within hours two men purporting to be Cambridgeshire CID officers had been despatched.

Harris was a forty three year old mechanic with thinning grey flecked hair pulled harshly back into a pony tail. He was summoned to see the wing supervisor shortly after 6pm and ushered into an interview room. Harris had little time for police officers and was disinclined to offer them any assistance. Nevertheless, the police don't make social calls at short notice without good reason. They politely offered him a cigarette. They then proceeded to grill him regarding his previous employer. What was in it for him if he co-operated? One of the officers told Harris that he was in a catch twenty two situation. If he helped, they would do what they could for him or Harris could walk back to his cell and do his time – and he would never know how much time he could have saved. Harris weighed his options and then decided to talk. Perhaps he saw an opportunity to finally gain revenge over his ex-employer.

Harris had been employed by JT Waterson (Transport) Limited from the spring of 1995, as a HGV driver. After a while, his suspicions had been aroused regarding some of the loads he was transporting, for example oral instructions to make two pick ups, with one set of documentation, which purported to show that both loads were from the same client. One day his curiosity was aroused to fever pitch and he examined his load whilst parked up at Watford Gap Services. He discovered he was carrying about forty thousand duty-free cigarettes and over two hundred bottles of duty-free bonded whisky. Harris later learnt that they were distributed through a network of contacts and sold into pubs, social clubs and working men's clubs across East Anglia. Frank Macintosh had purchased the business from the Waterson family five years previously, but had retained the goodwill of the family name. He lived in a five bedroom detached house just outside Peterborough. He owned a villa in Spain and drove a sixty thousand pounds Mercedes. Macintosh had a temper and was not a man to cross, as Harris had discovered to his detriment.

Once Macintosh had identified Harris as the culprit, skimming off the odd carton of cigarettes and appropriating the occasional crate of whisky that was mysteriously disappearing, he wasted no time in sacking him. There had been a heated exchange of views, whereupon Harris had threatened to shop his employer. Macintosh had apparently exploded at Harris' attempted blackmail and physically assaulted him, pushing him to the ground and kicking him repeatedly before Harris had the opportunity to vacate the premises, as quick as his battered limbs would allow. In the heat of the moment, he reported his suspicions to the local police.

It was at this point during the interrogation, it dawned on Harris that the police were angling for information regarding criminal activity significantly more serious than smuggled fags. His fears grew, as one of the officers asked if he knew anything about guns? Harris shook his head, in genuine surprise. One of them threw him a full cigarette pack as he stood to leave the interview room. As Harris had caught the pack of Silk Cut in his hands, the officer turned with an afterthought. "The name Charlie mean anything to you?"

Harris dawdled over the dregs of his cigarette. Perhaps the pricks in suits weren't so bright after all, he thought to himself, in a bemused fashion. "Ever been to Glasgow?" he asked cryptically. "The café owner in the TV show 'Allo 'Allo – work it out yourself smart arse."

I confess, when the clues were later divulged to me, I sat for a couple of minutes piecing the various segments together, before the eureka moment struck me like a bolt out of the blue, despite the spelling variations – *René and Glasgow* – *Charles Rennie Macintosh* – the famous Scottish Art Nouveau designer and architect.

An emergency security meeting took place in the early hours of Tuesday 29th April, with representatives from the Greater Manchester Police Special Branch and the Metropolitan Police Anti Terrorism Squad, senior officers from Cambridgeshire and West Midlands Police along with a representative from MI5. A trade off ensued between the safety of ensuring the Leyland Daff van never reached Manchester and the prospect of catching an IRA ASU red-handed. If the police moved too soon, MacKenna and Dennehy might escape. If they delayed too long, the deadly cargo might slip through their fingers.

This assumed the coveted Manchester City Council van had been transformed to a mobile mortar launcher and remained in situ at one of the Waterson's depots, before being moved either late on Tuesday or early Wednesday morning towards the target. With hindsight, this was a pretty Herculean assumption to make. However, it was a hypothesis based on hard intelligence gathered by Tara. Still sprayed white, the van would be driven from Cambridgeshire through the West Midlands and on to Manchester, where the white paint would be removed and the vehicle restored to its municipal burgundy.

The prevailing wisdom was that the final leg of the journey would not be undertaken until the early hours of Wednesday morning, as the Wolverhampton premises were deemed more secure than the lock-up. The only doubt concerned the co-ordinated series of hoax calls, which thanks to Tara, the police knew were planned for the rush hour of Tuesday morning, designed to block the main arteries of the motorway network in the South East. The authorities feared these were a cover to create the maximum possible confusion and congestion, diverting attention amid the traffic chaos, whilst allowing the ASU to relocate the converted van northwards.

Surveillance was increased at the two haulage sites. Undercover officers were pulled off reconnaissance at all other haulage depots as the emphasis shifted to the JT Waterson's sites. 5am Wednesday the 30th April was the appointed commencement time for the raids, provided no attempt was made to move the van from either site in the preceding hours. Tara revealed this information to me, after she returned from a briefing meeting soon after 7pm on Tuesday the 29th April.

29th April 1997

The IRA struck again today, paralysing traffic for the third time during the election campaign. Bomb threats were received in Kent, Surrey and Hertfordshire, as a 40mile stretch of the M25 was closed causing heavy congestion in the area around South Mimms services and routes to the Channel via the M20 and M26.

A slightly different approach was taken by Scotland Yard around the most heavily used stretches of motorway near Heathrow, the M4 and the M40 westerly section of the M25, which remained open whilst police officers checked for bombs. A spokesman indicated that the decision was taken after a professional assessment of the risk, following a number of hoax warnings over recent weeks. In addition, yesterday, a 7-mile stretch of the M1 and a 20-mile section of the M5 were closed for more than three hours. Sections of the M3 and M27 in Hampshire were also shut. There was also disruption at Southampton airport, whilst Terminal 2 at Heathrow and both North and South Terminals at Gatwick were partially evacuated.

I was engrossed in some programme or other on the television and didn't hear her key in the door, or her footsteps in the hall. I just had a gradual awareness, subconsciously, that I was being watched. Tara stood in the hallway, peering through the small gap in the partially opened living room door. Her head was angled slightly, hair falling loosely over her face, concealing her expression. "How long have you been there?"

"A little while," she said, with just a hint of melancholy. She made no attempt to intrude any further into the room – her hands tucked in the rear pocket of her jeans. Her body language betrayed weariness, maybe even sullenness. The signals were confused – her eyes disheartened, but a smile on her face. I recognised the bravado. When Tara forced a smile, the muscles at the corner of her mouth seemed to point upwards slightly more than usual, in a subtle hint of force. "It's over, Tom," she murmured eventually, under her breath.

I scrutinised her features, searching for clues. "What do you mean?" I moved from the sofa, approaching her. "What is it?"

Tara stood her ground firmly, her eyes closed mournfully. "Mission accomplished – they think they have found Charlie. Soon after five am tomorrow, this purgatory will end. They found the whistleblower in prison in East Anglia…" It took a minute for my overloaded brain to catch up.

"So there will be no mortar attack?"

"No," Tara smirked in triumph. "Finally we will stop an operation. That van won't get very far, although I'm told that Tony Blair won't come within a hundred miles of Manchester – just in case. Kieran and Fraser will be picked up at the same time, either at home, or at the depot, depending on which one of them decides to drive the damn thing. Apparently the GMP are being briefed tonight in preparation for dawn raids."

"Trust me, they don't require much practice." Tara giggled in a mixture of guilt and amusement. I was suddenly overwhelmed by the exhilaration of conquest. We had taken on the might of the IRA and, tentatively, it looked as if we had emerged victorious. I was buoyant, without drawing the logical ramifications. If Tara showed a degree of hesitation, I confess my sensitivity glands failed to discern it. "I suppose this means you won?" I beamed in Tara's direction.

"Don't be too eager," Tara cautioned. "Tomorrow morning remember."

"I know, but none the less this calls for a celebration," I countered, all of a sudden de-mob happy.

A minute or so later in the kitchen I was crouched forwards, my back to Tara, placing champagne in the freezer to cool. I felt the tender touch of her hand on my shoulder. The intimacy of her fingertips implored me to stop and listen. Her eyes examined mine, begging me not to force her to articulate the message she sought to convey. I regret to say I failed her. "Tom listen," her words were barely audible. Tara placed the palm of her hand on my face. Her fingers felt cold, as she traced her finger across my cheek, resting her index finger delicately on my lips. "It's over for me too."

The emphasis on the word 'me' finally revealed what Tara meant. I sank back against the fridge. "You're leaving?" It ought not to have come as a surprise. After all, it was a finite arrangement: a fake cover story of domestic bliss until the mission was accomplished, a place to stay and a pretend partner. In return we caught the bastards who murdered my brother. Now our obligations were fulfilled, I was free to resume a normal life, and Tara – she would have to confront the same demons she carried when she turned up on my doorstep that dark and wet Sunday evening.

"I hadn't reckoned on it being so soon," I answered, suddenly feeling rather deflated.

"The timing's not in either of our hands. If there's a balls up tomorrow, how long do you think it will take Kieran to figure out who the weakest link is? Powell wanted to withdraw me late this afternoon, given the timing of the raids."

"So why are you still here?" It was a crude turn of phrase that sounded harsher than I had intended.

I sensed the fire burning within, as she smarted from my verbal blow. "I thought you deserved to hear it from my lips. I figured that I owed it to you not to just disappear without explanation – again."

I pondered for a moment. "When?"

"They're sending a car, early tomorrow morning."

"So that's that then," I replied quietly, avoiding eye contact.

"I'm going to pack," replied Tara, firing her final arrow. "Like you said, mission accomplished. There's no reason to stay is there, even if I could?"

Tara's recently departed image still fresh in my mind, I experienced a myriad of emotions. In many ways, the previous few months had been hell. Any semblance of a normal existence seemed to have vanished. Now I felt the blessed relief of normality. The pain of Ben's loss was eased in the knowledge there would be some justice. Tara's presence served as a daily reminder of unfinished business, and constant guilt. I could relax, go on holiday and devote some time to my legal practice, sadly neglected like a middle-aged wife for the excitement of an affair. Standing in my kitchen, I knew only too well that passionate affairs were great in the heat of amorousness, but when it faded to indifference, you were left with nothing but cold comfort and a feeling of emptiness. Elation tinged with sadness. We had been cocooned in a world that very few others could ever share: fear, trepidation, jittery tension, adrenaline and, on occasion, euphoria. The prospect of her departure left me despondent and deflated. I didn't know what I wanted: for Tara to stay, which was impossible, or for her to disappear into the criminal justice system, which seemed logical, even moral, but at the same time perverse.

We sat on the sofa, eating Chinese food from aluminium trays and sipped champagne. "So what's next?" I asked.

Tara stuffed the end of a duck pancake into her mouth. "I wish I knew," she said, chewing her food. "They tell me there will be an extensive debrief. They will probably get the RUC to pump me on the IRA set up over there."

"And then?" I probed, picking up the last scraps of crispy duck from the silver foil and licking my fingers.

"You tell me, you're the lawyer?"

"I suppose they will make a decision on whether to prosecute you or not."

"Even if they don't prosecute me for Manchester, they will simply send me back to Northern Ireland to face the music there. One way or another I am not going to be doing this again in a hurry," she said, raising her glass in a resigned gesture.

"Will they want you to give evidence against MacKenna, Dennehy or Macintosh?"

Tara sat back on the sofa and thought for a moment. "We haven't discussed it, but I suppose they might...." She closed her eyes tightly. "Why do lawyers and courts scare the living daylights out of me?"

"More than MacKenna and Dennehy?"

"I guess not."

The champagne bottle emptied in line with my inhibitions. "This operation or mission, whatever you want to call it – you didn't really need me. You could've got a flat of your own and told them you were still seeing me."

Tara looked surprised, uncertain as to how to respond. "You really want to know why I involved you in the first place? Maybe I judged that living with you would give me more credibility with McDonnell and the others."

"There's nothing more to it?" I retorted, with a glint of cheerful smugness, our eyes reaching a mutual understanding.

A broad grin of anticipation crept across Tara's face, betraying a sense of mischief, as she sipped her champagne and lit a cigarette. She rounded on me. "I'll do you a deal. If you are really in the mood for honesty, I'll tell you why I wanted it this way, if you tell me why you agreed to go along with it?"

Why had I? "You first then," I stipulated, stalling for time. Tara positioned herself opposite me, close enough to touch. There was to be no comfort in physical isolation.

Tara began hesitantly, with a degree of uncertainty, ameliorated by the confidence of alcohol. She contemplated inserting her slender fingers between mine, but then thought better of it. "I could have done it without you," she began self-consciously. "Invented more stories and lies and it may have worked. But I wanted you to see what I was doing. I didn't want your last impression of me to be the callous bitch the police told you I was. An evil terrorist without humanity, that you would go though the rest of your life hating, smarting at my betrayal and always asking why? The person you knew in 1995 didn't fit that description. The only way I could prove I was sincere, was for you to enter the world I left behind. To say sorry without it sounding hollow, meaningless or trite. I couldn't bear for you to spend the rest of your life loathing me – even if it's deserved..." Tara's voice tailed off.

I was overwhelmed, but a deal is a deal, particularly when she had been so painfully honest. "I don't despise you Tara. When the police first confronted me, I was so incensed. I felt betrayed, yet I always struggled to reconcile the captivatingly beautiful, witty intelligent woman, I fell in love with and the psychotic bomber. I was putting my life back in some sort of order, when out of the blue you exploded back into my life with this incredible tale of the IRA, political violence and a road to Damascus conversion. One brief night and then you vanished. Like a tornado that tears up a house out of the ground and deposits it somewhere else, leaving a trail of destruction in its wake. I wanted to understand, to place you in context of what happened to Ben. Powell convinced me this was a once in a lifetime opportunity to play an active role in apprehending my brother's killers. So I jumped in feet first, without really working out the practicalities. I was a shit to you at the outset, but I didn't know how else to deal with the situation. You deserved better..."

Tara nodded, and acknowledged my words with a degree of humility, but her eyes probed further. "Don't hold out on me..." She sensed my honesty was not absolute and shook her head in frustration. "You promised. There's more..."

"...I owe you an apology," I began hesitantly. "When you reappeared, I screamed that I owed you nothing. That wasn't true." Tara looked inquisitive, occasionally wiping her eyes with her sleeve, before I placed my hand fondly into hers.

"You lied about the accident – I let it go at the time. I was too proud." I paused momentarily. "I landed in the water – it probably spared me a few more broken bones. There was no explanation as to how I had managed to drag myself onto the beach. You pulled me out and probably saved my life. I figured if you were really a heartless bitch, you'd have abandoned me to my fate – I had to reconcile these competing images." I stretched out my hands. "Terrorist and life saver...."

Tara appeared stunned and spoke only falteringly. "What I did was insignificant compared with ...what I didn't do – to that truck..." Tara paused, reliving the trauma of that afternoon. "You were so heavy in your wet leathers." She ran her fingers through her hair, uncomfortable with my honesty. "Whatever I did, it could never be enough..."

I hung my head low, brooding – recognising I might never get another opportunity, before finally I engaged with her. "Listen, you acted to protect your own neck. It was convenient for you to turn a blind eye to events under your own roof, and I think I understand why. If that was cowardice, the events of the last few months have proven you are no coward. I don't hold you responsible for Ben's death – rather those who conceived, planned and placed a bomb in a busy shopping centre, not caring who they maimed or the lives they destroyed. If your mission in including me in this venture was to ensure that I was left with an accurate impression of you, then I think you've been successful."

By now a steady flood of tears flowed down Tara's cheeks. I reached towards her and held her closely. We embraced warmly, sharing our relief and regret, taking solace in the restorative balm of our candour. When I pressed the first kiss on her salty cheek, it felt the most natural thing in the world. A product of the closeness we had re-established through adversity. Tara responded and moved her face slightly until our lips met and I kissed her tenderly, slipping my tongue into her mouth. Tara yielded before disengaging. "Stop," she commanded forcefully. "Is this really what you want Tom?"

I grasped her hand between my own. "After tomorrow, on four occasions now you will have entered and exited my life, leaving a trail of chaos...." My last comment drew a bashful smile. "Twice you have arrived unexpectedly and twice after tomorrow, you will have vanished. All I know is that tomorrow you won't be here and I have no idea how I will feel about that..."

I wished I had a remote control to press the pause button on the time machine to forestall morning as long as possible. Tara's response was unequivocal – the convergence of our bodies in the flicker of candle light. My fingers trembled as I unbuttoned her blouse, pressing kisses into the valley between her breasts. I placed my hand on her upper arm, massaging her shoulders, running my fingers wide down her back, cupping her breasts and softly stroking her firm stomach. I lay on the bed as she arched her back on top of me and I entered her. With each tender thrust, the pain of the last year softened into a world both delicious and sweet.

Afterwards, Tara, her head on my shoulder, gently stroked my chest. "There's been no one else," she whispered tenderly. In that moment, I was consumed with regret that I was unable to respond in a like manner – enough honesty for one night. The drunken encounter in the aftermath of my arrest existed only in a parallel dimension. So I held her close and lied. "For me either." Neither of us slept, as we watched the small hours on the clock slip slowly away towards five am, and imagined the simultaneous events taking place in both Peterborough and the other side of Manchester.

Chapter Thirty Nine

WEDNESDAY 30TH APRIL – I left home with a heavy heart, soon after 7am, for a trial in Leeds. I had anticipated that, by then, Tara would have been safely collected, but in a vicious twist of fate, after hanging on as long as possible, by the time I departed, there was no sign of her escort. Tara urged me to go. Neither of us particularly relished an emotional farewell in front of Tara's reception committee. We had rehearsed all our goodbyes the night before. My final vision was of Tara perched in quiet expectation on the edge of the bed, two small bags by her side.

As luck would have it, I negotiated a deal and settled the case at the door of court and arrived home shortly after 2pm. It took a few minutes before I perceived something was amiss. A sixth sense of foreboding, as the curtains in the study were firmly closed. In Tara's bedroom, sitting forlornly on the carpet, were her two bags. All the boys in blue had to do was send an unmarked Panda car to pick her up. How difficult could that be? It was only as I placed my cufflinks down on the dressing table, that my eyes alighted on the hastily scribbled note, with none of her usual finesse: "*Tom, Kieran got here first. Job's still on. Get help.*" It was signed with just the letter "*T*"

As I read her words, the bottom dropped out of my universe. I was winded and felt like I had just done twelve rounds with Mike Tyson. My entire body simultaneously broke into a cold sweat. I collapsed onto the bed. I tried to compose myself and think rationally. MacKenna and Dennehy possibly still at large? What if Macintosh had been apprehended and MacKenna knew? My brain was instantly awash with a nightmare vision of Tara being beaten senseless and summarily executed – her body hanging in the air for a second, before slumping forward. I screamed at the hidden microphones. "All you had to do was pick her up. Yet you still had to screw it up?" My voice was hoarse with shouting. I expected the phone to ring any second in response to my ravings, but it remained stubbornly dead. Why should I expect them to drop their pretence now? I fumbled for the handset with one hand, whilst scrabbling around for Powell's number. With each second that passed, I sensed Tara slipping further away. I punched the number and waited impatiently for a ringing tone. Powell sounded as calm as ever. "Tom, where is she? There was no one at the house when we arrived."

"No shit Sherlock. MacKenna beat you to her. Please tell me you have them in custody?" There was activity in the background, as Powell barked orders with his hand over the phone. As I feared, he had as little idea where Tara was, as I did. "What exactly is the point of eavesdropping, if the one time the information might be of any use to you, you ignore it? Or did you simply forget to install a microphone by the front door?"

There was a desperate silence at the end of the phone, which seemed to last for an age, before he replied calmly, ignoring my last comments. "We've got Macintosh. The airport is crawling with armed plain-clothes officers. This'll be the Provies' last stand." He spoke with resolute coolness.

"The only thing I'm interested in hearing about is how you plan to get Tara out of this almighty mess alive," I barked in exasperation. I'm not certain, but I think he had already hung up.

My mouth was dry and my head pounded like it was being smashed with a rather large sledgehammer. I was left with an uneasy feeling that Tara was no longer their top priority. She was expendable. Paranoia: too many conspiracy theories, right? In my despairing pessimism, I feared Tara would be caught in the inevitable cross fire. I paced the floor, impotent to alter events unfolding only miles away. I had little to contribute, yet felt compelled to be in close proximity to the airport.

I was clambering into my leather jeans when the doorbell buzzed. I figured using the bike would scythe through the Friday rush hour traffic. I stormed down the hall in irritation at such an unfortunate interruption, intent of getting rid of whoever was at the door. I was anxious not to be delayed, yet retained the faintest glimmer of hope it might be Tara. Instead I was confronted with a thunderous glare from Becky. I had no inkling what her problem was, knowing only her timing was highly inconvenient. Before I had a chance to fob her off, she had barged past me like a bull in a china shop. "Where is the murdering bitch?" she shouted, flying along the hall and poking her head around the door of each room, satisfying herself that each was empty, while I watched bemused in the hallway. "You'd better come clean before I haul your arse to the police, after I've given you a good slapping."

"If you're referring to Tara, I haven't the faintest idea where she is," I replied truthfully, but with little conviction.

Becky's nostrils flared at my audacity. "Give it up Tom," she balled in frustration. "I saw the two of you together – the other weekend on your bikes. I convinced myself even you couldn't do that to your own family. But I was wrong. Yesterday evening, I was out shopping and whom did I see, but our friendly local neighbourhood terrorist! So I followed her, right to your front door." She poked her index finger in my direction. "I hope she's a fine lay, now you've screwed her, as well as you've entire family." Becky quickened the pace of her poking finger in a stabbing motion and looked set to swing for me. "I almost confronted the pair of you last night, but I think I would have killed you both – and much as I'd like nothing better at this moment…" She hesitated slightly before adding, "…I think there's been one too many deaths in this family already, don't you?"

Becky seemed to crumple under the weight of my perceived betrayal, sitting at the bottom of the stairs, her head rested upon her knees in anguish. "Why Tom?" She wanted me to reassure her that she was mistaken, that an entirely plausible explanation existed. But I saw little point in further concealment, even if I had the time or inclination to construct an elaborate fabrication. Besides, I was sick of the deceit, creeping around like a fugitive, in case my family stumbled upon my houseguest. I refused to be ashamed. My actions had been motivated by the noblest of intentions. Well, almost all of them.

"She was here, okay," I conceded, in growing agitation.

"Conveniently, she left this morning did she?" Becky's tone was mocking with barely concealed scepticism.

My mouth was open and I was resigned to spewing out the entire sorry story in graphic detail. Luckily, the ringing of my mobile phone intervened. "Back in a second." I left Becky still mesmerised by my admission. I fumbled for the phone in nervous clumsy desperation.

"Tom, thank God." It was Tara. "Tell Powell to close the airport, Kieran will be driving a black Vauxhall Tigra. Fraser will follow in the transit. We're leaving in the next thirty minutes. The mortars will be transported from Wythenshawe down Shadow Moss Road. I'm the assigned getaway driver, only I'm going to bolt. Meet me behind the International Business Centre on Styal Road. There's an abandoned farm house, it's in the A-Z." I could hear the sound of a flushing toilet in the background.

"Hello." Nothing – damn.

Becky had been unable to resist eavesdropping and quickly deduced the identity of the caller. She approached like one very grizzly bear who wouldn't take no for an answer, upon being told there was no honey. "That was her?" I didn't waste time replying, punching Powell's number and relayed the message. "Will you tell me what the hell is going on?" Becky screwed up her face in frustration.

"Serious trouble," I replied gravely.

"Like I care about what happens to her?"

I shook my head. "You wouldn't say that, if you knew what was about to go down," I cautioned, pulling my boots on. "With any luck the rest of the IRA unit who bombed Manchester will be either in custody or dead within the next hour," I replied deadpan. I opened the front door and grabbed the bike keys. "Gotta fly, your timing is dreadful."

Becky charged down the drive after me, her eyes wide open, manifest with confusion, disbelief and for the first time the subtlest glint of glee. "Tom, will you please stop right now and tell me what's happening?"

"I'll explain when we get there."

Where?"

"Don't just stand there like an idiot," I replied, thrusting the Zephyr's bike keys into her hands. "Are you coming or not? Traffic will be dreadful." I threw Tara's leather jacket in Becky's direction and grabbed a spare helmet, before igniting the Bonnie engine into life, and accelerating rapidly. The speed cameras could go to hell.

Approximately ten miles away, the 'main event' of the IRA mainland tour 1997 had already commenced. MacKenna was due to scout the route for Dennehy, at the wheel of the van, now restored to its original

Manchester City Council burgundy. Abandoning his car, MacKenna would make a final sweep of the area on foot. Once he received the appropriate coded radio signal, Dennehy would drive the van onto the waste ground. The two of them would then pull back the canvas roof and set the ignition timers for the mortars. Tara was riding shotgun, closely guarding Dennehy's tail, before diverting into a side road. It was then only a short hop for Dennehy and MacKenna across a few back gardens to the waiting car, before slipping quietly back into obscurity. Fifteen minutes later a salvo of mortars would be shot onto the main runway. The final mortar was designed to explode, still sheathed in its tube, detonating the Leyland Daff van. The only record would be the devastation that would ensue within the perimeter fence of the airport.

Six co-ordinated raids had been launched soon after five am. My initial satisfaction that the police were at last about to destroy the real culprits' front door hinges, soon turned to despair when the police emerged from MacKenna's and Dennehy's flats empty-handed. They had spent the night guarding the lock-up garage containing the concealed van. It was later confirmed the lock-up utilised was not the same one MacKenna had used to spray paint the van weeks earlier. When the police forced the door they discovered nothing more than a few empty tins of paint. Tara was unaware of the location of the new lock-up until MacKenna collected her early that morning: a row of garages in Wythenshawe, adjacent to a block of flats.

The operations in the south of England proved more successful. At the sound of his front door splintering under the weight of a police battering ram, Macintosh attempted to make good his escape through a first floor bathroom window. He was apprehended in his bare feet trying to climb onto the roof of his mock Tudor detached home. In a hidden concrete bunker, beneath one of the loading bays at the depot outside Wolverhampton, they discovered a number of assault rifles along with a substantial quantity of ammunition, a Smith and Wesson .38 snub nose revolver and two hundred rounds of ammunition. A false ceiling in the Peterborough depot yielded half a kilo of Semtex and four detonators amongst a collection of other bomb-making paraphernalia: fuses, timers, batteries etc. Forensic examination revealed traces of nitrogen-based chemicals, believed to have been used in the preparation of home made fertiliser explosives.

Shortly before 3pm, Tara and Dennehy walked to the local shops, to purchase sandwiches. On the pretext of using the bathroom, they stopped into a nearby pub, The Jolly Sailor. This was from where Tara had telephoned me – in the ladies. Soon after 3.30 pm, Dennehy reversed the van out of the lock-up. In the back of the van sat five mortar tubes, each with a diameter of sixty mm and just over one metre long. The tubes were made of sections of pipe attached to a wooden frame. The equivalent military hardware would fire a shell 3490 metres – just over two miles. At that distance, however, the trajectory had to be altered in order to aim the weapon with any degree of precision. They had only one shot, as all five tubes would fire simultaneously. For precision, they had sacrificed distance. MacKenna had hired a black Vauxhall Tigra, using a false name and credit card. Tara was at the wheel of a three series BMW 2.8i 4-door saloon, "borrowed" from a garage forecourt in the early hours of the night before. Two minutes after MacKenna had driven away, Dennehy fired the ignition on the van. To his horror, the engine failed to kick into life first time. The second time it caught. He engaged first gear and released the clutch, wiping the sweat gathered on his brow with his sleeve.

Tara followed Dennehy, contemplating the surreal developments of the day. Her initial terror at MacKenna's appearance had given way to grim resignation. There was to be no safe haven, or last minute reprieve. Sitting in the elegant luxury of the top of the range BMW on leather seats, with the air conditioning blowing cool jets of air in her face, Tara felt far from relaxed, if a little insulated from the impending action. At every junction along the route, her head told her arms to swing the vehicle round. What hidden force compelled her to attend at a firework display she desired no involvement in? Park the car at the nearest police station. An automaton, she doggedly followed the distant tail of the maroon van, an invisible linkage holding the two vehicles in tandem. She'd survived this far, Tara reasoned. There was still a job to be done: ensuring the mortars remained, as now, silent. Her hand fumbled on the passenger seat a couple of times for her mobile phone to call Powell. Each time, she had second thoughts, paranoid that Dennehy might spy her in his wing mirror and become suspicious. Finally Tara lit a cigarette to calm her nerves. It took all her concentration to hold her hand steady on the steering wheel as she drew the glowing lighter towards her lips. She consumed the first euphoric drag, as MacKenna's voice cracked over the radio that he was approaching the target area.

I could see Becky hanging on to the Zephyr grimly through my mirrors. Her arms fixed rigidly to the handlebars and her teeth chattering with fear or anticipation. We nosed past the stationary cars at the lights, edging our way to the front of the queuing traffic. Words cannot describe the ominous sense of foreboding that overshadowed my every move. Like sand slipping though the palm of my hand, I felt increasingly that events were spiralling out of control – that any action I might take was utterly futile. Doing something, however, was better than nothing. I attempted to turn left onto the Styal Road at Heald Green, but the traffic was backed up in both directions. Little did I know that an elaborate wheeze was being enacted up ahead. Just over a mile before the airport, I spotted a flashing blue light. Great, do you want to shout from the roof tops any louder? Could they not have been ever so slightly subtler? I slowed the Bonnie as Ringway Road appeared on the right. I soon realised that the traffic jam was being caused by the closure of the right turn up to the airport. I lifted my visor, as I brought the bike to a stop next to a motorcycle patrol officer. "What's up?"

"Accident blocked the road," he replied, gesturing slightly impatiently in the direction of the airport terminal. "Follow the diversion."

The traffic announcement system in the BMW roared into life, as Dennehy and Tara approached the airport from Wythenshawe: *"Radio GMR Your voice for travel. There are reports of a serious accident on West Ringway Road approaching the airport from Heald Green. The road is closed near its junction with Styal Road. Police are advising motorists to find an alternative route and leave plenty of extra time if you are planning to catch a flight in the next few hours."* What the news reports did not reveal, for obvious reasons, was that all flights out of the airport would soon be delayed. No further planes would be allowed to land and were being diverted to Leeds/Bradford or Liverpool, upon receipt of word from Powell that the operation was underway.

A faint hope of an escape route materialised in Tara's mind, as she listened to the traffic update. She picked up the radio next to her. "You hear that?"

"Aye," was the instant reply from MacKenna. "Fraser, slow down, I'll check it out. Tara – wait with him."

As MacKenna indicated and turned right into Shadow Moss Road, he failed to observe the plain clothes officer ensconced in the rear of an anonymous dark blue Vauxhall Astra van on the opposite side of the road or the numerous concealed eyes that monitored his progress. At the "T" junction, he turned the Tigra sharply to the left, accelerating along Ringway Road. A hundred yards in the distance, he spied the rear lights of queuing vehicles. Within a couple of car lengths of the end of the queue, he mounted the pavement, bringing the car to an abrupt halt, before casually wandering towards the cause of the congestion. He scanned the scene, searching for any hint of a trap: major road traffic accident – head on collision. A red Renault Clio lay sprawled across the left-hand carriageway, its front end creased and distorted, surrounded by a mountain of broken glass, a tow truck slowly hauling a light blue Rover 800 onto a trailer. The impact had so disfigured the front offside wing and wheel that metal scraped on the ground, as the Rover eased painfully up the ramp. The wheel stubbornly refused to turn in its twisted agony. One ambulance, a motorcycle police officer and the tow truck – a couple of other civilians milled around, or sat on the pavement. Witnesses or passengers, MacKenna smirked to himself, before retracing his steps back up Ringway Road, increasing his pace to a jog and then a sprint, as he exited the peripheral vision of the police motorcyclist. Executing a three-point turn, MacKenna headed back towards the terminal buildings. There were considerably fewer cars passing in either direction, MacKenna noted, ever watchful for a sign that the mission had been compromised. He correctly surmised that there was a flashing 'congestion' warning sign displayed on the M56 motorway, warning traffic not to exit. In fact, at that very moment, the motorway exit was in the process of being closed.

Dennehy waited anxiously in a bus stop on Simonsway, fidgeting with the short wave radio nestled in his lap. Every few seconds he glanced anxiously in his wing mirror, desperate not to see the familiar white and coloured flash of a police patrol vehicle. Less than a hundred yards behind, the occupant of a BMW parked outside a newsagent prayed for the exact opposite – her hawk-like observation never shifting from the van in front and its curiously misshapen roof profile.

The silence was shattered by MacKenna's voice on the radio. "Alright folks, welcome to the party. We can do this right under the fucker's noses – move now." Dennehy acknowledged the command and pulled out hastily into the path of an oncoming Volkswagen, which applied its brakes sharply to avoid a collision and made an appropriate hand gesture. Any residual hope Tara harboured that the accident was a staged deterrent to persuade MacKenna to abandon the deployment drained away, leaving her mouth dry and her heart pounding like heavy artillery. Ahead Tara watched Dennehy turn right, easing the van into Shadow Moss Road. Once both the van and the BMW had passed the undercover officer in the Astra van, the road was sealed, closing the final main artery to the airport. No vehicles would now enter the target zone, aside from those containing plain clothes police officers, designed to give a rudimentary impression of normality, against the backdrop of the fake accident.

Reluctantly, I turned the bike around under the watchful gaze of the police traffic officer, as a 747 thundered overhead. Only three more aircraft would land before the command was given to close the runway. A couple of minutes later, our speculative expedition to find an alternate route ground to an abrupt halt, as we encountered the impromptu police cordon now situated at the end of Shadow Moss Road. I signalled defeat to the still bewildered Becky. We retraced our steps, navigating towards the rendezvous point. We rode as close to the farmhouse as possible and jogged the remainder of the journey, crossing playing fields and eventually farmland – the mutilated shadow of a ruined farmhouse growing ever larger on the horizon. Sat by the tumbledown wall, the interior wallpaper still visible in places, I waited uneasily, compelled to enlighten Becky as to the nature of the sordid gambit she had accidentally stumbled upon. Becky listened in stunned silence, before firing questions belligerently at me, with the grace and persistency of a Gatling gun. Her probing gave way to nervous silence, as the sheer enormity of events unfolding a mile or so north west of us dawned upon her.

Dennehy slowed for a car pulling out across his path from the industrial estate, the revs dropping on the van. It had precious little power when empty; now packed with its deadly cargo, it accelerated about as quickly as a tank bogged down in thick mud. Tara watched it lumber up the road, before cautiously reaching for her mobile phone, her hands wet with perspiration. She wiped them dry on her jeans and speed dialled Powell's number and lifted it into earshot only at the sound of the first ring tone. "It's happening now," were the first words that entered her head.

"It's under control," was the reassuring response.

"Tell me what the hell you want me to do then? This is way too close for comfort," Tara begged, trying to retain her composure.

"Just do your job. Let's not give them any clues...."

"Easy for you to say," she hissed, tossing the phone discontentedly onto the passenger seat and pushing down on the accelerator. Tara followed the trundling van, before turning right into Cornishway, left into Ravenscar Crescent and then right again onto Carsdale Road. She executed a three-point turn and reversed the car to the end of cul-de-sac, only a few hundred yards from where MacKenna watched the approaching van. Tara's eyes alighted on the neat semi-detached houses and trim lawns. To her left, Tara could hear the distant sound of children playing, to her right the faint hum of a radio tuned to Radio One – the epitome of suburban bliss. A tranquillity, she was mindful of, that was about to be shattered, as full of trepidation, she flicked ash through the open window and waited. She ignored her desperate need to pee and shifted restlessly in the driver's seat, searching for a comfortable position, adjusting her rear view mirror.

MacKenna's senses were heightened to full stretch in those final minutes before the point of no return. Crouched on the roof of a garden shed, belonging to one of the nearby houses, he was blessed with the ideal vantage point. The roof sloped slightly providing the perfect camouflage from observers from the road. Likewise it was protected from prying eyes at the window of the house by a garage and two large shrubs – of course he was unaware that the occupants had long since been evacuated. To his left was the familiar grunt of the approaching van – ahead, an occasional car passed every few seconds. He had to strain his ears for the instantly recognisable hum. He performed a final reconnaissance sweep across the horizon. Extracting mini-binoculars from under his shirt, he surveyed the scene, biding his time over anything unfamiliar. Looking for a subtle change in the environment that might reveal what had hitherto been concealed: a flash of colour, a strange reflection of light or a sudden movement.

The sound of the van grew quieter, its engine idling, before executing a right turn onto Ringway Road. Any second it would emerge into visual contact. MacKenna diverted his attention back to the view through the binoculars: trees, buildings, the blazing lights of the runway glistening against the evermore grey sky, but saw nothing. Abruptly he halted, why he wasn't sure – perhaps a faint registering of movement on the other side of the road, behind the bushes that separated the launch site from the target. He backtracked slightly as the van drove into view, through the gateway, lining up at the appropriate angle for trajectory onto the runway. Paranoia, MacKenna reasoned confidently to himself, peering through the lenses. Only seconds to the successful completion of all they had worked for, he reassured himself, as he scrambled down from the bitumen roof.

Quite why MacKenna undertook a final sweep with his binoculars before clambering the fence remains a mystery – whether a final precaution or a sixth sense of imminent danger? Perhaps he had residual doubts about the staged accident, or was concerned there were too few vehicles? Why did the undercover police marksman, hidden in the undergrowth, choose that second to move: an itch, or cramp or nerves knowing the contents of the adjacent van? What strange twist of fate conspired to choreograph the two events simultaneously?

Clutching his short wave radio, he bellowed to Dennehy. "Rifle at eleven o'clock – abort." His warning fell on deaf ears. The intended recipient had left his radio on the passenger seat. Only Tara picked up the message, with growing apprehension. Dennehy was already outside the driver's door, glancing round for MacKenna, preparing to prime the mortars. In desperation, MacKenna raised his head over the fence and screamed in his comrade's direction. "Fraser, get out – go now." Fraser heard his familiar shout and tried to identify his location. Having sensed MacKenna's anxiety, Dennehy panicked, torn between running to apparent safety and abandoning the van, its mission unfulfilled. Whatever his reasoning, those two short steps towards the driver's door proved fatal. A police marksman, acting on the assumption that the mortars were about to be activated, fired a single precise shot, which reverberated through the nearby trees and houses. It struck Fraser Dennehy in the forehead, just above his right eyebrow, penetrating his skull. He slumped forward – dead, landing on the soft ground, his eyes wide open, his jaw hanging loose. Kieran watched his body collapse in slow motion in an ungainly heap, his head rebounding softly on the ground.

The macabre scene fixated MacKenna's eyes for a second. In the BMW, the noise of the rifle echoed a chilling refrain that sent a shiver down Tara's spine. She looked anxiously over her shoulder, her eyes not trusting the rear view mirror, well aware her very existence was balanced on a precarious knife-edge, tottering as it glistened against the reflection of cold steel. Every sinew in her body begged her to drive away – torn between the desire to run and a fear of dereliction of duty. Absconding would be a betrayal – it ain't over till it's over. That fat lady hadn't yet sung. Tara vacillated, a gunshot changed the rules. Yet still the BMW remained obdurately motionless.

MacKenna's desire for life and the inherent stubborn arrogance that he would not die in this garden or that field, urged him back to reality. He felt the blood coursing purposefully through his veins and his heartbeat quicken, before jumping a fence and skirting across numerous gardens. He increased the stretch of his stride. Escape the only plan – survival the imperative. Do not fall into the hands of the enemy. The fight will go on – regroup and counterattack. The rhythm in the repeated mantra propelled him forward.

Finally, Tara's panic gene won the psychological battle. She had half-expected MacKenna or Dennehy to clamber breathlessly into the car, urging her loudly to move. When neither broke cover, Tara convinced herself naively that it was all over. Despite the sound of only one shot, she reasoned in a rare moment of self-delusion that her betrayal of the IRA would follow both of them to their graves. It was the only persuasion she needed to push the gearshift and release the handbrake – squeezing down on the accelerator, the BMW roaring forwards.

MacKenna had only a few desperate yards further to travel, when he heard the BMW slammed into gear. He ran, pumping his arms like a steam engine to match the car's velocity, in a desperate attempt to emerge into the road in front on her. It's possible this was the moment when his suspicions became reality. The fears he had never rationalised gaining a fresh perspective. Swiftly, he eased his right hand to the back of his jeans, simultaneously unzipping his jacket, confirming what he already knew from the sensation of cold steel pressing on his spine. Within seconds of the gunshot, the police entered phase two. Surprise, as a tactic, had been exhausted. A police helicopter lifted off from the airport only a few hundred yards away. It was airborne within forty-five seconds of the remains of Dennehy's skull touching the cold earth.

Tara's reaction was instinctive, pressing her foot hard on the brake pedal to execute an emergency stop. The BMW grimaced and screeched to an awkward halt a couple of feet from where MacKenna had suddenly careered violently into her path. In that split second of recognition, her illusionary tranquillity vanished, replaced by a haunting dread. Perspiration trickled down her spine, beneath her blouse. Why didn't she just run him over? Wasn't that simply another methodology for what was planned in any event? Tara cursed her reflexes, as MacKenna yanked the passenger door almost off its hinges and clumsily leapt in, shouting. "Go, go." Tara pressed forcefully on the accelerator, watching as the rev counter needle climbed and then fell, as she pushed upwards through the gearbox.

"What the hell happened?" Tara asked anxiously. "I heard a shot – Fraser?" She tried to disguise her all-consuming blind fear that MacKenna had guessed the truth.

"He's dead," he remarked calmly, leaning forward slightly, just enough to remove his gun.

"What happened?" MacKenna turned his head slightly, regarding her with distaste. Finally, he spoke, lifting the gun and gesturing towards her temple. "I was hoping you might tell me."

Tara instinctively relaxed her foot on the accelerator as she spied the weapon. "What the hell is wrong with you?" she screamed, as the car slowed.

"Shit," cursed MacKenna, craning his head to spy the whirring of chopper blades above them. "Just bloody drive." As if to emphasise the point, he thrust the barrel closer, until Tara could feel the cold ring of metal pressed firmly against her temple. She swung the car left onto Shadow Moss Road without even checking for oncoming traffic and pushed her foot down.

Tara's brain ticked over, attempting to formulate a plan. She had come too far to die. Not like this – not at his hands. Survival depended upon her being proactive. That was easier said than done, when driving at break neck speed towards a police roadblock whilst facing the wrong end of a gun barrel situated only millimetres from your brain. Ahead, at the junction, two police squad cars blocked the carriageway, their blue lights illuminated. "Now what – you gonna shoot them as well as me?" Tara forced the words out. With each passing second, the mobile barrier of police cars grew ever more imposing through the windscreen. Tara glanced down at the speedometer: seventy eight mph.

"Aim for the gap in the middle, but slightly to the left," he yelled. Tara could see the hand with the weapon in shaking slightly in her peripheral vision.

"Ram them?" Tara exclaimed in disbelief.

"You got a better idea? Like give ourselves up you miserable fucking tout." MacKenna was barely in control. His eyes glistened with anger and ruthless adrenaline. He seemed almost possessed – oblivious to the hopelessness of their situation. Tara hesitated, as the BMW approached the waiting police cars. She could see that there were at least four uniformed police officers stood adjacent to the cars, most of whom appeared armed. At least none appeared to be still inside the vehicles.

From the window of a house on the left of the street, a marksman clad wholly in black, sighted his sniper rifle with telescopic lens through the curtains. His orders were simple: take out the male suspect, do not endanger the life of the female driver. Watching their approach through the magnified sight, he focused on the vehicle, his finger poised on the trigger. He had a clear sight on MacKenna's head, but there were scarcely a couple of centimetres between them. In a moving object like a high-speed car, it was a chance neither he nor his superiors would countenance. Not that he knew why – to him they were both simply terrorists.

MacKenna reacted angrily to the slowing of the BMW by shouting and leaning closer towards Tara. "Do it or I swear I'll kill you." Tara could see the sweat streaking down his forehead, and knew in this state he was dangerously unpredictable, capable of unconscionable acts of madness. So she swallowed hard and jabbed her foot down, shutting her eyes tightly as her executive battering ram's velocity soared beyond eighty five mph. The waiting police officers executed a hasty retreat to the pavement when it became clear that the BMW was not minded to respect their barricade. They watched helplessly, as the BMW rammed the red and white marked Vauxhall Omega, striking it violently over the front wheel arch, sending it pirouetting to the left in a sickening crunching and scraping of metal. Tara braced herself during the impact, casting a sly glance to her left at MacKenna. It was only when she realised MacKenna wasn't wearing a seat belt that the nucleus of an idea formed.

"Have you ever considered that you're jumping to false conclusions?" she shouted. "You could've been tailed from the lock-up. Anonymous Irish guy you meet in the pub wants to pay cash to rent a garage. It's the ultimate cliché – a caricature of what they expect. Perhaps the transit was traced?" Tara bit her lip, refraining from naming Macintosh. "But no, of course it simply has to be my fault. It's never your bloody responsibility." She spat out these last words in the split second before the BMW hurtled into the police car. Tara struggled to control the steering wheel, as the rear end stepped out in a screeching of tyres, metal and crucified suspension, before accelerating along Simonsway.

MacKenna laughed a snide smirk that both repulsed and infuriated her. Tara had seen it before, as he stood over Drummond and coldly pulled the trigger in the face of his pitiful pleas for life. "You can't talk your way out of this, you stupid bitch. You and that boyfriend have played us for bloody fools for long enough. How much were they paying you to tart yourself?"

There was a queue of traffic waiting at the traffic lights ahead. Time to change tactics. Tara glared at MacKenna, ignoring the gun still pointing unwaveringly in her direction. "Fuck you, Kieran," she bellowed. "I have put my life on the line for this organisation. Who lured Drummond to that back yard? Who found McCleash? The British army murdered my husband. You think I'd betray you to them? You must be out of your tiny fucking mind, you paranoid piece of shit."

MacKenna's unshakeable belief seemed to waiver somewhat in the face of Tara's onslaught. Tara veered harshly to her right onto the opposite side of the carriageway to pass the stationary traffic. She contemplated closing her eyes and driving across the junction blind, better not to see death approach, she reasoned. Instead she focused narrowly on the tarmac ahead, entered the junction at over seventy-mph, causing at least two cars proceeding in the opposite direction to swerve and collide. Ignoring the now all too familiar crunch of metal, Tara swerved back onto the correct side of the carriageway and cleared the junction.

Tara looked in the mirror and tried surreptitiously to calculate the right moment. As the 'Heald Green' pub loomed large on her right hand side, she relaxed the pace of the car slightly. It was only a matter of seconds and a few hundred metres before she executed the plan conceived less than two minutes previously. Tara clenched her jaw tight in anticipation, but her nerves had dissipated, replaced by an uneasy, yet bizarrely soothing feeling of calm. What do I have to lose she asked herself?

"Speed up," barked MacKenna.

"It's over Kieran," she told him placidly. "You're fighting yesterday's war." MacKenna's eyes widened, as he processed the implicit confession, oblivious as to the reason for her apparently voluntary admission.

"I swear I'm going to kill you." He thrust the barrel of the gun viciously against Tara's temple. Tara's only reassurance was that she was not expendable whilst driving. MacKenna's brow furrowed and for a second Tara panicked he might actually pull the trigger. "Your dad will be turning in his grave."

Tara relaxed slightly. "Every bullet you ever fired in the name of the Republican Movement has been utterly meaningless – now that my father would have understood," she retorted.

Comforted by the hope this would be his final thought, Tara inhaled deeply. Surreptitiously, she checked her seatbelt was still fastened. With the BMW approaching Heald Green railway station, her eyes alighted on the target. By momentarily slowing down, Tara had created an empty piece of tarmac, into which she now accelerated. The wounded BMW screeched in protest towards the road-bridge spanning the railway lines below. When the front wheels drew level with the redbrick bridge, Tara jerked the steering wheel of the BMW brutally, thrusting her foot downwards until the throttle pressed rigidly against the floor pan. The BMW now propelled at over sixty five mph, screaming and skidding, lurched fiercely to the right. The piece de resistance was the addition of the handbrake, causing the BMW to almost fly across the carriageway, mount the pavement and ram the bridge with a gut wrenching ugly knockout punch. In the premeditated bedlam, the luxury saloon almost completed a one hundred and eighty degree turn before the near side front wing was bludgeoned into the brick and mortar. Seconds later the BMW was mauled in the rear by an approaching motorist, shunting it like a snooker ball along the table cushion. It scraped agonisingly along the wall of the bridge, before coming to rest in a mangled contorted heap. The violence of the initial impact had snapped the front axle, ripping the entire front wheel from the car, causing an excruciating ear-shattering whine, the exposed underbody grinding along the pavement, harmonising with the sound of shattering glass and crunching metal.

For Tara, the fleeting seconds between yanking the handbrake and the point of destruction seemed extraneous to the usual constraints of time and space. Transported out of the car, she hovered above the road – an uninvolved voyeur at a scene of carnage. The oldest cliché: your life passes before you, as the moment of death appears imminent. A rerun of all the bitter regrets that we torture ourselves with, interspersed with brief snaps of laughter, beauty, passion and love. Tara felt none of these emotions, as the world surrounding her faded, reassuringly insulated from the tornado of chaos that enveloped her. First came the relief of still feeling alive; quickly dampened by the threat to it, which was still posed.

The battering ram impact propelled MacKenna savagely into the shattering glass of the passenger door window, despite the inflated airbag. His pummelled torso slumped forward over the dashboard. Blood trickled from the glass fragments embedded in his face. Just as soon as the choreographed movement had begun, it was finished. The crushing havoc gave way to silence, as the vehicle's motion was reduced to sloth.

Tara was stunned, trying to gather her senses. Her survival instinct surpassed her capacity for pain. The adrenaline drowned out her brain's response to the messages being communicated from the blackened swelling growing on the right side of her skull, where she had struck the driver's door post. She remained blissfully unaware of the blood trickling down her face and the two cracked ribs, from the force at which she was thrown against the seat belt, until she attempted to move. Finally, her brain commenced pumping instructions: move. Struggling, Tara fought to open the driver's door. Her fingers trembled on the handle. Almost in tears, she pulled the handle in increasing frustration but to no avail – the mechanism was malfunctioning. To her left, MacKenna stirred. He was moaning, doubled over – his head resting in his crimson encrusted hands. A rising sense of panic engulfed Tara that she might be trapped – confined in this buckled heap of metal, with a wounded lunatic holding a gun. She had no desire to be around when he remembered where the trigger had been pointing moments earlier. The volume of MacKenna's moans became louder, as his eyes flicked briefly open and then closed again. Then there came a tapping noise. Out of the window, Tara saw that a passer-by was seeking to assist. "It's jammed," she shouted, pointing desperately to the door handle. Finally understanding, the man in his mid fifties, with greying hair and a concerned paternal expression on his face, wrenched at the handle from the outside. Tara corresponded from the inside. On the third attempt the creased door gave way with a loud cracking whine, rousing MacKenna from his concussion.

"What the hell happened?" MacKenna moaned, as Tara eased out of the driver's seat, assisted by the passer-by, her ribs screaming in agony with every movement.

"Thank you," she replied gingerly, casting an anxious eye back to where MacKenna had raised his injured head and was casting his eyes about, dazed and stupefied, but definitely alive. Oh no. "Can you help my friend?" Tara asked. "I need to sit down."

The passer-by poked his head through the driver's door. "Just stay there son. The door is trapped by the wall."

MacKenna moaned again, growing more alert by the second. Tara had to move. Relying on his injuries being more serious than hers was no guarantee. Engender some distance between them. A crowd had gathered, gawking at the mass of twisted metal. A fast-approaching police siren wailed in the distance. Cars queued in both directions anxiously trying to squeeze past the scene. Tara began to walk, or rather limp – slowly at first, concentrating simply on placing one foot in front of the other, overcoming the excruciating pain. She quickened her pace only when she heard a frantic shout from behind her. "He's got a gun."

Tara hastened her way through the crowd, using her jacket to wipe away the blood trickling down her face. Crossing the bridge, she turned down the footpath running parallel to the railway lines, which led eventually to the ruined farmhouse where Becky and I waited. It took every ounce of strength Tara could muster to keep moving. Her head was pounding and her ponderously heavy legs felt prone to imminent collapse. Every step sent shivers of electric pain through her chest – every gasp for breath bequeathed new agonies, like sprinting across a bed of nails. She pushed past the small wooden gate and into the open field, following the well-worn dirt path that passed to the rear of the adjacent houses. After a few feet, instinct compelled her to check her rear flank. To Tara's horror, MacKenna emerged from the crowd, half walking, and half jogging, his left hand still clutching his bloodied head. She pushed herself beyond the pain barrier, her heart sinking with despair, as she glimpsed MacKenna's right hand – the very same cold steel, only minutes before, had been pressed against the tender flesh of her temple. Sweat streaked down her face, mixed with congealing blood. She urged herself to become swifter, more agile, despite the smarting torment. Her only solace was that MacKenna was more seriously injured. For the next five or six minutes he pursued her – the hunter and the hunted – across the fields. The distance between them narrowed, as fatigue gripped Tara, and then widened, as determination triumphed over discomfort. Tire you bastard, she cried. She forced herself onward, urged forwards by flashbacks of Bridie McDonagh, Bill McCleash and Peter Drummond – determined not to share their fate. Still the distance separating them narrowed. The hunter's quest was now only eighty metres ahead.

It was Becky who spotted Tara first, from where she sat perched on the edge of a ramshackle wall. The buzzing of the police helicopter overhead and the sound of distant sirens distracted my attention. Good news or bad? The police presence must have been exposed – were they in custody or dead? What was the helicopter so blatantly searching for? I watched the chopper circle and move towards our position. Becky touched my arm. "Tom, what's that?"

"Where?" I asked, peering into the distance. I could see a dishevelled figure, attempting to run in our direction. Even at a distance of a few hundred yards, it was obvious she was struggling. "It's her," I called, breaking into a sprint, overwhelmed with a relief that Tara was alive, tinged with concern that she was injured. I bolted with as much despatch as my legs would allow. I watched from a distance of about two hundred metres, as she checked behind her. A figure emerged into view, barely recognisable as the man who had stood in my kitchen weeks previously: tall, dark curly hair…. The penny dropped – Tara was being pursued. Hovering above, the helicopter had spotted the chase and was closing in on MacKenna. Then from my left, storming from the path, which dissected the business-park through to Styal Road, I spied armed police officers sporting body armour and carrying rifles. We were all racing towards the same focal point. I had no inkling that MacKenna was wielding a gun. It was like the confused bewilderment of being dropped into an action scene from a movie in which I had no part.

The events that transpired in the next few seconds still haunt me – relived in both my conscious and sleeping hours – forever torturing myself that I stood by, helpless. The police helicopter thundered overhead, hovering only a few hundred feet above the green earth. MacKenna appeared oblivious to the chopper and the approaching police. The first police officers were within a few hundred metres, converging on him, when he slowed to a halt and lifted the revolver. To his right, a police loud hailer commanded that he drop the weapon. It was too late. He squeezed off four shots, before a police marksman, fired twice, felling MacKenna, as bullets penetrated his head and chest. Then there was nothing. The air hung heavy with reverberation and the acrid smell of gunfire. The only sound was the descending chopper.

I was less than a hundred metres from Tara when MacKenna had raised the weapon, stood with his legs slightly apart and eased down on the trigger. Consumed with blind panic, I screamed "no". Tara appeared oblivious to my screams. I watched the gun explode with a violent thud, the distinctive bark discernable over the sound of the hovering helicopter. Instantaneously, my world ended. Freeze-frame: no fields, no police officers, no helicopter, no MacKenna, no Becky, no farmhouse. Nothing except Tara, two bullets, and me suspended in mid air, like a scene from a comic strip. I reached out, stretching to grab her, to push her out of the line of fire. The distance was too great, no matter how I lunged and grasped forward. My efforts were in vain. Tara tumbled forward, midway through a step, crumpling onto the grass and the soft brown earth. I galloped towards her, shouting her name, dropping to my knees by her side and touching her face with my hands. "Hold on," I implored, desperate to believe my own assurances. She was barely conscious – blood oozed, soaking through her shirt, spreading by the second. The wound to her right shoulder wouldn't be fatal, but my heart descended into the pits of despair at the revelation of the wound at the base of her rib cage, just below her left breast. I hurriedly ripped off my shirt, trying to stem the flow of blood, as the paramedics approached. Tara opened her eyes briefly before losing consciousness. She no longer possessed the energy to speak, exhausted from her exertions, battered from the car smash and now fighting two bullets. I squeezed her hand, as the paramedics lifted her onto the stretcher and into the helicopter, jogging by her side, fully expecting her not to survive the journey. Words could not describe my feelings, as the swirling rotors lifted us from the ground. It seemed surreal – a hallucination. But the blood was real and so was the grief that consumed me with the torrent of a waterfall.

Part Five

Chapter Forty

EVERYONE HAS A story about the night of May 1st 1997 – Labour's landslide victory. It was an extraordinary night, at the end of the longest general election campaign in living memory: the first exit polls; the dizzying heights of Portillo losing Enfield; Martin Bell defeating Neil Hamilton in Tatton; and the five Tory cabinet members who lost their seats.

My recollections are vivid. I attended no parties, and enjoyed no celebratory drinks, nor did I dance in the street with unbridled glee. In stark contrast to the national euphoria, I sat in a darkened intensive care unit. Outside the door, two armed police officers stood guard, either to stop others getting in or to prevent Tara leaving – not that she was in any state to effect an escape. I sat by Tara's bedside, as she clung tenaciously to life, still unconscious, recovering from a six-hour operation to remove the two bullets from her broken and mangled body. One had shattered two of her ribs, missing her spleen by millimetres, but still causing serious internal damage. She also sustained a punctured lung when the BMW smashed into the bridge wall. Her right shoulder, smashed by the second bullet had to be reconstructed using a metal plate and pins. I didn't need to be told by any doctor that she was lucky to be alive.

Some time after 4am on election night, I had my eyes glued to the TV screen in the dim light, casting flickering shadows across the room. I stroked her hand as she stirred. She squeezed my hand softly in response. Her eyes barely opened, just a brief flicker of movement.

She enquired in a hushed tone, coupled with a faint expression of contentment. "He's dead?"

"Yeah, he's dead," I smiled. Reassured, she drifted back to sleep – a peaceful expression framed on her sedated face. I watched Peter Snow's swingometer from her bedside – praying that she would live to see our new Prime Minister.

Seven days after the operation, Tara was removed from the critical list. She slept mostly – a combination of physical exhaustion and obvious weakness following surgery. She remained in hospital for a further three weeks, while they monitored her slow, but steady progress. I visited most days, perennially running the gauntlet of the police guard, in case the IRA figured out their spectacular had been sabotaged. Not that Tara's location would have been easy to identify – her hospital records showed a false name and address. Thereafter, she was moved to a military convalescence home – the address of which I have promised not to reveal, where she continued with her rehabilitation. As she grew stronger, the debriefs commenced – initially lasting less than an hour, then growing to all day sessions, as her ability to concentrate increased. She was questioned on every aspect of her involvement in the IRA, both on the UK mainland and also Northern Ireland, including interviews with RUC officers, regarding two of their colleagues: Sgt Peter Drummond and Inspector William McCleash.

Once Tara was moved from the hospital, there was no contact between us for over a month. There remained a risk, however fanciful, that I might be tailed by the IRA and Tara's location revealed. Powell only informed me they were moving her hours before the unmarked police car with blacked out windows ushered her away from the rear entrance of the hospital.

With Tara in the convalescence home, I began to reflect on the events of the previous months, struggling to return to anything approaching a normal existence. The house felt empty and cold. I tried to ease the loneliness with work, and attempted to return to my old life. Whatever activity I undertook though, Tara was never far from my thoughts, as I was dragged back to contemplating the events of election-day.

When Powell finally made contact, I experienced a strange sense of déjà vu – back to the Little Chef just off the M6 months earlier. Powell greeted me in his makeshift office – a pile of papers and a laptop computer situated on a borrowed desk. After pleasantries had been exchanged, I asked him all the probing questions that needed clarification, acting more like a lawyer than a former lover. "You think we're callous, no loyalty to anyone but ourselves, right?" It was said with his tongue firmly in his cheek, but there was clearly a serious undertone.

I declined to rise to his bait – attempting to give the impression of professional detachment, whilst trying to peek at his computer screen. "Your words, not mine," I replied, wishing to sound non-committal.

"You think we'd abandon Tara?" Powell jibed accusatorially. "Hence you recorded every last detail."

Poker – high stakes. I wasn't about to reveal my hand, by confirming or denying his assertion – let him sweat. Powell waved his arm casually in my direction, a deliberate grin on his face. "No matter Tom. The fact is we offered her a deal – she turned it down. See if you have any more luck than I did."

Powell led me to a door off a near-deserted side ward. The room was blandly institutional: a simple bed, standard issue armchair and light green walls. A uniformed nurse pulled the door firmly closed behind me. Tara stood with her back to me, deep in reflection, watching out of the window. Physically she looked well, better than I had imagined. The familiarity of her presence was tempered by the changes I could discern. Her eyes seemed cold and dull: the endless hours of questions and the cumulative anguish of recent months. Tara appeared jaded – her limbs heavy with fatigue. "Powell says they offered you a deal?"

She nodded affirmatively. "He told you?" Tara returned her focus to the window – across the courtyard below. "I couldn't do it Tom. You of all people should understand." Tara perched on the edge of the armchair. Her steps were heavy and awkward, her words tinged with pessimism. "I walk away with a one off payment. It's as simple as that. Except I have to leave the UK and can't return. Of course I was tempted." Tara attempted a weak smile, putting on a brave face. "Who wouldn't be?"

"But?" I asked, already suspecting her response.

"I didn't do this for a get out of jail free card," Tara said quickly. It was obvious she had rehearsed the arguments endlessly, but still her voice was full of emotion, consumed by sadness.

"I know that," I touched her arm in reassurance.

"Don't you see?" Tara brushed her open palm against my face, her dejected eyes searching mine for recognition. "I'd always be on the run.

Constantly looking over my shoulder in the knowledge that one day either the RUC or the Provos will catch up with me. In the garden, watching TV, in bed, at work, in the supermarket, or a restaurant, never knowing whether the guy brushing past me in the queue or ringing the doorbell had instructions to do what Kieran failed to achieve. There'll be no peace. I told you before, I'm sick of running." Tara shook her head firmly. "I know it's trite, but at least I'll be paying my debt to society. The police won't be on my back, and I won't be banned from ever entering my home country."

"You know how long they are likely to send you down for?"

"I can think of little else," Tara confirmed, attempting to put on a brave face.

"What if I came with you?"

It was a spur of the moment suggestion. Tara looked up at me, inquisitive and curious. For a moment she was baffled. She mulled it over, shaking her head almost imperceptibly. "It doesn't change anything Tom. You can't protect me. I'd just be putting both our lives at risk. When the end comes, it will only be crueller…" Tara wiped her eyes and shook her head defiantly. "I won't have you throwing away your life, out of misplaced loyalty. What happens when you tire of me, of the life we're forced to lead – forever deflecting uncomfortable questions about our past, always on tenterhooks. You'd have to cut all contact with friends and family – try justifying that to Becky. One day, maybe not tomorrow or next month, you'll grow to resent me, for all the sacrifices you've been forced to make. Resentment would eventually turn to hatred. Once you've burnt your bridges Tom, there's no going back."

"Don't you think I know that?" I replied, in desperation. Tara pressed a kiss on my cheek that had a finality to it. A line was drawn under the discussion. I felt her lips soft on my cheek and the familiar fragrance of her skin, as my lips tasted her tears. She closed her eyes. "It would never work, Tom. You have to forget me." She allowed her hands to fall loosely by her side, placing her thumbs awkwardly in the belt loops of her jeans, swaying slightly. "It has to be this way," she said quietly, but firmly.

"You've made a unilateral decision." I was angry now, pierced by her rejection, after all we had survived and achieved. "Maybe, going to prison is the easy option – insulation from reality. You can sit in your cell and pretend it will ease your conscience. Impervious to the havoc you have wreaked." I knew she would not change her mind, but it didn't quench my desire to lash out.

"I think you'd better leave now," Tara responded quietly, displaying no appetite for further debate – her resolve absolute.

I stood to leave. Tara twisted back to face the window. I stalked towards the door, with the firm intention of walking away, yet felt compelled to stay, acutely aware I was unlikely ever to see her again. The harshness faded as she turned to face me and we embraced, pressing her face into my chest. I closed my eyes to ease the pain. "One day you'll see this was for the best."

"I love you," were the only words I could articulate.

"I know," she said, embracing me more firmly. "Speak to Stuart for me?"

"Lawyers – all parasites, till you need one?"

"You said it," she replied, attempting a faint smile.

Chapter Forty One

A WEEK AFTER I had last seen Tara, the debriefing sessions reached their end. Tara's usefulness was exhausted. No pat on the back, no tearful farewells and no golden handshake. Over time, I grew to understand why. I had, after all, lived through the insane paranoia of the last few months – if only second hand. I observed the toll it had taken on Tara to lead such a demented double life; forever cursed with constantly watching over her shoulder. She longed to stop running and not to have to lie – balancing the tight rope between the police and the Provies. Stubbornly, Tara chose the more onerous option.

Once the medical staff judged she had recovered sufficient strength, without ceremony, she was driven under police escort to Bootle Street Police Station, where she was formally charged with explosives offences for her part in the Manchester bombing.

Life occasionally throws seemingly unconnected events together. It was with a heavy sense of irony then that fate dealt the cards during the third week in July 1997, as Tara made her first appearance in court. Less than forty-eight hours after being charged, she was driven the short distance across the city to a heavily guarded Central Magistrates Court. There was extra security in abundance, from the armed cavalcade, which transported her with motorcycle outriders, to the laborious security checks before you could enter the building. Stuart joked that Joe Public believed the high security presence was to prevent the escape of a high profile IRA-suspect. In fact, our tax monies were being expended on protecting her from the vengeful army she had betrayed. After a five minute hearing, in which she spoke only to confirm her name and address, she was remanded in custody to appear at Manchester Crown Court, charged with conspiracy to cause an explosion. In the very same week the Provisional IRA released the following statement.

20th July 1997

"On the 31st August 1994 the leadership of Óglaigh na hÉireann (IRA) announced its complete cessation of military operations....After 17 months of cessation in which the British Government and the unionists blocked any possibility of real or inclusive negotiations, we reluctantly abandoned the cessation....We want a permanent peace...through real and inclusive negotiations. So having assessed the current political situation, the leadership of Óglaigh na hÉireann are announcing a complete cessation of military operations from 12-midday on Sunday 20th July 1997. We have ordered the unequivocal restoration of the cease-fire of August 1994..."

In contrast to the euphoria of August 1994, there was little flag-waving in Northern Ireland. After the previous cessation, the opportunity for peace had seemingly ebbed away in the senseless brutality of Docklands and the failure to agree a date for the commencement of all-inclusive talks. Ironically, the timing of the announcement, regarding the commencement of peace talks in the aftermath of the reinstated cease-fire, convinced unionists that the British Government was preparing to do a secret deal with the IRA. Sinn Féin was, however, excluded from the so called all party talks. The same old tired faces on both sides, trotting out the same old uncompromising mantras, whilst in perfectly choreographed scenes for the TV news crews, Gerry Adams and Martin McGuinness approached the padlocked gates of Stormont Palace – long the bastion of unionist rule – and posed for photographs gazing up at the imposing, but illusive talks venue. They too spoke of peace – only to those of us who had queued in motorway traffic jams, buried our dead, been injured or just watched our cities reduced to rubble, their platitudes seemed a little thin on sincerity.

Still, a new Government engendered a new hope. There was now a massive Labour majority and a new Secretary of State for Northern Ireland – Mo Mowlam. Yet the hope we all shared was qualified. Who was to say that the 'complete cessation' would not be as meaningless and temporary as before? There was an ever present fear that the politicians would filibuster and the paramilitaries would lose patience – scared that the gulf was too large, the wounds so gaping and that collectively they were simply incapable of compromise.

I was left with a feeling of futility. Precisely what had the resumed violence achieved? What advancement had my brother forfeited his life to secure? I succumbed to bitterness – we never learnt from our mistakes. We do all just travel in well-worn circles. If the cease-fire had never been broken, Tara would still be a teacher. I would still be her lover and my niece would have a father. I shut my eyes tightly, but all I could picture was the haunting vision of that final June evening we had all spent together. The warm elation of friends and family, in contrast to the lonely isolation that now overpowered me. In the dead of the night, I realised I had lost not only Ben and Tara, but a part of me also.

The sequence of events surrounding Tara's subsequent appearance at Manchester Crown Court began when I was summoned to see the now late Honourable Mr Justice Hammond, the High Court Judge who presided over Tara's guilty plea. He enjoyed something of a reputation in the legal world, as well as in media circles. He had tried a number of high profile celebrity cases and seemed to enjoy presiding over the media scrum. Politicians, businessmen, rock stars and actresses had all found justice of a form in his courtroom. Yet his reputation amongst lawyers was pretty impressive. He was the genuine article: an outstanding advocate and QC before his appointment. It was with a degree of nervous apprehension that I was shown into his retiring room, on a damp Thursday afternoon. The Judge was halfway through removing his red robe when he beckoned me in. "Third day of a double murder," he informed me, as if it was as mundane as his choice of tie. "Cocaine turf war in Moss Side apparently."

"I thought they were observing a cease-fire?" I replied. "The gangs, that is."

"Mopping up operation," he replied, in a matter of fact manner, straightening his suit jacket and slipping into his leather chair behind the desk. He smiled broadly, but I sensed his outward charm hid a deeper sense of curiosity. He reached over to the coffee pot and poured into two china cups and saucers of the Court Service's finest. He reclined in his chair and peered at me over the top of his gold rimmed glasses, pressing his lips together contemplatively, before breaking his silence. "You are something of a man of letters, Mr Flemming." It was a statement, rather than a question. The penny finally dropped, as he opened a file on the side of his desk. Before I had the chance to even glance at the top sheet, he launched into a soliloquy. "Twenty affidavits spanning a visit from an undercover police officer at an association football match, to what can only be described as a desperate shoot out on a field near Manchester Airport." He paused and regarded me inquisitively. "It's quite a story Mr Flemming," he commented, sipping his coffee.

"Every word is accurate," I replied, slightly defensively.

He smiled awkwardly, tapping his finger tips together. "May I call you Tom?" I nodded hesitantly. "I'm told you have a promising career. One hell of a risk you took."

"The truth is I feared Mrs O'Neil might be left high and dry. The authorities might assert public interest immunity, and she would receive no credit for putting her life at risk to right some of the mistakes she was being asked to pay for."

"A rather cynical perspective if I may say so," he commented.

"Perhaps," I replied, coolly. "But death has that effect on you."

"Point taken," he responded apologetically. "You needn't have worried." He pulled open his desk drawer and removed a large brown Manila envelope and opened the seal. "I'm going to show you this, because I think you deserve to see it, and I hope I can trust you as a member of the bar. I have never done anything like this before in my judicial role and I expect never to repeat it. I could be prosecuted under the Official Secrets Act for what I am about to reveal. You may read it. Do not, however, expect me to discuss its contents with you. Afterwards, you will not mention this to anyone else or reveal that you have seen it during my lifetime. Do I make my position clear?" He removed a six-page document and slid it across the table to me, before returning to his half-finished coffee cup. I glanced down at the official looking sheets of paper and began to read. It was addressed, '*Strictly Private and Confidential. Report on activities of agent Tara O'Neil codenamed 'Songbird'- undercover agent within the English Department of the Irish Republican Army...*'

The document concluded that without Tara's assistance there may have been substantial loss of life, and that the intelligence information she provided had substantially impeded the Provisional IRA's capacity to operate on mainland Britain. The point was forcefully made that the

English department was made up of the most dangerous, professional and ruthless operatives the Republican Movement possessed. This was the first occasion that the security forces had been able to infiltrate, and ultimately destroy so comprehensively, a cell operating on the mainland, since the Balcombe Street gang in the 1970's. I read the words with relish and then reread them to make sure I had not missed a word in my haste. Then just to be certain I read it a third time. "Thank you Judge." He glanced uneasily in my direction. "You will pass her sentence?" I asked. He nodded affirmatively with obvious unease. "I think I'd better leave now. Thank you for your kindness."

"Tom, you realise my hands are tied?"

"You have a public duty beholden of your office," I replied formally.

"It was good to meet you Mr Flemming," he added, returning to a more formal mode of address. "You realise that laws are made by politicians – when the politics changes the law will follow." I smiled an acknowledgement, a courtesy, as if I comprehended his words, although his wisdom soared way over my head. It was only much later that I understood the significance of the hope he was offering me.

I had no intention of attending Tara's sentencing. I had had a sneak preview of the final chapter and had no stomach for the inevitable climax. I couldn't bear to sit and listen to the events that had formed such an intimate part of my life, regurgitated for public exposure. However, when the day arrived, I felt a compulsion to be near. Not in a voyeuristic sense – I simply desired to see her one final time, even if it was only from the dock of a courtroom, behind a bullet proof screen. Whatever the terms of our parting, a part of me clung tenaciously to her, like an alcoholic drawn to the temptation of the bottle, or a moth to the light bulb. Perhaps on some level, I needed to share with her this final act. Still, I had no desire to relive or wallow in the gory details, as recounted by the prosecution, or to hear my Head of Chambers, William Boston QC, mitigate on Tara's behalf. So I slipped silently into Court Three in Crown Square, only seconds before the sentence was pronounced.

I had entered that courtroom on many previous occasions over the years – a familiar environment in unfamiliar circumstances. This was personal, not professional. My heart pounded so loud I felt certain that all around would be deafened. All I could see, from the public gallery was the back of Tara's head. She stared steadfastly ahead towards the

Royal Crest, her head bowed slightly, as she prepared for the inevitable. Her hair had grown slightly longer, but the nape of her neck was still visible above the collar of her blouse. So familiar and yet so distant – there was less than ten feet between us, yet she may as well have inhabited a different planet. I was pleased I could not see her face or she mine. "Stand up," barked the court clerk.

Mr Justice Hammond cleared this throat. "Tara O'Neil, you have pleaded guilty to an offence of conspiracy to cause explosions and have admitted to being a member of the Provisional Irish Republican Army. It is my duty to pass sentence upon you. I have listened to all that Defence Counsel has had to say so eloquently on your behalf. However, the crimes you have committed are exceptionally heinous. I accept you played no direct role in planting the explosive device that devastated the heart of this city less than a mile from where we now sit. I have to take into account, however, the fact that without your involvement that device may never have been detonated. I am obliged to consider the millions of pounds of damage, the businesses lost and the people injured. Most of all the fact that a person's young life was cut so needlessly, pointlessly short. The least sentence I can impose upon you is twelve years imprisonment. Take her down…"

Hearing the sentence articulated crushed me, forcing the oxygen out of my lungs, leaving me crestfallen, gasping for breath. I was stunned, with no time to react, as Tara was escorted towards the cells between two security guards. Tara simply bowed her head as she disappeared from view into the bowels of the building. Afterwards, I felt empty and numb, but there was to be no quiet reflection as the world closed in, like vultures ready to prey upon my sorrow. I returned home only long enough to pack a bag and escape the incessant phone calls. Some calls were from friends anxious to check how I was bearing up – others were less altruistic. The violation of my closely guarded privacy, exposed to the glare of the world filled me with total horror.

I rode the Bonnie to the airport, riding past Heald Green railway station, crossing the bridge Tara had struck with such force. I paused at the spot where the road and runway meet. Positive and negative: Tara and I had stood here together, gawping up at the aircraft in wonder, dreaming of flying away. Yet I was now slouched over the street sign, little more than a hundred metres from the site of Dennehy's last fatal stand. Was that a negative? He was responsible for Ben's death. Still, the thought of his lifeless body falling to the ground, blood weeping from the bullet's entry point, filled me with little satisfaction. I watched an Airbus A340 taxi down the runway and then accelerate towards me, the noise deafening, as the nose lifted gracefully from the tarmac. I always assumed revenge would be sweet. As a concept, I'd say it was overrated.

The lurid headlines in the following morning's papers failed to lighten my mood. "*Is this the most dangerous woman in Britain?*" screamed The Sun, underneath Tara's graduation photograph. The Daily Mail's "*Manchester Lawyer's double blow*" story regarding Tara, Ben, Becky, Hannah and myself, was the final straw. My stomach knotted, at the half-truths and subtly twisted account of the drinks that Tara and I had enjoyed with Ben and Becky the night before the bomb. Next to a picture of Ben and Becky on their wedding day, it read: "*The last supper – thanks to callous terrorist plot by brother's lover…*" I booked myself on the next available flight to Spain and lost myself for a couple of weeks.

Chapter Forty Two

EIGHT WEEKS AFTER her court appearance in Manchester, Tara was transferred to Maghaberry Prison near Lisburn, approximately twenty miles south of Belfast. On Monday 6th October 1997, she appeared at Belfast Crown Court, charged with one count of murder, in relation to Sergeant Peter Drummond and one count of attempted murder in relation to Inspector William McCleash. She pleaded guilty to both counts and received two life sentences.

When I first visited Belfast a couple of years later, I fell in love with the beautiful compact city, surrounded by mountains seemingly on all sides, the Belfast Lough and the giant blue and yellow cranes of Harland and Wolff, which dominated the skyline. I stood outside the fortified Royal Courts of Justice – the pre-war splendour of the old courts and the modern court complex, under construction within view of the river. The proximity between the hopes of the new Belfast – symbolised in the Waterfront Hall, and the sorrow of the adjacent fortified court building, was not lost on me. Tara's life sentence commenced at 11.46am on the 6th October 1997. A few miles outside the city, in Belfast's suburbs, only a day later, substantive peace talks began for the first time between Sinn Féin and the Ulster Unionist Party. Although the UUP only addressed the Sinn Féin delegates indirectly through the Chairman, Senator George Mitchell, another small Rubicon in the politics of Irish peacemaking had been crossed.

In the week before Christmas, at the end of a three-week trial, Frank Macintosh was sentenced to a total of sixteen years imprisonment, at

Norwich Crown Court for explosives and terrorist offences.

Over the following six months, life grudgingly returned to a kind of normality. We enjoyed a family Christmas – the innocent delight of Hannah on Christmas morning, raising all of our spirits. I practised law with renewed vigour. It kept me occupied, but engendered little zeal. The depressing truth was that there was little to fill the void of ambition, once it had died. No matter how far I travelled or how hard I strove, the past proved impossible to abandon. An invisible bond seemed to hold me fast, tightening its steadfast grip in the small hours of the night, when sleep evaded me. Caught in that limbo-state between consciousness and dreams, I would be tormented, with images of Tara confined to her prison cell. Her features were no longer discernible. I had to concentrate to dredge her face into focus from some distant recess of my subconscious.

Finally, I sought to exorcise my demons in the written word. I assumed, correctly, there would be no reply. This was of little concern, as eliciting a response was not my purpose. It was more that I was able to construct a semblance of rationality, only when confronting my inner thoughts. Tara believed, in time, I would lose interest in communicating with a dead woman. For that, I think, is how she came to regard her incarceration. My first letter set a pattern that continued into the spring of 1998. I wrote usually late at night, seeking solace from the dark and cold isolation outside my study window. I didn't write words that were especially profound, or of much significance. I felt no inclination to bear my soul. Some words are better left unspoken.

Meanwhile the peace process crept forwards at the pace of a very lethargic snail, until you foolishly believed there was a real possibility of progress. Then, you would be brought back to earth with a depressingly familiar bump, as the parties descended back into rancour, accusation and the recrimination of blame. George Mitchell wrote of the position as of December 1997. *"We had been meeting for a year and a half. For hundreds and hundreds of hours I had listened to the same arguments over and over again. Very little had been accomplished. It had taken two months to get an understanding of the rules to be followed once the negotiations began. Then it took another two months to get agreement on a preliminary agenda. Then we tried for fourteen more months to get an accord on a detailed final agenda....*"[4] He finally imposed a new deadline for a conclusion of the peace talks, in the hope of concentrating the minds of the negotiating parties. The 9th April 1998.

Still, the New Year dawned with little optimism that 1998 would be any different from 1997. On the 27th December, Billy Wright, leader of the LVF was murdered in the Maze Prison by the INLA. The LVF embarked on a pogrom – a Catholic killing fest, in revenge for Wright's death. The British Government announced that the troops, removed from the streets only weeks before as part of encouraging 'normalisation', would return, and 60% of loyalist prisoners voted to withhold their support from the peace process. In one of the bravest political acts ever by a Northern Ireland Secretary, Mo Mowlam personally visited the prisoners in the Maze, to persuade them to keep faith with the talks.

The principle that the parties to the talks were not involved in violence was blown apart in early January, when the UFF admitted that they had killed a Catholic taxi driver. On the 9th February 1998, an alleged drug dealer was shot in Belfast – suspicion fell on the IRA, acting under the euphemism of 'Direct Action Against Drugs'. The following day, a prominent loyalist was shot in his car in South Belfast, also allegedly by the IRA. Sinn Féin were excluded from the peace talks, despite a challenge in the Belfast courts. However, the carrot was left firmly dangling – providing there was no evidence of further breaches of the Mitchell principles of non-violence, they would be and were readmitted into the talks on the 9th March.

As March gave way to April, the pressure to compromise increased, like thumbscrews on all the participants. Not a day seemed to pass without a leak from the British or Irish Government or the political parties, as each attempted to wrestle the tactical advantage from their opponents. The press scrum at Stormont constantly reported the stumbling blocks in the negotiations. Throughout the week before Easter, both Tony Blair and Bertie Ahern personally took part in the negotiations. The imposed deadline of 12am on the 9th April came and passed, as the midnight oil burnt bright in the meeting rooms, where the protracted negotiations edged forward and the clock slipped unnoticed into Friday – Good Friday.

---

4   George Mitchell. Making Peace (William Heinemann 1999) p126

10th April 1998

A Historic day in Northern Ireland unfolded yesterday with the signing of a peace agreement. The peace deal is designed to end 30 years of political violence and over 3000 deaths. There will be a new power sharing assembly, new cross border bodies between Northern Ireland and the Republic of Ireland and new bodies, which represent all parts of the United Kingdom. The deal came at around 5pm after 33 hours of non-stop talking between the two Governments and eight parties. All emerged from the talks bleary eyed to face the cameras, tired but relieved.

All the paramilitary groups, including the IRA, will have to decommission their stockpiles of weapons, in co-operation with the International Body on De-commissioning, led by Canadian General John De Chastelain. In return, all paramilitary prisoners will be released on licence within 2-3 years.

David Trimble from the UUP is likely to be the First Minister. Under the power sharing arrangements, however, he is likely to have a nationalist deputy from the SPLD. The likelihood is that there will also be Sinn Féin ministers in the new Government.

Tony Blair summed up the feelings of many, speaking to the assembled press. "Today I hope the burden of history can at long last start to be lifted from our shoulders. Even now this will not work unless in your will and your mind you make it work – unless you extend the hand of friendship to those who were once your foes..."

As I pored over endless newspaper column inches, it became clear that by the summer of the year 2000, all convicted prisoners from the IRA, UVF and the UFF would be released on licence. The implications were monstrous. The magical futuristic millennium seemed on the one hand so distant, but the game plan had altered irrevocably. Mr Justice Hammond's words finally made sense to me. *"You realise that laws are made by politicians, when the politics changes, the law will follow."*

The politics of peace had revolutionised both the political, and my personal, landscape. Instead of a life sentence, within only twenty-four months, Tara would be free. After the initial euphoria, I felt profound unease. Could the political parties be trusted to make the peace work? Anyone could place their signature on a piece of paper – as testified by the number of marriage certificates signed each day, nearly fifty percent of which end in divorce. Would the IRA actually decommission their weapons? Would the unionists really share power with nationalists or balk at the final hurdle? Even the prospect of Tara's eventual release was tinged with dark reservations. How would I feel if MacKenna or Dennehy were still alive and were due for release? Macintosh, let back into society, before he paid what I considered to be an adequate penance? How would the family of Drummond and McCleash react to Tara's release? Would Becky resent the second chance Tara would receive, when Ben had been denied that very opportunity?

There was a harsh reality to face: peace is not simply a nebulous feel-good concept. It calls for individual sacrifices from each of us for a higher ideal. If they succeeded in making peace, I could live with Macintosh's freedom. As for Tara, I always believed she had more to offer society on this side of the prison wall, than trapped within its confines. I had just about grown accustomed to life without her. Twenty letters with no acknowledgement, it was time to call it a day. She knew the address.

On May 22nd 1998, the people of both the Republic of Ireland and Northern Ireland voted in favour of the Good Friday or Belfast Agreement, although the vote was substantially closer in the North. Two days later, an unassuming letter landed on my doormat. I had no doubt as to the identity of the author, well before I saw the prison postmark. I removed the two sheets of grey blue paper and glanced at the handwriting, taking in the loops and stems I was so familiar with. Then I returned the unread sheets to the envelope, in an act of supreme willpower. It was after 9pm, armed with a generous helping of Jameson's, the golden liquid glinting against the subdued light, before I finally absorbed her letter.

Dear Tom,

It is with some trepidation that I have finally put pen to paper, after the persistency of your many letters. It is, perhaps, tinged with a certain irony that you have remained stubbornly silent over recent weeks. I am fully aware there are two possibilities for your silence. If you desire not to hear from me, or have grown weary of my silence, I invite you to read no further. File these pages in the waste bin and return to whatever or whomever you were concerned with and think no more of me. I have assumed for the purpose of writing this letter that this is not your intention.

The second possibility is that in light of the events of the past few weeks, you are waiting for a response from me.

The Belfast Agreement represents the best prospects for peace in a generation – despite falling short of the IRA's avowed aim of a united Ireland…I hope that my actions of late have in some small way helped contribute to an environment where peace could be fostered. Despite the fact I took a more drastic approach than those who remained within the republican family, our goals have always been the same – a dogged belief that no one else should have to die for a meaningless concept like a 32 county united Ireland. The growing realisation that far from liberating the people of Northern Ireland, the paramilitary groups on both sides have enslaved them in a vicious cycle of violence. I welcome a partitionist, but democratic, solution over an armed struggle for a romantic ideal. Whether those still holding the guns (on all sides) feel the deep sense of remorse and shame I feel, only time will tell?

I hope that the events of the past few weeks mark a genuine sea change in the history of Ireland. I pray every day that those responsible for leading us forward into this brave new world will proceed in the same spirit of reconciliation, humility and compromise. For it will take nothing short of a miracle, if decommissioning is to deliver anything other than a token gesture. I fear they will talk the language of peace, but act as though still immersed in the heat of the battle.

The Belfast Agreement has profound personal implications for me. I arrived in these four walls, in the full knowledge that this was the end of the line. I had grown accustomed to the bleak despair that followed my convictions. There was no resentment, for I had willingly submitted to the system. Of course there were and are still days when I regret my decision. When the sun is shining, or when I long to feel the cool breeze on my face. Yet any sour feelings I have regarding my present predicament pale into nothing compared to the acts which have led me to this place…

Now I discover that far from this being the end of the tape, in the great scheme of life, it will represent little more than a brief tap on the pause button. The thought of freedom is sweet beyond belief. To be given a second chance is so much more than I ever expected or deserve. This is accompanied by guilt: I will have cheated in not serving the sentence imposed upon me. Rubbing salt in the wounds of those whose deaths preclude them or their loved ones from any form of release – peace or no peace. I have struggled long and hard with such sentiments. It is not my decision when and if I am to be released. I have no power to say yes or no.

A Bold Deceiver • James Hurd

All sides have agreed to the prisoner release programme, no matter how hard to countenance. If I am to be given a second chance, then I owe a duty to use it wisely and contribute to the sort of society we all desire. My continued confinement with the release of others will ease no one's pain. Perhaps you will welcome the peace, without welcoming my release? That I cherish a certain hope, is all I know to say,
  All my love, Tara

I savoured each word like the arrival of the rains on the barren Savannah, dancing in the dust, as the warm refreshing droplets soak you to the skin; cleansing and refreshing, revitalising the cracked and scorched earth. I could hear the gentle intonation of her voice, shadowed against her Belfast brogue. I had grown accustomed to the prospect that our paths would never again intertwine, until I read the final paragraph of her letter. Despite Tara's lofty ambition of contributing to the peace process, I was astute enough to discern that any input would be restricted by distant anonymity. The risk to her personal safety inevitably meant she would be a target. Tara's refusal to become involved in any form of IRA activity in prison, only served to heighten the case against her. She renounced her membership of the IRA and spent the final eighteen months of her sentence in segregation, along with other vulnerable prisoners. I later discovered Tara had been attacked with a broken bottle. On another occasion, IRA sympathisers poured boiling water over her, before she finally took the decision to be segregated.

The implications were clear – if I contemplated any form of ongoing relationship with Tara, my life would change beyond recognition. She would be vulnerable if either of us stayed in Manchester. If Tara left the country, would I leave with her? Was this a sacrifice I was prepared to make, away from the hothouse of impetuous emotion? I forced myself to weigh up my life: what I valued and what was dispensable. I had encountered the complete rainbow of emotions regarding Tara: infatuation to love, love to hate, alienation and resentment, which gradually gave way to a grudging respect, as she put her life on the line on countless occasions. The unspeakable horror of watching her felled, under a hail of bullets and the realisation in that second, everything I had ever cared about was being snatched away. I could return to my safe lifestyle and wake up aged forty, knowing I had settled for second best. Always wondering – what if? Sometimes, life compels you to take a risk, just to know you are still alive. I made my initial decision within five minutes of reading her letter, and then waited a month to cross-examine my judgement. The passing days only confirmed the strength of my initial conviction.

Tara,
We share a similar hope… Send a visiting order,
Tom

Tara replied within days, indicating that under no circumstances would she countenance me visiting Maghaberry. And although I vehemently disagreed with her, I was obliged to respect her wishes.

Dearest Tom,
I know you think me obstinate, but I don't want you to see me confined in this place, like a bird in a cage. Be patient. Our time will come. All my love
Tara

The eighteen month period following the receipt of Tara's letter passed slowly at first, but soon quickened in pace. We exchanged regular letters and spoke on the phone weekly, using Tara's hard earned BT phone cards.

From opposite sides of the Irish Sea and a prison wall, Tara and I scrutinised the highs and lows of the peace process, as the parties sought to implement the lofty ideals of the Good Friday Accord. It seemed at numerous defining moments of crisis that the whole peace process might collapse. My heart had sunk on each occasion opposition politicians called with reckless abandon for the prisoner early release scheme to be halted, in response to the lack of decommissioning. We watched in horror when the republican splinter group, styling themselves the 'Real IRA' exploded a device in Omagh Town Centre on the 15th August 1998. The optimism of the referendums and the peace agreement shattered into hopeless despair, at the pointless futile deaths of twenty eight people, including nine children. I reflected mournfully on the events of the 15th June 1996 in Manchester. What have we learnt in over two years: seemingly nothing?

Meanwhile, the politicians continued to squabble. It wasn't until September 1998 that David Trimble actually met Gerry Adams in a face to face meeting. In December, David Trimble and John Hume collected the Nobel Peace Prize, despite the lone prophets of doom crying in the wilderness that the peace was only halfway won.

March 1999 was supposed to be the deadline for the devolution of power to the new power sharing Assembly in Northern Ireland. In fact it took a "review" of the peace process during the autumn of 1999 to make a break through. On the 27th November 1999 at Belfast's Waterfront Hall, the UUP voted narrowly to enter a power sharing Government with Sinn Féin, on the understanding that decommissioning would follow thereafter. The euphoria at 3pm on the 2nd December was palpable as Northern Ireland had a Government made up of Catholics and Protestants for the first time since its creation in 1921. Martin McGuinness from Sinn Féin became Minister for Education and Barbara De Brun, Minister for Health.

The release of some five hundred paramilitary prisoners on both sides had commenced in August 1998. One of the first to leave prison was Thomas McMahon, responsible for the murder of Lord Mountbatten. The two hundred and seventy seventh prisoner released in June 1999 was Patrick Magee, convicted of blowing up the Grand Hotel in Brighton, during the Conservative Party Conference in 1984. The release programme reached its zenith in the summer of 2000: Michael Stone, who attacked mourners at an IRA funeral, followed by a further seventy-eight prisoners on the 28th July. Included in their numbers were some of the most notorious figures in the history of the troubles: Sean Kelly convicted of the fish and chip shop massacre in 1993; Thomas Knight, who had burst into a Catholic bar at Greysteel shouting "trick and treat", before killing eleven; and James McArdle who planted the bomb at Docklands in 1996. This left only a handful of prisoners in the Maze, which closed some months later. An institution steeped in grim republican mythology, thanks to the death of the hunger strikers in the early 80's, but also mass escapes and dirty protests, now itself confined to history.

On the 3rd January 2000, I visited Bill, my head of Chambers and handed him notice of my resignation. Sat behind his mahogany desk, the QC who would later be appointed a High Court Judge, read my letter in silence – a genuine look of sadness enshrined of his face. "Are you sure about this? It isn't the kind of decision you make lightly."

"I have thought of little else for the past year. It's not a spur of the moment decision."

"Where will you go?"

"Australia, New Zealand, the US. It depends, in light of Tara's convictions, who will allow her entry."

"I have contacts with the American Bar Association, if you choose to practise law there."

"Thanks, but I'm not sure it's what I want any more."

Slowly, but inexorably, I poured petrol over my bridges. I sold my house in May 2000. Most of the furniture was either bought with the property or went to a house clearance outfit that paid £900 for seven years worth of assorted junk. The distorted remains of the Fat Boy were sold to a Harley enthusiast from the bike club, and a classic car enthusiast snapped up the Alvis. The hardest moment was watching the proud new owner of my T120 Bonnie streak away into the distance. Every penny I could lay my hands on, after repaying the mortgage and cashing in my pension, was placed in an offshore account. I had an account number and a password – no name and no address.

Tara attempted in vain, via various Government agencies to make arrangements for her impending release. It will probably come as little surprise to learn that they were less than receptive to concerns regarding her personal safety. Whether the Northern Ireland Office was weighed down under the bureaucracy of prisoner licence release preparations or they had simply forgotten any obligation they owed to her, I know not? It is possible they were just not aware of the personal danger she faced; joined up government is a myth created by the politicians and officials who happen to currently enjoy the reins of power. Eventually, in desperation, I dug out the telephone number I had originally been given for Haydon Powell, over three years earlier. I rang the number and an anonymous official sounding voice answered. "I'm looking for Haydon Powell."

"How did you get this number?" The voice was icy and curt.

"Haydon gave it to me, some time ago," I began. "I need to speak to him," a subtle hint of desperation creeping into my voice.

"Name?"

"Flemming, Thomas. It's urgent." There was a grunt at the end of the line, as he made it clear he was not Powell's personal message service. I recited my number and he hung up.

Powell returned my call later that afternoon. He was sharp and to the point. No pleasantries or small talk. It was like meeting an old flame in a bar: yesterday's news when you have a new love interest. "Tom?"

"Tara is due for release in a matter of months. No one gives a monkey's about her personal safety...."

"Cut to the quick. What do you want?"

"Previously you offered her papers to get to a third country."

"Where you thinking of heading?"

"Anywhere that'll take her."

"Both of you?"

"I guess so."

"Leave it with me. No promises."

Chapter Forty Three

THE FINAL PIECE of the jigsaw, as I prepared for Tara's release, slotted into place on the 15th June, when I collected my brand new Triumph Bonneville. It was exactly four years to the day since the accident. It represented the end of a chapter in my life, even though that date will always carry a brutal sadness for my brother.

I stood outside the showroom with a broad smile on my face. Seventeen years after production had ceased, when Triumph went bust, I had manage to secure one of the first of the new 790cc models to roll off the production line. Gone was the vibration of the old model, the handling was fantastic – and most amazingly, it did not leak oil like a beached supertanker. I also purchased a new set of leathers and posted them to HMP Maghaberry.

Tara was released on the 15th July 2000 – two weeks prior to the mass exodus from the Maze. She had spent three years, two months and fifteen days in custody, if you count the day an armed guard was placed outside her hospital room, on the eve of Labour's landslide general election victory.

Leaving Manchester soon after 4am, I rode to Liverpool. The sun was rising behind me, causing the reflection in my mirrors to glow with a pinky orange hue. It was warm, but at over seventy mph the wind was biting cold, until the sun rose, warming the earth around me. By the time I had stowed the bike on the ferry for Belfast, however, the cloud was thick and swirling. Sitting in the cafeteria sipping strong coffee, I contemplated what lay ahead. Other than a fleeting glimpse in the courtroom, I hadn't seen Tara for almost three years. What if she'd changed? What if I'd changed? I wouldn't have been human, if a nagging voice in my head wasn't asking if I was doing the right thing? I watched, as the coastline of northern England gradually faded into the mist, until all I could see was the greeny blue of the sea and the swirling white of the wash in the wake of the ship. Later, I watched from the bow, as the coast of Ireland appeared in the distance – the craggy rocks that had once been joined with the Scottish Highlands and Islands. I drank in the scene, as we slipped up Belfast Lough. It occurred to me that I was undertaking the exact journey in reverse that Tara had made in early January 1994.

I was so nervous as I disembarked, I stalled the bike. It took an age to select neutral and restart the engine, much to the annoyance of the car driver impatiently waiting behind me. Slicing my way through the Belfast traffic, I eventually found the M1 junction and headed south towards Lisburn. Leaving at junction nine – the exit for Moira – I dawdled over the final three miles, as I was a little early. I rode down the road a couple of miles before doubling back and pulling into the prison car park. The building was larger than I had anticipated. I knew it housed all of the female prisoners in Northern Ireland, although its capacity was only forty-two. I had forgotten it also held up to six hundred and eighty nine male prisoners. Lifting off my helmet, I reached into my leather jacket for a mint. I hadn't seen Tara for three years – the last thing I wanted was bad breath. I loosened the spare helmet from where it was secured over the pillion seat, and awaited my future.

I sat with my eyes glued to the main doors, waited and watched. At exactly six minutes before midday, a white van emerged through the gates and the rear doors swung open. No ceremony, no goodbyes and no looking back. Out from the shadows, stepped Tara. Her hair had grown, returning to a length similar to the day when we first met; the colour returned to rich dark brown. She stepped back into society with only a small rucksack, already mounted across her shoulders. She lingered for a second, sucking in her first taste of freedom – determined never to take it for granted. Her reflection lasted only a second, before she raised her head. I watched her eyes dart around until they alighted on me. Her hesitant saunter developed into a steady sprint, as she sped across the tarmac. As Tara closed the distance between us, her face emerged into focus: those large soft green eyes, shapely nose and delicate cheek bones. The lines that had materialised around her eyes added a certain harshness to her features that only the austerity of incarceration can breed. Most of all though, I recall the glint of ecstasy that shone across her face at the exhilaration of liberation. Eventually I found my feet and strode towards her. We embraced. "You're a sight for sore eyes," I smiled. I felt the touch of her cold pale skin on my cheek, as I pressed a kiss onto her lips.

"Not here," Tara indicated, nervously gesturing towards the backdrop of the prison.

I threw her the helmet and pressed the ignition button. "View's not up to much is it."

"Nice bike," Tara observed approvingly. "Hope she's quicker than your Harley. I feel the need for speed," were the last words I caught, before they disappeared under the deafeningly sweet noise of the exhausts. "Faster," Tara urged, gesturing with her gloved hand, as I yanked opened the throttle on the Bonneville. Standing upright on the pillion pegs, the breeze whistled thought her helmet. Her arms gripped my shoulders, whooping with excitement, as life began once again to course through her veins – and with hers, mine also.

In the highly unlikely event that Hollywood ever gets its mucky paws on this story, my guess is that they will probably choose to cut the movie at this point. Against the backdrop of the closing credits, will be the rear of a motorcycle on a desert highway at sundown. Riding to freedom against the backdrop of a brilliant orange setting sun, accompanied by whatever soft rock guitar band is in vogue, singing some uplifting melodic ballad about love and the freedom of the open road. No helmets and no rain – just two pairs of designer sunglasses and Tara's hair flowing in the wind, as she hangs on tightly, her arms slung round my waist. As the image of the bike and riders gets smaller and the camera pans back along the road we have travelled, the screen will turn black and the final credits will roll. The audience will gather their possessions and leave, smiling at the romantic upbeat feel-good ending.

Forgive me, I digressed. Leave the movie theme, sunshine and the desert on the cutting room floor and step back to reality. The swirling clouds gathering overhead turned darker and descended, as the rain began cascading from above, yet not even a force ten gale and flash floods could have dampened our delirium. From the prison, we proceeded swiftly to the ferry terminal. Despite the incessant rain, we leaned over the handrail on the upper deck, and laughed as the ferry slipped its moorings, bound for Scotland. The open expanse of the sea and the sky, she had so often dreamed of, seemed to intoxicate Tara. As the hungry rain droplets bounced off the lifeboat tarpaulins, we danced and smiled, our hands tightly intertwined. We would talk later, endlessly, covering the entire spectrum of life from the serious to the stupid, the momentous to the frivolous. Some moments, however, are to be cherished – never forgotten. The temptation is always to worry and fret, ever anxious about what tomorrow may hold. Sometimes, you just have to celebrate the present, disregarding the complications of the future. We were grasping freedom and each other, my fingers stroking her wet face, as we giggled like helpless teenagers. We held each other, never more than a few centimetres apart, lest it should all be snatched away – revealed as a cruel illusion.

I chose an idyllic setting in the Highlands in the West of Scotland, on the banks of Loch Sunart on the Ardnamurchan peninsula. A secluded cottage proved the ideal place to recuperate, less than a hundred yards from the gently lapping water's edge. I paid cash, placing the deposit in my mother's maiden name. We enjoyed long walks in the open air, swimming in the loch, fishing, and planning the rest of our lives. Looking back, those weeks seem magical – a brief interlude of tranquillity. In the evenings, we would stroll the mile down the single track to the local pub, avoiding the midges. To the outside world, we appeared like any other holidaymakers. After three years without alcohol, Tara became tipsy at the merest sniff of a drink. On the first night, we drank champagne by candlelight, entwined in each other's arms. Within minutes, Tara was giggling, savouring the taste of liberty. If I close my eyes really tightly, I am transported back: the old-fashioned TV, standard lamp and bookcase stacked with well-thumbed paperbacks; the large open fire place and fresh supply of logs; the smell of fresh fish cooking; making love by candle light; the softness of Tara's touch and the sweet eagerness of her kisses. Later in the afterglow, as we lay arm in arm, Tara wept – either tears of happiness, the joy of the present, or a lament for wasted opportunities.

Tara stood at the open front door, contemplating the night sky, gazing towards the darkened loch. The stars, partly visible were half-obscured by wispy cloud formations. She pulled her slip tighter around her shoulders and laid her head against my chest. "Have you ever wanted anything so much it hurts? I mean really wanted it, to the point where physically you will perish without it?"

I nodded, but made no attempt to answer her question. "What is it you want so badly?"

"This," she replied, as I embraced her, wrapping her in the safety of my arms. "I could shout I am so happy," Tara said in jubilation, reaching for her wineglass.

"We're miles from anywhere. No one will ever hear us."

"And swim naked right now," she said high spiritedly. And so we did, splashing each other with the freezing cold water, until we collapsed exhausted on the beach, intoxicated on more than just the wine. It felt like we'd been born again.

Despite this initial euphoria, in subsequent days Tara proved more reserved, even suspicious, as if we were strangers. If I was impatient with her, she forgave me without a murmur. Tara was not the same person I had watched cling to life by a thread. Who could have survived the past three years unchanged? I was different too. What divided us though, was insignificant compared with what united us: a bond that had been tested in the fire of separation and not found wanting. Slowly, hesitantly, she relaxed, letting down her heavily guarded defences – the layers of protection peeled away. She hated speaking about her experiences in prison and wished only to forget. "Can't we just talk about the future," she would beg, and I cared too much to press her further.

On the Friday of our second week we received a visitor. Shortly after 3pm, just as arranged, Powell arrived in a dark green Range Rover, carrying a brief case. I showed him inside. "Long time Tara," he said, entering the living room. Tara hung back, keeping her distance. She acknowledged him with a slight nod, but gave no audible response. She was so fiercely independent, she found it difficult to accept assistance graciously. It grieved her we had to resort to Powell and the Government he represented – or perhaps she resented the invasion of her new found privacy? She eyed Powell suspiciously, while I made the small talk. "You're looking well," Powell added, when she emerged carrying a tray loaded with coffee.

"Not many late nights recently," she replied caustically. That brought an uneasy smile to all of our faces, and appeared to break the ice.

"I can't stay long," he began formally. "I'm expected back in Glasgow this evening. I have to catch the last flight back to London." He lifted the black leather briefcase onto the small coffee table, retrieving a white A4 envelope. He pushed it across the table to Tara. "Never let it be said that we abandoned you."

He spoke sternly – whether resentful that we had ever doubted his ability to keep faith or a subtle dig at my affidavits. Payback, for the two bullets received under his command.

Powell raised his eyebrows. "Not may countries will accommodate ex-cons with terrorist links. You're bloody lucky that the Clinton administration takes such a keen interest in ensuring the survival of the peace process. You'll find new passports, drivers' licences and birth certificates. Two air tickets, visas and one year work permits for the USA. There is $20,000 in an account with City Bank, Phoenix, Arizona. You've been enrolled on a teacher exchange programme. Term starts in eight weeks." This seemed ironic, given Tara's lie to McDonnell about the chance of a lifetime opportunity to teach in the United States. We had so many questions: who, where, how and why? He anticipated them all. "It's all in there. Call if you need me."

With that, he downed the rest of his coffee, shook hands and disappeared. We both stood shell-shocked in disbelief at the reality of this brave new world, as the Range Rover disappeared down the farm track.

Dumbfounded with fear and excitement, and daunted by the enormity of what lay in front of us, we were apprehensive – reluctantly clinging to the shabby lives that were so familiar. Eventually, like excited children on Christmas morning, curiosity overcame our inhibition. "Oh my goodness," laughed Tara, reacting with childish glee, as she scanned her new passport. "Mrs Katherine Richardson. I'm married."

"To me," I added, opening the fresh burgundy passport with the golden royal crest. "John and Katherine Richardson."

"Kate," corrected Tara. "And John, not a chance – Jack."

"Kate and Jack." It tripped off my tongue with eager satisfaction. We rolled on the floor, laughing – rejoicing, until the tears streamed down our faces, calling each other by our pseudonyms and practising scrawling our new signatures on scrap paper. Our new lives spread out before us. "Why Phoenix?" I wondered out loud.

"Who knows," Tara replied, returning her concentration to studying the documentation. "I have to attend an interview…" There was a hint of disappointment in her voice.

"Powell said term started…"

"I know…but…"

"I suspect it's just a formality."

"You want to teach?" I asked, stroking her silken hair.

Tara nodded. "I think so. More than anything."

"Anything?"

"Well, almost," she smiled coyly, as I planted a kiss on her lips.

Later, Tara was more reflective, unable to settle. As the sun set, spreading a shimmering orange glow across the water, Tara sat forlornly on a large rock, hiding behind her sunglasses, while I tried unsuccessfully to skim flat stones across the fiery reflection in the water. "What's wrong?" I asked, plonking myself down beside her.

Tara eyed me for a second, before returning her vacant stare out across the loch. I placed a reassuring hand on her arm. "I'm scared Tom," she confided finally, removing her glasses. "Of what will happen to us…"

"I thought this was what you wanted – would make you happy. After everything…"

"It is," she said, reflectively, almost morose. "It's just not that easy is it? We just fly away, leave it all behind. We have a past as well as a future."

"You've lost me Tara," I replied, growing slightly exasperated. Tara buried her head in her hands and slowly massaged her eyelids, with a slight moan.

"I think what I am saying is, it's not too late – to change your mind." Tara removed her sunglasses, eyeing me with concern. "I'm scared you'll end up disappointed Tom. It's a hell of a burden, knowing the sacrifice you're making…" Tara barely moved her lips, resting her chin on her clenched fist. I attempted to interrupt, but she stopped me. "Let me finish – if this is some guilt trip you signed up for three years ago and now you've changed, I understand. No obligations. I'm not holding you to any kind of commitment."

"There comes a point in life, where you have to analyse what's important. You taught me that." I peered into her searching eyes. "The day I received your letter, I made my choice. Am I scared – who wouldn't be? Do I have regrets? Many, but about this, I've never been more certain. Oh and by the way the name is Jack."

Tara squeezed my hand and smiled, brushing her hair from her cheek in the cool evening breeze. "Jack…I'm sorry. I couldn't bear it, if we built a life, then you changed your mind. I swear you'd break my heart."

I stroked my hand across her cheek and caressed her hair. "No regrets Kate." We walked hand in hand, our bare feet lapping in the icy cold water – and watched the last rays of the sun disappear over the horizon in relaxed contentment.

Chapter Forty Four

LESS THAN A week later, Kate and I boarded a Virgin Atlantic flight at Heathrow, bound for New York. It was a poignant moment for both of us, awash with hope, expectation and nervous apprehension. We were leaving behind the grey drizzle that hung like a damp blanket over England. As we taxied from the departure gate, my thoughts turned to what we might find across the Atlantic Ocean. Like generations of inhabitants from these small islands, we were travelling the well-worn footsteps of those who had set sail for the New World, for a better life – free from the tyranny of the past. My own ancestors had abandoned Ireland for Liverpool at the height of the potato famine. For a brief interlude, I entertained how different things might have been, if my predecessors had travelled west instead of east? My daydream was disturbed, as the thrust of the engines gathered pace, thundering down the runway, before lifting us effortlessly into the sky.

We carried only two rucksacks – all the possessions we could hoard from our old lives. Clothes for a few weeks and assorted personal effects: photographs of Ben, Becky, Hannah and my parents; half a dozen CDs I couldn't bring myself to part with and my leather jacket. An ill fated attempt at sleep, two movies, one very average in-flight meal and three Jack Daniels later, we touched down at JFK, in blazing sunshine.

We stayed in New York only for a few of days, anxious to extinguish any remaining links with the flight from London. As tourists, we stood absorbing the magnificent view from Liberty Island, taking photographs looking back towards Manhattan. We succumbed to the same delight that must have quickened the hearts of centuries of weary refugees, as their ships finally steamed past the welcoming embrace of the Statue of Liberty.

We purchased two second-hand Harleys from a dealer on the south side of Manhattan: a 1998 Road King and a 1997 Ultra Classic Electra Glide complete with forty watt per channel sound system. The only problem in the otherwise smooth process was arranging insurance cover. There was a glitch with the computer system, according to the girl behind the counter. There followed an anxious wait, while she inputted our personal details for a second time. I turned white as a sheet as she informed me with a puzzled expression: "We have no record of your names…" Uncovered, found out and exposed – sent home in disgrace to an uncertain and unpredictable future. All these wild fears I entertained in the nervous seconds before the insurance clerk realised she had simply inputted the wrong driver's licence number. Kate remained cool throughout. Like she remarked afterwards, I was sweating enough for both of us.

I have always been passionate about road movies – films that symbolise freedom, rebellion, Route 66 and the wonder of youth; the empty road, shimmering in the distant heat haze. The best of them all is Easy Rider. Now I'm no Peter Fonda and Kate was no Dennis Hopper, but as we rode the highway out of New York, I was humming Steppenwolf's 'Born to be Wild' in my head. We rode south to Philadelphia, on to Pittsburgh, Columbus Ohio and Indianapolis, and then south through Kentucky to Tennessee. We visited with Elvis at Graceland, drank beer and sang the blues in Memphis, paying our respects at the Lorraine Motel, where the Rev Dr Martin Luther King was shot. Across the Mississippi, Arkansas to Dallas, Texas, El Paso and Albuquerque, New Mexico until we finally reached Arizona. The cover notes to Easy Rider state that it was the story of a man who went looking for America and couldn't find it. We enjoyed a little more success in a quiet suburb of Phoenix, Arizona.

The interview was a formality for the exchange programme. A UK teacher goes to USA for a year and vice versa. Heaven knows where the US teacher ended up – not HMP Maghaberry, I bet? Although the position was for a year, the Principal told Kate that there was a possibility she could be kept on, if her immigration paperwork was in order. Kate taught classes in English and History and seemed to lap up every minute of it, grabbing life with both hands and refusing to relax her grip. Her enthusiasm for the kids she taught was boundless, whether marking papers or watching high school baseball. Having been given a second chance, you never forget. Every day, you wake up and give thanks you're alive. You embrace life with passion – an insatiable zest. Kate's excitement was infectious on all those who surrounded her, her classes, her colleagues, our neighbours and me.

We rented a modest house in a quiet suburban neighbourhood. To us, it was a palace – three bedrooms, sun deck, double garage, a little white fence and neatly manicured lawns. Slowly, we constructed a life for ourselves. It took time to grow accustomed to telling people my name was Jack and my wife Kate. It took serious discipline and concentration not to slip up and get caught out. Even when we were alone, we insisted we should not lapse into old ways. Don't get me wrong, we didn't live our lives like fugitives. We simply tried to live our lives as Kate and Jack Richardson, rather than Tara O'Neil and Thomas Flemming.

Re-inventing one's self is an art. It's a pity I had to resort to the extremes of a new identity and crossing continents to realise it. Once out of the rut of lawyering, I turned my hobby into a business. Small initially, but expanding over time, I started an on-line motorcycle vacation business, aimed mainly at European tourists. It was simple really – we picked holidaymakers up from the airport and put them up in a motel for the first night. We provided bikes, gave a half day's orientation and then away they were. Maps, accommodation and insurance all provided. They had California, San Diego, LA and San Francisco to the west. To the north, there was the Grand Canyon, Nevada, Vegas and Reno. Ride south to Tucson and Tombstone and east to Texas. For the slightly less adventurous, we also organised guided tours.

In the summer months, Kate and I were on the open road most weeks, camping around an open fire, meeting bikers from the four corners of the world. We started with the two Harleys we had purchased in New York and acquired a few more bikes over the following months. Within a year there were fifteen bikes. I got to spend my winter renovating the bikes, instead of being trapped behind a desk or stuck in a courtroom. The fifteen became sixteen when my Triumph Bonneville was eventually shipped from England in a sealed container. That bike was special. It symbolised our hope, the spirit of reconciliation and second chances. I refused to part with that bike for love nor money.

A Bold Deceiver • James Hurd

Speaking of which, love that is, Kate and I finally got married – officially. We already had a fake wedding certificate and shared the same name. But there is no substitute for authenticity. I proposed over Christmas, whilst we vacationed in Mexico. We were married the following spring, at a little Baptist church, not far from where we lived. The ceremony was small – the guests consisting of a few of Kate's work colleagues and some new friends we'd made: Joe from the local bike shop, a great mechanic when I was out of my depth, along with Pete, Jen, Rob, Caroline and Frank from the local Harley Owners Club; our neighbours, Jeff and Barbara from next door, with their kids; and Mike and Laura from across the street. I shall never forget our wedding day – from the moment Kate walked down the aisle, to exchanging vows with the woman I loved, to the party that seemed to last until dawn.

We spent a week at Lake Tahoe on our honeymoon, learning to sail, swimming, making love and gambling. We never took it for granted and we never became complacent. Drawn together in adversity – now we prospered in the tranquillity of the sanctuary we had created. Life seemed so sweet and I never realised just how fragile it could be. You never think beyond tomorrow do you? We made plans like any couple: buying a house, new business ideas and vacations. We planned to start a family. The future seemed so bright, so full of glorious promise. Upon reflection, perhaps if Hollywood ever comes a calling, they will conclude the movie at this point. It makes some sense I suppose – a happy ending set in the good old US of A.

28th August 2002, a day that began like all the rest, but ended like no other. There was nothing in the preamble, which served to place either of us on our guard. It was an ordinary Monday. We'd been up late the night before, but not that late. I was up early – before Kate – to go running, before the sun was too hot. I remember my head felt a little sensitive and perhaps I was a little slower than usual, my feet a little heavier. Whilst supping my second mug of coffee, I remembered that one of the returned rental bikes had a cracked rear taillight. I had this inkling in the back of my mind that I had seen a spare one, hanging around in the garage in a box of spares I had picked up at an auto junk sale, a few months previously. Hence I was still poking around in boxes in the garage when Kate appeared, to tell me she was leaving for work.
"What are you looking for?"
"Taillight for a soft tail."

"Not seen it," she offered, taking a step towards the driveway, as I continued to rummage in the box.

"Hey." I turned back to face her. Kate reached forward and kissed me.

"What's happening tonight?"

"I've got to pick up some clients at the airport at three."

"Meet me in Uncle Sam's?" A favourite downtown hangout, serving great food and cold beer.

"Six-thirty okay?"

"Sure."

I watched Kate, as she approached our old Chevy convertible on the driveway. It possessed the acceleration of a snail and drank fuel quicker than a space shuttle. I remember standing, smiling, thinking how beautiful Kate looked. You know, like if I walked past her on the street, she would definitely turn my head. My hand was still probing the bottom of the cardboard box for the taillight cover. I heard the car door open and the metallic clank as it closed. I didn't actually see either, to my eternal regret, as my back was turned. Maybe, just maybe there was something I could have done. Perhaps not, but that doesn't make it any easier to live with. Eventually, I retrieved the taillight, only to realise it was the wrong size. I tossed it back in the box and moved towards the other side of the garage.

Less than three seconds after Kate turned the key in the ignition, the booby trap device concealed underneath the driver's side floor panel activated. I had no time to react. I was standing less than fifteen feet from the Chevy, when a fireball struck me with the intensity of a bulldozer, consuming the garage. I was tossed backwards by the force of the explosion – careering helplessly into the rear wall, where I passed out. I recall coughing – the smoke, thick and black, heavy with the stench of burning rubber and paint, acrid with melting plastic. I tried to edge forwards to reach the car, to pull Kate out, but the relentless blistering heat and smoke filling my lungs, continuously drove me back. It didn't help that I had smashed my kneecap, although the pain in my leg was of little consequence at that moment. The unbearable realisation that there was no prospect of her surviving an explosion of that magnitude, at such a close proximity. I screamed "no," till I was hoarse and every ounce of energy in me was drained. I was consumed with grief, frustration and despair – a sense of complete and utter fucking futility. I vaguely recall the siren of a fire engine, in the seconds before I passed out, overcome with exhaustion, agony and smoke inhalation. Kate died instantly and felt no pain. Unlike those of us left behind.

To this day, I am tortured by not knowing how they tracked her down. I have no conclusive proof, but I am convinced it was the IRA. Or rather, renegade hawks within the Republican Movement, righting perceived wrongs. Settling old scores and taking their bloody revenge – peace process or no peace process. Had we said or done something to give ourselves away? Had some inept gaff on my part let some vital piece of information slip? Perhaps they had traced us via the Bonneville – noted the registration number from the day of Tara's release? Impossible – it was in storage for months and was shipped in the name of Jack Richardson, not Thomas Flemming. Had someone recognised us? Had a tourist captured Kate in home video footage – a chance holiday snap, recognised in the old country? For months, I consumed myself with such thoughts.

It made no difference – Kate Richardson, Tara O'Neil, my wife was dead. After all we had been through, all we had survived. To travel so far, achieve so much, to be shown such a fleeting glimpse of happiness and then to have it all so cruelly snatched away. I had stood at the vantage point, perched on the mountain summit and looked out across the fertile plains and valleys of the Promised Land. But it was never to be my inheritance.

Postscript

There were many developments on the political front in Northern Ireland during Tara's imprisonment, our subsequent time in the Unites States, and in the period since her death.

Amidst the height of optimism, surrounding the peace process, on the 24th November 1999, the rebuilt Manchester city centre opened to the public. The promises, in the aftermath of the bomb, that Manchester would be revived, bigger and better, proved accurate. The new Exchange Square, New Cathedral Street, with its medieval pubs, and the brand new Marks & Spencer's store: a glass palace that rose from the ruins and debris of a demolition site. A symbol of our new found peace: Ben's peace.

But the aspiration of reconciliation proved, like so many things in Northern Ireland politics, to be transitory, as the pendulum swung back towards deadlock. Power sharing was suspended on the 11th February 2000 – the political parties collapsing back into recrimination over decommissioning. The deadlock was broken only in May 2000, when it was agreed that the IRA would open its arms dumps to third party inspection. This paved the way for the even narrower vote, on the 28th May 2000, in favour of a return to devolved government. On June 27th 2000, it was revealed that Cyril Ramaphosa and the former Finnish Prime Minister, Martti Ahtisaari had inspected a substantial amount of IRA weaponry, including explosives. On the 23rd October 2001, with the peace process seemingly again tittering on the edge of collapse, the IRA for the first time in its history, decommissioned a quantity of arms, ammunition and explosives.

A second quantity of arms was decommissioned on 8th April 2002. However, the staggering peace process seemed doomed to collapse, as the Good Friday institutions were once again suspended, following allegations of an IRA spy ring at Stormont in late 2002. A third quantity of decommissioning, in October 2003, did nothing to break the impasse. The Northern Bank raid, where £26.5 million was allegedly stolen by the IRA in December 2004, and the murder of Robert McCartney in January 2005, only confirmed the suspicions amongst unionists that the IRA continued to plan for war, despite talking peace.

However, on the 28th July 2005, the moment came that many of us thought we would never see, when the IRA released the following statement:

"The leadership of Óglaigh na hÉireann has formally ordered an end to the armed campaign. This will take effect from 4 pm this afternoon. All IRA units have been ordered to dump arms. All volunteers have been instructed to assist the development of purely political and democratic programmes through exclusively peaceful means. Volunteers must not engage in any other activities whatsoever…"

This was followed on the 26th September 2005, by a historic announcement from General John De Chastelain that the IRA had put all of its weapons beyond use, commenting that: *"We are satisfied that the arms decommissioned represent the totality of the IRA's arsenal."* Regrettably, despite being witnessed by church leaders, and the inventory destroyed being consistent with security service estimates, such was the lack of trust between the two communities, that the absence of photographic evidence of concrete being poured over weapons, still caused unionists to doubt the sincerity of the Republican Movement.

The decision by Sinn Féin, on the 28th January 2007, to support the Police Service of Northern Ireland, however, paved the way, against all expectations, for the culmination of the peace process. On the 8th May 2007, two days before Tony Blair announced the timetable for his resignation, and only days after the UVF renounced violence and placed its weapons '*beyond use*', a new devolved power sharing executive in the Northern Ireland, was sworn in. Dr Paisley, the DUP First Minister, was shown on our television screens, joking easily with his Sinn Féin deputy Martin McGuinness – former adversaries, across the political and religious divide – now in Government together.

I recognise a significant number of you will have felt distinctly uneasy at Tara's release, after serving such a short portion of the tariff imposed upon her. You will have been troubled by the Good Friday or Belfast

Agreement from its inception, and its provision for the early release of prisoners. You may have regarded it as a perversion of justice, designed for and by the political expediency of politicians – a shabby deal to appease the paramilitaries with no quid pro quo. In the end, you may think justice was done. Those who live by the sword must die by the sword. She sealed her own fate, in joining an organisation committed to violence. I vehemently oppose such sentiments. No one, whatever their crime, deserves to have their life brutally snatched away in the way Tara's was, or Drummond's, or Ben's. I had to stand by helpless, as a terrorist bomb took away that which was most precious to me. No one should be forced to endure that.

For the second time in my life, I found myself in hospital, attempting to reconcile my injuries, the death of a family member, and facing the daunting prospect of life without Tara. The galling pain of having found her again, only to lose her, was almost too crushing to endure. If I could turn back the hand of time to the beginning, would I change the course of my life? It's idle speculation, of course – we're only ever given one chance. There is no dress rehearsal in which to practise all our mistakes. Do I have regrets? I regret that I never had the chance to grow old with Tara. Our time together was so short. The many things I would have said, had I known I would never be blessed with another opportunity. I regret we never had children. I regret I no longer have my brother and I miss him, more than I can ever say.

I have no regrets about loving Tara. There are many people who never find that all-consuming passion that makes this life worth living. It's a gift. And you don't always get the opportunity to be choosy about the details. I found such a bond with a former terrorist, and for that I offer no apology, only an explanation. And the life I have now, I also owe to Tara. In the aftermath of her death, I confess almost losing my appetite for this world. I spent weeks in hospital and then sitting around, following the operation to repair my damaged knee. With Tara gone, there seemed little point in carrying on.

In the months that followed however, as my leg recovered, my mood brightened. Although I will never be able to run a marathon, at least I can ride a bike. In my deepest lows, I hear her quiet comforting voice, clear and calm. Something of her will to live – her exuberance for life was imparted to me. During my recuperation, I became increasingly aware there was unfinished business. I felt compelled to return and face the cowardly strangers who were still killing in the name of a united Ireland. I refused to sit in Arizona and hide away. I was determined to be in their faces, to confront their mind set. Only my fight was not with guns and under car booby traps.

I sold half the bike business to Joe and we entered a partnership. He runs the US operation and I run the European end. Every summer, I spend a couple of months touring with various groups around the USA. I'm no e-millionaire yet, but that's not the point – it never was. Every bank holiday weekend, at the end of August, I return to Phoenix, where I sit by her simple grave and lay flowers, and I tell Tara about my year. The rest of my time is spent in Belfast, where I teach at a non-sectarian college. My hope is that a new generation of young people will not grow up in the fear, ignorance and terror of a violent and divided society and that religion may be a healing, rather than a divisive force. And if that happens, even in some small measure, I will be content. Then Tara's life and her death will not have been in vain.

The devolved Northern Ireland Assembly has responsibility for education. Caitriona Ruane, a Sinn Féin MLA is the Minister for Education and Martin McGuinness is the Deputy First Minister. He was allegedly a member of the IRA Army Council, second in command of the Derry IRA on Bloody Sunday in 1972 and one of the most senior members of the IRA. He is now committed to the peace process and the power sharing executive that will hopefully see the gun banished from Irish politics forever – both are my ultimate bosses. Now there's a delicious irony that Tara would have adored.

Glossary of Terms

Armalite Lightweight, small-calibre assault rifle

Army Council The IRA's seven man ruling body

ASU Active Service Unit

DUP Democratic Unionist Party led by Revd Dr Ian Paisley -regarded as more hard-line than the UUP (see below) and the largest political party in Northern Ireland since 2005.

GMP Greater Manchester Police

Green Book IRA Training Manual. General Headquarters General Army Orders: (revised 1987) No 1(1): *"Membership of the Army is only possible through being an active member of any Army Unit...Any person who ceases to be an active member of a Unit or working directly with General Headquarters ceases to be a member of the Army. There is no reserve in the Army. All volunteers must be active."* General Order No. 3(1) *"All Applications for readmission by those who were dismissed or who resigned from the Army, must be submitted to the Army Council or delegated authority, who alone have the power to sanction reinstatement."*

IRA Irish Republican Army

Long Kesh Internment camp near Lisburn which became the Maze Prison in 1976 after the construction of H-Blocks and the scene of the 1980-81 hunger strikes by republican inmates.

Loyalist A supporter of paramilitary unionist groups (see below for definition of unionist)

LVF Loyalist Volunteer Force (loyalist paramilitary group – which broke away from the UVF- see below)

MLA Member of Legislative Assembly for Northern Ireland

Nationalist A supporter (usually Catholic) of greater autonomy from Great Britain for Northern Ireland or peaceful constitutional change, but can also refer to any expressions of nationalist sentiments, including cultural.

Óglaigh na hÉireann Irish for IRA which translates as Soldiers of Ireland

OC Officer in Command

Peeler Slang term for a police officer

Provisionals / Provies/ Provos Refers to Provisional IRA following a split in the Republican Movement in 1970

RA Republican Army (abbreviation of IRA)

Real IRA Republican splinter group formed after 1997 IRA cease-fire

Republican A supporter of a single republic covering the whole of the island of Ireland and those prepared to use physical force to achieve this political goal but also associated with left wing politics

RIR Royal Irish Regiment (British army unit formed in July 1992 by the merger of the UDR (see below) and the Royal Irish Rangers).

RUC Royal Ulster Constabulary – which changed to become the Police Service of Northern Ireland in November 2001

SAS Special Air Service

Saracen 6 wheeled armoured personnel carrier used by the British army – capable of carrying 9 soldiers plus driver and commander

SB Special Branch – A division of each UK police force which deals with intelligence and amongst other things counter-terrorism – working alongside MI5 (The Security Service) who were given the lead role in combating the IRA in 1992.

SDLP Social Democratic & Labour Party – predominantly Catholic moderate nationalist party, which opposed paramilitary violence, led by John Hume from 1979-2001

Sinn Féin Political party associated with the Provisional IRA – translated as '*We Ourselves*' or sometimes '*Ourselves Alone*' – led by Gerry Adams (President) and Martin McGuinness

SLR Self loading rifle

Tout Derogatory term of abuse / slang for informers

UCBT Under car booby trap

UDA Ulster Defence Association – largest Loyalist Paramilitary Group. Members also operated as the UFF (see below), when claiming responsibility for the killing of Catholics from 1973 onwards, during the period when the UDA was a legal organisation. The UDA was proscribed or declared illegal in August 1992.

UDR Ulster Defence Regiment (Part-time locally recruited British army regiment, amalgamated in July 1992 with the Royal Irish Rangers to become the Royal Irish Regiment (RIR)).

UFF Ulster Freedom Fighters (loyalist paramilitary group – cover name for the UDA (see above))

Unionist A supporter (usually Protestant) of the preservation of Northern Ireland's status as part of (or union with) the United Kingdom

UVF Ulster Volunteer Force (loyalist paramilitary group)

UUP Ulster Unionist Party – moderate unionist political party, formally led by David Trimble (1995-2005) and the largest unionist party until the 2005 general election

Author's Note

The characters and events in this novel are entirely fictional, and any likeness to actual persons or events (aside from those detailed below) is completely coincidental. However, I have tried to set the story, as accurately as possible against the backdrop of the Northern Ireland peace process and actual events in the northwest of England in the 1990s – most notably, the IRA bombs in Warrington in 1993, Manchester City Centre on the 15th June 1996 and the bombing campaign in the run up to the general election of 1997. Fortunately, in reality, no one died in the Manchester bomb, although many were seriously injured.

Each of the news type articles throughout the book are based on actual contemporary reports, aside from the 19th June 1996, announcing the death of Ben Flemming and the earlier references to a man in intensive care. Each of the terrorist incidents in the run up to the 1997 election, described in Part Four actually occurred, apart from the attempted mortar attack on Manchester Airport, which is entirely a figment of my imagination.

No one has ever been charged with terrorist offences arising out of the Manchester bomb or the IRA campaign in the run up to the 1997 general election.

I would like to thank Clive Gregson for allowing me permission to reproduce the lyrics of the song "(Don't Step In) My Blue Suede Shoes" in Chapter 3. The song is published by Gregsongs, administered by Bug Music Ltd, UK. Clive has also asked me to add that the song is available on "The Best Of Clive Gregson & Christine Collister" (GottDiscs GOTTCD 054).

The quote from George Mitchell's Making Peace, published by William Heinemann Limited in Chapter 42 is reprinted with the kind permission of the Random House Group Limited.

Many thanks to Ben Jones for the fantastic job he did on the cover design.

I would also like to extend my thanks to the many people who have encouraged me to persevere throughout the writing, and seemingly endless redrafting and editing of this novel. I would particularly like to thank the following people, who read the manuscript and provided helpful suggestions on each chapter – my sister Debbie Hurd, Jennifer Pleavin, Maureen Keast and Alisan Bilsland.

Most of all, I would like to thank my wife Jo, for her insightful comments, suggestions and ideas, her diligent editing and proof reading skills, her boundless inspiration and encouragement to keep writing, when I lost faith, and for her patience in losing a husband to a word processor for seemingly unending hours.

Selected Bibliography

There are numerous books available on the history of the troubles in Northern Ireland and the subsequent peace process.

I have been greatly assisted by a number of first hand accounts of life inside the IRA as undercover agents for the police and the authorities – amongst them Eamon Collins' (with Mick McGovern) *Killing Rage* (Granta Books 1997), Raymond Gilmour's *Dead Ground Infiltrating the IRA* (Warner Books 1998) and *The Informer* by Sean O' Callaghan (Bantam Press 1998).

I would highly recommend Martin McGartland's two books, *Fifty Dead Men Walking* (Blake Publishing 1997) and *Dead Man Running* (Mainstream Publishing 1998) for an account not only of life as a double agent in the IRA, but his account of life thereafter.

On the other side of the divide, *Phoenix Policing the Shadows* by Jack Holland & Susan Phoenix (Hodder and Stoughton 1996), the story of the police officer in charge of counter surveillance unit in Northern Ireland, before his tragic death in the helicopter crash on the Mull of Kintyre in 1994, provides compelling reading.

A number of more general books on the IRA and the peace process were indispensable, particularly in relation to the bombing campaigns on the English mainland: Martin Dillons' *25 Years of Terror* (Bantam Books 1994), *Bandit Country The IRA and South Armagh* by Tony Harnden (Hodder and Stoughton 1999), *Provos The IRA and Sinn Féin* by Peter Taylor (Bloomsbury 1997), Brendan O'Brien's *The Long War The IRA and Sinn Féin* (The O'Brien Press Updated edition 1999)) *Northern Ireland since 1968* by Paul Arthur & Keith Jeffery (Blackwell Publishing 1996 (Second Edition) and *The Northern Ireland Peace Process 1993-1996 A Chronology* by Paul Bew & Gordon Gillespie (Serif 1996).

James Hurd • *A Bold Deceiver*

For a deeper insight into republicanism, I would recommend *Rebel Hearts Journeys within the IRA's Soul* by Kevin Toolis (Picador 1995) and *The Trouble with Guns Republican Strategy and the Provisional IRA* Malachi O'Doherty (The Blackstaff Press 1998).

I would also recommend two biographies, *John Hume Man of Peace* by George Drowner (Vista 1995) and *Man of War Man of Peace? The Unauthorised Biography of Gerry Adams* by David Sharrock & Mark Devenport (Macmillan 1997).

I was greatly assisted in creating what is hopefully an authentic female IRA volunteer by Margaret Ward's *Unmanageable Revolutionaries: Women & Irish Nationalism* (Pluto Press 1989/1995).

Finally, for a gripping account of the making of the Good Friday agreement, I would recommend Senator George Mitchell's *Making Peace* (William Heinemann 1999).

About the Author

James grew up in South Manchester, before attending the University of Birmingham. He has a legal career, practising as a barrister in Manchester and writes in his spare time. He is married to Jo and has a daughter Christina. *A Bold Deceiver* is his first novel.

ISBN 142513272-3